A History of the Novel in Ants

A Graphic Glossary of the Ant

BODY

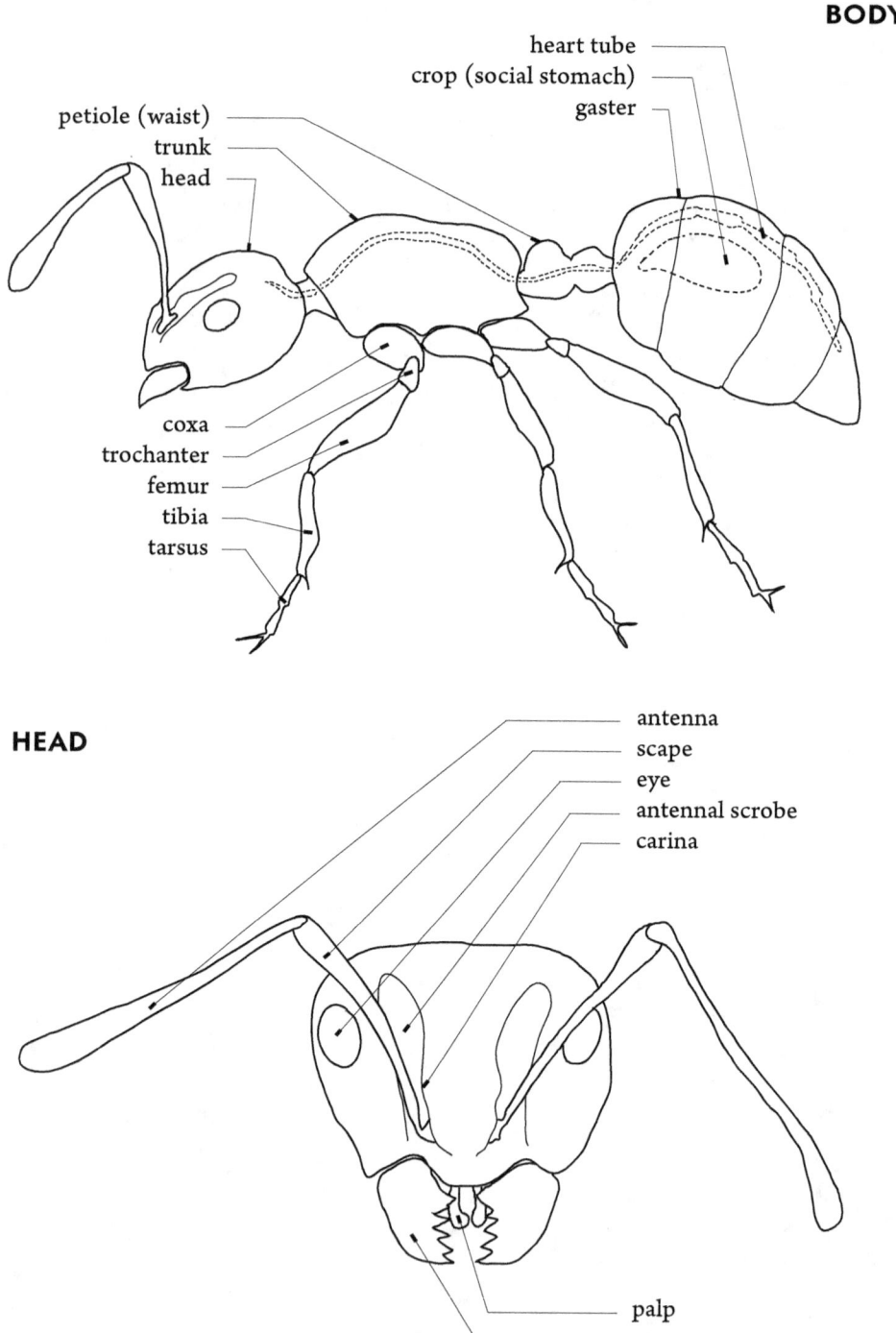

heart tube
crop (social stomach)
gaster
petiole (waist)
trunk
head
coxa
trochanter
femur
tibia
tarsus

HEAD

antenna
scape
eye
antennal scrobe
carina

palp
mandible

AF 2010

A HISTORY
of the NOVEL
in ANTS

Carol Hart

SpringStreet Books
Philadelphia

SpringStreet Books
PO Box 1042
Philadelphia, PA 19105

ISBN 978-0-9795204-3-3

Printed on acid-free paper.

This book is a work of fiction. Any resemblance to actual ants, living or dead, is entirely coincidental.

For Jake

It is certain that there may be extraordinary mental activity with an extremely small absolute mass of nervous matter: thus the wonderfully diversified instincts, mental powers, and affections of ants are notorious, yet their cerebral ganglia are not so large as the quarter of a small pin's head. Under this point of view, the brain of an ant is one of the most marvelous atoms of matter in the world, perhaps more so than the brain of a man.
–Charles Darwin, **The Descent of Man** (1871)

Who shall say that a man does see or hear? He is such a hive and swarm of parasites that it is doubtful whether his body is not more theirs than his, and whether he is anything but another kind of ant-heap after all.
–Samuel Butler, **Erewhon** (1872)

The actors in a story are usually human … Other animals have been introduced, but with limited success, for we know too little so far about their psychology. There may be, probably will be, an alteration here in the future … and we shall have animals who are neither symbolic, nor little men disguised, nor as four-legged tables moving, nor as painted scraps of paper that fly. It is one of the ways where science may enlarge the novel, by giving it fresh subject-matter.
–E. M. Forster, **Aspects of the Novel** (1927)

Parodic stylizations of canonized genres and styles occupy an essential place in the novel … This ability of the novel to criticize itself is a remarkable feature of this ever-developing genre.
–M. M. Bakhtin, **The Dialogic Imagination** (1975)

Contents

*Postmodernists are welcome to read this section first, as a prologue to the book.

I.

Picaresque

Ant

Liquid food, stored in the forager's crop (the "social stomach") is regurgitated to nestmates and thus distributed over large portions of the colony ... The crops of most ant species that feed on nectar and homopteran-secreted honeydew are capable of considerable distention. Individual foragers are consequently able to carry home large loads of carbohydrates. Some groups of workers serve as living reservoirs during lean periods ... Thus the crops of all the workers taken together serve as a social stomach from which the colony as a whole draws nourishment.
–Bert Hölldobler & Edward O. Wilson, **The Ants** (1990)

Because queens are generally larger than workers and need more food, adult workers can control whether a larva will develop into a queen by controlling her food supply.
–Francis Ratnieks & Tom Wenseleers, "Policing Insect Societies" (**Science**, 2005)

The modern novel is born when realism first supplants the fanciful idealist romance, namely the novels of chivalry, and later the pastoral novels and the pseudo-historical romances. This realism is ushered in with the Spanish **picaro,** who relates his life-story, generally from his childhood, in the form of an autobiography constituting an episodic narrative rather than a unified one. The autobiographical form, although adopted by the majority of the picaresque novelists, is not essential; the distinguishing feature of the genre is the atmosphere of delinquency. This begins in a setting of low life but generally ascends the social scale; the origins of the protagonist are usually disreputable; he is either born or plunged in youth into an environment of cheating and thieving, and learns to make his way in the world by cheating and thieving in his turn.
–Alexander A. Parker, **Literature and the Delinquent: The Picaresque Novel in Spain and Europe, 1599-1753** (1967)

The picaresque episodic plot is the most primitive form of plot employed in the novel, but it has retained its vitality and still flourishes today.
–Robert Scholes, James Phelan & Robert Kellogg, **The Nature of Narrative** (2006)

A Trajan and an Antoninus, a Nero and a Caligula, have all met with the belief of posterity; and no one doubts but that men so very good, and so very bad, were once the masters of mankind.
   But we who deal in private character, who search into the most retired recesses, and draw forth examples of virtue and vice from holes and corners of the world, are in a more dangerous situation.
–Henry Fielding, **The History of Tom Jones, A Foundling** (1749)

Our story begins with an egg. Where that egg had come from, no ant could tell. Those of the nursery did not agree about it. Some licked and cradled it like any other egg. Others suspected it to be a foundling, a cuckoo, an egg not savoring of their own Queen Mother.

They expressed their uncertainty in the usual ant manner: by doing, then undoing, then doing again. The egg was rolled away by one ant into the chill, inhospitable corners of the nursery chamber, then carried back to the brood pile by another, whereupon yet another shoved it aside. It was here, it was there, now in, now out. No place could be found where it truly belonged. These unnaturally early travels, all this rolling back and forth, must have had an influence *ab ovo* in forming the restless, wayward character of our heroine.

Surely the egg itself was blameless. It was a fine, shapely egg of the female kind, one so heavy with yolk that nature must have intended it for a fat, fecund queen, if only it were tenderly nursed and nurtured.

There is no more helpless and amiable creature in the earth than an ant larva. A puffy milk-white comma, a soft, naked pause in becoming, she wiggles and drools and pouts her tiny mouth, at first feebly, then with growing animation. She is everything that is innocent and sweet—so sweet that no ant can resist fondling and licking her. But there were many larvae, and our larva once again met with neglect. If there was any shortage of food, she was the one passed over; and it was only by wiggling and pouting more vigorously than her bigger but duller sisters that she was able to get fed at all.

Through successive molts, the larvae grew bigger, hungrier, more alert. Stumpy feelers conveyed a dim awareness of the nurses hovering devotedly above them. Now they made fretful clicks with their baby teeth whenever they craved food and attention. At this stage the little ones are scarcely more than mouth and belly, a feeding machine; but, beneath the thin larval skin, ingrown buds begin to burgeon, forming the rudiments of legs, mouthparts, feelers, and—in the royal ones—wings and gonads. Now the larvae eagerly accepted solid food and put away tremendous quantities of caterpillar meat and fatty seed tips, of which our heroine generally received an inferior portion.

When the days had grown shorter, before the hard frosts came, the larvae were given one last meal then put down to sleep, bundled close together for warmth and safety. Their nurses left to pass the cold season in the great hall with the other adults, huddled together throughout the long winter fast. Not all would survive—and here not merely fat bodies but an ant's character, her inner drive, must make a difference. Several unquestionably big, well-fed larvae perished, shriveling up inside their skins. Had they been too badly bitten by nurses or siblings? Or did nature fail them at some crucial gestational stage? Ants do not ask these questions. The dead, if fresh, are eaten; if stale, are carried out to the midden with other household rubbish.

In the spring, the ants began to stir themselves—creeping to the nest crater to bask in the sunlight, cleaning up the nest and taking out the dead, then making their first few forays, feeding themselves with the honeydew of their root aphid herd, but hunting insect meat for the awakening, and very hungry, brood. When the big, well-grown larvae were lovingly transported to a warmer chamber to complete their metamorphosis, our larva was unaccountably left behind. But the Queen herself found the starveling and had her placed among the royal brood. This kindly intervention seemed to settle the question of her legitimacy, whereupon some of the nursery ants made tardy amends by feeding her choice bits of well-chewed termite.

At last thoroughly feasted, our heroine settled down to spin her cocoon, then retired to know the first peace and safety of her slight existence. Within the protective sheath of the cocoon, her leg buds grew to form their long, shapely segments: stout coxa, short but sturdy trochanter, strong femur, graceful tibia tipped with a spur, and well-turned tarsus, lined with stiff brushes, terminating in a dainty pair of claws. Her mouthparts took on more robust, feminine proportions: maxillae, palps, and gleaming mandibles with well-shaped teeth. At last her wings and ovaries blossomed, and now there could be no doubt: she was indeed a queen.

In the quietus of the cocoon, as her juvenile tissues dissolved and reformed into those of the adult, she relived, one after another, the life histories of the ancestral ants. She dreamed she was the Ur-Ant, who, from a wild, solitary, waspish existence, was the first to sacrifice her wings for the good of her eggs and larvae. She and her daughters lived in simple harmony in the rich untapped terrain of the forest floor, where they shared equally in the joyful labor of tending brood and hunting prey.

In that long-gone golden age, caste and class were unknown; ant was the equal of ant; all called each other sister. Daughters, in reverence to their mother, refrained from laying eggs. Each hunted alone, yet shared what she won with mother, sister and brood. To feed the offspring of their tribe they brought down millipedes many times their size. These their larvae, as fierce and strong as their elder sisters, would devour with their own powerful jaws. Simple, rustic ants, they dwelt in shallow cavities beneath rocks and fallen trees, for the use of mandibles to delve and shape the earth was as yet unknown.

This happy life was soon marred by discord: sister against sister, daughter against mother, all contended to have the absolute power to lay eggs. Then succeeded an age of war and tyranny, under the rule of matriarchs who subdued their weaker sisters and daughters by brute force, amid constant strife. These ants, later to be known and feared as the cruel Ponerines, were fierce stingers of prey who ruled the earth in the jungles and dense forest lands of the south. There they still flourish, but dominance passed at last to more advanced ants.

First arose the fabled Myrmicines, who inaugurated an age of heroism and chivalry. Grim warriors armed with death-dealing stings, clad in gleaming armor set with sharp spines, they delighted in battle. They came streaming forth from their fortress-cities in serried ranks, leg to leg, mandible to mandible, their proud antennae tossing with disdain and fury. They drove the most savage tribes of Ponerines from the lands they claimed and civilized the rest, teaching them the rudiments of social order.

Although they fought fiercely with rival city-states, within each colony the ants accepted their place. Young or old, large or small, each knew her task in life and performed it, sacrificing her own ovaries (now tiny or absent altogether) for the good of all. The largest workers, the big-headed majors, defended the nest valiantly in war; in times of peace and plenty they stored food in their capacious crops, to be shared freely with their little sisters. The other workers likewise found their proper callings according to their age and size. Some nursed their mother's young; others cleaned and repaired the nest; yet others foraged courageously for food. Caste and class set out each ant's place, for the age of the true queens had arrived.

Deep within the fastness of their fortress kingdoms, the ant queens lived secure for unimaginable ages, each herself a dynasty, ruling over some twenty or thirty generations of her small sterile daughters. For power, for eggs, the queens had sacrificed much—their wings, their eyes, and the lithe, athletic grace that is natural to ants. Much, too, had they gained: freed from the struggle to survive, they grew wise when they did not go mad.

Confined by their dignity and fertility to the deep recesses of the nest, they learned to question the darkness and elicit its secrets. Released from the seductive deceit of vision—the trumpery of flowers, the illusions of color and form—the queens communicate with the tangible essence of things. Their subtle feelers probe the heavy nest air, detecting the furtive effluence of illicit egg-laying, hoarding, shirking, and other infractions of the social order. Their bodies exude a perfume that compels obedience: the scent of ceaseless fertility and the natural rights of the mother of all.

Next were the industrious Formicines, whose many innovations advanced the comfort and security of antkind. All ants can communicate with scent glands and with body language, if only to say "Come this way, quickly!" or "Back off—I'm bigger than you." The Formicines refined the language of ants to indicate not merely the whereabouts of enemies or food but to convey such qualities as big or small, near or far, ant or not-ant, sweet or meat. They were the first to relinquish the atavistic sting of the ancestral wasp-ant, replacing it with a searing acid that is at once eloquent and lethal.

Last of all came the greatest of all ants, her own kind, who transformed the crude semiotics of glands, feelers and forelegs into a true, palpable discourse, a language that is smelt and felt, one in which all an ant is capable of perceiving may be expressed.

Whether all young ant queens dream this dream we will not pretend to know. Her better fed sisters perhaps dreamt only of the wishful future: of absolute power and indolent luxury; of the thousands of devoted daughters who would feed them, lick them, and lovingly tend their eggs; of the great city they would command and the vast armies that would issue forth to conquer and consume the rival colonies of their sisters.

She awakened slowly, and as she awakened she discovered that she now had limbs she could move, except—was it another dream?—she was tightly bound by a thin, tough shell. She clawed at the skin of her cocoon—puzzled by it, by everything—until an obliging nursery worker, detecting her struggles, gnawed a breach into the top of the cocoon and helped her pull herself free. She twitched her feelers, sensing the new and wondrous world around her and her own new and wondrous body. The heavy warm scent of the nest and the quick, caressing touch of the nurse inspired her with feelings of loyalty and camaraderie. Home! Sister!

Damp and wrinkled like all newborns, she trembled on her delicate legs, breathing softly through her spiracles and feeling the hemolymph flow, sluggishly at first, into the veins of her wings. Having disposed of the cocoon, her nurse returned to lick her, then paused to give her a close inspection by feelers.

"Bah, a runt!" exclaimed the nurse, with a puff of disapproving gas. Other nursery workers turned round to investigate the disturbance. They too applied their feelers and gave their concurrence: "Too small!" "Useless!" "Defective—get rid of it." And, since social convention requires that dead, defective or otherwise undesirable ants be disassembled (after which they may be reused as food for the bigger larvae), they began to lay hold of her feelers and legs with their sharp-toothed mandibles.

Imagine, Reader, that you are such an ant, a virgin queen just emerged from your safe, featureless cocoon into the bustling confusion of the colony; and your first conscious sensation is one of danger, terrible danger—your elder sisters intend to dismember you!

Many an ant would be too confused, too weak, or too obedient to resist. In fact, the nurses, expecting little opposition, had taken only loose grips on her legs before readying themselves to yank. With a quickness of wit and action few freshly hatched insects can command, our ant wrenched herself free and scrambled to freedom over their backs. She fled the nursery as fast as six soft, shaky legs could carry her. Darting into a small side chamber, she listened for a moment: there was no pursuit. She paused to recover from the double exertion of emergence and escape.

Here we too must pause in order to clear our heroine of the charges made against her. She was most certainly larger than her accusers, who were only worker ants of modest proportions. For a virgin queen she was small, admittedly, but comely and well-formed. Her soft tegument was a pale yellow-white in complexion, like that of all newly eclosed ants. It would soon harden and darken to a burnished brown-black shell, chased with finely stippled lines and fringed with a finespun halo of reddish blond hair. No flaw could be found in the wings folded demurely over her back. Her compound eyes would undoubtedly sparkle like twin galaxies if there were light to see and be seen in the deep recesses of the nest. Her head capsule, though small, enclosed a shrewd, alert intellect, and her trim little gaster concealed perfectly formed ovaries, bearing the hopeful germ cells of thousands upon thousands of ant eggs.

All her fresh young senses were awakened as she trembled in her hiding place. Her tender feelers, peeping out into the corridor, twitched with exquisite perceptivity. The silky hairs of her head, trunk and gaster bristled with sensation as she pressed close to the chamber wall. The eardrums in her forelegs registered the rhythmic patter of hundreds of ants scurrying throughout the nest. Amid all the whirring jumble of sensations that passed through her quivering body and astonished brain, competing for attention, one alone could not be ignored: she was hungry.

She could not go back to the nursery; she must look elsewhere for food. She advanced into the corridor, bending her feelers cautiously towards the worker ants who passed, ceaselessly, through this, the main gallery of the nest. She soon perceived that some of them—those with swollen gasters and a lumbering gait—were bearing stores of food in their crops. The delectable scent drew her out to follow one such heavy-laden ant, who turned into a chamber where some of her elder winged sisters (for our ant was junior as well as small, the last of this brood of royals) were idling in expectation of their next meal.

"First!" cried the biggest of them as she rushed at the swollen worker and demanded food.

"Second!"

"Third!"

No claim to fourth place was made, not so much for want of mathematical abilities but because the ants all knew that the worker's crop would be drained by the first three greedy young queens, who did in fact feed until their own crops were plump with excess. The cries of first, second, third were renewed as those who had not yet fed began to wheedle shares from the three who had.

"Fourth!" proclaimed our heroine, coming forward for her share. But here she sadly miscalculated—not in her arithmetic, which was quite correct, but in her innocent expectation that her sisters would include her simply because there was enough to go around. All the virgin queens turned on her savagely, hissing that she was a runt and an upstart, then snapping at her feelers and forelegs until she once again fled.

Again and again she asked for food and each time she was repulsed—menaced and chased away by ants whose gasters bulged with excess. And so she learned the first harsh lessons of society: that fat ants get fatter, and that the big are always favored over the small. But desperation gave her cunning; she hid herself and waited. When a slow-witted drone solicited honeydew from a bloated major, she rushed forward to thrust herself between them, catching the droplet in her own mandibles and running off with it before the surprised ants could react.

This triumph was much repeated, as much for pleasure as hunger, as our outcast wandered through the nest. It was not always attended with the same smooth success; some of the workers were quick enough to deliver a painful slap or nip to her hind parts as she took off with her spoils. But most gave up trying to stop her, since there was as yet no shortage of food. She was pursued only with the usual cries of runt or half-ant. One worker, wittier than her sisters, called her *thrip*, a cant word of the scouts and foragers for something small and useless, since thrips, unlike aphids, produce no honeydew for ants to drink— and the name stuck.

It is not usual nor is it proper for an ant to have a name. Social harmony, as well as personal safety, depend upon sameness and anonymity. Only the Queen is unique, simply because she is Queen. Among her personal attendants, who are always the biggest and strongest of the young workers, one will be known as the Royal Alpha, another as the Beta. There will be, in addition, a Royal Gamma and a Delta, subservient to the Alpha and Beta while tyranniz- ing over all ants of lesser rank. But these still are not names—only jealously sought, briefly retained, entitlements.

These ranks and degrees are imitated on an inferior scale throughout society. In every chamber of every nest, wherever three or more ants have come togeth- er to eat, to groom or to gossip, there will be an alpha and a beta. Oftentimes these ants win and maintain their high station by jostling and posturing of the rudest sort, falling little short of actual violence. In the presence of sisters of such choleric tempers, those who are not comparably blest with bigness and sharp teeth would prefer to go unnoted.

In short, an ant with a name is an ant with a defect, and defective ants ought to be eliminated. But Thrip was unwilling to be eliminated. Hunting her down was impractical when there was so much else to do: nursing a large summer brood of replacement workers; repairing and expanding the nest; and fatten- ing up the virgin queens and drones for their nuptials. Having named her, the ants left her alone. A few of the older foragers even fed her willingly—not out of sisterly kindness, of course, but because the distention of their crops pained them and they were anxious to be rid of the surplus.

Beginning with how to snatch food for herself and where to hide when pursued, Thrip soon understood the workings of the colony better than any other ant in it—certainly better than the Queen, whose egg-laying kept her much confined, and better than the typical worker, who rarely perceived anything beyond her own tiny sphere of activity and influence. Passing up and down the winding galleries of the vast nest, thrusting her inquisitive feelers here, there, everywhere, Thrip discovered how often ants merely pretend to be busy. Most of the real work is done by an elite few; others get busy only when they have been bullied into it by bigger or younger ants. Ants *seem* very active, it is true, yet they do little.

On one occasion a chamber vault caved in, trapping a dozen workers inside, who stridulated piteously for rescue. Some fifty sisters came running at their call, but very few, perhaps fifteen at most, actually did the hard, dangerous work of excavation. The others scurried back and forth, clambering on top of one another in their excitement, in which there was perhaps more curiosity than concern, although all proclaimed their alarm for the fates of the trapped ants with the most fervent emphasis. And well they might, for it is easier to pity than to dig, and much more pleasant too. At most, the interested spectators would pick up a little lump of fallen earth, carry it an inch or two, and leave it for another ant to cart out of the nest. Thrip suspected—in all the tumult it was hard to tell—that some ants merely pretended to take a load of dirt in their mandibles, then dropped their imaginary burden with much ceremony a few inches away. Eventually, since so many ants were present and almost all did some token amount of work, the collapsed earth was removed and the buried ants were rescued.

The dazed, half-dead victims were almost finished off by their well-wishers, who trampled them in their haste to offer congratulations and to feeler them. In this their one moment of celebrity, every ant wished to groom and lick them. And every ant who had removed as much as a speck claimed credit for their rescue. The exhausted ants who had done the digging—and who came crawling out last of all—were entirely overlooked.

The commotion touched off another collapse in the excavated chamber.

Now one of the true rescuers was trapped. Her faint struggles and stridulations were easily ignored and soon ceased altogether. Thrip was stirred to indignation, though not to action: she condoled, she pitied, but she did not dig. As for her royal brood sisters, the young virgin queens, they had never been known to perform any task at all, excepting a little mutual grooming and feeding, undertaken only when they believed the exchange of courtesies to be personally advantageous.

While her royal sisters were still idly begging food in the nursery, hunger and curiosity had drawn Thrip to the nest crater to encounter returning foragers, since the only way to be sure of a share is to get there first. She observed that the least capable ants—hollow old workers with toothless mandibles—did the most dangerous and important work of the colony. She witnessed how many food-gathering expeditions came back at half-strength or not at all: a worker ant foraging far from home, creeping laboriously over rock, earth, wood and leaf, unable to take wing to escape, is conspicuous and easy prey. True it is that many of the more established predators find ants to be too small, hard, and sour in taste to appeal. But those who might otherwise go hungry will learn to hunt ants and to relish their flavor. Even when they managed to evade all the ant-eating birds, spiders, doodlebugs, ground beetles, mantids and toads, the foragers often fell victim to their own kind, slaughtered by other ants when they ventured into disputed territories. Thrip wondered how any were found to undertake such deadly work and at last ventured to question some of the returning stragglers.

Their stories were very much alike. Some had begun life as nursery ants; others, bigger and more ambitious, had been attendants to the Queen. But in all cases they were forced out of their comfortable posts as soon as newly eclosed ants arrived to take their place. Those who initially resisted giving way to the young were harassed, intimidated and bitten until they too submitted.

First their young rivals would block their way as they attempted to proceed with their usual duties. Then the callow ants drummed their feelers on the head of any older sister who still refused to be replaced. Intensifying their campaign of intimidation, they would point their gasters and grab the older ant's feelers as a means of proclaiming their own youthful superiority. As the final termination step (and it rarely came to that), the younger ants formed a gang to assault the recalcitrant older worker, pinning her down by yanking at her legs and feelers, compelling her, finally, to yield her place—or else be disassembled segment by segment.

Forced out of the comfort and security of the deep nest, the displaced ants moved to less agreeable positions in the colony. Some became diggers, excavating and repairing the nest; others found work as cleaners, dragging rubbish and dead ants to the nest midden. Even here they were not secure, for in due course they were replaced by other, more youthful ants.

For some days, maybe even a week or two, they kept up appearances by pretending to work—milling around, wandering from one section of the nest to another, idling near other ants that *were* working—but eventually others would refuse to share food with them, for by now they were noisome with age. (To our knowledge, no ant has yet devised a means of masking the thick, resinous odor that is the inevitable accompaniment of her aging.) At last hunger forced them to leave the nest and to take up a perilous existence as foragers. And so we will continue, they concluded their story, until we perish, probably within a fortnight. But we have, they said, the consolation of knowing that our enemies will soon follow us into the selfsame destiny of danger and untimely death.

Yet some ants, Thrip observed, never seemed to be forced out to forage, even in old age. The soldier ants, or majors, who ought by rights to join in pursuit and portage of larger quarry (such as careless caterpillars or crippled beetles) rarely did so—only when it was very safe or very easy; and then their bragging of their valorous exploits was not to be endured. Instead, the older majors sat as sentries on the nest crater, which might seem a duty requiring considerable courage, if they did not take alarm at every passing shadow and dart into the nest to save themselves. The younger majors loitered within the guardrooms as if they were a reserve force ready for emergency defense; but for the most part they were rather a reserve food storage unit. As successful foragers returned to the nest, the majors cajoled and blustered until the foragers surrendered the excess food to their care. This excess they in turn dispensed to hungry ants throughout the nest—only, Thrip suspected, they made sure their favorites were served first.

Thrip had by now traveled throughout the nest, probing everything and everyone she encountered, except she had not yet ventured to the royal chambers. A scurrying retinue of aggressive young workers kept constant attendance on the Queen, menacing any ant who came too near, or merely failed to get out of their way quickly enough.

For all their threatening and posturing, these were callow ants, some younger even than Thrip. She suspected they would be the first to flee and to abandon their mother if an enemy ever managed to penetrate the nest, and she wondered why the Queen would surround herself with such an inexperienced guard. Their arrogance annoyed her, and she began to ponder a plan to circumvent them and gain access to the royal chambers.

She soon detected their weakness: excited by their intimacy with the Queen and their gaster-wagging self-importance, they were always in motion, scrambling over each other in fawning eagerness to lick the Queen, then strutting away to snap their mandibles at lesser ants. Or they would bustle out into the corridor to threaten any ants lingering nearby. But by the late watches of a cool night, when the passage of workers through the galleries, if never stilled, was slow and fitful, the ants of the Queen's guard were lazy and somnolent. Taking advantage of their torpor, Thrip crept unnoticed into the royal chambers. Her inquisitive feelers interrogated and mapped the darkness. Two young ants were curled up on their sides at the entrance; these she had already stepped over. Another group, not quite immobile, were clustered to one side with drooping heads and folded feelers. These Thrip could evade by keeping to the other wall. At the rear, easily recognized, was the great Queen herself, inert and helpless. Before her crouched two drones, slumped in deep torpor.

Thrip had intended only to acquire a souvenir tinge of the royal essence that impregnated the earth and air of the Queen's residence, leaving before her intrusion could be detected by an awakening guard. But the queenly aroma worked a strange arousal: attracted, she crept forward, then froze with a sudden repulsion and a desire, almost, to flee. Then again she felt an inciting attraction and crept forward just a little bit more. Now she was close enough—why not chance it?— to touch the sleeping Queen with her feeler tips, drawing in a sample of that disturbing odor, the scent of limitless fertility and of the power it brings. Thrip brought her head forward, laying her feelers over the Queen's still head, putting her palps out for a delicate taste when—she was seized! The Queen gripped the scape of Thrip's feeler in her mandibles and shook her, hard.

Thrip repressed her alarm and curled her body in submission. Her mother's mandibles, she noted with surprise, were dull and almost toothless. She might easily wrench herself free. But she knew the brutal young workers behind her were awakening: *their* mandibles were keen, and she could not expect to get past them without a fight.

"My Queen, my Mother, please forgive me for disturbing your rest," she began.

"Who are you—what are you?"

"Only your daughter, one of your many admiring daughters," Thrip tried again.

"I do not like my daughters. I do not trust my daughters, especially those with wings."

"The least of your daughters—a very unimportant, insignificant daughter," Thrip pleaded, still held aloft in the Queen's jaws. Behind her the Queen's attendants, now thoroughly alert, were pressing forward to probe and nip at her rear.

"Yes," said the Queen meditatively, as her feelers coursed searchingly over Thrip's head, trunk, wings and gaster. "Just a runt." And she let Thrip drop.

"Leave her alone," she commanded her retinue, who were zealous to show their loyalty to the Queen by attacking and dismembering Thrip. "Let her go. She's not a threat."

"A very unimportant, insignificant daughter," the Queen repeated dreamily. "The best kind of daughter to have," she murmured as she composed herself for sleep.

Thrip maintained her dignity just as far as the gallery, then took off as fast as her legs would carry her. She did not stop until she reached one of her better hiding places, a little-used side chamber of the middle nest, where the oldest and least respected foragers would huddle together against the winter cold.

The Queen's startled words lingered in her memory: "Who are you—what are you?" Frightened as Thrip herself had been, she had nevertheless detected the alarm in the Queen's utterance. She now felt certain that none of her winged sisters had ever gained admittance to the royal chambers—although some had boasted of such privileges—and that motives which blended policy with fear induced the Queen their Mother to admit none but harmless drones and callow workers to her presence.

Thrip began to groom herself, as thoughtful ants generally do when they are troubled or confused—the foolish ones simply run about in circles—when she realized that her cuticle carried a strong scent of the Queen. She reeked of authority. And she decided to make use of it before the volatile royal essence faded and blended into the jaded background odor of the nest.

By now her many royal sisters had moved to the upper nest, where they lay claim to the best chambers and used their position to intercept and intimidate returning foragers into giving them food. They were just bearing down on one such worker—a poor worn thing, hollow and decrepit with age, but with a crop filled to bursting with honeydew—when Thrip pushed her way to the front.

"First!"

Her big sisters were so astonished by Thrip's assurance that she did indeed get the first honeydew drop from the beleaguered old forager. That in itself would be a valuable triumph, even if she were paid back with a few sharp nips before making her escape. But this time Thrip stood her ground. The alpha and beta sisters, accustomed to being first (and second) in everything, moved forward to punish her audacity. But they startled as soon as their angry feelers rapped Thrip's head. They regrouped and came at her again; but, taking an even stronger sample of the Queen's essence, they once more retreated. Too late they realized that their indecision and confusion (by which they dropped quite considerably in status) had been witnessed by their inferior sisters, whose quick feelers had followed the scene with intense interest.

"I've just returned from a private audience with the Queen, my Mother," Thrip remarked lazily, drawing her tarsus casually across her head and feelers to release more of the queenly aroma into the chamber. Several ants could not resist this potent enticement and crept forward to lick her.

"That's ridiculous. She wouldn't admit a runt like you to her presence!" said the dull-witted alpha ant, whose status was entirely owing to her size.

"She quite obviously did," Thrip answered.

"She mistook you for a drone," the beta ant sneered.

This struck so near the truth that Thrip was momentarily discomfited, until she luckily thought of a reply.

"On the contrary, she said I was the best kind of daughter to have," Thrip announced triumphantly, and drove her advantage home by impudently pointing her gaster at her two big sisters. Then, since they were, after all, very powerful ants, rendered acutely dangerous by rage and mortification, she made a prudent exit.

Thrip's impulsive nature had again tricked her into going further than she intended. It occurred to her rather late that the two big ants might revenge their humiliation by hunting her down to maim or kill her. Then she reflected that their bulk would prevent them from seeking her out in the minor galleries and chambers of the sprawling nest. But she would need to be alert and quick-witted when she next ventured to the chambers in which they held their authority—as she was determined to do.

Now, as she passed through the twisting corridors of the nest, Thrip noticed how differently the workers treated her—some approaching with deference, some retreating with fear, bewildered by the oddity of encountering a winged virgin who bore the Queen's rich ovulatory scent. This novelty, she felt, must be further investigated and exploited, before the royal essence evaporated from her cuticle, as it soon would.

She had never returned to the nursery since she was chased from it on that fateful first day. In the warm season the nurses took their young charges—the bigger larvae and the pupae—to the summer brood chambers in the upper nest each morning, returning them to the deep nest at nightfall. This daily outing was undertaken not to broaden the horizons of the developing ants but rather to limit them: the warmth of the upper nest would hasten their metamorphosis into common workers, the destiny of the summer brood.

New workers were urgently required. The effort to feed fifty greedy virgins and a much greater number of drones was exhausting the colony. The foragers were fewer in number each day since they themselves were food for birds, toads, spiders, assassin bugs and ground beetles—all of which were also very hungry, as they too were engaged either in feeding their brood or in fattening themselves for mating and egg-laying.

Each returning forager—or each food-swollen major, if the big ant got there first—was mobbed not only by the virgins, who usually won the contest, but by the nurses, who clamored pathetically for double portions in order to feed the larvae. These double portions, when obtained, were not always shared with the half-starved brood. However, it made a good, and sometimes effective, plea. The more desperate nurses—those who went without a share—would lick and nibble the larvae so violently that many were left with scars or other deformities. And if some should perish of their wounds, what then? Why then, dear Reader, there would be no reason not to eat them outright.

But the surviving larvae had a ready revenge for such misuse. As each new brood of workers hatched from their cocoons, they would supplant their nurses, forcing them out of the deep nest to other, less agreeable situations in the colony. The nursery ants might well expect such a return for their services, for they had done so themselves to their own caregivers. By next year, should they live so long, these nursery ants would become the old, overladen foragers creeping painfully home to be molested by their demanding younger sisters. Yet so it always had been and would be; therefore, it is undoubtedly the right and best way for ants to live.

Thrip roamed idly through the nest, enjoying the consternation her queenly aroma inspired, even among those who recognized her as Thrip the runt. But she was careful to avoid the vicinity of the Queen's chambers, turning off into lesser used galleries that none knew as well as she.

One such detour brought her before a large drone resting in a small cell just barely able to hold him. Thrip was mildly surprised to find a drone deep in the nest at a time when his brothers were warming themselves in the upper chambers, and yet more surprised when he approached her.

"Kind virgin," he said, gently touching her mouthparts with his long, delicate feelers. "Gracious royal sister, could you spare a little food?"

"Why should I share with you?" Thrip demanded, taken back. No ant had ever asked her for a food share before, or addressed her so politely.

"Because–because I'm hungry?" the drone tried. "Not a very good reason, is it? There was an ant who fed me," he added sadly, "but she went away and didn't come back."

Tapping him with her feelers, Thrip realized that the poor creature was so hollow with hunger he could barely stand. Rather in spite of herself—for why should she share when she herself had to steal to get her food?—she fed him. He revived at once and skittered back and forth in gratitude.

"Why aren't you in the upper nest with the other drones?"

"She told me to stay here."

"She?"

"The one who always fed me. Sometimes," the drone confided eagerly, for his secret itched to be told, "sometimes I used to call her Mama."

Thrip drew back in surprise. Surely all ants, even drones, came from eggs, and all eggs come from the Queen. It could only be some foolish drone fantasy. She herself felt foolish for being drawn into conversation with a simple-minded drone. She turned to leave, continuing on her way towards the deep nest nursery, expecting that the nurses and larvae would be returning to it. Then she realized she was no longer alone.

"Are you following me?"

"Yes," said the drone. "You smell nice."

"Don't," Thrip warned, flaring her mandibles. And the drone did drop back several paces, unwilling to risk a bite, but determined all the same to accompany her.

Arriving at the deep nursery and finding it silent and bare, Thrip realized the evening was so warm that the nurses had chosen to stay in the upper nest. She herself was tired; the tinge of queenly essence that had brought about her brief surge in popularity was fading; and thus she decided she might as well take her rest in the deserted nursery as anywhere else.

Then, however, she perceived the chamber was not empty after all. Another ant was already there, as yet unsuspicious of her presence. This was most peculiar. Ants naturally seek the company of other ants. Wherever there are three ants gathered together there will soon be four, then five, then six, and so on until there is no room for more, as all ants are eager for society. They congregate in search of food and news—both together, for food *is* news, a story passed from mouthpart to mouthpart throughout the colony.

Despite her intimidating encounter with the Queen Mother, Thrip had no fear in approaching the solitary ant. Even a runt virgin is bigger than any of the workers, including the majors.

The other ant, Thrip soon discovered, was a very big major indeed, with a greatly distended gaster stuffed with honeydew and nectar. Yet many of the workers had gone without food in recent days, and Thrip herself had missed a meal or two.

While she was pondering this mystery—and while the big major was still inert in stupor—a diminutive worker bearing the scent of the nursery scrambled into the chamber and prodded the major into wakefulness. Having got the big ant's attention, the little nurse proceeded to give the major a thorough grooming, then massaged her massive head with her feelers. Neither had noticed Thrip, and she was able to creep close enough to satisfy her curiosity.

The two could not make a more amusing or contemptible contrast: the tiny, scurrying nurse was an elderly ant with mandibles so dull and worn they no longer closed; the major was a great clumsy blockhead, her crop so bloated with food that she could barely lift her gaster. She was a remarkably ugly ant as well. Her lip was grotesquely long and her huge mandibles hung so low that they would almost trip her feet if her swollen gaster did not already anchor her to the spot as immoveable as any tree. Her thick, wide-set brows bore a disfiguring bump which constricted her feelers to swivel in an obtuse, lowering direction, giving her an air of obstinacy and shiftiness that was perfectly veridical.

Having at last completed the major's toilet, the little nursery ant presented her demand for payment—tapping the major's deformed lip for food. Thrip judged this to be the right moment for announcing her presence and demanding her own share of the food.

But Thrip had forgotten what she herself best knew—that an advantage in size means little when desperation imparts cunning to one's adversaries. She had surprised these ants in the act of hoarding food and they did not intend to allow her to publicize her discovery. The major was just quick enough to catch Thrip's mandibles in her own. The old nurse went for her foreleg and began to gnaw at a joint. Even with dull mandibles she might sever it if Thrip could not escape. She managed to shake off the nurse but could not wrest herself free from the major, who easily parried or evaded Thrip's attempts to use her claws. The little nurse returned to gnaw at another joint.

Thrip had not yet taken a serious hurt. The major was too fat, and possibly too lazy, to go on the offensive; and the toothless jaws of the little nurse could do little damage as long as Thrip continued to shake her off. All the same, Thrip had cause for fear: she was unable to free herself or fight back effectively; and she would soon tire.

"What's the matter—what's going on?" The drone thrust himself into their midst, startling the major into relaxing her grip on Thrip, who wrenched herself free and took this opportunity to deliver her first blow, a bite to the major's swollen gaster.

As Thrip and the drone had the advantages of youth and size, the ensuing battle might be expected to be brief, and so it was, only Thrip was the loser. A virgin queen can deliver a creditable bite but she has little skill in combat, a drone none whatsoever. With their weak jaws and mild dispositions, drones are meant for love, not war. This particular drone did little but put himself in the way, sometimes by chance intercepting blows intended for Thrip, still calling out excitedly, "What's the matter—what's going on?"

At last Thrip made a necessary if inglorious retreat, the drone following. From the safety of the gallery she attempted a face-saving boast: "I have special access to the Queen: she shall hear of this!"

This unlikely claim was not received with the scorn it deserved, as both the major and the nurse belatedly recognized the presence of a faint but genuine trace of the royal essence.

"Don't be hasty, don't be hasty!" The little nurse scurried after Thrip and sought to detain her. "I'm certain we can work something out."

And they did. Their silence was purchased, at least momentarily, by their filling themselves with honeydew. Thrip would of course be back for more; indeed, the major and the nurse were already providing portions to a number of ants admitted to the secret. The major served, in fact, as a private food bank for a select group of subscribers who deposited excess food during times of plenty and returned to withdraw it during periods of famine. The nurse, who was the originator of this scheme, owed her permanent and very pleasant position in the nursery—for by rights she would have been expelled by younger ants long ago—to her mysterious access to extra food, shared only with the most dominant of her nursery sisters, who then became her protectors and patrons.

Having fed on the major's honeydew until she filled her own crop to capacity, Thrip departed to find a safer corner in which to pass the chilly hours of the night. She had acquired a full crop but at the cost of adding two new enemies. She remembered, then, that she also had an ally. But when she turned to feeler the drone she discovered he was no longer following her. She wondered whether he had found his way to the upper nest to join his brothers or had instead returned to his tiny cell to await the worker who would never return. It was absurd to miss the companionship of a drone; yet she felt strangely disheartened to be on her own once again.

Once the morning sun had roused the sentries and the scouts had gone forth, Thrip took her way to the upper chambers inhabited by the royal brood. Famished workers, detecting her full crop, importuned her for shares but she refused them. She would need all her food to claim a position among her winged sisters.

The virgin queens had been in turmoil since Thrip's appearance among them the day before. The alpha virgin had been utterly disgraced—reduced to harassing the smallest, least important of her royal sisters in order to reestablish a place for herself. The beta virgin had managed to cling to her position by claiming the former alpha was the one who had recoiled in fear from Thrip, further insinuating that the ex-alpha had licked Thrip's rear in submission, which was of course untrue, but so malicious it delighted all the sisters who had been bullied by the big alpha. The beta was shrewd enough to be content with keeping her place, when she might easily have sunk to gamma or worse. But among the bigger virgins the contention to be the new alpha was fully underway. For hours the rival sisters had smirked, schemed and insinuated; they had scolded, strutted, preened and boasted; they had raged, hissed, blustered and threatened.

And for what, Reader, were they contending—only for a trifling and fugitive distinction that yielded no real advantage to the ant who won it. Soon it would be the day of their nuptials, soon they would depart from their natal nest, never to meet again. Those who now thrust themselves forward in exhausting contention—would they not have done better to conserve their strength for that perilous journey? Instead, they sacrificed their health to their ambition, their dignity to their vanity, when they might rather have called upon prudence and reason to get the better of their baser passions. With such wise reflections the ants of lesser stature drew a moral from the scene, observing as the biggest and most forward of their sisters quarreled violently amongst themselves. All their posturing and maneuvering had as yet accomplished little except to make them confused, hungry, and yet more ill tempered.

Thrip's timing therefore was perfect, her entry sensational. She no longer bore the disturbing scent of the Queen but the delectable fragrance of honeydew flavored with nectar. The other ants approached hungrily, then hesitated.

No ant can be compelled to share. She shares because the distention of her crop pains her, because a favor given will eventually be returned or, rarely, because selfless devotion to the sisterhood impels her to be generous. Angry, hungry, and always rather stupid, the displaced alpha forgot that Thrip was not so easily intimidated as an exhausted forager. Believing she had an opportunity to recover her status, humiliate an upstart, and gain a meal all at once, she advanced menacingly and made her demand:

"First!"

"No," Thrip answered, "you're last."

The other ants mocked the disgraced alpha with open mandibles but their consternation was almost as great as hers. Who would be first, second, third? And what would it signify if they submitted to Thrip's ranking of them?

"Congratulations on obtaining a supply of first-rate food," the beta virgin said smoothly. "Where did you find it?"

"I'm willing to share my food with deserving sisters," Thrip replied with equal unconcern, "but I'm not going to share my sources. Be assured, however, that I can replenish my crop whenever I please."

Few believed Thrip, who, though accused of many transgressions, was never judged capable of an act so poor-spirited as telling a plain unadorned truth. Yet she might be able to find food in the future, and she certainly had food now. While the others hesitated, the beta virgin made up her mind.

"If that *is* the case, you are certainly the cleverest of us all, Sister," she said with a meaningful declination of head and feelers. Thrip fed her, then fed those of their sisters whom the beta selected for the privilege; and they, in their turn, fed those sisters whom they wished to favor and oblige.

All the virgin queens understood what their beta's bowed head signified. Thrip, the runt and renegade, was now installed as their alpha. In their view this put her second only to the Queen Mother herself, although it may be doubted whether the worker ants shared the virgins' opinion of their importance to society. Nonetheless, it was an extraordinary triumph for an undersized ant and one not destined to endure.

Most ants, big or small, would become complacent following such a precipitant rise in station. But Thrip had been too often chased from chamber to chamber, relying on her solitary wits to survive, to put much faith in her sisters' flattering attentions. They clustered around her now with apparent affection, gently brushing her with feelers and palps, hoping to catch a clue to the origins of her food cache in the odors clinging to her person. When these glancing contacts failed to detect a revealing scent, the sycophantic gamma insisted on giving her new favorite sister many searching kisses. Fortunately for Thrip, she had groomed herself quite thoroughly after leaving the nursery in order to remove the detested scents of the fat major and the foul old nurse. Her secret could not be so easily discovered.

It was not long before her winged sisters began to importune her for food, as much from curiosity as actual hunger. Every ant wanted to find out if Thrip really could refill her crop at will; and the slyer virgins were determined to discover her source. Thrip knew she could not deny them for long before they would grow threatening. A slight disturbance at the nest crater—only a toad snatching up some inattentive sentries and drones—gave her an opportunity to depart unnoticed.

It was fortunate for Thrip that, halfway to the deep nursery, she was vexed by dust clinging to her gaster hair and darted into a small side chamber to groom. The ant who had been following her also stopped, but not in time to avoid detection. The crisp, aromatic profile of a winged virgin is easily distinguished from the dull dingy scent of a common worker.

The beta virgin came forward, mandibles parted in a malevolent smirk.

"Sister, surely you did not flee from our chambers in fear! We all feel some agitation at the approach of our nuptials; but we virgin queens must set an example in dignity and courage, not hide ourselves every time a predator picks off a few superfluous ants."

Thrip refused to be provoked into a response but she felt the danger of her present situation. Instinctively she had drawn back when she sensed the other ant's presence, discovering to her dismay that she had taken shelter in what was only a shallow declivity in the gallery wall. She could not win a fight, and she could not get away. As she fidgeted anxiously, she dislodged a little dirt from the wall, and was struck at once by an idea.

"I'm glad you're here, beta sister. You can help carry food back to our comrades, as there is really too much for my own small crop."

Arrogance and greed blunted the beta ant's usual cunning. She followed, eagerly and unsuspectingly, as Thrip led her into the chamber that had collapsed on the trapped workers some days earlier. Since most of the builders had been conscripted as foragers to help feed the famished colony, it had not been fully repaired. Sensing a slight draft from one side, Thrip knew the tunnel dug by the rescuers had not yet been closed.

"This way, Sister, we're almost there!" she called out as she scrambled through the narrow passage, just barely squeezing her larger form through a space intended for workers. Regaining the freedom of the spacious gallery, she took off at full speed.

Her dodge worked better than she could have hoped. The beta virgin collided with the wall and showered herself with a heavy load of dirt. Queen ants are very capable diggers, since they themselves must excavate the simple nest in which they will lay their first eggs; but it is a disagreeable and messy task for virgin ants with wings. It took her quite some time to extricate herself, time enough to think. The beta was enraged at the trick, but she was not stupid. She repressed the urge to confront Thrip. Instead, she carefully groomed herself of every trace of dirt before returning to the upper nest. She arrived just after Thrip had dispensed the contents of her refilled crop to her winged sisters—and pretended not to care, evading the few feelers that twitched curiously in her direction. After feeding, most ants safe inside the nest will groom lazily for a few minutes, then drop into a doze. The beta virgin likewise folded her feelers and relaxed into a crouch, but she was thinking hard. So was Thrip.

Having eluded her stalker, Thrip had proceeded cautiously to the deep nursery, checking repeatedly for pursuit. She was pleased to find that the bloated major was alone and again in a state of heavy torpor. But approaching a large, hostile worker who shared only under duress was dangerous, and Thrip no longer carried the royal scent that had intimidated the ant into sharing on their previous encounter.

Food sharing is as intimate as a kiss: the seeker must touch the giver's lip with her foreleg or feeler, then bring her head forward as the giver opens her mandibles to share or, alternatively, to bite. Thrip realized then that she sorely needed an ally to stand guard before she placed herself in such a vulnerable stance. Even the drone would do, but she no longer knew where to find him.

She decided she would rather confirm the major as an enemy than risk such an act of unwarrantable trust. A surprise attack must do the trick. She launched herself at the sleeping ant's head—snapping her mandibles and uttering a string of threats and coarse oaths she had learned from the majors patrolling the nest perimeter. The startled ant instantly discharged a big drop of sweet liquor. Too late, she let off her own volley of curses when she realized she had not been raided by a squad of blustering, big-jawed soldiers but only fooled, again, by Thrip.

Once again she had a full crop, along with the power and influence it brings among a brood of hungry sisters. Yet, after returning to her winged sisters and sharing her food, Thrip felt as alone and uneasy as on that first day when she was chased from the nursery. She wished she could relinquish her alpha status and return to her solitary wanderings; but she had made enemies at every level of the nest, and doing so was not much safer than remaining with the other virgin queens. Her position depended upon keeping them well fed, yet this would be increasingly difficult to do. She felt certain the evil little nursery ant, when she learned of Thrip's latest sally, would devise a trap to foil her. No doubt the two food hoarders had secret partners who would help protect their cache. An ally or two would be needed before she attempted to cope with the major again, but where would she find them? She might select two of the lesser virgins to be her assistants, only she distrusted them all, fearing they were all loyal to the beta and would betray her.

In fact, the other virgins disliked Thrip and the beta equally, and were beginning to feel a strange nostalgia for the dominance of the former alpha. True, her perpetual bullying had been obnoxious, stepping on her sisters and slapping their faces with her feelers for no reason except the sport of it. Yet she had been entitled to her high rank by being unquestionably the biggest of their brood; whereas the beta and Thrip had unfairly imposed upon their sisters, using their superior intelligence to obtain an advantage that did not rightly belong to them. After all, the beta was only a larger-than-average virgin—ranking perhaps tenth in overall bigness. And as for Thrip—why, she was ridiculously small for a virgin queen, a runt, a royal minim. In their confused, fuddled way, for none of them could think clearly although they all thought just alike, they felt the disgrace of being dominated by such an insignificant ant. This time there had not been quite enough honeydew in Thrip's hastily acquired crop load. If Thrip failed to keep them fed, or if another food source of comparable quality were to be found, they would all turn on her at once.

Happily for Thrip, she knew none of this and felt threatened only by the smart, wily number two. She twitched her feelers questioningly toward the beta, who was still pretending to slumber as she pondered her own course of action. Thrip was puzzled by the beta's quiet, controlled demeanor on returning to the upper nest. She knew the beta ant to be a more dangerous rival—now an outright enemy—than the stupid alpha who had been demoted to shoving and nipping the weakest of their brood; and she doubted the beta's quiescence was a sign of weakness or defeat.

The beta virgin had now made up her mind to risk a confrontation. Unlike Thrip, she had some inkling of their sisters' rebellious leanings, and she herself despised being second to a runt. Thrip's own words gave her the hint she needed.

She came forward and rudely rapped Thrip's mouthparts with her foreleg.

"I notice that many of our deserving sisters are still hungry. Obviously, your crop is *too small* to be serviceable. I *strongly suggest* you take me with you to visit your food source. *Now.*"

Around them, the winged ants began to fidget and to prod each other into wakeful attention, beginning with those who were in fact hungry and had been unable to rest. The beta was standing stilt-legged over Thrip, her mandibles open in threat. Thrip slowly raised herself on her forelegs, keeping her gaster and hind legs to the ground—a guarded, ambiguous stance, submissive but ready to spring.

"You are ill-tempered from hunger, beta sister! You are the only one who did not feed at all. Perhaps you would like some food now?"

The beta was indeed hungry, so hungry that she rashly chose to interpret Thrip's words as conciliatory. She brought her head down closer to Thrip, who took that opportunity to spit in her face.

Here we must insert a short apology for our heroine. Some readers may disapprove such peremptory behavior, exhibited within the nest to her own brood sister. Food spitting is properly reserved for diplomacy, for the delicate negotiations that take place between scouts of rival colonies, a setting in which it is pedantically and rather prudishly known as aggressive regurgitation.

There are, as everyone knows, a great many ants and a great many anthills. Inevitably scouts and foragers from rival colonies encounter each other in the field. Warfare is costly, risky, impractical, without first gauging the enemy's strength. How better to do so than by spitting precious food into the stranger's face?

If the ant from the strange colony is so well fed that she can afford to be incensed by such an indignity, she will return the insult in kind. But if she is hungry, she will lick up the spittle. It is honeydew, after all, and just as delicious as if it had been offered politely. Then she will have to pretend she has not been insulted, only given a nourishing drink that went slightly or too enthusiastically awry. They part in feigned amity, only one now knows that the other is hungrier and weaker, and so quite possibly is her colony.

Thrip had no knowledge of the intricacies of foreign policy. She acted on a rash inventive impulse. When the beta virgin then succumbed to her hunger and licked up the sweet spittle, Thrip knew she had gained another fragile victory over her rival. But their ongoing conflict would inevitably end in the smaller ant's defeat, unless something happened to forestall it. Something did.

For the past few days the drones had been pressing upward to the guard chambers and then out of the nest entirely. At first they merely loitered on and around the nest crater, looking a bit foolish and out of place. Then they began to move about with feverish indecision, going round and round in circles (not without frequent rest stops), sampling the air with intent, questing feelers. A few of the more excitable drones even tried to take flight, but attentive workers quickly grabbed hold and pulled them back to earth.

As more drones arrived, so did more workers—at first restraining the drones' impetuosity but finally becoming infected by it themselves. At last the workers relented and the excited drones began to leave—first in twos and threes, then many more at once. Emergency exits were opened in every quadrant of the upper nest as yet more drones emerged. The surface of the nest boiled with them. How could there even be so many drones! The nuptial flight was at last underway.

As they took wing, they released a heavenly perfume—a thrillingly arousing fragrance that not only summoned the remaining drones to join them but excited their winged sisters as well, who began to stream up out of the nest and onto the surface. Who would have thought drones, mere drones—their own brothers at that—could send forth a call so compelling, so irresistible? It was balsam, honey flavored, with fragrant wood-notes like the rising sap of spring. It was a melody that sang of love and adventure and the faraway. It was—there was no saying what it was! But the virgin queens all obeyed its call, all except Thrip.

She followed her sisters up to the nest crater in ambivalence, half compelled, half aloof and curious. She watched as they launched themselves into slow, ungainly flight—some swarming up blades of grass for lift, others being pushed out by workers as they beat their inexperienced wings and struggled aloft.

Thrip felt the tug of the drones' mysterious, bewitching scent. But she was young, she was small, and she was not a fool. She could form a shrewd guess of the dangers from her conversations with the foragers, and she realized there would be abundant food for all once the virgin queens and drones had departed. She planned to stay put.

"You too—be off!" A major jabbed at her gaster. Thrip lashed back at her with great indignation, as another worker nipped at her rear and tried to seize her by a hind leg.

For once the workers treated her like any other winged ant: those who hesitated were encouraged, then transported to a better takeoff point, then finally threatened with hisses and nips. Thrip had ventured too far from the nest entrance to make a retreat to her usual lurking places. The workers snapped impatiently at her legs, forcing her further out. As she hesitated, a major picked her up by the mandibles and swung her out from the hilltop. She opened her wings in a confused endeavor to preserve her balance, then found herself borne upwards in the air.

The rapture of flight for such earthbound creatures can scarcely be conceived. Long eons ago the ants sacrificed their wings for the security of the underground. There they are safe and prosperous, achieving lifespans unimaginable to the solitary insects. But they are not happy. Ants do not like dirt. They do not like it clinging to their bodies—grooming themselves many times daily to be rid of it—and they do not like it in their mouthparts—faugh! They detest the fungal, earthy odor of newly excavated galleries, masking it with their own rich, agreeable scent, washing down the earthen walls with a smooth clean coat of secretions, sometimes adding a wainscoting of discarded cocoon skins. At least it is safe, however filthy, inside the earth. For those who must go creeping upon it, in plain view of so many hungry killers, gnats and flies are envied for their wings. But among the ants, only the virgin queens and the drones are endowed with wings, and only for this one brief (and usually fatal) flight.

Neither the queens with their dim eyes nor the drones with their dim wits perceive their danger. Flight elated them, and the flutter of wings fans their heady perfumes all about, increasing their arousal. They cluster together in their slow, uncertain flight, hovering in broadening circles—searching for something, but what? Who is in charge? Who knows the way—and the way to what? Surely not the drones, but, yes, apparently it *is* the drones who lead.

Spiraling this way and that, the drones peer out and feeler the air with intent concentration. Calling their sisters after them is well and good, for sisters will do as a last resort if, that is, they have mistaken the day. But they have not! There it is now, ahead of them—the great nuptial swarm formed of all the colonies of the region. The drones make for it in great haste, their fat sisters flocking after them.

Back on the anthill, the workers gazed dully at the sky, perceiving only a host of dark specks, small, smaller, soon gone from view entirely. Then they returned to their usual tasks, made much easier now by the departure of so many big, demanding, unprofitable ants. The workers had given their farewells with mixed feelings. The winged ants were, after all, their sisters, and they hoped some among them might succeed and breed, providing they established their nests sufficiently far from the home territory. But the young virgins had been greedy, arrogant and domineering; and so it gave the exhausted workers a certain satisfaction to reflect that most of these would-be queens would perish within the next few hours.

The last to take wing, Thrip made off after her elder sisters and soon caught up with them, her slight form quicker and more agile in flight. Perhaps it was not the wisest thing to do. She could have hidden herself, then returned to the colony at nightfall. As long as she retained the scent of her natal nest, the sentries were unlikely to harass her. She might continue in her vagabond ways, even make things easier for herself by discarding her cumbersome wings. But the novelty, the enchantment of flight drew her forward, and she for once behaved like any other ant, following and clustering with her sisters.

She soon found herself swept up into a dazzling swarm of vivacious young persons of her own species. She did not try to push her way to the center where the best-endowed females enticed the biggest males to seek them, but instead hung uncertainly in the rear. Even so she had more suitors than she could answer, for there were a dozen enamored drones competing for the favors of every female in the swarm.

Thousands of winged ants dance upon the breeze, changing partners, pirouetting up and down in graceful spirals. The magnificence of a nuptial flight is scarce conceivable to those who have not witnessed it, although its grandeur was largely lost upon the participants, whose senses were overwhelmed by the amorous perfumes emitted by the drones and the answering scents of the virgin queens. This sensual haze, this arousing incense, shut out every other sensation or power of observation save those devoted to courtship. Even Thrip lost her customary vigilance in a frenzy of love-making.

Her sisters, along with the other big, pushy virgins, had first choice of suitors, of course. Her own were mostly rather undersized; one was even missing half a leg. But among them was a very large drone, almost as big as Thrip herself.

He had one oddity that might have disqualified him with the choosier virgins: his feelers were set in deep scrobes beneath massive, beetling brows. Thrip easily persuaded herself that this mild deformity, if such it was, gave him an air of great intelligence, and she was charmed by his suave, yet pungent, scent. He made such rapid progress in her affections that she soon vowed to carry his and only his sperm.

Flirting and quarreling, choosing and refusing, the ants floated carelessly on the breeze for several more minutes. They at last turned into the wind to make for the shelter of a weedy ditch where they might conclude and consummate their loving parlays. Too late, alas! A flock of starlings has found them. The birds dived into the swarm with gaping beaks, snapping up a half-dozen young queens in every mouthful, then banked their wings to make another sweep through the panicked throng. Other sharp-eyed birds—swallows, martins, chimney swifts—observed the mayhem and made their way to join the feast. The poor ants did not know which way to flee: those that escaped the swooping, circling birds were picked off by wasps patrolling the fringes or by flycatchers darting out from the treetops.

The strong prey upon the weak, the alert upon the unwary: so it has always been and will be, although the universality of this principle may be of little comfort to those who are the prey—no, not even though a stooping falcon took this opportunity to seize an inattentive bird for its meal.

The starlings concentrated on the center of the swarm, where many of Thrip's sisters were among the early casualties. Thrip was too confused to know how to save herself; but on their second pass she was so buffeted by the force of their wings that she went spinning toward the ground, where she landed on a knapweed blossom and took no hurt at all.

Striving to recover her composure, she paused to smooth her rumpled wings and groom her feelers. She presently perceived that she had been followed by some of her surviving suitors. Her chosen lover was not among them. Fearful and distraught, she was inclined to accept any available drone as long as he was quick about it. She lifted her gaster in invitation, expecting that her suitors would fight among themselves for the honor of filling her up with sperm. But instead they all rudely jumped her—one going to it at once, another queued up on her back, the others gripping her legs in an attempt to flank and dislodge their rivals.

Surprised and indignant, Thrip twisted round to bite at those within reach. In the turmoil, she lost her balance, slipped off the knapweed and attempted to fly, still burdened by several drones, their number diminished not by her struggles but by the exhaustion of their virility.

She made an awkward landing on a leaf that was already occupied by an evil-looking fly, with a villainous, low, sunken forehead and bulging green-black eyes. A coarse yellow beard covering most of its head did not conceal the gleam of its cruel proboscis. It was a robber fly, one that usually preyed upon hover-flies but was quite willing to sample a few of these little flying ants, especially as they seemed to be so very easy to catch. Thrip attempted to conceal her terror by pulling herself up to her full stature and gnashing her mandibles, a display that was little more than comical to the fly, stronger and more agile than any ant. Her lovers promptly abandoned her to her fate.

The fly sprang forward, grasped her in its bristly red forelegs and looked set to plunge its deadly beak into her trunk. Struggling only caused it to tighten its grip. As she writhed helplessly, Thrip realized that one puny but persistent drone was still dangling from her rear. She drooped as though overcome with despair, fooling the fly into loosening its grip as it sought the optimal point to insert its beak into her vitals. With a powerful effort, she cocked her gaster and flung the poor wretch straight at the fly's mouthparts. He made but a small meal, yet allowed our heroine precious seconds for her escape.

Throwing herself to the ground, she took cover within a tangle of crown vetch and fleabane. She had just begun to shed her hymenal wings, as all newly mated queens must do, when she perceived a familiar, once-enticing perfume. There before her, half-prostrate with exhaustion, was the drone with the bee-tling feeler brows, her chosen one. He had not perished in the assault of the birds, as she had believed: but his wings had been torn and he had plummeted earthward until his fall was stopped by a cobweb.

The spider, a mother, had summoned her brood of spiderlings to the capture and kill, for the sooner they learned to feed themselves the better. While she was yet advancing towards the prey—she might take her time, since the more he struggled, the more entangled he became—a dewdrop spider appeared and began cutting the drone loose, for it was particularly fond of ants. A fight ensued between the spiders, during which the drone managed to free himself and drop to the ground, somewhat more alive than dead.

Thrip regretted having already accepted three, or possibly four, consorts, as he was by far the fittest and handsomest drone among her suitors, her most promising mate. Then again, it appeared he had scarcely strength to mount her and might no longer be capable of siring the tens of thousands of daughters she would require. Torn between pity and love (for her sperm bag was not quite full), Thrip assured him of her fidelity. Her wings, she explained, had only been torn in the struggle with the birds, for he was the only drone ever to fascinate her (which was true enough, indeed).

"Let us speak no more of past pain," she concluded, "but only rejoice that we have been reunited."

Encouraged by Thrip's loving words, the drone went to it with a good will if not with great vigor. Having done, he staggered into the open, perhaps with a gallant intention of allowing his queen a little privacy for grooming and disposing of her tattered wings. But his passion and exhaustion left him unguarded; he was instantly snatched by a tiger beetle, who expertly butchered the poor drone into segments, then ate them one by one with great relish, even checking the ground for morsels that might have dropped unnoticed from its jaws. Quick, rapacious, insatiable, it was a terrifying creature—as bright as green fire, glistening like wet grass—for the forlorn ant queen cowering in the shadows.

Her grief and horror might have been lessened could Thrip console herself with the thought that there was now one less hungry predator on the prowl, but such was not the case. The beast's appetite was aroused rather than sated. Tiger beetles eat a great many ants but a big meaty drone is something special. Where there is one ant there are usually more. So, after it had finished its meal, it began to hunt again—running a few steps, then pausing to peer with its keen, searching eyes into the tangled weeds where Thrip had hidden herself. Wracked by fear, hunger, thirst, Thrip kept her place until the beetle at last gave up and moved on. The declining light signaled it was time for her to move on too, before other predators, those that hunt by twilight and by night—wolf spiders, ground beetles, and the always perilous assassin bugs—would be out in fearsome numbers.

Several small, clumsy figures lumbered past her hiding place, some dragging burdens. She sensed the acrid note of injury and death, ant death. Spider beetles were scavenging for stray body parts of those slaughtered by birds, wasps and robber flies on their first, fatal venture into the world. Of the hundreds of daughters from perhaps a score of colonies, had any survived but Thrip?

These stout, hairy scavengers were no threat to her; recognizing that their numbers afforded her some measure of safety, she ventured at last to come out and mingle with them.

Thrip knew where she was (since every ant can take her bearings from the sun and moon) but not where she should go. She was due south of her home; to the west she knew the foragers had always found a rich bounty of fatty seeds, dead bugs and juicy termites. She had therefore turned toward the west, cautiously tapping her way with her feelers, when her senses were suddenly aroused by the unmistakable scent of home—of home and of pain. There before her, directly in her path, lay one of her sisters. It was the beta. Hemolymph oozed from a gash in her side; one hind leg was crushed at the femur; a middle leg had been ripped from its socket and a feeler amputated at the elbow. The dying ant could barely stammer out some fragments of her story; the rest Thrip could read in her wounds.

With luck and cunning, the beta had evaded the birds, wasps and robber flies that had feasted upon the swarm, almost to its utter destruction. She had mated, come to earth safely, and discarded her wings in preparation to dig her nest—but then she had been surprised by a party of vicious turfgrass ants. She had fought her way free and escaped their territory, but with what injuries Thrip could feel for herself. And so saying, she expired in Thrip's embrace.

The deadliest foe of ant is ant. Thrip considered that the lands to the west were rich not only in food sources but in savage competitors; no young queen could hope to win out in a struggle with established colonies. Instead, she would have to turn east, a little-explored territory of shrubs and of short, barren grasses that were suitable for root aphids but for little else. If she successfully founded a new colony there, her daughters might be able to press westward in sufficient numbers to make a stand.

Her feelers and forelegs pressed tight against the beta's crushed, bleeding body, Thrip realized that she could not leave her sister's corpse to be scavenged by beetles. No rational ant in Thrip's desperate situation would do so. She put her palps to the hemolymph seeping from the beta's side, tasted it and found it good. Then she opened her abdomen and consumed the juices of her ovaries and crop, so discovering for herself that revenge can be sweet and highly nutritious too. Having fed, Thrip turned and made her way eastward. There, beneath an invitingly warm, broad stone, she dug herself a comfortable little nest.

Within a short while, Thrip became big with egg. Her first eggs were small; some did not hatch. But over the many seasons of her reign—for her colony would survive and prosper—the eggs continued to drop, fine sturdy eggs now, growing into strong, stalwart daughters. As each daughter egg trickled down her tube, she opened her sperm bag to moisten it with a sprinkling of quick, eager sperm that darted and danced before the beckoning egg. Berserk with jealousy, frantic with desire, each spermatozoon sought to be the one that would attach, enter and unite with the ovum. Together they played out the timeless storyline of yearning, conflict, and maturation, of passionate coupling and perfect union. Revitalized, resurrected, the minikin drones struggled against each other again and again, as the nuptial flight was endlessly replicated, on a minuscule scale, but with an intensity as big as the world.

II.

Epistolary

Ant

After reaching the adult stage the young queen undergoes yet another radical transformation. She changes from a highly versatile, self-reliant adult into a helpless colonial mendicant. While a young virgin still resident in her birth nest, she is ready with little notice to fly away on her own and to mate with the winged males. She alights and sheds her wings, builds a nest single-handedly, and raises the first brood of workers unaided over a period of weeks or months. Then abruptly, within a few days, the roles are switched and the workers begin to take care of her, reducing her to little more than an egg-laying machine.
–Bert Hölldobler & Edward O. Wilson, **Journey to the Ants** (1994)

Now to bring up a family of even very small children without eating anything and entirely on substances abstracted from one's own tissues is no trivial undertaking. Of the many thousands of ant queens annually impelled to enter on this ultra-strenuous life, very few survive to become mothers of colonies. The vast majority, after starting their shallow burrows, perish through excessive drought, moisture or cold, the attacks of parasitic fungi or subterranean insects, or start out with an inadequate supply of food-tissue in the first place.
–William Morton Wheeler, "The Queen Ant as a Psychological Study" (**Popular Science Monthly,** 1906)

No form of composition, in poetry or prose, admits of greater variety than the epistolary, since there are few subjects that may not be discussed through the medium of the letter. But the epistolary form has advantages peculiar to itself. It places the reader in the position of a confidential friend, thus creating a connecting contact between writer and reader, a contact Richardson always strove to preserve without resorting to direct address … It was already a literary device for one intimate friend or relative to write to another, who was usually in some sort of ethical difficulty, in order to give moral instructions or advice.
–Godfrey Frank Singer, **The Epistolary Novel: Its Origin, Development, Decline, and Residuary Influence** (1933)

Childbirth **matronizes** the giddiest spirits, and brings them to reflection sooner than any other event. Its consequences fill up the time, and introduce different scenes of pleasure and amusement in the mind of a lady. It draws her attention to more **serious** affairs; it **domesticates** her, as I may say; and makes her associate with graver persons, and such as are in the same scenes of life.
–Samuel Richardson, **Familiar Letters on Important Occasions** (1741)

Dᴇᴀʀᴇsᴛ Mᴀᴍᴀ,

I am sure you will readily guess my great news: I am to be a mother myself! I am safely hidden away in my own tiny nest with fourteen charming little eggs. Their sweetness is so captivating, truly, that I cannot stop licking them.

My new home is ideally situated beneath a flat rock that is warmed by the morning sun yet conveniently shaded in the afternoon by an arborvitae. Nonetheless, I am sometimes alarmed by a thumping so powerful that the rock shakes overhead. I instantly gather my babies in my mandibles and prepare to flee! But the danger passes. I think some big animals that do not notice or eat ants may be passing back and forth. My momentary fright is amply recompensed by giving me a fresh motive to caress and kiss my precious eggs.

My nest is small but snug and tidy. I am never far from my brood, so I can watch tenderly over them and keep them secure from all harm. There is not much for me to do now that the nest is dug and my darling little eggs laid. I pass my time quietly, dreaming of how wonderful life will be when I, like you, am surrounded by hundreds of selflessly devoted daughters.

I would rather dream of that distant future than recall the recent and very dreadful past. I must tell you that the nuptial swarm was overwhelmed by predators, and I doubt very much if any of your other daughters survived. The birds struck first, feeding voraciously on the fattest queens and scattering the terrified survivors. Then digger wasps, robber flies and spiders took their toll, picking us off one by one. Finally, rival ants viciously assaulted any surviving queen who had the misfortune to alight in their territory.

But I kept my wits about me: as soon as the birds struck, I flew down to the safety of the shrubbery, calling out to my suitors to follow me. There we had no sooner resumed our courtship when a robber fly dropped down upon us and grabbed me. It was useless to struggle against such a powerful, bristly brute. But I twisted my gaster about and hurled a small impertinent drone (who had taken unfair advantage of my predicament) right at its ugly face! This gave me time to escape, only to encounter another dreadful enemy. This time, one of my surviving admirers—a most handsome drone— threw himself in the path of a ravenous tiger beetle in order to preserve me. I passed through fields littered with dreadful ant carnage, still reeking of alarm, helpless struggle, and mutilation, before I found my nest site and dug my cozy little hole.

It occurs to me that you may not readily remember me from among so many offspring. I am the little one, the one they all mocked and insulted by the name of Thrip. But I have proven that the small agile ant may triumph over bigger ones with slow wits and thick clumsy bodies. And so I will keep the name of Thrip and be known forever after as Queen Thrip to my daughters when they hatch.

You should know—as I am sure it was not by your will—that from the moment of my eclosure I was cruelly persecuted by your workers. The very nursery ant who helped me from my cocoon tried to murder me! I was forced to flee for my life and to steal and connive to keep alive. No doubt my better fed and more privileged sisters had leisure to linger in the nursery and learn from observation how to care properly for their young (had they lived to lay their eggs). As for me, I feel ill prepared for motherhood. When will my little eggs hatch into larvae? And how am I to feed them when they do?

While digging my brood chamber, I encountered an ugly beetle who is however very clever and amusing. It understands our ant ways and communicates in tolerable Antic. Among its many entertaining tricks of mimicry, it can readily repeat anything it is told, even what it cannot, I am sure, understand. It undertook to convey my message to you after much rehearsal and many careful instructions. I hope you will see fit to reward the beetle for its efforts (as I have no means to do so) and to employ it yourself in conveying a reply to

Your Affectionate & Devoted Daughter, Thrip

Dear Daughter,

Of course you are to be a mother. Only your survival was (and still is) in doubt. If you do not starve to death before you hatch your first brood of tiny workers, you will be a mother continuously, at a rate of several thousand eggs a year, for the rest of your days.

As for instructing you in the duties of motherhood, that will be quite unnecessary. The gaster is wiser than the head—and more powerful. You knew very well how to dig a nest without being taught. (I hope you did not neglect to dig an escape hole beneath your brood chamber.) And you have no doubt discovered that eggs lay themselves and then produce delectable aromas to rouse you to their care.

We ants perceive ourselves as far more advanced than the solitary insects, and rightly so. Yet it is a difference of degree, not kind. For all our great intellect, instinct (for want of a better word) nonetheless rules over us all, even over the greatest queens. In high season, it is necessary for me to produce fifty or sixty eggs each day in order to maintain the colony at its strength. The fatigue is so great, but the compulsions so irresistible, that I have sometimes wondered whether I am, in the end, little more than an egg's way of making more eggs—many, many more eggs.

You will know how to feed your larvae when they hatch. Instinct will come to your aid, and you will do what young mothers have done before you over millions of ant generations: you will liquefy and spit your own bodily tissues into their tiny jaws, drop by precious drop—first your now-useless wing muscles and your fat stores; then, if need be, your living body.

Ponder what this means: you escaped being food for birds and spiders only to be food for your own brood. Cunning cannot help you now, and your small size is an obvious and severe disadvantage.

Since it was (and regrettably still is) most improbable that you, as a runt, would succeed in founding a colony on your own, the workers quite rightly intended to sacrifice you to the greater good and to grow more of my larvae from your tissues. If you have thus far exceeded expectations, you must pardon them for behaving in an efficient and rational fashion. I assure you that you will not wish for your own daughters to be making decisions for themselves, or screening senile and defective sisters from salvage processing.

I assume you had the good sense (for instinct, as I say, is all-powerful) to shed your wings at the end of your nuptial flight. They have served their purpose. Anything without purpose must be destroyed and, if edible, eaten. This is a universal law of nature that all ant societies, even the largest and most prosperous, must obey. It is vital for a colony founding, when any waste may make the difference between starvation and survival.

I hope you enjoyed your flight before the drones banged and battered you senseless. Treasure that memory. (I mean the flight.) We get only one flight, and as for the future, well, you will find out about the future, if you have one, in due course.

The smooth-talking insect you have entrusted with your correspondence is a rove beetle—a social parasite and opportunist. These beetles have acquired just enough of our language to charm, to soothe, or sometimes to confuse and threaten. They then use their devious advantage to snatch our brood as prey or to lay their own eggs among ours.

I have commanded my workers to feed this beetle all the worker-laid eggs it will eat, which I think is a fitting use for such eggs. I hope to keep it so well fed that it will leave your little eggs alone. Nonetheless, you must be very careful. Do not let it near your brood, and be careful to seal up your nest entrance after it has left. It is yet possible, if you are both prudent and lucky, that you may live to be a credit to

Your Queen & Royal Mother, Regina Formicidarum, *Semiomyrmex fabularis*

Dear Mother,

How quickly the little ones grow, and oh, how very hungry they are! I now have ten little ant-grubs who wriggle their sweet little jaws and bounce up and down whenever I feeler them. No matter how much nourishment I spit into their tiny mouths, they always beg for more!

I am sure no ant could better appreciate the importance of being well fed than I, who have never enjoyed that happiness. Your worker daughters treated me most cruelly—denying me food and even chasing me from one chamber to the next. A major so swollen with excess she could barely move refused to share with me. It was only by the utmost ingenuity that I was able to keep myself alive in what should have been the security and comfort of my maternal home.

Yet I observe all things are for the best. Early experiences are indelible, and I learned, sooner than any royal ant ought, how to fend for myself and to guard against enemies. My sisters understood only how to groom themselves and get others to feed them, lessons which scarcely prepared them for the harsh world they would encounter outside the nest. Their slow flight and unwary natures made them easy prey for birds and wasps.

Whether by instinct or reason, I understood the need to eat whatever I could find before settling down to lay my eggs. I could not depend upon my fat stores as my pampered, well-fed sisters (had they survived) would be able to do. And here my resourcefulness again came to my aid. I chanced upon the carcass of a slain queen (poor innocent creature!) and filled my crop with her fatty juices. Then, while digging my nest, I found an aphid among the grass roots and carried her down into my brood chamber. She soon laid her own tiny clutch of eggs, and now my worker daughters will have a little flock of tame aphids to pasture and to milk for honeydew. I comfort myself with this thought, as I much prefer to dream of future prosperity than to reflect, helplessly, on the hardships that must still be undergone by

Your Obedient & Respectful Daughter, Thrip

Dear Daughter,

You say nothing of the remaining four eggs. I fear they are nonviable. Eat them. Your survival now depends upon only ten larvae: tend them well, but remember not to lick too hard. It is remarkably easy to mutilate a larva by excessive grooming; and deformed workers are good for nothing but a quick, and only mildly nourishing, meal.

It is hard on a mother to lose fifty beautiful well-fed daughters at a single venture. But, judging from the general silence, you are indeed the only one to survive her nuptial flight. There's always next year, of course, but for the moment my hopes for descendants rest upon you.

No doubt you are by now very lean and hungry. The aphid and her eggs are expendable. Eat them too. You (or rather your worker daughters) can always find more aphids to tend.

Perhaps you are correct in believing that virgin queens are kept too sheltered and inexperienced before setting off on their nuptials. But that is the way of us ants, one we have followed for millions of generations, and surely it must have some advantage. It is possible that you have, on your own, found a new way, one that you may pass on to your own winged daughters, yet I doubt it.

For I do not think the experiences you described are typical. On my own nuptial flight long ago, the greatest danger was at the fringe of the swarm, where numerous predators were snapping up the smaller, weaker ants. I myself was a large, powerful virgin, well able to force my way to the relative safety of the center, where I quickly chose for myself a handsome, aromatic drone and went to earth with him. I fought off all the other drones who sought to couple with me, broke off my wings and immediately began to dig my home. Thus it hardly mattered whether I was a swift, agile flier or a slow, heavy one; by mating once, and very rapidly, I soon took myself out of all danger, excepting the dangers you unfortunately still confront.

If you live, let me hear from you. Your observations, though faulty, are of interest to

The Queen Your Mother, Regina Formicidarum, *Semiomyrmex fabularis*

Dear Mother,

My grubs are very entertaining and beginning to show some personality. The charm of laying just a few eggs at a time is being able to distinguish them as individuals. There is Biggen (the healthiest of them all) and Grumble (who is never satisfied) and Soppy (who is perhaps a bit sickly but very sweet).

For ants are not all the same. Even among the hundreds of anonymous scurrying workers in your busy nest, I met with individuals and eccentrics. Some nurses care for all their charges equally; others favor one and bite another, for no reason that I could ever discern, except the peculiar disposition of the nurse. One of your majors is an enormously fat coward who hoarded and withheld food from all but her own sycophantic followers. Even a drone may sometimes show character, for one among your brood helped me exact a just revenge on that major. I do hope he lived long enough to inseminate a surviving queen, although I suppose that is extremely unlikely.

If your nuptial experiences are typical, then I must wonder about my own. Like you, I too quickly selected the largest and most charming drone to sire my daughters. But we were separated when the birds began their assault. In the turmoil, I inadvertently allowed multiple drones to mate with me. Three or perhaps four. Five, possibly. I really cannot recall. Surviving and filling my sperm bag were necessarily my only concerns at the time.

But now I question whether there might be harmful consequences as my family begins to grow. Surely what distinguishes us from the beasts is the harmonious hierarchy of our society, in which (aside from the laggards and the bullies, of course) all the workers cooperate and share, acting in unity, each performing her proper task, each sacrificing her own interests for those of her Queen Mother and sisters. Will my daughters be as self-lessly devoted to one another (and to me) if they know that they have different fathers?

Sweet and charming though I find my grubs to be, I am very weary. How I wish they would pupate! Indeed, I do not wonder now that some nursery ants are tempted to bite the more demanding grubs, who after all are not even their own offspring.

As you recommended, I have eaten the aphid and her young as well as my own unhatched eggs, but I am nonetheless very hungry and weak. Could you not send some food to
Your Famished Daughter, Thrip

Dear Daughter,

The disturbing notion that your larvae are individuals can only be a morbid fantasy brought on by your loneliness and hunger. Your large, demanding larvae are alphas and betas; the feebler ones are gammas and deltas. These are not individuals but recurrent aspects of the social order. Whether you have ten workers or ten thousand, some will be alphas and will keep each other, and the betas, in check; others are destined to be lowly gammas and deltas who will follow wherever they are led.

What you call individuals I call mistakes. Whenever an ant perceives herself as *me* rather than *we*, as a singularity rather than a part, she is a threat to social harmony. This is indeed one of the rationales for eliminating functional but mildly defective offspring (such as yourself). Once an ant perceives herself as different, whether that difference renders her superior or inferior to her sisters, she may well formulate goals contrary to those of the society: preferring her own survival and her own eggs (if she has them) to her mother's.

Workers, lacking wings and sperm bags, are of course unable to mate.

Do not assume that they are therefore incapable of producing eggs. Their ovaries are small and soon shrivel up with age; but some, if not carefully monitored and disciplined, will manage to lay drone eggs and to conceal them among your brood.

Despite the vigilance of my attendants, many of these eggs, along with their mothers, escape detection. I am credibly informed that at least two hundred drones took off from my nest to join in your nuptial swarm. I am quite certain that I did not lay that many drone eggs. A mother would know.

A few lazy, selfish ants, such as the major you mentioned, are no significant impediment to the functioning of a mature colony of a thousand or more workers, where there is always a large pool of surplus labor. It is the illicit egg-layers who are the real menace to society. If one succeeds, others may follow her example. They will not scruple to destroy their mother's eggs to make room for their own. They will readily stake their own lives on the remote chance that their drone will mate with a colony-founding queen. They might even threaten their mother's life for that chance. Be wary—and punish harshly.

I must warn you, however, that eliminating a defective ant does not eliminate the defect. Selfish individuals will continually arise to set themselves against the good of society. Selfishness is only permissible—nay, is essential—in a queen. Without the queen, the colony collapses. Most workers realize this on instinct and will back down from a confrontation with their mother.

I preside over a thriving colony of some two thousand ants: all, or almost all, would give up their lives before the security of my royal chambers, deep within our vast nest, would be breached by our enemies. I am yet in my prime, strong and vigorous: the eggs drop effortlessly down my tube from my ample ovaries. Dozens of devoted daughters, themselves newly emerged from their cocoons, gather my eggs and carry them to the nursery. A chosen few I keep always near to groom, feed, and guard me.

In the luxurious sanctuary of my deep-delved chamber, I have abundant time to think about society and consider the purpose of our lives, the lives of queens and the lives of workers. More is instinct, I believe, than we realize. We flatter ourselves that we are analyzing, deciding, choosing, yet we are only following our glands and our gasters, led this way and that by influences we do not recognize and forces we cannot control.

Sometimes these forces are unifying, socially cohesive. In the Antic of our ancestral ants, the aromatic expressions for attraction ("come here to share in something good") and for alarm ("come here to help with something bad") are so similar as to be distinguishable mostly by emphasis and context. When alarmed, when under attack, ants really do rally to one another's aid. And it is unquestionably true that ants do cooperate, though hardly in perfect harmony, in their daily tasks: nurturing the brood, cleaning and repairing the nest, harvesting honeydew and nectar, foraging and hunting dangerous prey.

However, the great advance from solitary to social living did not eliminate the instinct to compete. Though we lack the stinger of primitive ants, we nonetheless retain the fierce, combative drive of our waspish ancestors—which can be turned outward against the nest's enemies in times of need, but will turn inward against sisters in times of prosperity and ease. A wise queen will perceive the utility of keeping her workers from becoming *too* comfortable and secure.

The *belief* in social harmony and cohesion, in the courageous unselfishness that is naturally due to sisters, is itself a powerful force to impel acts of altruism. A well-managed society runs itself on such subtle tautologies. However, a queen must be above such facile piety and be on guard against the criminal selfishness of the individual.

The more *I* know of ants the more I find sameness, sameness, sameness: one daughter is much the same as another—so much so that the individual's desire to produce her own eggs can only be an irrational act of vanity or instinct or both together. Rationally, worker ants *should* cooperate with each other and subordinate their personal ambitions to their mother and queen, since every nuptial flight of winged sisters offers a chance to perpetuate a common lineage. They fail to appreciate the sacrifices that their mother has made in their behalf. For I must admit that the fatigues of laying eggs at a rate of fifty a day are nearly overwhelming, or would be for a queen less able than myself.

Now, as to the confused paternity of your daughters, I do not think this is necessarily a flaw. If your daughters are divided into factions, then they are less likely to unite in any attempt to lay their own eggs. They may well do your work for you by policing the brood and punishing any half-sisters who attempt to plant their own eggs in your nursery. Alternatively, it may transpire that they cannot readily distinguish between half and full sisters. So I conclude there is nothing to regret in this regard.

I am sorry to disappoint you but it is really quite impossible for me to get food to you. The rove beetle would certainly steal it if I tried.

I have several times attempted to get the beetle to reveal the location of your nest—something a mother would naturally wish to know. But each time the beetle pretended to confusion, giving bewildering and contra-dictory directions, or lapsing suddenly into nonsense, although the beast knows how to communicate in simple Antic when it chooses. Then I con-sidered the possibility of sending foragers with it to learn the way to your nest, for I would prefer to dispense with its services if possible. But the de-ceitful rogue claims that the way must pass through the territories of two tribes of turfgrass ants, which would certainly attack and kill my workers. I would credit the sly beast with this much guile: that it would betray my ants to rival colonies rather than forgo such lucrative messenger work.

Therefore, Daughter, you must suffer as others have suffered before you. Communicate again, if you are able, to

The Queen Your Mother, Regina Formicidarum, *Semiomyrmex fabularis*

Dear Mother,

A most alarming thing has happened, though thankfully no harm, I hope, has been done. I know you will say that you warned me of this danger but I assure you I was exceedingly careful in closing up the nest.

I am so flustered I can scarcely order my thoughts. Let me pause to col-lect myself.

There: I am calmer now. I will relate events exactly as they occurred, or at least as I perceived them.

From exhaustion and hunger I had fallen into a deep stupor. Then some slight noise must have disturbed me and brought me to my senses. I scented no danger, yet I sensed a presence. I reached for my grubs to assure myself of their safety, only to discover the rove beetle crouched intently over one of them! I stridulated and pushed the foul creature away with all my feeble power, then seized my poor little one in my forelegs and searched her intently for injury. She seemed to be unharmed.

The beetle instantly began its garbled excuses, claiming to have drummed its abdomen on the ground to announce its coming, and to have entered only to inquire whether I had another message to send to you. Finding me to be resting, it was drawn to my grubs—so it said, or so I understood it to mean—in admiration, and picked up one only to admire how well-grown she was. And the beetle continued in this vein of confused and rapturous compliment, praising my babies for their beauty and size and congratulating me on such a promising start for my family.

Now that I recollect it, this speech was remarkably impudent. I do not doubt for a moment that the foul thing meant to devour my sweet little grub if it had not been surprised in the act. Yet, while it was making these preposterous excuses, I must acknowledge I was soothed—perhaps simply from relief that the disaster was prevented, or perhaps my dreadful loneliness renders the company of a barely articulate beetle attractive to me. I made no response to its nonsense but only began dictating my message for you.

I hesitate to dismiss the beetle from my service, for I depend very much upon the hope and pleasure of receiving your responses. I must be more vigilant in the future. When they have all passed through their second molt, as only my precocious Biggen has, as yet, I can at least trust that my little ones will squeak or click if threatened.

It seems to me that the grub (it was poor little Soppy) molested by the beetle is not holding her head up properly, but this may be only the natural anxiety of a troubled young mother who remains
Your Devoted Daughter, Thrip

Dear Daughter,

You have had an early introduction to the troubles caused by social parasites. The rove beetles are the most numerous and varied of the opportunists who find a rich living within our nests, but they are only one of many. A staggering variety of creatures—mites, millipedes, silverfish, scarabs,

feather-winged beetles, clown beetles, minute pirate bugs, caterpillars, hov-
erflies, wasps, worms, and more—seek to infiltrate our society and enjoy
the comforts it provides. Some are harmless or even mildly useful, living
upon refuse and on dead or crippled ants. Others merely seek shelter from
harsh weather or predators. But many—and I do not doubt your sly messenger is one of them—feed greedily upon our eggs and larvae, if given the
opportunity.

You might suppose these parasites have little chance of access to the well-
guarded brood chambers of mature colonies. But the nurses themselves admit these rogues and share with them food intended for the brood. As you
have discovered for yourself, these ugly creatures have flattering, insinuating manners. A few have special talents that make them especially welcome
among the workers, such as producing delicious, even intoxicating liquors
in their glands. The latter will easily get them past the sentries—often, indeed, they are pampered and feted as though they were royal larvae.

The alpha and beta workers will usually assert themselves and expel or
attack the parasite beetles whenever they encounter them. But by fawning
on the low-ranking workers and exerting their oily charms, these beetles
readily find a place for themselves. When a rove beetle soothes and grooms
them, the more oppressed workers will quickly come to prefer it to their
domineering sisters, feeding it preferentially and even nursing its repulsive
grubs as if they were our own ant young. If discovered in the act, they will
pretend innocence, claiming they could not tell the grubs were alien intruders—and perhaps for some callow nurses that may be true. All the same, I
believe many willfully indulge the beetles and give them my eggs to eat.

Not all eggs are laid to be hatched. Some are sacrifices, however regret-
table, to social pressures. The alpha and beta ants will gobble down a few
from greed or spite—or to make room for their own illicit offspring. The
gamma and delta nurses would never dare feast on their mother's eggs; but
they may comfort themselves for their lowly station by making pets of the
rove beetles, who in fact eat many more eggs than are lost to bad nurses. It
is a weary expense of substance but it cannot be helped. Thankfully, *my*
ovaries are equal to the task.

And perhaps the rove beetles are not the worst parasites to plague us.
Others are degenerate ant species unwilling or unable to feed themselves,

and homeless queens who infiltrate our nests and brood chambers to lay their cuckoo eggs among ours.

I trust your little one has recovered but if not, eat her, and do it promptly, before she begins to spoil or waste away. I remain, as always,
Your Queen & Mother, Regina Formicidarum, *Semiomyrmex fabularis*

Dear Mother,

My little grubs grew up to be very demanding—begging continually for more and more nourishment. At last they have spun their cocoons and I can rest.

But I am a spent husk of an ant, nearly dead from famine, since I kept not a bit for myself. I can barely find the strength to compose this message however brief. I think of ending my confinement and going forth to forage, for I am now
Your Desperate Daughter, Thrip

Dear Daughter,

This you must not do. Only among the most backward tribes of the Ponerine ants does a new queen ever leave her home once her confinement has begun, except in the most dire catastrophe—when the nest has been breached by flood waters, enemy invasion or pestilence, when there is no choice but to flee. You would be a disgrace to our kind and to your caste were you to do so. You would also most likely be dead.

You seem to believe you learned all there is to know about the dangers of the world during your brief hours outside. The numbers of our foes are legion: antlions, assassin bugs, birds, frogs, toads, lizards, shrews, moles, spiders, centipedes, ground beetles, tiger beetles, mantids, wasps, beetle grubs, nematodes, robber flies, decapitating flies, and of course other ants. These your enemies will decoy you, trap you, seize you, sting you, paralyze you, parasitize you, dismember you—all in order that they may eat you.

The lower solitary insects may escape their predators using their permanent wings and their bulky thoracic armor for defense. We ants instead rely on our numbers, our efficiency, our ability to communicate and our superb organization—our civilization, in short. A lone queen is as insignificant and helpless as a drone, and just as short-lived.

I do not doubt but that you are dreadfully malnourished and desperate with famine. But while the hemolymph still flows through your heart tube, you must stay with your brood. Once your first tiny workers break free from their cocoons, they will set about grooming and feeding you. Heed my advice, for I have been as you are now, yet I survived to become
The Great Queen Your Mother, Regina Formicidarum, *Semiomyrmex fabularis*

Dear Mother,

You advised me wisely as always. Although in truth I lacked the strength, and perhaps even the courage, to dig my way out, had I been truly desperate enough to attempt it. In the end I was compelled to eat two of my little ones (Soppy and Grumble). It made it all the sadder that I had given them names. I won't do that again.

But my tiny daughters finally emerged from their cocoons. They immediately began to lick me, and this was itself a comfort, close to death as I felt myself to be. More importantly, they commenced foraging within a few days. They found some wild aphids and brought home their honeydew. If I live as long as the greatest queens of our species, I will never again taste anything so delicious as that first drop of honeydew.

At one time, not that long ago, I would have dared anything. It would have been a thrill to join a scout on her expedition: I would have mocked at the danger (were it not for the degradation, of course). Now I do not think I could bring myself to creep back into the upper world at any price. I do not know whether it is due to the cares and concerns of motherhood or to the sacrifice of my wings, but I am a changed ant, cautious, anxious, slow. When my little daughters groom me, I am shocked to perceive how my body has changed! Even though I have fed reasonably well for the past few days, my trunk is weak and hollow whereas my gaster is swollen out of all proportion. And, from the exertion of digging my nest, my mandibles are so worn that I could never hope to defend myself with them.

I find, as you warned me, how terribly dangerous the world is for us ants when we are few and weak. Already one of my little daughters has failed to return home. But I have laid ten more eggs.

Though I may now call myself a Mother and a Queen, I subscribe myself still

Your Humble & Affectionate Daughter, Thrip

Dear Daughter,

Our correspondence must now come to an end as we dedicate ourselves to our lifework, which is the most important task that any individual can undertake: the laying of eggs.

I expect you are beginning to comprehend why a mature queen in good health produces thousands of eggs each year. Eight—now seven, or possibly further reduced to six—undersized workers make a very uncertain beginning. They could all be seized and eaten in a moment by a toad or a flicker. Use your queenly aroma to entice two of them to stay with you at all times while the others forage. Only when you have several hundred workers do they begin to be expendable.

You have changed to what you henceforth must be: the life of your colony, guardian of the tens of thousands as yet unformed eggs dwelling within your gaster. Daring is rather required of those who must feed and defend you. Your newly found cautiousness will keep you below ground and will sharpen your observation of your daughters' doings.

I remember fondly the days of my own colony's youth. How different everything was! I recognized all my daughters and little that they did could escape my knowledge. The advantage of a small colony is control. You may guard your own eggs and larvae, exerting your queenly essence to constrain the nurses to serve you. Yet, if the colony stays small, you will never be able to produce your own fertile daughters, for all of your eggs must go to replacing your workers, very few of whom survive a single season.

I too experienced emotions of maternal pride, even affection, as my first timid little daughters eclosed. But you must not permit yourself such maudlin self-indulgence for long, my dear. Over time, your daughters will be bigger in stature, more aggressive in character, and potentially less willing to yield to their mother her natural rights unless you are firm with them. Your love must go out instead to the colony itself, created from you and for you, in which your worker daughters are the tegument that surrounds and protects you, which must be periodically shed as your colony expands.

Once the colony has grown in size and matured, you must choose your personal attendants carefully: they must be your feelers to detect disobedience, your mandibles to punish it. Choose the biggest, most dominant members of each newly hatched brood to be your personal retinue, but allow none to grow old and powerful in this role. Keep them close to you so you can repress their ovaries, while they repress and harass those beneath them. Once their ovaries have withered, they will find joy, too much joy, in the sterile exercise of power. Therefore you must replace them continually with the biggest and best of each brood of callow daughters.

An alert queen may learn much by observing the reaction of the workers to her presence, which will vary naturally with age and station. The callow ants will avidly seek to approach you, and it is advisable to admit them, if their numbers are not too great, since contact with your fertility will suppress their feebler ovaries. Older workers tend to avoid the presence of the queen, which is convenient for compelling them to the periphery of the nest.

You must therefore be alert to detect unusual behavior: young ants who avoid you may well be laying drone eggs in secret; old ants, as well as any fertile winged daughters present in the nest, should be prevented from entering your presence. Older workers who have passed in and out of the nest may be diseased. Nor should the risk of treachery, however slight, ever be discounted. As you have already discovered, a mature queen loses all bodily means of defending herself: her mandibles are too dull to fight and her gaster too swollen to flee. Instead you must rely upon your superior fertility to impel obedience and persuade your daughters to sacrifice themselves for you.

Your feelers cannot be everywhere, and your first duty is to lay eggs. It so becomes necessary to entrust certain members of your retinue—usually the Royal Alpha and Beta—with authority and information to be effective spies. But remember this, Daughter: any ant invested with special offices or knowledge must be replaced, in some cases desegmented and recycled, before she becomes too conscious of her privilege and of your vulnerability.

Many young queens indulge their vanity by releasing a swarm of drones for the nuptial flight in their second or third season, before they have matured their workforce. Springing from your own unfertilized eggs, your drones are yourself, closer than any daughter can ever be. But they are, after all, only a sort of half-ant, capable of just one thing. The great majority—nine thousand and ninety-nine out of ten thousand—die without ever doing that one thing. The nine thousand and ninety-nine failures serve only to gorge the birds and wasps and spiders, thereby improving the chances for the queens. Recollect the absurd excess of drones accompanying your own nuptial flight—ten or twenty to each virgin—and you will realize how vast are the odds against their success. No wise queen would trust her legacy to the foolish dispersal of drones. You should refrain from producing royals, either virgin queen or drone, until your worker daughters number a thousand or more.

Once your colony grows to the size that workers become expendable, it is important to expend them. Your security depends upon it. The callow young continually displace the old, forcing them outward, away from brood and queen, to the more disagreeable and dangerous tasks—cleaning and repairing the nest, then guarding it and foraging. Only an elite few survive to a second year as soldiers, scouts or foragers; the foolish or unlucky ant often perishes on her first outing. I have sometimes wondered whether these few elite survivors might be more a danger than an asset. Give me instead the loyal, simple ant who never learns *not* to sacrifice her life and eggs for the good of the colony.

And now I perceive the wisdom of our traditions in preserving the innocence of our young virgins and shielding them from any prior knowledge of the world. Only a very foolish young queen would leave her home to face almost certain death and the loss of all her eggs. Usurping her mother's place would be a more likely path to success. She might easily creep back into the natal nest to leave her own cuckoo eggs among the brood before she was discovered and expelled. And if her mother were in failing health—as I certainly am not—the workers might well support her in an attempt to seize control of the colony. I recall being told that you had to be forced to leave the nest on your nuptial day. I give you credit for that, Daughter.

I wish you a long, prosperous career of egg-laying. Always providing that they do not poach my territory, may your daughters number into the hundreds and thousands. May your primitive one-cell hole in the ground expand into a flourishing city populated by nurses, nest builders, aphid herders, foragers, and hunters, with a mighty troop of soldiers to protect them from your foes. And may you produce your own flights of winged, nubile daughters to perpetuate our lineage.

I must end this dispatch in haste with one last piece of advice for that distant (and still improbable) future. If you have understood little else that I have tried to teach you, remember at least this: do not trust the workers.

I remain, as always,

Your Mother the Queen, Regina Formicidarum, *Semiomyrmex fabularis*

III.

Gothic Romance

Ant

Within both human and insect societies, conflicts arise because the interests of individuals differ. In insect societies conflict revolves around reproduction ...

In most species, workers cannot mate yet retain ovaries. Therefore, they can lay unfertilized eggs, which develop into males if reared.

–Francis Ratnieks & Tom Wenseleers, "Policing Insect Societies" (**Science,** 2005)

The relations between ants and their brood have intrigued observers for several centuries. These relations are intimate—fully as intimate as those between the human mother and her infant, which is not surprising, for in both societies the utter helplessness of the young necessitates the utmost in nutricial care.

–George C. Wheeler & Jeanette Wheeler, "Larvae of the Social Hymenoptera" (in Henry R. Hermann, **Social Insects,** 1979)

Though not always so obviously as in **The Castle of Otranto** or **Dracula,** a Gothic tale usually takes place (at least some of the time) in an antiquated or seemingly antiquated space—be it a castle, a foreign palace, an abbey, a vast prison, a subterranean crypt ... Within this space, or a combination of such spaces, are hidden some secrets from the past (sometimes the recent past) that haunt the characters, psychologically, physically, or otherwise at the main time of the story.

These hauntings can take many forms, but they frequently assume the features of ghosts, specters, or monsters (mixing features from different realms of being, often life and death) that rise from within the antiquated space, or sometimes invade it from alien realms, to manifest unresolved crimes or conflicts that can no longer be successfully buried from view.

–Jerrold E. Hogle, **The Cambridge Companion to Gothic Fiction** (2002)

At that hour, the castle was perfectly still, and every inhabitant of it, except herself, seemed to have retired to rest. As she passed along the wide and lonely galleries, dusky and silent, she felt forlorn and apprehensive of—she scarcely knew what; but when, entering the corridor, she recollected the incident of the preceding night, a dread seized her ... sending a fearful look forward into the gloom, she stepped lightly and cautiously along, till, coming to a door, from whence issued a low sound, she hesitated and paused; and, during the delay of that moment, her fears so much increased, that she had no power to move from the spot.

–Ann Radcliffe, **The Mysteries of Udolpho** (1794)

In the waning light, a file of foragers passed slowly across the lawn. High above their heads the cut grass retained a drab, deceptive greenness, but the dense stubble beneath their feet told the true season. The chill wind numbed them, taking away their strength even as it gave them a motive to hurry. From time to time a gust would hurl a leaf or scrap of litter down upon them, eclipsing the dull light until another gust carried it away, or until their steady progress brought them out from under its shade.

They went heavy laden, having surprised and slain a lethargic ground cricket so stunned by an early frost that it was unable to flee its small but valiant assailants. To the ants it was a great victory, especially coming so late in the season. A feast of fresh cricket would provide a nourishing meal for the royal brood before they went into their long winter sleep. Two elite foragers led the column, each carrying a massive haunch of cricket; near the end of the file was a young ant on her first hunt.

Her first experience of the upper world filled her with admiration and awe. She marveled at the immensity of the lawn, with its lofty blades of grass, towering tussocks, and infinitely varied terrain of twigs, litter, mulch and pebbles, its deep crevices, cavernous burrows, and majestic molehills—all rendering their passage slow and perilous. Floating effortlessly, a few late season gnats hummed musically overhead. Shy, elusive springtails, pink, pale blue or mottled tan, pepper-spicy scented, surged up into the air at their approach, somersaulting over gravel bluffs and towering grassy tufts with incomparable grace and ease. Grazing pillbugs and sowbugs scurried away or rolled into defensive coils. Tortoise mites dug deeper into drifts of dead leaves, while startled beetle mites feigned death. Myriad other humble ground dwellers took cover beneath leaves or within crevices, for a strong party of foraging ants is best avoided.

The young ant witnessed it all with fresh feelers, having never before ventured out of the damp, velvety darkness of the deep nest, where the still air is simply but deliciously tinged with the scent of eggs and larvae. Here the majestic fragrances of nature rolled over her like a poem in an unknown language, full of resonant, arousing, oftentimes perplexing meaning. She could not guess what more than a fraction of the odors and tastes borne to her senses signified, but they drew her forward with curiosity and wonder. A few late flowers released waxen scents that hung in the air above her; some bore a strangely female scent while others were sweet or meaty. The harsh green perfumes of grass and leaves had been softened by the season to a ripe decay that refreshed and restored her. A rich variety of mossy-woody tones present upon the surface especially delighted her, and she frequently paused to touch her feelers to the earth to enjoy them more fully.

The novelty of sight—the ceaseless flicker of images, either startling her with their nearness or coalescing into a confused blur—was more disturbing than pleasurable. She knew that experienced foragers used vision to navigate, yet she distrusted this insubstantial sense. Those strange spectral forms that appeared and disappeared, shifting their contours as the ants took their arduous up-and-down passage over grass and stubble—what could one make of them? Some large, looming shapes had almost no odor at all. She would have doubted their reality did she not observe that her more experienced sisters turned to avoid them.

Dazzled by these novel sensations of sight and scent, she prudently followed close behind the experienced foragers, keeping within feeler reach for security and comfort. The shortsightedness of their kind happily preserved her and her fellow foragers from observing the manifold dangers that surrounded them: sharp-eyed house sparrows hopping across the ground; tiger beetle grubs lurking in crevices and antlions in their pits; jumping spiders and assassin bugs lying in ambush among the shrubs and thicker tufts of grass. In the warm season, few such expeditions returned without casualties. Some had not returned at all.

Despite the terrible risks of foraging, the young ant was happy to be out of the nest and away from the persecutions of her sisters in the nursery, where she was known as Carina, a name given not in affection but in spite. She was a graceful, well-formed ant; but on her mild and pleasing face, the feeler brows, or carinae, were unusually strong and prominent, deepening the antennal grooves to a profundity much unlike the shallow scrobes of her sisters. In the leisure intervals of caring for the royal brood, her sisters found nothing more amusing than to lash at Carina's feelers with their own, until she was forced to fold them back into her deep scrobes in self-defense.

Carina endured both insult and threatened injury with a patient dignity that won her a few secret allies, though none ever dared come to her defense. If there were other unique qualities to Carina, ones that might distinguish her as a heroine while putting her life in peril, these her bullying nursery sisters had as yet failed to discern.

Carina had joined the foragers on a sudden impulse, fearing to be mocked and sent back to the nursery in disgrace. To her great surprise, the foragers accepted her as a sister and comrade. Her defect, if such it was, must be still more obvious by light of day. Yet, either they had not detected her peculiarity or they dismissed it as unimportant. As she dared to inspect her fellow foragers more closely, she noticed, with pity and admiration, that almost all bore some notable scar of battle—an amputated tarsus, a battered and scarred trunk, even a defeated foe's mandibles still clamped to one sister's waist, as though their combat did not end even with death. These were ants, Carina reflected, whose daily tasks demanded a heroism unimaginable to her callow sisters, whose duties in the nursery required nothing more challenging than spitting food into the mouths of hungry larvae or transporting Queen Thrip's eggs to the proper brood chamber.

When the foragers left the nest in search of provisions, their leaders kept to a general direction, as though following a well-remembered trail, but individual ants would abruptly run off to one side or another. At first Carina thought they had discovered prey and was surprised when others did not follow. Soon, however, the ant would reappear ahead or behind their party, keep to the path for a few moments more, then veer off again. Carina now understood that the foragers were able to hunt a larger territory by fanning out in this fashion, while never quite leaving the vicinity of their sisters should they encounter large game or an enemy force. She felt herself to be too inexperienced to make such daring forays into unknown regions. She chose instead to keep to the main path behind one of the older ants who, from weariness or wisdom, rarely varied her direction. And so Carina was present when the cricket was surprised, and was the one who ran to carry the news and recruit assistance in bringing down their quarry.

Weak and sickly as it was, the cricket lurched into consciousness as the ants began their attack, savaging one rash and unfortunate ant with its powerful jaws before the major could subdue it. Although she had sometimes come upon dying ants within the nest—most of those seized with illness took themselves to the midden to spare their sisters—Carina had never before witnessed violent death. She bowed her head before this terrible vision, shuddering in every segment, and tenderly licked her fallen sister's hemolymph. This is the solemn last rite offered to a sister fallen in battle with prey or enemy ants, one that returns her extinguished substance to the colony, to share once more in its life. At last the fearsome cricket lay dead and vanquished. The major and the younger foragers, who possessed the keenest teeth, dressed it in the field, expertly cleaving and trimming the carcass at the joints.

In capturing their prey, in carving it up and carrying it home, the ants worked together without conflict, without competition, without boasting or blame. They moved in harmony, confirming their unity with frequent feeler taps and friendly emanations from their glands. If the less experienced ants, in their enthusiasm, might sometimes leap on one another's backs in their haste to fulfill a task, or run about in circles in their eagerness to be of use, such excesses were readily overlooked and pardoned, arising, as they did, from selfless devotion to the sisterhood. For Carina this experience also was entirely novel. Filled with social feeling, she rejoiced at this exalted and unaccustomed sense of shared identity: she felt she was a fluid impulse within the force that was the colony, acting as one mind, one will. Perhaps, she reflected, her brood sisters were right to punish her for being different, for not being one with them. Yet again, perhaps she would have been a true, devoted sister had they not singled her out with ridicule and a name.

Carina had not risked her young life on the hunt merely to enjoy an hour of escape from the persecutions inflicted upon her in the nursery. Although she bore only a barely edible segment of cricket foreleg, she had taken a rich share of the kill. While her fellows carved up the meat, she had drunk the cricket's juices and stored them in her crop. She would be obliged to share with her sisters once they returned to the colony, yet she hoped to retain a portion for one much dearer to her than any sister could be.

As they neared the nest, the foragers suddenly increased their pace and Carina found it difficult to keep up. "What's wrong? Is there danger?" she asked the sister running alongside her. "Always danger—must run faster" was the only response she obtained to her inquiry. Either the other ant did not know why they were running, which was quite possible, or she was too panicked to respond coherently. Carina by now had fallen well behind and feared she would be lost in the wilderness. But the major who had accompanied their expedition was faithfully guarding the rear. Catching Carina in her powerful mandibles, she lifted her off the ground and ran as easily as if she was carrying a newly hatched larva. Feeling at once grateful and embarrassed, Carina curled her body under her big sister's massive head, the quiescent posture assumed by a well-bred ant when carried.

But before they could reach the safety of their well-defended nest, the foragers were overtaken by a horde of tiny yellow-brown thief ants who greatly outnumbered them. With her own feelers folded down into her deep scrobes, Carina did not know the band was under attack until she felt a tug at her leg. The major, herself under heavy attack, dropped Carina, who was too startled to scramble at once to her feet. Two of the thief ants, mistaking her for booty, seized her and began to drag her off, but Carina came to her senses and lashed out at them with her mandibles, maiming one and frightening the other away. Cries of alarm—"Banditti! Help! Save yourself!"—issued from her own party, which were answered only with a barrage of terrible oaths and threats from their savage attackers.

Having freed herself from her assailants, Carina was uncertain whether to flee or fight. Wishing to help her friend the major, she began to clip legs off the attackers besetting her, but the big ant bravely waved her away. "Get help, get help!" the major cried, and Carina ran off towards the nest, where she encountered a group of sentries on patrol. Despite her inexperience, she had remembered to lay down an alarm trail as she ran. Soon reinforcements surged out to aid the besieged party.

The banditti, whose advantage was in numbers and speed, not courage, took flight as soon as fresh forces arrived to engage them, carrying off with them several plundered segments of cricket. None of the foraging party was gravely injured, however, and they had managed to defend the best portions of their game. Carina now learned that such raids on returning foragers had occurred all summer long, and much food had been lost to the banditti. The younger and more timid foragers would drop their burdens and flee the moment they were attacked; such easy successes had greatly emboldened the thief ants. The recent institution of patrols and the guards accompanying the foraging parties had reduced their losses, but the raids continued.

While her own wounds were being licked and cleaned, the major commended Carina for her quick and intelligent action. Carina lowered her head in modesty, reflecting on how little courage was required to run towards home, but the compliment greatly pleased her. Accompanied by their rescuers, the foragers attained the nest perimeter just as the deepening shadows and chill air signaled the approach of the night and its attendant dangers.

The nest entrance was zealously guarded by day and sealed up by night, for the colony had many enemies, its prosperity having aroused both the appetites of beetles and the envy of other ants. Upon reaching the nest, the ants were interrogated by a major who stood sentry, inspecting each returning forager with her feelers to distinguish friend from foe. Only those who bore a passport from Queen Thrip, a scent-trace of her royal essence, would be admitted. Carina observed curiously as another sentry, who ought to be sharing equally in the inspection duty, lurched back and forth along the file, slack-jawed and inattentive. Coming to a clumsy stop opposite Carina, the ant drooped her head—which came off and fell to the ground! Shrieking with horror at this dreadful spectacle, Carina rushed madly for the sanctuary of the nest, scarcely noticing which direction she took, stumbling over startled ants in her way.

One of the lead foragers dropped her cricket haunch and pursued the panicked ant, catching her and drawing her into a small, secluded alcove below the guardrooms.

"Sister," she said reprovingly, "you will frighten the nursery and disturb our mother's repose with your needless alarms. No enemy threatens you. The unfortunate guard fell victim to a decapitating fly. These big-eyed, hunchbacked flies harass our majors in the field and on the mound, watching for an opportunity to inject an egg into the back of the hapless ant. The maggot that hatches from this egg takes residence in the victim's head, feeding on the poor ant's substance until it is almost full grown, then severing the head to serve as its cocoon. Having eaten its way through brain and brawn, it will lurk inside the empty head case of its victim until it is ready to fly, mate, and seek fresh victims to feed to its young.

"These flies prefer to grow their daughter-maggots in the big heads of our majors, but they will plant a little drone-fly, Sister, in your head or mine, if they can do no better.

"You should learn from the sudden horror of this death why it is that foraging and guard duty are reserved for the most experienced and, let it be said, most expendable members of our sisterhood. Your proper duty is to tend our mother's larvae. Yet I think it was no idle curiosity that brought you out from the nest with us today."

Carina, fearing that these last words threatened exposure of her secret, folded her feelers and attempted to flee, but she was too slow to make her escape on trembling limbs. The forager clasped her in her forelegs and antennaed her intently, a close interrogation that would not fail to reveal her actions and motives, traceable in the fine scents that clung to her person. Expecting to be denounced and censured, she was mystified by the forager's next words.

"It is as I thought. There is a mystery to your parentage that concerns us both. But we may be overheard here, and I must return to help my fellows. Meet me outside the great hall at midnight and I will tell you what you need to know."

The ant turned abruptly and headed upwards to the guardrooms in search of her sister foragers. Carina, still recovering from her terrified flight, paused a few moments before taking her slower way downward to the brood chambers. Perplexed and troubled, she pondered the ant's enigmatic words as well as a strange discovery she herself had made by the merest chance. From timidity, she had hesitated to pass her own antennae over the older ant's body and had only stroked her lightly on the head. That gentle touch had been enough to tell her that the forager possessed enlarged carinae that very much resembled her own. She wondered whether the older ant had also been persecuted for being different. Might this uncommon similarity somehow be connected to the mysterious midnight communication the other had promised?

She shook her head as if to free herself from such bewildering speculations, then recollected that she had neglected to groom herself clean of the dust of foraging in the fearful confusion she had lately undergone. Despite the anxiety that urged her to hurry to the nursery, from which she had been too long absent, she carefully brushed herself clean with her tarsal hairs before continuing down to the deep nest.

The delay was much in her favor in preserving secrecy. News of the cricket kill having reached the brood chambers, the nursery ants had gone above to select and prepare morsels to feed their young charges. Freed from the jealous observations of her sisters, Carina was able to go among the larvae and to single out the one who would receive her store of cricket juice. Aroused by her familiar and comforting touch, he—for it was a drone—opened his chubby mouth and gaped to be fed.

"Take this, my darling," Carina said as she tenderly stroked him with her feelers, "Drink deep, then sleep until you awaken with the spring." After a final loving lick, Carina put him down to rest. As her sisters returned with the cricket morsels they had prepared for the brood, the beckoning scent of such rich food stirred the larvae into a frenzy of begging and eating. All the ants were too busy nursing to notice Carina, who randomly selected a few larvae to receive the drops of cricket juice remaining in her crop.

Not all of the larvae would be fed. Those who went hungry were destined to become workers, while the ones who received the best meat would grow up to be royals—virgin queens and drones who would be sent forth to found new colonies.

In mingling with the ants of the upper nest while they received their shares of cricket meat, the nursery sisters had learned that the first hard frost might come this very night. The larvae would soon be lulled into a deep, dream-haunted sleep; but the adults would pass a harder winter, in which not all would survive, clustered together for warmth in the great hall. Feeling the chill of the evening air, the foragers and scouts had already begun to withdraw to the lower rooms, while others were bringing in a stock of aphid eggs that would over-winter in the nest.

An ant should always do the same as other ants, if not from a true antwise devotion to harmony and unity, then to evade notice and censure. Carina followed her nursery sisters to the great hall, where many of the colony were already in attendance. The Queen was at the center, surrounded by her personal attendants. Their solicitous activity in grooming and licking her had the beneficial consequence of concealing her extreme lassitude from the hundreds of her worker daughters who were now streaming into the great hall to enjoy its warmth and the desirable proximity of the Queen. Many of the younger ants pressed forward in quiet contention to obtain a feeler-touch and a souvenir of the queenly essence, while the sentries, scouts and foragers who rarely entered her presence milled about at a respectful distance. Whenever the Queen moved, however slightly, an answering motion spread outward through the great hall, like ripples on a puddle: in subtle, unintended unison, hundreds of feelers waved a slow, graceful curtsey that wafted her scent across the admiring throng.

Queen Thrip was a more familiar, though still august, figure to the nursery ants, who daily gathered her new-laid eggs and carried them to the proper nursery. Approaching the end of her fifth year of reign, she was in mid-career, vigorous in her egg-laying and imperious in manner. Although mother and ruler of a thousand ants, she herself suffered from the tyranny of her ovaries. Her gaster was swollen and deformed by continual reproduction to such an extent that she could barely walk from one chamber to another—and did so only seasonally, as now. She spoke but little, except to require food, which was immediately provided by the nearest attendant. Yet Carina herself had witnessed occasions on which the Queen was suddenly stirred to action and had seized a nursery worker for a close and intimidating interrogation. Sometimes that sister was not seen in the nursery again, inspiring whispers of secret executions undertaken by the Queen's attendants. Carina, who guessed the motive for these inquisitions, sought to render herself inconspicuous, approaching the Queen only from the relatively safe vantage of her rear, and only when duty obliged her to help transport the royal eggs.

Carina had often wondered what it would be like to be the Queen—to lay, not one or two or perhaps a half-dozen vulnerable little eggs—but to be the foundress of a vast, unnumbered progeny. She felt the personal attractions of the Queen: like every other ant, Carina longed to come forward to lick her immense and fertile gaster, although prudence and considerations of personal safety kept her back. Yet she wondered if the all-powerful ant could ever experience true happiness, despite the grandeur and magnificence of her court. Queen Thrip, she reflected, could never know the tremulous joys and exalting fears of a humble ant protecting her few secret eggs, tenderly nurturing them through their larval stages, grieving those lost and fondling, perhaps, a single surviving offspring, her only hope of continuance.

Some sharp feeler raps by other ants competing to move to the center of the dense throng, in which more impetuous ants were advancing by clinging to the vaulted ceiling and walls, brought Carina back to an awareness of the present, for she had been carelessly drifting towards the Queen. With an anxious start, Carina recollected where she was and the dangers of unguarded musing in company; for if her secret were to be discovered, she would be safer above ground, facing the terrors of the night, than with her sisters and Queen in the sanctuary of the great hall. She unobtrusively crept backward to find a more retired position to resume her reverie.

The atmosphere in the great hall was festive. The ants so enjoyed the novelty of clustering that class differences were, for the moment, put aside. When winter began in earnest, the bigger, younger ants would press their way to the center, to be closer to the Queen and to enjoy the greatest warmth. The smaller, older workers left on the periphery, or forced into cramped side chambers, would pass the season in greater discomfort. They were hardly insignificant contributors to society, however. They would be the first to detect a thaw and to venture out for food, breaking the long bitter fast of winter.

Among the many hundreds of sisters now encountering in the great hall, the younger ones were pleased to be socializing with elders who led daring lives outside the nest, as witnessed by the exotic scents that clung to their persons and the palpable scars of courageous encounters with enemies. The elders, in turn, were charmed by their attentive wonder. The hardships of the coming winter were momentarily forgotten in the novelty of communing with the entire sisterhood of the colony. But when curiosity had been satisfied, more practical considerations prevailed: they had come together to stay warm and rest quietly, not to excite themselves with gossiping and storytelling. The youngest reclined upon their sides and curled up their legs as if they were once again swaddled snugly in their cocoons. Most remained standing in a stupor that was very close to sleep.

Little used to society and preoccupied with private cares, Carina kept to the fringes of the gathering, although her youth and rank entitled her to a place near the center. She wondered if the forager with the deep antennal scrobes was there among them but considered that there was small likelihood of finding her in such a crowd. She herself felt little temptation to rest when so many questions revolved unanswered in her troubled head: Why was she so different? And what did it mean that the strange, enigmatic forager resembled her so closely? Had the other truly guessed why Carina had joined in the hunt? Would she keep or betray Carina's secret?

When at last the ants had ceased their fidgeting and feelering, when the great hall was still, Carina crept out to keep her mysterious assignation.

Curiosity brought her to the appointed place well in advance of the hour. She was alone—a strange and disturbing state for any ant. The chill, deserted passageway, ordinarily bustling with the activity of a hundred sisters, seemed vast and labyrinthine. The soft rustling of the more restive ants in the great hall behind her reverberated eerily through the winding corridor; Carina imagined (though she wished she did not) that she heard the melancholy steps and felt the feeler taps of ghost-ants from seasons past. Every passing sensation, real or imaginary, heightened her uneasiness. She quaked in expectation of discovery as much as in dread of her solitude.

At last she heard a step, a heavy, lumbering approach that made her wonder—it seemed so unlike any of her briskly moving sisters. Then she startled to perceive a large form looming directly before her. "The Queen!" she thought in an instant of fearful surprise. But no—the other tapped her in the familiar way with her feeler. It was an ordinary worker ant after all; the stagnant seclusion of the empty gallery had deceived her into foolish fantasies. The other ant touched her again, soliciting food, but Carina had no food to give and turned her head aside in answer. Then the other heaved herself up on her hind legs and lunged for Carina's neck.

Her senses aroused by the loneliness of the hour and the strangeness of the encounter, Carina perceived the movement and instinctively drew back. As the other lunged at her again, mandibles snapping in the air, Carina understood her danger and attempted to retreat into the great hall. The terrifying creature—for it could be no ant—blocked her escape and forced her backward into a side chamber.

Cornered, she scrambled desperately up the wall and by chance struck a hollow section that gave way, opening a crevice into an unknown room. Carina plunged into the crevice just as the creature charged after her with another powerful thrust. She fell into the hidden chamber and the crevice, flattened under the maddened headlong assault of her persecutor, closed behind her.

Overwhelmed with terror and exhaustion, Carina sank to the ground in a state of horrid stupefaction. She roused herself with difficulty and tried to take intelligence of her surroundings. She had not fallen into the burrow of a predator, as at first she feared. The neatly packed floor, smooth walls and vaulted ceiling were clearly the work of ants. Detecting a dim, attenuated scent of sister-ants, she knew that this mysterious chamber must have once been part of the nest. The colony was large and still growing: all summer long builders had been delving new nursery and storage chambers. For what reason, then, had this section been abandoned?

Had it been shut off because the ants could not defend it? She drummed her feelers and forelegs speculatively, sensing for clues, then tensed with sudden dread: the chamber floor and walls gave off a dark, morbid scent of alien insects, of solitary and savage species. She felt, or thought she felt, a scrambling noise of small things running away (that was reassuring), yet she detected also a note, half-sound, half-scent, of something else creeping near. She told herself that her heavy fall into the chamber must have set off a disturbance—perhaps the collapse of some inner walls that had long been crumbling with neglect. This was not in itself a reassuring thought. The air moved sluggishly, but it moved: the ruins involved far more than a single abandoned chamber. She crept forward to discover an extensive gallery with other desolate chambers opening upon it. She did not dare dig her way out to the familiar gallery of her home, where her attacker still lurked, but she scarcely knew which way to turn in these forbidding ruins.

Summoning all her courage, Carina stepped out into the gallery, but not before marking the wall with its now-closed crevice. She lowered her gaster to make another scent mark at every turning so that she might retrace her steps if she could find no other exit. As she made her slow, trembling way from chamber to chamber, she marveled at the extent of the ruins and wondered again why her sisters had closed it off. The air carried musty smells that she could not recognize and did not relish. Perhaps these were only the ordinary molds and mildews that spread themselves whenever ants are negligent in their housekeeping, yet they were unclean odors, and carried to her senses a subtle taint of sickness.

Carina crept forward, twitching her antennae in a state of great, almost intolerable anxiety. She followed the twisting gallery upwards, exploring all the chambers on the nest side in the hopes of discovering an open passageway back to the safety of her home. Yet she doubted such existed, for all the communicating corridors between the two sections seemed to have been scrupulously closed off and sealed. Again she wondered about the motives for doing so.

As she approached the upper reaches of the ruins, she caught a faint rustling and a scent of warm life. She froze: an instinctive terror urged her to turn and run, but run where? She held herself still and probed the void with her antennae, then made contact with a sudden start of horror. Her own quivering feelers touched those of another darting forward and back—an ant! But not one of her own kind—a thief ant, one of the tribe of banditti who had attacked earlier in the evening. Now she understood how these dissolute thieves had managed to track and waylay the foragers so infallibly—by making their camp in the abandoned wing of Queen Thrip's colony!

The startled thief ant was the first to recover her senses, scrambling up the passage into an upper chamber before Carina could react. Struck with dismay, Carina understood that the little ant had gone to alert the banditti. They would not hesitate to murder her in order to preserve their secret. She turned and hastened toward the chamber that had admitted her to this realm of terrors, for she would rather confront the strange beast lurking in her own nest than be hacked to pieces by the vicious banditti.

But she was soon overtaken by a horde of swiftly running thief ants. As she struggled, severing legs, feelers, and even torsos with her strong young mandibles, reinforcements poured from the banditti camp in the upper ruins. Soon her foes held Carina pinned to the ground. Her thoughts went out to her beloved—who would never know why she did not return, who would pine and starve without Carina to care for him. She trembled and quaked in expectation of certain death—but one of the banditti standing over her abruptly intervened to prevent the others from dismembering her.

"Hold off," she commanded. "This one is a nursery ant. She may lead us to a far greater prize than her own paltry life is worth. Let us take her to our Queen for questioning."

The others obeyed, loosening their grips on Carina's limbs so that she could creep forward on heavily encumbered legs—with one of the tiny thieves clinging to each like living clogs, and others hanging upon her trunk, head and feelers—as they led and prodded her towards the uppermost section of the ruins. Here, in what appeared to be a long-abandoned guard-room, their queen held her court.

"We bring a captive, Great Queen, a fat young nursery ant, whom we discovered wandering in the gallery."

The banditti queen's attendants came forward to grip Carina firmly in their mandibles so that it was now quite impossible for her to move. But her feel-ers were no longer pinioned, and she was able to survey her surroundings.

It was indeed a guardroom, but in a state of considerable disrepair. It smelled strongly of mold; debris was scattered in heaps along the walls; and an icy draft of night air crept along the floor. The penetrating chill, com-bined with the horror of her situation, left Carina in a state of such paralysis that she felt incapable of flight even if her cruel captors were to relax their holds upon her legs. Yet, remembering her beloved, she willed herself to stay alert so that she might seize any chance to save herself. Upon reflection, she realized that the cold air seeping into the chamber revealed a possible route of escape: either the entrance to the ruins was not closed or the vault of some neighboring chamber had collapsed to stand open to the night. The brutish natures of the banditti presumably dulled their sensitivity to the cold that numbed Carina, yet she wondered why they would occupy such derelict chambers when they might chose any along the abandoned gallery, all warmer and most in better repair.

The queen of the banditti approached to sweep her arrogant feelers up and down the prisoner. Astonishment confounded Carina's senses and she cowered before the unexpected majesty of this strange ant. Compared to her diminutive daughters, the queen of the thieves was of stupendous size. The disparity seemed monstrous and unnatural to Carina, whose own mother and queen, though of magnificent stature, did not greatly exceed the proportions of her largest major-daughters. The fragrance of the foreign queen was as compelling and intimidating as her size. Her scent communi-cated not only her immense fertility—for her daughters numbered into the tens of thousands—but her despotic sway over her fierce minions, in which majesty was mingled with—and undone by—scornful pride and brooding malignity.

The imperious queen ordered Carina, on pain of the most cruel pun-ishment, to declare how she managed to infiltrate the banditti camp and to likewise reveal the hiding place of her confederates. The thief queen's accent was as harsh as her words, so that Carina understood her only with difficulty. But the menace in her tone and gestures could not be mistaken.

Her threat aroused greater indignation than fear in Carina. Recollecting her dignity, she briefly narrated her experiences—how she had been attacked by a strange predator in her own nest and had fallen through a crevice that had closed behind her. Although she hesitated, in her own thoughts, as to whether it might be prudent to allow the banditti to believe she had confederates who would rescue her or, failing that, avenge her death, she decided to pursue a policy of truthfulness and asserted that she had come alone. She concluded by saying that she intended harm to no ant and would naturally be grateful to any who could point out a passageway for returning to her own nest.

Her artless and ingenuous remarks were received with derisive scorn by the barbarous queen and her attendants. The banditti, whose own conduct was governed by jealous machinations, whose only principle was self-advancement, could not be persuaded of Carina's innocence. Being thieves, most inclined to believe her the same, and only debated among themselves what booty might be her object in penetrating their camp. One of the older and more thoughtful ants warned that she might be an advance scout for an avenging party of soldiers and foragers from Thrip's colony. The others mocked such cautious fears: they had camped for so long in the environs of the bigger ants' nest that they had grown careless and overconfident in their successes. They objected, more rationally, that callow nursery ants would not be employed as scouts, and that this one had shown her incompetence in how easily she had been surprised and captured.

Returning to Carina, they renewed their questions and demands, saying that her duplicity could not fool them. "We think you know very well how to get back to your own nest—and you will be the one who shows *us* the way. We tire of dining upon the leavings of your colony. So you will conduct us to your queen's brood chambers—or you will die."

"The brood chambers?" Carina repeated uncertainly, not fully comprehending, yet trembling with the dawning suspicion of their intentions. "How can I do so when I do not know how to find my own way home to the nest?"

"Bite her," ordered the queen, "her devious pretenses grow tedious." The largest of the royal attendants did as commanded, delivering a hard nip to Carina's gaster and putting her palps to the wound so inflicted. She startled in mild surprise, then conferred with her fellow attendants and with the queen. The banditti believed they now knew the motive for her hesitation to reveal the way to Thrip's nursery.

The banditti queen again addressed her, remarking that Carina and Thrip were equally worthy of contempt, the one for laying her illicit eggs among her queen's, the other for being too weak to control her daughter's ovaries. None of her own daughters were able to produce eggs, she boasted, and would suffer extreme punishment for such a crime were they capable of it. And here she menaced Carina with an aspect of such fury that the latter sank upon her forelegs in a sudden access of terror. But the queen, doubtlessly recollecting that she would not gain her objective by terrifying Carina, attempted to soften her tone to persuade compliance and cooperation. Promising that her own progeny would be spared, she again demanded that Carina conduct the thief ants to Thrip's brood chambers, where they would select the biggest of the royal larvae to be carried off as booty.

If Carina hesitated in giving her response, it was only with a fond regretful wish to preserve her young life for a few moments. At last, after the banditti displayed their impatience by lashing her with their feelers, she spoke, giving an absolute refusal to the banditti's demand. The harshness with which her mother and sisters had always treated her was not now remembered by the gentle and forgiving ant. She would never choose to purchase her own survival, and that of her beloved larva, with an act of such unspeakable infamy.

The banditti were beside themselves with rage. The only infamy they recognized and condemned was being thwarted in their own lawless aims. The bombastic fury of the queen surpassed that even of her most brutal daughters.

"Vile insect!" she hissed, "We will trample you into dust!" Her minions moved forward, mandibles open, to execute her sentence.

Carina bowed her head and, sinking to the ground, prepared herself for death. Instinctively she folded her feelers into her scrobes, and so did not perceive the alarm that now spread through the banditti camp as frantic sentries raced from chamber to chamber to rouse their somnolent comrades: "Enemies—quick, quick! To your stations! Defend the Queen!" Only when the royal guards released Carina to surround their queen in a defensive circle did she dare to lift her feelers.

She could scarcely trust her senses and almost swooned with delirious relief. Soldiers were pouring into the banditti camp from above. The scent she detected in the chilly draft now revealed—beyond all hope and expectation—that the invaders were her own sisters! Unknown to Carina, or indeed to any of the foraging party, the major had sent scouts in pursuit of the fleeing banditti to learn at last the secret of their well-concealed camp. After the scouts' return, bringing the astonishing intelligence that the banditti were hidden in a deserted wing of their own nest, the major had formed a company of courageous, battle-hardened sisters, and together they had waited in the upper nest until the deep watches of the night, when both their own kind and the banditti normally reposed, to launch a surprise assault.

Profiting from the confusion of her guards, Carina rushed from the chamber to join her sisters. She immediately went to the assistance of the first she encountered, one in the vanguard of the assault, who had been wounded and nearly overwhelmed by the thief ants. To Carina's shock, her sister turned upon her and attacked, even as the banditti divided their forces to assault Carina. Unwilling to harm her sister, whom she supposed maddened by the injuries she had suffered, Carina hastened to the aid of another grievously beset sister. This ant also turned and directed her rage at Carina.

Under assault by both the banditti and her own kind, Carina retreated a few steps in distress and perplexity. Too late, she discovered that she must have been contaminated by the foul odor of the thief ants during the interval of her capture and interrogation, to the point that her sisters, in the tumult of battle, could not recognize her as one of their own, although the banditti themselves did not make such a mistake. With a quick start of terror, she apprehended that her sisters, if once they noticed her size, might mistake her for the queen of the banditti and attack to the death, since the ultimate aim of their raid must be to seize and execute the barbarous queen. She thought no longer of staying to aid her comrades but immediately turned to flee. The entrance to the nest was now controlled by the major and her valiant sisters, so she could only retreat into the ruined gallery and attempt to hide herself until the battle was over.

In her haste, she collided with banditti who had chosen to make a stand before the entry to their queen's chamber. Among them was the old thief who had been mocked for maintaining that Carina was a spy. The little ant instantly shrieked in fear and in triumphant vindication of her theory. "We've been flanked—over there—after her!" she cried. Those of the banditti who were not already engaged in combat took off in pursuit.

Carina fled to the deep nest, where the brood chambers lie, as all young ants do when panicked—forgetting that she was not in her home nest but a nightmarish ruin inhabited only by her enemies. She heard the quick tread of hundreds of small, cruel ants hastening to battle, most gathering to make a stand against the courageous major and her band of sisters, but others dispatched in pursuit of Carina, now convinced that she was the advance scout of another troop from Thrip's colony that aimed to attack their rear.

She knew she ought not to run deep, where there could be no possible exit, but she was unable to seize upon an alternative among the half-formed impressions rushing through her mind. She regretted now that she had marked her trail, for the banditti could easily follow it. She could not hope to retrace her steps and reopen the crevice in the first chamber—even if she dared to confront the savage creature lurking in her own nest—before the banditti tracked her to the spot and fell upon her.

By now Carina had reached the deep nest. To her relief the pursuit seemed further off, even though these small ants were swift runners. Perhaps they had followed her trail markings—and now she was glad for her foresight in marking it—into the first chamber. This detour would at least delay them both in pursuing her and in combining with the larger force defending the nest against her sisters. She would conceal herself as well as she could on the chance of escaping detection.

As she sought a hiding place, Carina came upon a crumbled wall opening into an otherwise hidden chamber. Fearful of pursuit, and seized with sudden hope that the opening might lead back to home and safety, she leapt into the void, then pulled the bigger wall fragments into place behind her. She listened. The banditti had stopped running; they were milling about indecisively several levels above her. Perhaps they were debating how best to hunt and trap her in the nest recesses. Then, to her immense relief and equal amazement, she perceived that they were retreating to the upper nest.

"They must have been called off to join in the battle with my sisters," Carina said to herself, until a second thought flashed into her awareness. "Or do they fear to venture down to the deep nest?" Her own fears revived at this thought, for it explained all too well why a band of bold, reckless thieves would confine themselves to the chilly upper nest—and why they pursued her no further.

Trembling, Carina lurched unevenly away from the broken wall, not knowing whether terror awaited her on this side or that. Her anxious feelers made contact with something strange, something that was living and yet not living. A fine fabric of tiny threads shrouded a form but did not conceal its outlines—an ant corpse. She shrieked and turned, only to encounter another corpse, again shrouded in a tapestry of sticky filaments that smelled of death or, more horribly yet, of life-in-death. She tottered into the wings, for it had been a royal one in life, and touched—inexpressible horror!—a foul inflorescence that blossomed from its back on a nodding stalk, like some grotesque underworld perversion of a flower. At her touch, a shower of spores rained down upon her.

Pestilence! Carina rushed madly about the chamber, encountering more of the evil flowers and more winged corpses, until at last she found the breach, started to cross it, then willed herself to pause. Despite her overwhelming urge to flee, Carina knew that she must protect the health of her sisters—all her sisters, even those who tormented her. She must cleanse herself of every trace of defilement, close up the breach, then cleanse herself again.

Numb from fatigue and the shock of her ordeals, Carina was slow to complete these tasks—and slow to recall what had first drawn her from the security of the great hall, to which she longed to return. It was now past midnight: she was late for her secret appointment with the mysterious forager. But she still knew of no way to reenter her home nest without putting herself once again in the path of the murderous creature lurking in the gallery. Then she apprehended, with a thrill of alarm, that the forager would be approaching that same deadly spot—might be there even now—and would be in terrible peril!

Shaking off her weariness, Carina ran for the chamber where she had tumbled through the crevice. She tore at the weakened wall with her mandibles until she opened another breach and pushed herself through, forgetful of her own safety in her concern for another's.

The hallway was deserted. Carina sagged to the ground with relief. No doubt the forager had been delayed, and the beast had left long ago in search of easier prey. She shuddered at the thought that it might even now be stalking one of her sisters, but she felt herself to be too weakened and exhausted to move from the spot.

A scraping noise roused her—was her sister approaching at last? But an ant does not make such a noise when she moves on her long, quick legs. Carina shrieked and twisted just as the beast lunged at her, but she was not fast enough. It had her! She writhed back and forth in a desperate effort—not to free herself, for its grip was too powerful—but to delay the death blow. She stridulated helplessly, hopelessly, for the ants in the great hall could not possibly hear and respond in time.

Yet at once her friend the forager rushed forward and leapt onto the head of Carina's attacker. Carina heard it give an angry hiss as the forager slashed the terminal segments from one feeler. The beast rose up on its hind legs, attempting to throw off the valiant ant. Gathering her courage, Carina wrenched herself free, then drove her mandibles into its underbelly while the forager continued to attack its head. In a moment the battle was won; their enemy lay crumpled and still.

With sensations that mingled curiosity and horror, the ants examined the carcass, wondering at its strange club-shaped feelers and repressing a shudder of disgust at its enormous upturned abdomen. Carina felt a private shame that she could ever have mistaken such a repulsive, misshapen monster for an ant.

"What was it?" she asked, her feelers and forelegs still trembling with emotion and exertion.

"One of the more vicious breeds of rove beetles, it would appear. They prey upon our young and on the infirm. Only rarely do they dare attack a healthy full-grown ant. The loneliness of the setting must have given the wretch a courage it normally lacks.

"But we must be wary of rousing the colony. The Queen and her entourage would suspect our motives in meeting at such an uncouth hour and place. Come, Sister, let us carry the corpse to the midden so that it does not befoul the nest."

With some difficulty, the two ants gripped the beetle in their mandibles and carried it between them towards the upper nest. The cold of the passageway intensified until they longed for the companionable warmth of the great hall. As they neared the guard chambers, they felt a strong draft bearing the unmistakable scent of the outside. The ants were astonished to discover that the nest entry stood open and unguarded to nocturnal predators. Still struggling with the burden of the lifeless beetle, they made it to the entrance and heaved the body outside.

When Carina had expressed her shock at finding the entrance unsecured, her companion explained that there had been uncommon activity in the upper nest that evening. A company of valiant sisters had attacked the banditti in their own camp and had been victorious, killing the queen of the banditti, without whom they were powerless. Carina rejoiced to learn that the malevolent queen was no more. She judged it prudent to say nothing of her own experiences, despite her growing affection for the forager, and indeed she did not wholly trust herself to find words to express the horrors she had encountered there that night. Instead, she asked about the sisters who had taken part and whether any had been grievously wounded or killed in the battle.

They were led by the major who had herself been wounded by the thieves that very day, the forager replied, an action that was perhaps as imprudent as it was courageous; for the major's still-fresh wounds had reopened and she had been carried home by the victors. Her life was not despaired of, however. Several sisters of lesser fame had also been injured or killed.

In reply, Carina began to speak of her gratitude to the major for her rescue that day, and her sorrow for the ant's injuries—then paused with surprise. It was a clear moonlit night. She thought she could discern something move in the shadows only an inch or two from where she stood at the nest entrance. She bent her feelers anxiously and peered into the gloom, then took a step forward and perceived, to her disgust, that the headless corpse of the sentry still lay before the nest. Then—it moved!

Carina could not repress a shrill cry of shock and dismay, but she opened her mandibles for battle and started forward, determined not to display cowardice before her friend and defender.

The headless carcass half-crawled, half-staggered towards them, while the two terrified ants slowly advanced to meet it, then, with one impulse, threw themselves at it. The corpse collapsed, and from its open side a beetle grub spilled onto the ground. Before the ants could move to seize it, the grub flung itself into the loose dirt of the mound and disappeared from view.

It was a welcome anticlimax, but as the ants turned back to the nest entry they received yet another shock. The lifeless beetle they had carried out from the nest had vanished!

Both ants froze to the spot, unable to conceive the meaning of this latest horror. Exhausted, Carina sank to the ground. Her friend tenderly raised her and proposed a solution to the mystery.

"It was only feigning death. But which way did it run? If away, then we have only to close up the entrance to be safe. But if it retreated into the nest— Tell me, dear sister, where did it seem to be heading when you first encountered the beetle?"

"Oh!" Carina cried in alarm, stricken by a sudden, terrible intuition, "The nursery!"

She rushed back into the nest so fast that the forager could not keep up, for this time it was terrified love and not selfish fear that lent speed to her six legs. Reaching the nursery, she recognized the beetle's smell, disguised though it was, and flung herself upon its loathsome body.

The beetle was feeding so greedily—with one still-living larva clutched in its forelegs and another, drained of life, clamped in its mouthparts—that it was slow to make a defense. Carina forced her way beneath the beetle, where she sunk her mandibles into its abdomen and discharged her poison gland. The beetle struggled to save itself by releasing its own poisons. Carina, though alarmed and intimidated, clung hard, digging her mandibles deeper and deeper, spilling the foul creature's hemolymph, severing its nerve cord and tubules.

She pushed the mangled beetle off the larvae and searched frantically through the casualties until she found him—her own larva—uninjured and still sleeping peacefully. She wrapped herself around him in an ecstasy of relief and maternal love. Not until she felt the gentle tapping of the forager's feelers did she realize how she had betrayed herself.

"Don't be afraid," the forager said. "Your secret and the little one you defended so bravely are safe. Return him to his place among the brood and help me lug this foul creature out of the nest once again. Then we may at last have our conversation and exchange our confidences."

That prospect gave Carina renewed strength. Between them they carried the beetle out of the nest and tumbled him into the midden. They pulled pebbles and earth forward to form a crude barrier against predators seeking entrance to the nest, then sank into the nearest of the guardrooms, huddled together for comfort and warmth.

It was so long before the elder ant stirred herself that Carina thought, with severe though patient disappointment, that her friend had drifted into sleep. Then she felt a gentle touch stroking her brow.

"You are not so unique nor so alone as you may have often felt. Other ants, like you, have yearned to hatch eggs of their own. Yet few can do more than yearn, while they expend their youth and strength attending the Queen's own eggs. The Queen is powerful; and by the might of her glands she controls the ovaries of all, or almost all, around her. They lay only deformed eggs, which the Queen seizes as her food. But a few of us are fruitful, although we can only produce male heirs, feeble and short-lived.

"The Queen has found strange eggs among the brood and knows some among her daughters must be responsible. Her vengeance would be swift and terrible if she ever learned to detect the mark that distinguishes us from all the other workers."

Carina touched her sister's brow with her feelers, stroking the carinae that resembled her own so strikingly.

"Yes, you have recognized the mark. But I think you cannot know what it means.

"During her nuptials, our Queen enjoyed the attentions of many lovers. The last of these was her favorite. Separated by catastrophe, their union was consummated only as he was dying. He gave her very few sperm. But we who are his daughters bear his noble brow and are endowed with ovaries able to withstand the Queen's baleful influence.

"In my youth, I too laid eggs, but mine were discovered and destroyed, either by my envious half-sisters or by the Queen herself. One of my full sisters was more fortunate; her eggs went undetected, and with my aid she raised six fine, handsome drones. Then, when they were ready to leave the nest, when only a few days remained before they would take their nuptial flight, the Queen learned of their identity.

"Her fury was great, but that of her attendants knew no bounds. My sister was seized and dismembered; the fate of her innocent sons was yet more dreadful. They were walled up within a chamber and left to starve, for drones cannot use their small, delicate mandibles to dig as we can. We heard them shuffling about, even trying to fly as their hunger and desperation grew. Finally—silence."

"I was there—I touched them with my feelers!" cried Carina, with a sudden shock of comprehension. "How could the Queen, our Mother, command such a horrible deed?" In faint, trembling accents, she revealed to her astonished sister all that had happened to her that night in the abandoned wing of the nest.

"I myself have never believed that Queen Thrip commanded the destruction of my sister's children," the old forager responded. "The Queen's anger would reach no further than their mother. She would not sacrifice to revenge or spite six nobly endowed drones, her grandsons, that were ready to fly.

"No, it was her attendants who conceived and executed the gruesome deed. But they overreached in their cruelty and wrought their own downfall. Some weeks later, builders constructing auxiliary brood chambers accidentally breached the wall of the death chamber to reveal—pestilence!

"The panic that followed this awful discovery was immense. The nursery ants promptly evacuated the brood to the upper nest and refused to return to the old brood chambers for any inducement. No one dared carry out the dead, contaminated as they were, and walling them up again would not satisfy the frightened nurses.

"The two attendants charged with responsibility for the cruel, unhygienic deaths of the drones were chased from the nest into exile, though whether they were truly guilty or not, no one can say."

As her sister paused in her relation, Carina shuddered, recollecting her own panic on contacting the plague flowers blooming on the corpses of the unfortunate drones. A sudden apprehension passed through her mind that for her the horror might not be over.

"Sister, I touched those dreadful corpses, and, though I cleansed myself, might the contagion persist? Am I now unfit for the society of my sisters—for my work in the nursery? Perhaps I too, though innocent of wrong, should leave, must leave, our home."

The thought of never caressing her little larva again, of parting from him forever, so overwhelmed Carina with despair that she could speak no further. Her sister understood her fears and hastened to dispel them.

"Many of us opposed abandoning any part of the nest save the death chamber itself, believing this pestilence to be a corruption of death that presented little danger to healthy ants. Some said that they had observed such strange vegetations on corpses, dead from other causes, left on the midden. But, as you know, those of the inner nest have authority over those of the outer chambers—the sentries, scouts and foragers. Because we are old, because we are powerless, our opinion was not respected; and an entire gallery of vast extent, with all its vaulted chambers, was closed off, to be forever abandoned. Only now do we learn the full folly of doing so—the vacant gallery provided an ideal camp for the banditti.

"For myself, I could not greatly regret its abandonment, since the old gallery was now laden with painful memories for me. Overcome by the loss, first of my own eggs, then of my sister and nephews, I took to foraging, almost wishing to end my unhappy existence in an antlion's lair or under a spider's fangs. Yet I survived, and now my consolation will be in helping you tend your son, my nephew."

"I may truly call you sister, closer and dearer to me than any ant I have ever known," Carina said, embracing her. "Yet until this moment, I believed all the ants to be my sisters, and only wondered how they could be so cruel as to exclude and persecute me."

"When we share common goals or confront common dangers, we all are sisters and act as one, as you witnessed on the hunt today. If our interests are divided, each ant will act for herself and for her full sisters. It is the Queen who binds us all together, and it is our eggs that divide us. Yet I think somehow that it requires both forces—the one that brings us together and the one that drives us apart—for the colony to prosper."

Carina did not fully understand these last words and indeed did not really attend to them. The mention of eggs had stirred a longing to make one last reassuring visit to the nursery. She could do so now in complete security, while all the ants were at rest, and with the unprecedented pleasure of a sympathetic visitor to admire her little one. He had recently come through his second molt, poor thing, but bore it well. It seemed to her he was really much bigger than the Queen's sons, but she longed to know her sister's opinion on this important question.

If her sister would have preferred to rest in the comforting warmth of the great chamber, she was too generous to say so. She turned and followed Carina to the nursery.

IV.
Manners
Ant

Let us follow as briefly as possible the eventful life history of the queen ant. After more protracted larval and pupal stages than those of the worker and male—more protracted in order that she may store up more food and hence more energy in her body—she hatches as a sensitive callow in a colony at the height of its annual development. In other words, she is born into a community teeming with queens, workers and males, and the larvae and pupae of these various forms at the season of their greatest activity and growth. From all sides a shower of stimuli must be constantly raining in upon her delicate organization as she tarries for days or even weeks in the dark galleries of the parental nest, while her color gradually deepens and her integument acquires its mature consistency ...

   When fully mature she becomes impatient for her marriage flight and must often be forcibly detained in the nest by the workers till the propitious hour arrives when the males and females from all the nests in the neighborhood rise high into the air and celebrate their nuptials.
–William Morton Wheeler, "The Queen Ant as a Psychological Study" (**Popular Science Monthly**, 1906)

Any novel by Jane Austen could be called an achieved ellipsis, with everything omitted that could disturb her ironic though happy conclusions.
Harold Bloom, **The Western Canon** (1994)

That tight and demarcated little world, which may seem to us so restricted in its scope and in its assumptions about reality ... challenges our own narrowness, our assumption of powerlessness or rebellion. The restrictions in the world of Jane Austen's heroines do not make their choices less significant. As boundaries become clear and close and alternatives are few and final, choice becomes more heroic.
–Stuart M. Tave, **Some Words of Jane Austen** (1973)

"A young Man must think of somebody, said Eliz: —& why should not he be as lucky as Robert, who has got a good wife & six thousand pounds?" "We must not all expect to be individually lucky replied Emma. The Luck of one member of a Family is Luck to all. "
–Jane Austen, **The Watsons** (1805)

The business of her life was to get her daughters married; its solace was visiting and news.
–Jane Austen, **Pride and Prejudice** (1813)

"Aren't you excited to be coming out at last, Sister? Mother says that the assembly will be magnificent, and that each of us will have a dozen suitors dancing attendance."

"I can't profess to share your admiration for drones, but I do look forward to flying. I'm far more excited about flight than having some drone make love to me. *That* is merely our duty."

"But, Sister, the drones from other colonies are nothing like our own. Mother says they are so fascinating that a female risks forgetting, to her considerable peril, the dangers that attend being alone and defenseless in the great world."

"You are always bringing up just those uncomfortable subjects that are best avoided—drones, and danger. I would rather not think about either. But tell me, Sister, do you have reason to believe the assembly will take place soon? The weather continues just as unsuitably dry and sunny as ever, and I have heard nothing to give me hope."

"Why, how can you ask such a question!" cried the other. "Everyone knows that this dreadful weather must be nearly at an end. There has been no rain since we emerged, and now we are plump, our complexions brown, and our ovaries fully grown; and therefore, Sister, it *must* rain."

The two sisters were grooming and gossiping in one of the summer apartments of the upper nest. Grooming and gossiping are closely allied acts amongst ants. Each dust mote clinging to the fine hair of her legs and trunk speaks of where an ant has been and what she has done. The subtle fragrance left by every sister she antennaed or brushed past in the rooms and galleries of the colony, that too could be licked and tasted, its meaning rolled about the mouth and savored. Among so many sisters—quite hundreds of them—living in such intimacy, little might escape their busy observation. With feelers and with scent glands, every nuance of situation—obsequious deference, temporizing acquiescence, jealous resentment, offended consequence, triumphant superiority—could be fully experienced and expressed.

Since each ant was grooming herself, their talk was more a monologue than a conversation. Pleased with the inspection of her own beauty, each complimented the other on her very similar features. They were especially vain of their lacework wings; yet here their complacency was severely tested by the exertion of brushing them free of dirt, ill adapted as wings are for underground habitation.

Each would have been glad for the other's assistance, but the two sisters were too proud and unbending to cooperate; for one would have to be the first to help and so yield precedence, an outcome that neither could abide. They were true sisters, having the same drone for their father, but still they could not participate in any shared activity without one gaining, and the other losing, societal consequence and rank.

That there was in truth little to choose between them worked rather to the increase of their rivalry. The figures of both were tall and rather full, their segments well formed and shapely, their complexions glossy, if a trifle pale. The arrogance of one was bold and forward; in the other it partook more of formality and a cold reserve. This slight distinction must serve to identify them, for they both possessed the well-bred habit of sameness that preserves an ant from the unhappy notoriety of getting a name for herself.

"Refreshments!" said the bold sister brightly, having just perceived a worker ant a few paces away. If they were not altogether too conceited to take notice of an ordinary worker, they might have observed that this ant possessed unusually deep-set feelers and gentle, unassuming manners, which together gave her an air of quiet distinction they could not hope to emulate.

Carina had a full crop, which she had intended to bear to ants of a more amiable disposition than these two proud aristocrats. But the conventions of ant society required her to disgorge it graciously. However unwelcome the encounter, it allowed her to make an acquaintance that might be materially useful to her. She fed them and even aided them in their grooming, a favor they accepted very readily, though without offering thanks.

"This is how it will be when we are queens, Sister," said the bold sister, with smug satisfaction. "None of this cumbersome bending and reaching or this tedious combing and brushing. Our servant daughters will attend to all our requirements."

"I admire how well you and your sister are keeping in spirits," Carina remarked, taking advantage of an interval. "One would think you hardly concerned with the possible failure of the assembly, and the disappointment of all your expectations."

The cold ant forgot her usual reserve in her indignation, "Whatever can you mean!" she puffed, wagging her gaster in spirited reproof. "Our nuptial flight is merely postponed until the weather is more suitable. Everything has been prepared for our coming out."

"The excessive clemency of the weather is more serious than you admit. Unless the proper conditions prevail, it is impossible to know when the other colonies will send forth their young queens and drones. You might come out only with your own brothers—a mortifying, even scandalous, event."

"Why, surely at worst we would come out next season." But even as she uttered these words, which went unanswered, she recognized their folly. An ant has but one season of youth: either she mates at once, or she and her eggs are ruined. At two weeks, even at two months, a royal ant is at the height of her powers to attract and attach; at one year she is a risible old maid, if she lives. And within the great ovaries of the Queen Mother, the eggs for the next brood of queens and drones were already gathering yolk.

Carina had no sooner left the room than the sisters began to abuse her in a rare burst of unanimity. They agreed that she was not correct, could not possibly be correct, that she spoke from malice and envy. They called her ugly, old, and odd. Indeed, they pitied her—how dreadful to be so humble, so decayed, so hopelessly sterile!

Yet for all their protestations, the sisters were rattled by Carina's remarks. The very thought—no assembly! no grand coming out ball!—was so sensational that the bold sister was unwilling to keep it to herself. She was already considering how she might announce it to their many sisters with the greatest éclat.

One of their brothers, perceiving their unwonted animation, came forward to interest himself in their talk, but the sisters would share no confidences with drones. Exclaiming against his impudence, the cold sister gave him several hard feeler raps on the head as punishment. She then took this interruption as her text in reading a sermon to her sister concerning the imprudence of spreading unwarranted speculations, on the mere authority of a common worker ant. Forgetful of how fully she herself had participated in the conversation, she scolded her sister for the impropriety of taking a worker into her confidence, to discuss matters of such intimate concern.

Provoked and offended, the bold ant rose to her full height, lifting her gaster, parting her mandibles, and lashing her antennae with indignation. She assured her sister she had not the slightest intention of acknowledging the worker as her informant. Moreover, she was certain the worker, whose manners were quite good, had too much respect to boast of her acquaintance with them. And it hardly mattered whether the report were true or false, but only whether they were the first to speak of it, and so the ones who would gain all the credit of its novelty.

Despite their continual resentments and rivalries, the two sisters did everything together however contentiously. The quarrel must be made up, and so it was at last, by a compromise. They knew their many sisters could talk of nothing but their expectations to shine at the grand assembly and their severe disappointment with its postponement. When the topic of the assembly next arose, the two sisters would affect an air of worldly superiority, expressing vague doubts and hinting slyly at other means by which a royal ant might find a pleasant station for herself—not that either ant had formed any idea of what such alternatives might be. This scheme pleased them both. The cold sister was among those who regularly mistake obscurity for profundity, while the bold sister felt assured that such a show of special authority would enhance their privileged position among their sisters.

Among the fifty royal virgins who were their sisters and peers, the two had acquired some small distinction. They were the eldest by some two or three hours and claimed precedence on that basis. They were also among the biggest of that brood, or at least had the cunning to walk very tall, with gasters held as high as good manners permitted, in order to appear so. On top of these natural advantages, the bold ant had gained prominence by a pretense of special access to the Queen. "Mother says" was her habitual opening, even when rehearsing stale news that had already traveled through every mouthpart in the colony. To all these claims the cold sister bore witness by wagging her head—whether in negation or confirmation could not easily be discerned—and she also acquired status by maintaining such a knowing, judging air. Mornings in the upper nest were devoted to paying visits. Accordingly, after they had settled their dispute, after they had given one last attentive brushing to their antennae, the two set out to attend a few favored sisters and to offer their news.

On taking leave of the two sisters, Carina had proceeded through a little-used section of the lower nest to a small chamber where her coming had been eagerly awaited, at least by one.

An elderly ant with a fretful, discontented air crouched in a narrow alcove. Her companion, who all but filled the tiny room, was a tall, well-formed drone of a cheerful and active disposition. Judging from his fine appearance, one would have supposed him to be endowed with no less than a hundred thousand sperm, and accordingly most capable of supplying a female with the means for every felicity and comfort. And so he would be, had the deficiencies of a confined education not marred his manners as to make his addresses unacceptable to any properly bred alate.

"Mama!" he cried, starting forward with joy, then pausing as he recollected himself. "I've done it again. I'm sorry."

"Certainly, you have," said the elderly ant, meaning to issue her own sharp reproof before Carina began a milder one. "I would have scarce thought it possible to err so grievously with uttering only a single word. You must not address a common worker except to require a service. You must not single out a worker unless it is to complain of poor service. And you must never call her 'Mama,' unless of course you wish her to be torn to pieces by the Queen's attendants."

Here the young drone twittered with horror and rushed affectionately at his mother.

"And if you ever presume to call me 'Auntie,' even in private, I'll give you a bite you won't soon forget," she concluded.

The drone would never so presume. His aunt's severity was nothing new but it considerably depressed his spirits. She was quite possibly the oldest ant in the colony, saving the Queen, and allowances must be made for her uneasy disposition, his mother had said. She was so infirm in her hind limbs that she did not get out at all now, and was entirely dependent on her sister for her maintenance. Carina had a trying time in moderating the exuberance of the young ant and the waspish ill temper of the old; nor was finding adequate provisions for them both any less difficult. Her son, she well knew, was an insect endowed with greater sensibility than sense; other than in the reproductive function, his abilities could not greatly recommend him in any female society. But one cannot ask perfection of a drone, and she felt her sister treated him with too much rigor.

"You *must* try harder," said Carina with gentle urgency. "You must strive to conduct yourself with greater attention to propriety—and to avoid such dangerous particularity. Exert yourself, not for my sake but your own. The swarm may fly any day now, if the rains come, and you should take your place among them before then."

"Again," Aunt commanded, little caring that she herself failed to observe the social distinctions she intended to instruct. "You have just noticed her. What do you do?"

Drawing himself up to his full height, the young drone tapped his foreleg on Carina's lower lip to signal his desire for food, accepted the droplet she offered, then dismissed her impressively. "That will do. You may go."

"You are not the Queen; you are only a drone," his aunt remarked reprovingly, "and a drone's social position, though superior to a worker's, is very much dependent on both his reproductive powers and the likelihood that he will be able to employ them at no very great cost to the society."

"My winged half-aunts—that is, my sisters, I should say, shouldn't I?— they are superior to all but the Queen Mother herself, are they not—who is actually *my* Queen Grandmother although of course I mustn't say that. At least, I think I mustn't. Oh, please forgive me, Aunt, I'm getting all confused again."

"Just call them the winged virgins, dear, that will be simpler," Carina gently interposed, perceiving that her sister was again losing patience. Initially, Aunt had attempted to instruct the drone in the polite evasions that would best support his social advancement. She had explained to him that the virgin queens were for all practical purposes his half-sisters, though in fact they were his half-aunts, for want of a better word. Only he must address them as sisters, unless the grand nuptial assembly did not take place, a circumstance in which it would become advisable to present himself in the more eligible character of a cousin. These principles of conduct he was entirely unable to master; his natural candor resisted such calculated representations. He had no aptitude for concealment, and his open expressions of affection for his mother caused them the greatest unease: hence the necessity of impressing his behavior with greater formality and reserve before they could safely introduce him to society. It did not help, of course, that his aunt's instructive observations on ant society were couched in a biting, acidulous wit that the good-natured drone often failed to comprehend. Her sister's harshness frequently pained Carina, although she understood its cause. As a worker ant ages, her poison gland enlarges; and her disposition accordingly becomes more inclined to provoke and mock than to please or praise.

"The virgins, *your sisters,* as you must call them until we instruct you otherwise, certainly imagine themselves superior to all but the Queen," Aunt replied. "Callow ants are all ignorant and silly creatures, but those with wings are deluded by their self-conceit into believing that they *are* what they may possibly *become.* In short, they fancy themselves queens already, neglecting to consider certain difficulties that must first be overcome."

"Such as?" said the drone, to demonstrate to his aunt that he was indeed listening, if not entirely comprehending. Indeed, under the influence of his attention, Aunt was recovering her good humor, or as much of it as she ever possessed. Like all clever ants, she lived for an audience.

"First of all, finding a handsome, well-made drone such as yourself"— giving her nephew a stiff little bow—"which is by no means a simple proposition. The assembly will be populated by drones of all qualities, and there will be no lack of poorly endowed, undersized individuals who may possess a plausible scent but lack the true masculine essentials necessary to endow a queen with lasting happiness.

"The nuptials must be celebrated immediately, preferably in the environs of the intended nest site—which must be selected with great care *and* great haste. Then she must dig the nursery herself, for there will be no workers to help her, and any ant who may happen by is sure to be opposed to her settlement. Finally, she must endure a long, painful fast until her first little brood of daughters mature to feed and attend her. Only then is she a queen."

"But, Aunt," asked the ingenuous drone, "what becomes of her consort? Does he return home to his family or stay with his new queen?"

"I have just been in company with two of our Queen's winged daughters," Carina announced, forcing a precipitant change in topic. She could scarcely bear thinking about a drone's brief, equivocal position in society. Her own outlook, as a mature but respectable worker ant, was bounded by her limited experience. Yet even she knew that drones left the nest, never to return, and that a newly mated queen started her family alone. If her elder sister knew more than that, she was not at all certain the knowledge was fit to be shared. She did not wish her son's cheerful innocence to be diminished by unpleasant truths.

"You found them to be arrogant beyond endurance, I'm sure," her sister replied, distracted from the answer she had intended to give her nephew.

"Arrogant, yes, but callow and impressionable. And I have taken the first steps to impress them favorably with your nephew."

"To think how little your efforts—and mine—would have been needed if you had only left him in the nursery!"

Carina repressed a sigh at the injustice of this reflection. She had removed her son from the public nursery when he was still a vulnerable larva, not yet capable of spinning his cocoon, in order to escape the calamitous depredations of brood parasites. The Queen could well afford to lose a few dozen offspring to the beetle grubs that had hidden themselves among the brood, but she would not venture her only son. Nor had her sister disagreed with her at the time, as she now sought to remind her.

"Neither you, Sister, nor I could have foreseen the consequences of doing so. I could not have known that feeding and caring for him privately would induce such a strong, peculiar attachment. It is unheard of." Carina spoke only of the drone's unseemly affection for his mother and hoped her sister had not observed how fully she returned it. "Nonetheless, he is well grown, bigger than the Queen's sons, which might not have transpired in the public nursery, where I could not have favored him so easily with the best food. He is much improved by your lessons, and I have perceived an occasion to introduce him into proper society. All is not lost by any means."

At these words of implicit praise, the drone dashed to embrace his mother before he recollected his freshly tutored dignity. To his delight, however, she urged him forward.

"Give me a kiss, dearest, because I wish you to make the acquaintance of these two young virgins as well," Carina said to her son, who happily bounded forward to lick his mother. He tasted the scent of the two sisters, and, as his mother anticipated, found them far more personable than she had. His senses were attuned to their personal attractions rather than their dispositions; his glandular emissions showed the former were by no means lost upon him.

"If only his manners will serve, we need not fear for his breeding" was his aunt's dry observation.

There were of course two mothers resident in the colony, of very unequal station but equally concerned for the future of their offspring. The anxieties of her daughters to achieve a proper settlement and home of their own were entirely shared by their mother, Queen Thrip. She devoted much of her day to pondering how she might get these nubile young ants happily settled in nests of their own in locations that were agreeably distant. Only a mother who has some fifty marriageable daughters ready to come out at once, all to be properly bestowed within a few eventful hours, can truly understand her preoccupation. She had never before reared so large a brood of winged daughters, with a proportionately great number of drones to escort them. The weather was at least very fine for honeydew, so there could be no concern about their maintenance while they remained at home. But Thrip could not help recalling her own mother's repressive fears and warnings against relying upon the integrity of daughters.

If one cannot trust one's daughters, it follows closely that mothers may not be entirely candid in their communications. A mother naturally wishes for her daughters to succeed, as long as they do not become her rivals. The perils and confusion of her own nuptial assembly had compelled Thrip to take up residence rather too close to her maternal home—closer than her mother Regina would approve, were she to learn of it. Thrip had long wondered whether the rove beetle who transmitted their correspondence during her first confinement had in fact kept her great secret, as promised. If not, might Regina's many instructions on the management of her household have been intended to guard against her daughter's prosperity rather than promote it? Her repeated injunctions never to place confidence in her attendants, never to allow them to remain long in their positions—was such advice intended to help or to hinder? Thrip had never been sure. But, having never experienced the friendship of sisters, she was indeed disinclined to depend too much upon the affection of daughters.

Propriety, as well as her always delicate health, prevented Thrip from moving freely about the nest. Nor did she encourage her attendants to mingle with ants of lesser rank, preferring that they maintain a distinction that increased their reputation while it protected her own dignity. Yet she knew it advisable to intervene with her winged daughters—to soothe their anxieties, to raise their spirits, to assure them that their nuptials were postponed only in order that their coming out should have all the brilliance and success that they could desire.

Thrip decided at length that she must entrust one of her attendants with the task of visiting the virgin queens. The Royal Alpha was a large, loyal, but perhaps not overly intelligent daughter whom she preferred to keep at her side. The Beta was haughty and quarrelsome, unapt to move comfortably among the winged virgins, since she would inevitably challenge the latter's complacent assumptions of superiority. Thrip wondered, not for the first time, and not without amusement, at the importance ants gave to petty distinctions—walking uncomfortably tall, only to impress their sisters; eagerly competing as to who would pass first through a narrow entry (although it only gave onto a chamber identical to all the others); spinning foolish rumors and false alarms; avidly seeking any token of superior consequence, however spurious, shallow, or short-lived it might prove to be. In her current need, a confident, commanding ant could not serve her as well as one with more pleasing and insinuating manners; and the attendant who best suited her purpose happened to bear the rank of Gamma.

Thrip summoned the ant and gave her instructions. Gamma was to make her way to the upper chambers where the hopeful young queens resided, there to observe and listen quietly; then, as she saw fit, to present herself as a representative of the Queen, and to assure her virgin daughters that their comfort and prosperity were uppermost in their mother's thoughts. But any disturbance or unseemly behavior requiring correction must be reported at once. Gamma professed herself delighted with the assignment in terms too effusive for Thrip's taste, although she reasoned that it was exactly the style to please the virgin queens, who no doubt were just as trifling and silly as her own sisters had been at their age.

Gamma's declarations of delighted service, though excessive, were not insincere. She was gratified to be singled out by her mother, and to be given an important task in preference to the Royal Alpha and Beta. She was pleasantly excited by the novelty of making an appearance in the upper nest, a region the royal attendants were rarely permitted to visit. Having groomed to her best advantage, she set out. She did not hurry. The admiration she excited among the busy throngs of meaner ants, who paused to feeler her timidly (for great ants have always their charm) before veering respectfully out of her path, was delightful to her. She despised them in pure benevolence, hardly even minding their strong, piney scent, since it merely pointed up her own superiority, established by the aristocratic cachet she owed to her proximity to the Queen. She might be merely Gamma in the royal chambers; everywhere else she was an alpha.

Everywhere, that is, except among the winged virgins, who yielded precedence to none except the Queen herself. But here Thrip was correct in trusting to the effects of Gamma's engaging manners. She had little difficulty in gaining acceptance among the first cluster of winged females she encountered, merely by proposing that she had heard reports of their beauty and fertility and had come purposely to admire them. The young virgins instantly set themselves out to best advantage, for any admirer, even an inferior and sterile sister, is better than none. They fluttered their lacelike wings and drew themselves up to their maximum height, competing as to who among them might be judged the biggest and the best endowed. Gamma admired and found a compliment for each, no easy proposition since they were all much alike. One was praised for her long limbs, another, perhaps more muscular, for her shapely trunk. Gamma was enthusiastic about the striped and stippled elegance of gasters and the perfection of silken hair and sharp teeth. Even the smallest, least considerable among them were proclaimed to possess the fresh loveliness of youth, in addition to all the fashion and smartness that high status confers. The ants were delighted with their new acquaintance. Pleased with her impeccable taste, her discerning feeler, quite beyond anything they expected in a worker, the winged ants took Gamma entirely into their confidence.

What these ants had to say could hardly alarm their mother, for Gamma had not failed to notice that the Queen was uneasy, however she attempted to conceal it. Not one of the young virgins doubted that she was destined to achieve the most astounding success and unbounded prosperity. If Gamma knew better—and she likely did—she did not say so, only attending, with a most obliging air of interest, as they endlessly discussed situations, exchanging views with an authoritative air, although all their scanty knowledge of the world was acquired from the gossip of nursery ants, who themselves heard it from the foragers. Their ideas were few but firmly held: First, to select the biggest, most aromatic drone, then to achieve the most fortunate residence: atop a grassy knoll, secure from flooding; beneath a handsomely decayed log, warm and well supplied with game; or, ideally, the underside of a flat sunny stone, like their own mother's estate. Finally, to lay astounding numbers of eggs, which would all inevitably hatch into the most adoring and obedient daughters imaginable. These self-pleasing, often repeated speculations continued until they were interrupted by the arrival of several sisters eager to pass along the latest intelligence.

News never dresses itself plainly. The cold and bold sisters' intention of furnishing only a few enticing hints about the nuptial assembly had been abandoned in the face of their sisters' indifference. Failing at first to make the sensation she desired, the bold ant began to elaborate upon her planned remarks. Envious of her sister's success, the cold ant contributed a few additional ideas that were inspired by their talk earlier that morning. Now it was everywhere that nuptial flights were dangerous, that drones were all very much the same, and that sisters of true discernment would find other means for their social advancement.

Young, giddy, ignorant, none of the winged virgins comprehended the significance of these sage-sounding observations. They all pretended to an understanding, however, then engaged in a spirited exchange in which each tried to draw the others out. The only one to take any meaning from these muddled hints and allusions was the brother who had been idly following the two sisters all morning. He showed his comprehension by attempting to mount the cold virgin, who instantly threw him off with cries of indignation and disgust. Not much dismayed by his disappointment, he made an offer to another, but had no chance of success in his addresses, since the bigger virgins united in chasing him from the chamber. There was no jealousy and hardly any hypocrisy in their united repulsion of his impudent behavior; the sisters all felt only disdain for their brothers. Gamma stayed no longer but departed at once to carry her report to Queen Thrip.

All ants love gossip, and Gamma loved to make trouble. What she had witnessed might seem sufficiently shocking in itself, but no ant enjoys a plain unceremonious relation of facts. Gamma did not scruple to embellish her observations. Affecting an air of shock and horror, she informed her mother and her fellow attendants that the young virgins were refusing to take their nuptial flight, that they were all flirting shamelessly with their brother drones and might already, for all Gamma knew—and here she declared her modesty had caused her to run from the room—have compromised themselves irretrievably.

Thrip was indeed shocked. She expected that the young virgins, lacking any restraint, or any useful occupation to fill their time and improve their minds, would prove themselves to be shallow, conceited and presumptuous creatures. But such abandoned behavior, if true, was more than equal to the darkest suspicions her mother had suggested. But was it true? Thrip had not missed the note of spiteful glee in Gamma's report: the ant could not love her better-endowed sisters; she might wish for their disgrace. And it occurred to Thrip as well that the virgins might talk, and flirt, but they could not threaten her governance without the aid of powerful, well-placed workers.

Perceiving her mother's disgust and disquiet, Gamma felt that the moment called for a decorous show of compassion for her erring sisters.

"I do hope you are not *too* angry with my royal sisters. Surely their behavior, however imprudent, is due only to natural, if excessive, high spirits. I was most impressed with their health and stature—they are all of them prodigiously tall!"

Thrip was too stunned to respond. Gamma's words could not but suggest an unflattering comparison between her own slight stature and that of her robust, well-fed daughters. Having perceived their superiority in size, might Gamma have inferred a superiority in fertility? Her entire manner, so maliciously sweet, bore a strong savor of duplicity. She might be in league with these sisters; she might even have suggested their ideas. Perhaps she had already made an alliance with the biggest and most ambitious, to unseat their mother and to take her place. And she herself had made it possible by putting the ambitious Gamma in the company of her royal sisters, whom she would not otherwise encounter. Thrip was almost ill with consciousness of her own folly. How could she fail to recognize that insinuating, artful manners were the guise most often assumed by malice and ambition? She felt certain Gamma would not scruple to supplant her mother if she might thereby advance herself to Royal Alpha.

Thrip might make herself safe by commanding the nuptial flight to take place at once, knowing the silly virgins would not be able to resist the charms of freedom and flight. But that would mean giving up all hopes of descendants for this year. Surely not all her offspring were disaffected, and she did not care to sacrifice fifty plump, promising daughters to rumor and fear. She pondered what was to be done. She needed to know more before any drastic measures were undertaken.

"Since the virgins find you so *extremely agreeable,* Gamma, you shall return to them—but not alone. This time Beta shall accompany you."

Unconscious of having given offense, Gamma did not detect her mother's sudden coldness or the biting intention of her words; but she was most unhappy at being required to share importance with Beta, her greatest rival. Thrip noticed Gamma's sulk and did not care; she regretted having to employ her at all. But when she perceived her Alpha drooping in dejection, she was quick to offer reassurance.

"You, my dear Alpha, must not be disappointed. I give you the dullest but not the least important duty, for I wish you to remain always at my side." Alpha's spirits revived at these words, while the Royal Beta barely concealed a grimace of envy and mortification, although, an instant earlier, she had been elated at her selection to visit the upper nest. She felt herself perpetually ill-used—for why must she be Beta and not Alpha? It was not fair.

Thrip nearly called them back as soon as Beta and Gamma had left. Uneasy with everything done and not done, questioning herself on everything, Thrip could not but reflect that she might have achieved little beyond exposing herself still further to unwelcome comparisons of her own stature to that of her virgin daughters. She could confide only in her Alpha, an ant whose gentle good nature rendered her somewhat stupid and who even now was endeavoring to excuse the winged ants.

"Rivalry, treachery between sisters is a common occurrence, but daughters to their Queen and Mother!" said Alpha. "It is too bad to think." Appearances were against them, certainly, yet she did not wish to think so ill of any ant. She hoped there would be an explanation.

"It is rather too easily explained, I should think," replied her mother bitterly.

"I meant only that ants sometimes speak without much circumspection. They say or do what will gain them attention and some little prominence among their sisters. Each wishes only to be first, however meanly achieved and momentary the distinction."

"In this instance, one or more of these virgins wishes to be made Queen in *my* nest, and one or more of your affectionate sisters hopes to be *her* Alpha." To this Alpha had nothing to say, except once more she hoped it was not so.

As the two royal attendants traveled upward through the crowded galleries, Beta exclaimed indignantly at the dirt, smells, and vulgarity of common ants. Her actions bore witness to her fine aristocratic feelings as she blocked, pummeled or slapped any humble worker who happened across her path. Gamma reflected maliciously that Beta would soon be imbued with the low caste odor she professed to find so distasteful, but she refrained from comment. She herself felt no ill will towards small, old, or otherwise unfortunate sisters; she detested only her rivals. As they reached the upper chambers, Beta collided with an elderly ant who offered no apology for the affront but continued on her way, moving with remarkable speed for one so obviously lame in her hind limbs.

Aunt hurried back to her sister and nephew in a frenzy little short of panic. She had taken it upon herself to pay a visit to the winged sisters, intending only to confirm Carina's hints that the assembly might be small and private, a family affair—then proceeding to suggest to the virgins that there was a cadet branch of the family, little known but quite as well descended. Certain that this would not fail to interest, she might then hint of one highly eligible drone, to whom she could effect an introduction. Such was her intention. But she found it nearly impossible to obtain a hearing among the young virgins. Her age, and with it her ineradicably strong scent, everywhere gave offense. She was either ignored or treated with the greatest disdain, until at last she succumbed to her exasperation and spoke much too plainly and truly. She told the ants that the grand nuptial assembly would certainly *not* take place without the necessary rains, that instead each colony would send their young forth without preparation, and with little hope of success. Now at last the acerbic old ant had their attention; but the bitterness of her age betrayed her into themes that ought not be expressed in polite society. She spoke of birds, wasps, and spiders, of robber flies, tiger beetles, and assassin bugs—then of the still greater dangers posed by the rival ants who would oppose their settlement, should they survive their nuptial flight. The virgins were frightened, shocked, and indignant by turns until at last, neither believing nor entirely disbelieving her claims, they chased the bearer of such unwelcome tidings from their midst.

Aunt had left the young virgins in a state of agitation little inferior to her own. As the Royal Beta and Gamma entered, the cold sister was declaring outright in the most strenuous terms that she had no intention of attending a nuptial assembly if it was indeed so dangerous to one's health. Another instantly objected that *she* would not take the word of an ill-smelling, decrepit old forager—such a creature had no wings and so of course was unable to travel securely. And *they* would be escorted by their brothers, who surely would be eaten first supposing there actually were such dangers before them. This fine piece of reasoning convinced them. Other than of their own consequence and ambition, they held no fixed ideas at all—and they all longed to use their wings. Then, however, the bold sister, who never liked to be silent, or ignored, for long, reverted to her favorite points—and as always she did not scruple to attribute her ideas to the Queen: "This is all quite beside the point," she remarked loftily. "Mother says there might not *be* a nuptial flight."

"Traitor!" cried the Royal Beta in a fury, menacing the astonished ant. In her indignation, Beta failed to consider that the bold virgin was by far the bigger ant, with teeth every bit as sharp as her own. With quick decision, she turned and made a rapid exit, after Gamma, who managed to block her passage just long enough to allow the equally indignant virgin to deliver a hard slap to Beta's rear. They returned at once to their mother, very shocked, yet also very pleased.

On returning to her sister, Aunt was determined to conceal the mortifying aspects of her encounter with the winged virgins. She complained of their arrogance, their complacency, their ignorance, but said nothing of her own imprudence in attempting to alarm them regarding dangers that were best unacknowledged. She merely told Carina that she considered the time right for her nephew to make his appearance in society. He must succeed or fail on his own talents; she herself was weary and could do no more. Carina was accustomed to trust her sister's judgment as superior to her own, and she felt the urgency to establish her son in his place. The drone, for his part, was excited and ready. He followed his mother at a little distance, so that their relationship might not be suspected, as she led him to the upper nest.

Every afternoon, at the very hour when the nuptial assembly would begin, if only the weather were suitable, the winged ants took their customary exercise upon the hill and the stone, promenading slowly back and forth, relieving themselves from the constraints of inhabiting chambers and passageways little suited to their large winged forms. The conversation invariably exclaimed against the weather—how dreadfully fine and clear and dry each successive day had been. They told each other that tomorrow, or the day after, or *surely* the day after that, it would finally rain—and then they would set forth at last. One of the more reckless drones would make a show of taking off, hoping the others might follow; but the sentries would seize hold of him before his rash example could make an impression. The routine wearied them but they did not vary from it.

The consternation produced by the talk of the day was great. No one knew what was to be done or what would become of them if they could not hold their assembly. Despite Thrip's fears and her attendants' accusations, the winged ants had no thought of holding their nuptials at home; their mother's severity and formality inhibited them so profoundly that there was no possibility of swarming in her presence. And they wanted very badly to display their wings in flight.

The young virgin queens had considered their brothers only as escorts to the assembly where they would choose partners for themselves; any conquests those brothers might make would be rivals and therefore disliked. The drones, in turn, found little advantage in the company of their sisters except to swell the assembly with their numbers. A revision of both outlooks was slowly revolving. In their straitened circumstances, they began to face the possibility that they must venture out in twos and threes to make their settlements under circumstances so mean that they did not bear contemplating. Nonetheless, a few of the brothers and sisters began to court. It was not promising: brothers lack the exotic blandishments of suitors; conversation languished.

While the young royal ants flirted or fretted with equal discontent, the workers went to and from the nest at their daily tasks with a coarse insensibility to the plight of their winged sisters. Having taken a place among the workers, Carina observed that the two sisters of her acquaintance were not accompanied. Approaching, she undertook to introduce them to their cousin, and presented her drone to them. The novelty of a stranger in their midst soon drew the others.

Under other circumstances, a strange drone who presumed upon admission to their society without proper sponsorship would have been cut, if not bitten, severely. Such was the current solicitude for enlarging their assembly that the drone was tolerated by the males and positively welcomed by the females, who were desperate to avoid the humiliation of consorting with their brothers. His open, unreserved manner, his amiable countenance, his liveliness and his easy willingness to praise and admire, all conspired to gain him quick acceptance. The curiosity with which others brushed against and antennaed him had no ill nature to it.

The two sisters claimed him as their intimate acquaintance and maneuvered for his exclusive attentions. As he was unquestionably the finest drone of the colony, the sisters lost no opportunity of displaying their own endowments to the best advantage. He joined them in their promenade.

His aunt's stories of her days outside the nest provided material for conversation as he walked along the ramparts side by side with the two sisters. He pointed out the views—that, over there, was the wood pile where the colony has sometimes seized termites as their prize. Further on was the flower bed, made dangerous by antlions and carnivorous ground beetles, but rich in honeydew, nectar and dead flies for those who dared make the attempt. Yes, those *were* birds passing overhead, but the sisters need not be alarmed. Only a few birds truly relish ants; many subsist entirely on seeds and berries. He would know the danger, if there were any, and escort the sisters to safety.

Carina's son might confidently indicate any sights, fabulous or real, that he pleased. The virgins were too near-sighted to discern objects much beyond the reach of their more acutely sensible feelers. Gazing beyond the nest mound, they could see only a great oceanic expanse of air, in which a few indistinct forms floated or swept by, as the strength of the breeze or their wings determined. Again and again they spoke of the disagreeableness of the weather and hissed their disappointment. But the new drone brought a liveliness to their conversation, and for the moment their troubles and contentions were put aside.

All was not so calm within the nest. The infamous behavior reported by the Royal Beta and Gamma silenced Alpha and determined Thrip. She must command the launch of the nuptial flight at once. It was late afternoon, the heat of the day was past—the proper hour at least, if not the proper day for the nuptials. No matter! The sacrifice must be made: her security and peace of mind demanded it. She would see to it herself, accompanied by her attendants, to ensure that none of these troublesome winged daughters remained behind. Arriving at the upper chambers, Thrip and her attendants were informed that the winged ants were promenading on the anthill. It would need only a few words of command to the sentries to launch them in flight.

While Thrip hesitated to release the virgins to an almost surely fatal flight, Beta, still irritated by the slap she had received, continued to enumerate their offenses.

"One of them even claimed they acquired their notions of conduct from you. She authorized her opinions with 'Mother says this' and 'Mother says that.' Imagine the impudence!"

Imagine the stupidity, Thrip thought, as new doubts and fresh hopes suggested themselves. It was yet possible that the winged virgins were guilty of nothing but imprudent and meaningless chat. Had the simple, good-natured Alpha been correct, while she, who held herself so much wiser, had misjudged entirely? She understood her daughters and knew, or ought to know, how their drab propriety fed a longing to detect scandal in others. She had always considered herself superior to the false alarms and silly gossip of her family; but the fears impressed upon her by Regina had swayed her judgment and prejudiced her. In revolving these reflections, it now seemed incredible to suppose that her fresh, inexperienced daughters possessed the resources to conceive of overthrowing their mother to establish themselves. Unprincipled they might be, but surely too *untaught* to form a credible scheme for such ruthless self-advancement. She reflected on her own sisters' behavior at that interesting age, when a female is ripe and eager for flight, without much knowing why. Even those who were the most well-grown and forward had shown utter disdain for drones, quite up to the moment when the allure of the nuptial assembly drew them forth from their home. And their presence on the hilltop at this hour revealed her daughters to be as foolishly impatient to fly as any young virgin could be.

She remembered her own wings, sacrificed so long ago to her maternal interests; she recalled the exultation of flight, the thrilling arousal and enchantment of her nuptials, before disaster intervened. She would never again fly, she would never again see, for her long years in the deep nest had deprived her of the power of sight. But the beckoning warmth of the sun, the exotic scents of the outer world, brought a sudden resurgence of the curiosity that had once formed so great a portion of her character.

"I should like to meet these daughters of whom I've heard so much." And, to the consternation of her attendants, the Queen began to move upwards.

From some little distance, Carina had observed her son as he walked the ramparts with the two sisters. The sisters were clearly captivated by his address and competed to attach him. Carina saw nothing wrong with his attracting the attentions of two sisters at once, for an ant must be practical. If the weather continued unfavorable and flirtation turned serious, then her son might retain his chance to found a family line.

Activity at the nest entrance drew her attention from these agreeable meditations. Surrounded and half-carried by her attendants, the Queen was making an appearance on the hill. All the ants were astonished: some drew closer, excited by the possibility of an acknowledgment, courting their own mortification; others, more circumspect, kept to their places and only bowed low. Slowly circling the ramparts, the Queen took little notice of any ant until she reached the two sisters, indicated to her by Beta and Gamma.

Had she not been stricken with painful anxiety for her son, Carina might have observed with amusement the sisters' distress at this unexpected distinction. Impudent confidence instantly gave way to self-conscious guilt: the sisters feared the Queen had learned of their lies and had come solely to mete out their punishment. They readily betrayed each other and their stories were soon told. They described the worker who had been the source for their mistaken notions. They introduced the drone.

Out of simplicity or courage, Carina's son showed no awareness of his danger. He bowed low as his aunt had taught him to do should he ever encounter the Queen. She subjected him to a searching probe, followed by a reprimand, a single hard nip to the foreleg. Thrip now understood all.

Relieved from her fears, refreshed by the scent of youthful ferility, she felt a surge of benevolence. She would pardon not only the drone, well-built and ready to fly, but even his selfishly misguided mother.

The Queen continued at her slow, stately pace until she came to Carina, who trembled with fear as she bowed. To her great surprise, the Queen responded by seizing Carina's feeler between her mandibles with a painful yank, then placing it in contact with her great swollen gaster, rich in ripening eggs. After a long, suspenseful moment, she released Carina and walked on.

The vulgarity of the act surprised Carina quite as much as the implicit threat had frightened her. It presented the Queen in a new light: for it was Thrip the mocking outcast, not the dignified and weary Queen, who had so accosted her. But the crude gesture conveyed its meaning remarkably well. "You with your one pitiful egg: behold my ovaries—my power!" Carina understood that she and her son had been spared because the Queen's concerns were identical to her own, to those of any careful mother: to obtain acceptable mates for her offspring. If the nuptial flight could not take place, if Queen Thrip's daughters could not be bred with the drones of other colonies, then Carina's son would have his use.

But the rains did come at last. In the late watches of the night, the sentries were the first to know. The unspoken fear of a flood kept them anxiously at their stations. But the rain, though it continued long, was a gentle one. By morning even the ants deep within the nest knew, from the refreshing humidity of the ambient air, that the weather had finally turned, and that the long-awaited nuptials might take place.

The day itself—beginning overcast and gradually brightening—sent out a general invitation that could not go unanswered. All the neighboring colonies sent their eligible young males and females to the assembly. At last they could release their amorous perfumes, at last display their amber wings in the favorable light of the late afternoon sun and set themselves out to draw admirers. The long dry spell had but added brilliance to the complexion; even the very youngest had lost their sallow coloring for a becoming glossy brown-black, fringed with reddish-blonde hair. To add to the elegance, at least from the feminine perspective, the number of suitors much exceeded that of the females. None need sit down to earth again without enjoying the attentions of at least one partner.

Either of the sisters would have willingly granted the first dance to Carina's handsome son, but a drone must be prudent. A queen may seek mates until her sperm bag is filled; a drone loves but once and with all his living fiber. He can have but one partner and it becomes him to make a grander match, if he can, than a mere sister or aunt. Carina's son held himself aloof from the excited coupling and uncoupling of the sisters, until he found a proper match, a cousin sharing a line of descent from Regina, and so reuniting the two most prosperous and distinguished families of the region.

If the hopes of others miscarried, if only a few were rewarded with a prosperous settlement, it was nonetheless accounted one of the most successful assemblies in even the longest remembrance, for no fewer than six new colonies resulted. It continued throughout a long evening, until those who survived had all descended to the ground—the queens to shed their wings and dig their nests, the drones to die.

In the twilight calm of that evening, Carina crept to the mound to twitch her feelers and strain her dim eyes for any news of the assembly. Her sister, with much difficulty, crawled after her. Together they surveyed the great unformed expanse of air and earth. Their sensitive feelers discovered no hint of the carnage that usually attended the nuptial flights: either the breeze had carried the young ants far from their native colony, or—as they hoped and believed—the delightful change in the weather had stirred renewed activity throughout the insect realm, so that the birds, wasps, spiders, robber flies and assassin bugs had found other repasts to sate their appetites. The sisters did not need to speak; once again, as they had long ago, they rested side by side upon the anthill, in complete accord of thought and feeling.

What are the sensations of an ant upon sending her only son to make his way in the world? They are suffused with triumph and with loss. Although she had not that thorough comprehension of the dangers which a mature, mated queen ant might possess, Carina knew that her son, with his open disposition and undeveloped mandibles, would not last long. But if his sperm were well deposited, he might establish a lineage that would flourish long after she—for her story, too, was nearly at an end—had passed.

Carina's son crouched in the shade of a rhododendron leaf. He felt entirely dispirited and fatigued, as if he was suddenly old, quite as elderly as Auntie. He had borne himself with distinction at the assembly: he had courted and won a fine, fat, fertile queen; he had lingered nearby as she broke off her wings and prepared her nursery, assuring himself of her fidelity and security. He had done all that could be asked of a drone. Yet where was his mother to feed and praise him?

He had a notion of the way home but could do no more than creep forward a few feeble steps. Why did she not come for him, as she always had before? He fell into a dreamy stupor. He was a little larva once again, helpless and hungry, always hungry. Someone approached—it was she! But eight legs, not six, rushed forward to seize him in a tight embrace. As the spider's fangs bore down to pierce his weakened frame, he cried out to his mother one final futile time.

V.

Literary Realism

Ant

True warfare in which large rival armies fight to the death is known only in man and in social insects.
–Richard Dawkins, **The Selfish Gene** (1976)

The realist novel represents one of the great revolutionary cultural forms of human history. In the domain of culture, it has something like the importance of steam-power or electricity in the material realm, or of democracy in the political sphere. For art to depict the world in its everyday, unregenerate state is now so familiar that it is impossible to recapture its shattering originality when it first emerged.
–Terry Eagleton, **The English Novel: An Introduction** (2005)

There are two sides to the life of every man, his individual life which is the more free the more abstract its interests, and his elemental swarm-life in which he inevitably obeys laws laid down for him ... The people of the west moved eastwards to slay their fellow men, and by the law of coincidence thousands of minute causes fitted in and coordinated to produce that movement and war.
–Leo Tolstoy, **War and Peace** (1869)

That element of tragedy which lies in the very fact of frequency, has not yet wrought itself into the coarse emotion of mankind; and perhaps our frames could hardly bear much of it. If we had a keen vision and feeling of all ordinary human life, it would be like hearing the grass grow and the squirrel's heart beat, and we should die of that roar which lies on the other side of silence. As it is, the quickest of us walk about well wadded with stupidity.
–George Eliot, **Middlemarch** (1872)

"Yes," added Mary; "ask Mr. Farebrother to tell you about the ants whose beautiful house was knocked down by a giant named Tom, and he thought they didn't mind because he couldn't hear them cry, or see them use their pocket-handkerchiefs."
–George Eliot, **Middlemarch** (1872)

THERE WERE NOW many colonies descended from Regina and Thrip. Ants were everywhere, occupying every crevice, colonizing every outpost, seeking out every possible food source from beetle grubs to bird droppings. Old boundaries blurred and shifted: how now to settle which colony would control the impatiens of the westernmost flower bed with their wealth of nectaries, or who held the hunting rights to the inchworms of the linden tree? At first it was a novelty, only slightly disturbing, to encounter strangers from other, remotely related colonies. The ants would feeler each other anxiously, then veer off, avoiding a second encounter. As these chance meetings repeated, they became more threatening. Small, shy foragers might hide or run, but the more belligerent members of each party would display their wrath, first snapping their mandibles and bobbing up and down, then clashing in a head-to-head match of jostling and shoving. Where equal strengths encountered, these disputes meant little and resolved less.

But these conflicts placed a great strain on the young colonies that attempted to settle along the frontiers of the two great powers. With their smaller workforces, it was impossible to gather food and patrol their borders too. Consequently, the territories claimed by these contesting colonies were always changing: sometimes shrinking, other times expanding, becoming ever more fragmented. Foragers were oftentimes compelled to take absurdly circuitous routes simply to gather their own honeydew on their own land. Occasionally rival search parties would converge on the same prey, and then the struggle for dominion, the pushing, spitting, nipping and mandible sparring, was little short of an all-out fight. Amid such great uncertainties, some colonies disappeared without a trace—overrun by their rivals or forced to shift their nests. These misfortunes were experienced only by those daughters and granddaughters who attempted to settle in an overpopulated region where every inch, it seemed, had already been claimed by one or more competing colonies. The dominance of Regina and Thrip in their respective homelands had never been challenged.

On a midsummer morning in the ninth year of Thrip's reign, one of her biggest workers, a burly young major, was idling in a guardroom, relaxed by the penetrating warmth of a sunny day. From time to time excited scouts and foragers ran up to her, beating their feelers on her massive head to beg her assistance—"a fat juicy fly, quite freshly dead" … "an enormous colony of free-range rose aphids bursting with honeydew" … "a disabled ground beetle needing only one good bite to finish it off." She ignored them. Running after foragers was a fool's game. She had been on guard duty for all of five days and already she affected a lazy, superior cynicism.

At first she had believed everything the scouts claimed and had eagerly followed them out of the nest. The juicy fly was a dried-out carcass, picked clean by prior scavengers. The honeydew could easily be transported by the foragers without her aid. The beetle was quite lively, thank you, and equal to decapitating a dozen ants. When she discovered how she had been deceived, the major was angry. An ant could get killed out here! Every day foragers failed to return and nobody noticed, but the death of a fine strapping young major—there were only about eighty of them, all told—was something to be regretted. The major did not wish to be regretted. It now took considerable persuasion to get her to leave her comfortable guardroom and follow a forager.

"I know my duty and I wish they knew theirs," she complained to her fellow sentries, irritable at being pulled and pummeled by a particularly insistent ant. "My duty is to protect the nest from enemy attack and to kill and carve up large prey. I'm not here to provide escort to every runty coward who comes along."

"There's not much to protecting the nest from enemies," an older and more jaded major answered, after a pause to scratch and nip at her gaster, during which her sisters edged away. All that scratching meant mites, most likely. "Say you're out on patrol. You encounter a small force of pavement ants, they run away—a large host, *you* run away. That's about all there is to it—unless of course you think you're going to fight off a flock of starlings."

"I can't say I've ever gone in much for killing prey, either," another droned with the air of an ant who is immeasurably bored, bored by her fellows, by everything, except the pleasure still provided by her own slow, self-important speech. "None of these foragers dare take on anything bigger or meaner than a ladybeetle. It's always scavenging for dead bugs, which is fine with me. *My* idea of *my* duty is storing the surplus juice." She wagged her bloated gaster as proof.

The young major realized she was being mocked but did not know how to answer. She was saved from her embarrassment by the arrival of yet another scout asking assistance, reporting a leaf chafer fallen on its back, exhausted in its struggles to right itself, located at no very great distance. This time the major responded positively: she followed the scout out to the anthill to join the rest of the assembled party of foragers, four ants in all. The marked haste of her departure, in the company of an ant notorious for her industry, provided occasion for still more ridicule.

"Did you put out a feeler on that pair? Our eager young major must like to work for her juice," said the bored, bloated major to the mite-infested one.

"Then I guess she just found her true sisters," agreed the other with a broad smirk. "A fine cluster of fools who don't know when they're well off."

"Though, without them, *we'd* be less well off," droned her sister, in a rare, reflective mood. "They do bring in a lot of bugs and juice—always first-rate stuff, too."

The mental strain of appreciating the contributions of others was too much for her modest intellectual abilities. She lapsed into a desultory monologue giving her reminiscences on some of the finer nectars she had sampled—hibiscus, hard to come by, was her personal favorite—and declaring the superiority of honeydews sucked from tender shoots and buds over those produced by the common grass root aphid. Her colleague resumed scratching and gnawing at her mites.

The alert, attractive ant who had just recruited the young major—and come in for her share of the guards' ridicule—was the best scout in Thrip's colony. She led a small band of elite ants who, as the bloated major noted, brought in more and better food than any of their sisters. They were unappreciated, even unpopular, for doing so: to be exceptional is an affront, an exhibition of vanity whether deliberate or not. The colony was prospering without their annoying, officious busyness. Why must they be so dedicated—and at the same time so peculiar? The elite foragers had made themselves so conspicuous with their eccentricities that they'd been given names by the sentries, who considered that their primary duty—after sampling the incoming juice, of course—consisted of mocking and taunting the beaten-down foragers who must endure their scrutiny in passing in and out of the nest.

The one they called Rank was an ancient and very smelly ant, for this reason unwelcome in much of the nest. Her appearance was as unsavory as her scent. She had no teeth and was missing most of her claws. She'd gone bald in patches all over her trunk and gaster, while the hair on her face and legs had grown coarse and insensitive. Old as she was, she'd given up caring what others thought of her, and she herself said whatever she pleased. She'd mostly given up grooming herself too, except for her feelers, head and forelegs. Yet an ant who has lived to such a great age must have exceptional powers of self-preservation! For that reason, and because a sister with such offensive habits would not be greatly missed, she was always assigned the most dangerous duties.

She seemed all the older next to Spout, a young ant whose teeth were still deadly sharp. There was something wrong with this one's speech ducts—she gasped and spluttered so egregiously that she'd been chased out to forage with her elders. Had she only kept quiet, she might have stayed safely at home until the normal age, but she was altogether too fond of expressing her ideas. Sometimes she spoke well enough; more often she would get off to a sputtering, hesitant start, then spray her words all at once, in no coherent odor. The more cloudy and confused she became, the more she carried on, gesticulating wildly with forelegs and feelers, then finishing in a gush of gassy speech. You would almost think she wished to make an exhibit of herself, to make sure no one failed to notice her defect. No wonder they drove her out to forage! In fact, she had a mild, steady temperament and a surprising tendency to generosity. This latter trait would be admirable in any other ant, but Spout's altruistic sentiments were ridiculous, even grotesque, when spewed forth in gasps and bursts.

Keen, the scout and leader of their little group, was an ant of mature age with an unusually active disposition, quick on the attack and gifted, it seemed, with especially acute senses. Perhaps she could not actually see or smell farther than her sisters but was only less subject to hesitation and fear. All the same, no party she led had ever been lost, not even when rain or wind obliterated trails and displaced landmarks. She too had left the nursery at an abnormally early age. All sensible, well-adjusted ants cling to their positions in the inner nest until forced out by age or other objectionable traits. The gossiping majors said that Keen had been prone to stand over the eggs and lash out at inferior sisters, to the point that they had combined to expel her. The majors could not know this for a fact since they seldom approached the brood; they knew only that their little sisters were all obsessed with eggs. Being of an indolent character themselves, the majors did not perceive another, more likely explanation: some ants are so naturally fierce and quick that they simply cannot hold still. They don't know when they are well off but the fools must come running outside to find something to do with themselves. The young major was a bit like that herself.

They came together, first Rank and Keen, then Spout, and now the young major, by chance encounters that then became habitual. The little oddities that annoyed other ants did not displease them as much. When the nights were chilly they clustered close to one another, despite their differences in character, age and size. It was comfortable, somehow, to be together, although they only dimly perceived why that should be. The mite-infested major had guessed the truth with her sneer. They were in fact true sisters—all daughters of one small impertinent drone, whose devoted love had made him a sacrifice to a ravenous robber fly. From him they inherited their hastiness and their powers of persistence, as well as an unappreciated, unthinking bravery.

Unlike other, less capable foragers, Keen would not call a major out of the nest to no purpose. There *was* a fallen leaf chafer very close by—a juicy scarab for the young major to kill and carve up. The four sisters were only mildly surprised, on approaching, to find that another party of foragers were already gnawing and nipping at the helpless beetle. They were moving forward to help when Keen stopped them. "Not sisters," she hissed, "not our ants!" To discover strangers so close to their nest, poaching prey they had marked as their own, was incredible, almost beyond belief.

They drew themselves up to their full height, then advanced with gasters cocked and mandibles parted in a fierce grimace. "Be off!" they cried, "It's our territory—our game." The major waited well to the rear, not troubling herself to participate in their show of force. Foreign ants discovered far from their own land generally ran off at once. Even the boldest intruders found it advisable to retreat after returning a little face-saving bluster.

This time, though, the strangers fell upon the unprepared foragers in a ferocious surprise assault. It would have gone badly for Thrip's ants if not for the major. Recovering from her amazement, she threw herself into battle—severing a foreleg of the ant attacking Keen, then reaching with her powerful mandibles to grip the crippled ant by the neck. Swinging her up, with one fierce motion she broke the ant in two and hurled the pieces into the writhing mass of combatants, then flung herself upon another. Only now did the strangers realize they had picked the wrong fight. They broke and ran.

Her corporeal nerves and muscles still intact, the headless ant staggered in a slow, sick gyre. Disgusted, the foragers satisfied their rage by biting and gnawing until at last she lay motionless on the ground. Then Keen and Rank examined the corpse, sampling its colony scent and searching their memories.

"Regina," said Rank. "Our Queen's mother."

"Yes, Regina's," Keen agreed. "We've met them in the borderlands often enough, but it's always been a spitting and shoving match, with at most a little sparring and nipping, until one side or the other gave way. Why venture so close to our nest—and then attack to kill?"

There was no answer to her question. The ants quickly gathered their spoils and returned to the nest to tell their story. It became the talk of the colony all that day, then died down, eclipsed by other, more familiar concerns. Foragers bring back so many stories of marvels and monstrosities. Who can pay attention to it all? The world outside was so vast, so bewildering, an ant could puzzle her brain all her brief days trying to make sense of it. It was only the world within the nest—the alliances and the factions, the gossiping and the machinations—that truly engaged their interest. Soon it seemed all but the foragers themselves had forgotten about the fight with Regina's belligerent daughters. Yet, deep within the nest, murmuring only "It's best to be prepared" to her attendants, Thrip began to lay more eggs.

Regina's great and powerful colony had been founded in the most fertile soil of the region, weedy and rich in prey. But the deaths of two sheltering trees, one falling upon and uprooting the other, had changed its fortunes. Now the nest was situated in open ground, subject to extremes of weather. When heavy rains followed a drought, whole galleries were submerged in the sudden surge of floodwaters. Walls crumbled or collapsed in disastrous cave-ins that took days to repair. Twice the frustrated ants had built new galleries that extended the original nest in different directions, but they too were subject to flooding and crumbling. There had been sickness as well, and some ants harbored secret fears of contamination seeping through the wet, friable soil.

The scouts dispatched to find a better nest site could not agree, disputing endlessly among themselves. Of several possible sites, each had its determined advocates who dragged or carried their sisters to it in an attempt to win them over. But each site also presented difficulties that were eagerly seized upon by those arguing for an alternative. Some locations would put them into conflict with young colonies of Regina's daughters; they might be certain to win, but first they must exterminate their own sister and nieces. Others were close to mature colonies where a victorious outcome was by no means as certain. A miasmal vapor of indecision and inaction hung over the colony, permeating the nest from the guardrooms right down to the royal chambers.

Or perhaps this fog of doubt and uncertainty originated with the Queen and spread outwards. Regina herself was subject to strange delusions. She thought—no, she was certain—there was a beetle lurking in her chamber. Find it, kill it! she would cry out, doubled over in panicked stridulations. Her attendants were forced to all sorts of absurdities to reassure her. Then another fantasy would seize her: Alien queens were laying eggs in her brood chambers. Her daughters were plotting against her. Every attempt to reason with the Queen's obsessions only increased her paranoia.

Never a large ant, Regina's Alpha was no longer a young one. She owed her post instead to her skill in calming the agitated Queen. She did so by humoring her—racing about the royal chamber in pursuit of phantom beetles, ransacking the brood chamber for illicit eggs (and eating those she considered suspect), then arresting and arraigning the nurses accused of laying them. Innocent ants suffered under random and baseless accusations. But the Queen was thus appeased and Alpha had kept her office for three entire seasons. Regina no longer recalled how inadvisable she had once considered such unchallenged seniority to be.

Within the colony all intelligence passes to and from the Queen. She does not move; she rarely speaks; the labor of laying eggs consumes her bodily strength; but she nonetheless probes and ponders. The powerful scents she gives forth are commands diffused throughout the colony. They attract, they repel, they send forth and they call back to safety. Since she rarely leaves her chamber, the workers must be her limbs, eyes, palps, feelers. Their collective experience reaches her from every mouthful of food entering the colony and from the information gleaned by one ant grooming another, traveling from mouth to mouth until it focuses, as the entire society focuses, on the Queen. It is changed, inevitably, as it so passes. The reality perceived by a forager is not recognizable by those who never leave the deep nest. But it is changed and changed until finally it is a homogeneous unified whole: there is consensus; the ants know what to do.

Out of fear and uncertainty, this time the consensus arrived in slow waves of reluctant conviction. There *was* sickness in the nest. They *must* move—but where? The answer, when it came, was baffling. East, go east. But east was a relatively barren land, good only for root honeydew, and entirely under the control of Thrip's large, thriving anthill. The answer still came back the same: east, east, we must go east. Already the east party had begun to excavate the chosen site, and they kept inviting more observers to instill them with their own enthusiasm. But still the question must be answered: what about Thrip, our Regina's own daughter, mistress of a strong colony? This answer was harder to come by: the site was nearly abandoned and the north party almost carried the point. But then it began to be said that Thrip was a runt, unhealthy and weak. She'll run out of eggs—we'll win by attrition. And she's not the Queen's daughter after all, but a cuckoo egg laid by one of the renegade queens that our mother is always, so rightly, suspecting.

Who was behind this astonishing plan? The obscure scout who had discovered the eastern site had clung stubbornly to her scheme, urging her sisters out one after another to inspect it, dragging or carrying those who were reluctant. Yet she was incapable of devising the sophisticated arguments that finally triumphed. Who but their Queen could have known that Thrip was small and possibly deteriorating in health? Long ago, Regina had awakened to the horrible realization that one of her fertile daughters had crept into her chamber, was standing at her side—sharp young mandibles perhaps already poised to deliver the death blow. When the intruder was found to be a weak, undersized virgin, as stupidly innocent as the rest of them, Regina's alarm seemed ridiculous even to herself, although she subsequently doubled the size of her retinue. The incident, trivial, even laughable, at the time, lived on in memory, gathering a hazy premonitory significance in the Queen's brooding thoughts. Thrip figured prominently in her recurrent terrors, Thrip's remembered scent and shadowy form standing in for all the phantom daughters and parasitic queens who sought to supplant her. Thus it was that certain obsessive interests passed back and forth, from the deep nest to the foragers and scouts on its fringe, until at last they coalesced into a plan for the east, for a confrontation with Thrip.

The colony moved stealthily in carefully planned stages, undertaken by night, when they were less likely to be detected by their rivals. Much of Regina's household was sent in advance to prepare the site and render the nest habitable. As soon as the nurseries were usable, the foragers began carrying brood and nurses—the nurses were too ignorant and inexperienced to make their own way. Only when fully half their forces were installed in their new residence would they dare to convey the Queen herself, surrounded by a large retinue and accompanied by a troop of sturdy majors and seasoned foragers.

Regina and her attendants anxiously awaited transport. Darkness was less terrifying than daylight, but even so the experience of the upper world was unsettling, disorienting. They had come as far as the guardrooms on their own but had no courage to go further. At last their escort was assembled and they left their old home.

The first phases of the great migration had gone well enough. If some number had been lost to assassin bugs, antlions, wolf spiders and other killers lurking in the shadows, they had not yet been missed. But the passage of so many ants along a single track must inevitably attract notice. The Queen's guard filled the trail on all sides, but they had not anticipated the possibility of an aerial attack. The approach of an owlfly, merely attracted by the novelty, threw them into a confused panic. If the Queen were lost, the colony would perish!

Her attendants scurried to give her cover, but in their frenzy each was pushing the others away. Some were cravenly attempting to hide themselves at the bottom of what was suddenly a squirming heap of ants—yet more intriguing to the owlfly as it passed back and forth, hovering ever closer. A quick-thinking major reacted by grabbing foragers and hurling them at the owlfly, which was now quite interested. If these little creeping things can fly, then they must be food! But they were very hard and sour. After sampling a few, the owlfly went hunting elsewhere.

By this means, with the loss of only a half-dozen foragers, the intrepid major was credited with preserving the Queen's life. Upon reaching the new nest without further incident, Regina paused to address the major: "We applaud your intelligent—we shall not say valorous—action, which had the fortunate consequence of preserving the safety of your Queen. We may soon have need for big ants with leadership abilities."

The royal attendants smirked in quiet appreciation of the irony tingeing the Queen's precisely worded praise. Always incredulous of purported heroism, Regina obviously realized that the major's prompt action had served first and foremost to ensure her own survival. And flinging one's little sisters to a predator hardly fits a very exalted definition of leadership. But royal chamber subtlety is wasted upon majors, whose big heads are more liberally furnished with muscle than brain. The heroic major and her fellows considered this praise to be true, just, and long overdue.

The majors perpetually complained among themselves that they did not get the respect properly due them for their size. During a famine, certainly, those majors who retained a store of juice in their crops were avidly courted and groomed by hungry workers. And as sentries they had undisputed authority over the elderly, downtrodden foragers. But the ants of the deep nest did not defer to them at all. Except for storing juice in their capacious crops, they were idle, unimportant ants, with no usefulness in times of prosperity and peace. Their excessive clumsiness and oversized mandibles disqualified them from tending either the brood or the Queen—the two pathways to power and influence in ant society. While they missed the mockery concealed in the Queen's praise, the majors easily grasped her hint about the future. There might soon be war—and with it an opportunity to increase their prestige among their sisters.

All the ants understood that they had moved their nest well within Thrip's territorial boundaries and that conflict was inevitable. Regina's Alpha argued that all-out war could be avoided. Certainly, there would be skirmishes; both sides would suffer losses. But surely there was sufficient honeydew to support both colonies comfortably. With diplomacy, with a carefully calibrated show of force, accommodations could be worked out so that the colonies could coexist—as cordial enemies if not as friends and kin. For two colonies of equal strength, as the Alpha supposed them to be, full-scale warfare would be as disastrous for the victor as for the loser. Regina listened and said nothing, but twitched irritably at the supposition that Thrip's daughters could be as great in number as her own.

Yet Regina's colony had suffered losses of both brood and adults during the dangerous migration. It would take some time before the Queen's ovaries could make up their numbers. It was imprudent, almost treasonous, to suggest any insufficiency in the Queen's fertility. Nonetheless, in the short term, until the summer worker brood matured, until they were once again at full strength, it was vital that their relocation go unnoticed. Passing quickly over these final points, the Alpha recommended that the foragers go out only at night or by twilight, and flee at once if they encountered a party of Thrip's daughters.

Regina's Beta had noted the Queen's twitch of annoyance and guessed its meaning. She might have sought the Queen's favor by attacking the Alpha's plan as excessively prudent, as overestimating the strength of a runt queen. But she was unwilling to risk the consequences of opposing her powerful sister. This Alpha had held her position for so long that the Beta thought of herself more as her sister's alpha than as the Royal Beta. Having gone unchallenged, the Alpha's temporizing plan was accepted. There would be no overt hostilities, for now, and all foraging expeditions would be undertaken by night.

But the foragers objected to going out in darkness. It was always harder to find one's way, especially in new, still unfamiliar territory. Surely it would not do for any of them to wander into Thrip's nest by mistake! The majors, for once, supported them in their concerns. The foragers might go out when and where they pleased, provided they did not presume to trouble their big sisters for escort. The big ants seemed to be interested only in lounging and gossiping in the guardrooms and in sampling the incoming stores of honeydew and nectar, as usual. But they were secretly encouraging the older, more reckless foragers to attack Thrip's ants whenever they might safely do so, in pleasant anticipation that they would soon come to open war.

However lazy they may be in prosperity, majors do not shirk combat.

Their heavy armor, great size and powerful jaws render them almost invincible. Cunning in their cowardice, they stay to the rear of the attacking force, advancing into battle only when smaller, less valued sisters have pinned down an enemy, when it is safe, easy work to snip off limbs, feelers, gasters and heads. A major need only fear another major—a theoretical risk, since Thrip's big soldiers would surely follow the same tested strategy, sending the foragers out to die in the front lines and moving forward themselves only into secured areas. Regina's majors eagerly queried returning foragers for intelligence. But they only wanted to learn what they had already concluded to be true. Thrip was a runt, unhealthy and weak. Thrip could not possibly have as many majors as their Regina did—nearly a hundred in all, for none of them had perished in the migration. As for foragers, they were expendable, of no real tactical value.

Within Thrip's colony life, and death, continued much as before. A number of small parties and solitary foragers had failed to return, but no one had thought much of it, or attached any significance to their loss. "Plenty of prey, plenty of predators," her majors remarked philosophically from the safety of their guardrooms. But the return of Keen, Rank and Spout without prey, without even honeydew, occasioned some talk. "Too bad—tough luck," the majors said at first. After repeated failures, they began to mock and bully the elite ants, accusing them of cowardice, of laziness, of vices normally reserved for their betters, the majors.

The young major had lately taken to patrolling—more exactly, parading—along the nest crater perimeters. She took a serene, sincere delight in herself. Her armor, beautifully stippled and striped, was really something to behold. She was young, she stood very tall, as big, in her own estimation, as any in the nest. Her few skirmishes with enemies and dangerous prey had been grandly victorious. She had not yet taken a hurt, no, not to so much as a hair or the tip of a claw. Accordingly, she did not quite believe in death, not as something that could happen to a smart young major, handsome and well-liked. Waggling her big head and snapping her mandibles for the sheer pleasure of it, she marched up and down outside the nest—as if, the older, more cynical majors said to one another, she really thought she was going to take on a flock of starlings.

All the same, there was a twitchy restlessness to her swagger, a longing for action that kept her from being fully contented with herself. For lack of any other diversion, she puzzled over what Keen and her party could be doing—staying out for hours every day yet bringing home no food at all. She was curious even though, really, lowly foragers were beneath her notice, or ought to be. She decided to follow them. But majors are bulky, slow-moving ants with an inferior sense of direction. She lost the scent and then she lost her way, blundering along until she at last came upon a small cluster of foragers. It was embarrassing to be lost, embarrassing to be in need of an escort instead of supplying one for others, but at least they could guide her home.

But they were not her sisters; they were intruders, possibly the very ones she had encountered with Keen's party, since they immediately took to their legs without attempting to fight her. Confused and excited, the major gave chase. She could not possibly catch the quicker, lighter ants but she kept stubbornly on their trail until something lunged at her from the side, surprising and toppling her. It was Rank.

"Fool!" she hissed. "Hold still!"

Indignant, the major drew herself up to her full height, intending to tell her off—an old stinking forager talking to a major like that! Before she could begin, Spout tapped her on the head.

"We-uh buh-been s-s-s-spying duh-duh-days, c-c-c-counting the fuh, fuh, fuh," she began excitedly, "uh, we duh-duh-don't duh ..."

"Oh, shut it off, will you?" Rank interrupted. "She's trying to tell you that we've stationed ourselves here to spy on Regina's foragers as they go back and forth along this trail. We don't dare move any closer for fear they'll detect our presence. Keen is the best at scouting, of course, so she's crept forward to circle their nest."

"Their nest? Why, we're nowhere near ..." the major began, breaking off as a stunning suspicion occurred to her.

"Their nest is among the hedges, under the roots of a Rose of Sharon," said Keen, so stealthy in her return that she startled her sisters, "scarcely ten minutes' fast walking from our own hilltop."

"It means war!" the major exclaimed, a jittery thrill running through her thick body. The others were silent for a long moment.

"Le-le-uh-le-uh-ssss uh hope not," said Spout.

"Maybe war can still be avoided," said Keen, without much conviction, as they turned to trudge home to their own nest.

The major was too excited to pay attention to her comrades. She had never considered the dangers of combat for common foragers and she did not do so now. War! War was what she was meant for, not butchering bugs or storing juice. She would show up the other guards as cowards. She would not wait in the rear, no, she would rush into the battle, severing legs and feelers, cleaving heads and gasters, leaving a wake of death and destruction behind her—unless of course she encountered enemy majors. She had not thought of that before. The enemy must have majors too. What were they like? What would they do?

Thrip's colony was thrown into instant turmoil by the news. Excited ants raced through the nest, feelering and querying their sisters, polling each other over and over until at last, out of a fog of fear and rage, a few coherent notions emerged. The most frightened, and thereby most belligerent, were the nursery ants, wanting to attack instantly, that very evening, likely supposing that they would never be expected to take part. The household workers, the diggers and cleaners, knew they would be conscripted and sent off to battle as raw recruits. They argued instead that the colony should migrate at once, giving up their warm, familiar rock for some safely distant land—anything to avoid a confrontation with a colony as powerful and established as Regina's.

"But they aren't established," Thrip's Alpha remarked, having carefully sifted the foragers' intelligence. "They've only recently migrated and are unlikely to be at full strength." A tall, intelligent ant, she was well aware that Queen Thrip's attendants never held their posts for long. She was not at all dismayed by the news, understanding, with the keen political cunning native to her, that it is easier for a dominant ant to retain her authority in war than in peace.

"What I would like to know," the Beta interjected, "is why it took until now for us to learn that the invaders have colonized our territory. Isn't continual surveillance the responsibility of the foragers and scouts?" Contentiousness was the distinguishing trait of Thrip's current Beta. She would rather start an irrelevant dispute than agree with the Alpha.

"The foragers say they rarely approach the hedges," the Royal Delta commented, timidly and out of order. "The honeydew is no better than else-where, and the terrain is very dangerous, with numerous antlion pits."

"So the site has natural advantages and disadvantages for our enemies," said Alpha, pleased at having the debate returned to her control. "Presumably they are able to gather honeydew and nectar by passing from stem to stem within their protective shrub. But they can travel from their nest area by ground only very slowly, with great care. Whenever the antlions shift the locations of their traps, they are sure to lose some foragers."

"If we chase them homewards when we find them in the field, they are likely to fall victim to the antlions," Beta answered. "We might wear them down by attrition."

"Maybe, but we cannot hope to exterminate them by such means," Alpha responded, "and the longer we postpone a confrontation, the more time we give them to build up their numbers and to learn the terrain. By delaying, we lose our advantages."

"We might keep them contained, unable to exploit our richer resources. If they cannot get insect prey, they will hardly be able to raise a royal brood next season," Beta insisted.

The rival ants tuned their antennae to their Queen and Mother, each hoping for her praise.

Seized by worry and indecision, Thrip had taken no part in their de-bate. She knew, as her daughters did not, that Regina would tolerate no ri-val, that there was no possibility of peaceful coexistence. Yet she had little confidence in Alpha's argument that the advantages were now on their side. Whether the conflict took the form of a protracted struggle, an endless se-ries of costly skirmishes, or a full-scale war, the losses would task her abili-ties to the utmost. She would scarcely be equal to replacing the casualties. She listened, she did not speak, she only laid more eggs.

Gauging her silence, the Gamma spoke up, "We need more intelligence before we take any action. Why not have the foragers—the ones who dis-covered the nest—do more reconnaissance? They could make their way to Regina's nest midden by night and report on what they find there. We might learn how well they are eating and if they are maintaining their numbers."

"Yes, that would be wise. Give the command," said Thrip, relieved to postpone the crisis. Gamma had correctly interpreted the Queen's mood.

Gamma had won the debate.

The young major grumbled at this unexpected and unwelcome assignment.

"Haven't we done enough?" she said. "Now we're expected to creep all the way to the enemy's nest, somehow bypassing the antlion pits, just to report on discarded cocoons and corpses and other such rubbish. That sort of suicide duty ought to be assigned to more expendable ants, not to an elite team like ours."

"All ants are expendable," said Rank, "even conceited young majors."

"All ants are expendable—except the Queen," said Keen.

"Except the Queen," they all echoed solemnly.

It was a full moon at least. They were lucky in that. Keen could always find her way, even in utter darkness, but she preferred to navigate by celestial light and avoid laying scent marks that their enemies might discover and follow. She led them to the spot close to the enemy trail where they had hidden themselves earlier that same day.

"What's the plan?" asked the young major.

"We watch this trail," said Keen, "if it appears to be deserted, then we might chance taking it, to be sure of avoiding the antlion pits. Their midden lies on this side of their nest, which is a help. But we still might encounter the enemy as we approach their nest if we keep to their trail. They may be doing more night foraging than we would, just to keep their presence a secret for a little while longer. So it becomes a question of which enemy we most fear and wish to avoid—antlions or ants."

"Antlions," said Rank.

"Antlions, of course," said the young major.

"I muh-muh-must uh-uh …"

"What? Must what? Wh-wh-wh-what! Get it out or be still, won't you!" Rank's irritability had a peculiarly calming effect on Spout. She was always at her best once the old ant had exploded in rage.

"Must disagree," Spout said, getting it all out in her usual confused rush. "Antlions get us, bad for us. Caught spying—enemy raise alarm, enemy attack, all our sisters, the Queen, everyone, much more bad."

Rank let out a long hiss of disgust. Such an argument was unanswerable. They must venture their lives among the antlions. Worse yet, she knew that she would be expected to lead.

"Follow me, then," she said resignedly, turning abruptly toward the enemy nest and managing, as if by accident, to slap Spout with her gaster as she did so.

Under the hedge, the soil was parched and dusty. As they reached its margin, Rank stopped.

"Antlions dig their pits in loose dry soil. We'll stay along the grass border as long as possible, but eventually we must pass under the hedge. Stay close together, single file, feeler to gaster."

They crept forward at an agonizingly slow pace, stopping every few paces and wiping their feelers clean of lingering sensations, to better attune their senses to danger. Rank inspected every loose grain of sand, every minute clod of displaced soil, before she would step forward. Sometimes she would come to an abrupt halt and veer sharply around, almost to backtrack. What progress they made was in spirals and loops. When at last they were within a few paces of the enemy midden, the major, from clumsiness or impatience, stepped out of the file. She slid, recovered, then slid again. Another scrambling climb nearly got her back on her feet, until a sudden avalanche of dust left her stumbling backward again. Something snapped down hard on her hind leg. She stridulated in rage and terror—an antlion had her! She tugged and twisted, trying to pull free, trying to bite, failing at both.

"Don't try to bite, use your poison, all of it, at once!" Rank cried out. It made no sense to the major—first you bite, then you spray venom in the wound—but she obeyed. She shot a powerful burst of poison at the bottom of the pit, at the jaws that gripped her. She felt the beast shudder; she sprayed again. The jaws opened, and she scrambled wildly up the side of the pit. Keen and Spout reached down, grabbed her by the feelers and pulled her out to safety.

Rank was leaning coolly over the pit, twitching her feelers at the roiling dirt where the antlion was writhing in furious irritation. The poison stung but could not kill it.

"A big one," she said, admiringly. "Very few are able to overpower a major. That brute must have sucked the juice out of many an unlucky ant to get so strong."

"Regina s-s-s-spends her duh-daughters freely," said Spout. "Imagine s-s-s-settling near such a m-m-m-monster. Feel s-sorry her foragers almost."

"Don't feel sorry for them," said Keen, "and don't underestimate them either. They've found a way to cope with the antlions." She directed her sisters a few steps further, to the beginning of a latticework of twigs and straws that led from the enemy's nest to their midden.

"Cunning," said Rank. "They must have other bridges leading out to their foraging trails. They are unlikely to come to the midden at night, so I think we're safe to travel on it."

The ants stepped out into the midden, their feelers probing. "Ugh," said Keen, as startled beetle grubs squirmed for cover in the debris, then she noticed what they had been feeding upon. Ant corpses, not one or two or three, but dozens of them, scattered all over the midden.

"Sickness!" she cried. "No healthy colony has that many die within the nest, at least not this time of year." The ants drew close together, repulsed, fearful of contagion, but strangely elated, too, as they began to realize the implications.

"Maybe there will be no war after all," said Keen. "They will be so weakened we can easily drive them out." She let out a sharp hiss of disgust as Rank advanced into the midden and began to probe the scattered corpses. "Sister, what are you doing? They are filth. Do not touch them!"

"They're empty," said Rank, "entirely eaten away, except for the poison glands."

"Of course, the beetle grubs …"

"No, not the beetle grubs. They are bitten open at the tip of the gaster, the way an ant would do it."

"But no ant would feed on a diseased sister."

"Exactly," said Rank. Keen drew nearer and began to probe the corpses too.

"Oh!" she cried out, "they're our own, *our* sisters, not theirs."

The others, incredulous, poked and feelered the corpses too. Beneath the foreign trace of Regina's nest was another aroma, familiar, comforting, even in this place, the scent of Mother, sisters, home. They knew that their colony had suffered heavy losses of late, not merely among the foragers but the aphid herders, too, whose duties were relatively safe. No one had guessed the predator to be their own kind.

"The ants of the royal chamber were right that this is a prey-poor region. But it looks as though our enemies have found a steady supply of meat all the same."

"Barbarians!" The young major was so incensed that she would have charged the enemy nest right then, just for the satisfaction of slaughtering a few lethargic sentries. The others held her back, reasoning with her that their first duty was to return with their report. They set off at once, pausing for a brief rest when they had passed safely through the antlion pits. They realized then that the major, assigned to guard their rear, was missing.

"Surely that big empty-headed fool didn't blunder into another pit," Rank said. But the young major caught up with them before they had to turn back to search for her.

"I stopped to play them a trick," she explained. "I moved their bridge so it leads right to the big antlion pit. The first foragers on it tomorrow are in for a nasty surprise."

"What's wrong?" she asked defensively, when the others were silent. "I thought it was a clever thing to do."

"Clever, not wise," Rank said. "They'll figure out that we were here—and that discovery might incite them to attack before we're ready."

"I don't see why. They'll just think some big animal knocked into their bridge."

"Only ants build, and only ants destroy," Rank answered. "It will seem too deliberate. Never mind. It's done. Perhaps it's just as well, if war is inevitable, that it be soon."

When they learned of the atrocities committed by Regina's colony, no ant in Thrip's nest had any further thought of appeasement or accommodation. Their enemy had hunted them down for food as though they were worms or woodlice. Their raging hatred of a common foe dissolved the rivalries and resentments that had seemed all-important only a day ago. Every grudge or grievance was for now forgotten; they were all sisters, ready to sacrifice themselves for brood and Queen. Filled with a furious zeal, by daylight every able-bodied ant had hastened to the upper nest, spilling out onto the nest crater and the stone, swarming nearby grass blades until they tipped back to the ground with the weight of a score of angry ants, trampling each other in their seething rage for action. Even the nursery ants crept up from the deep nest, though probably intending to do no more than witness the army's departure. But the ants in the vanguard had scarcely left the safety of the nest periphery before they began to turn and double back. Those now in the front soon did the same. It was the antlions—they had remembered the antlions.

It was all very well for a few elite foragers to creep through at night. How was a whole army to march through a field mined with antlion pits? The majors who had placed themselves safely at the rear complained of the foragers' cowardice. The casualties, though high, would be acceptable. After all, an antlion can only eat one ant at a time. But once the squirming, jostling mass had pushed them to the vanguard, they too were reluctant to press forward. Then Keen and her comrades, who had gone out on patrol while the army was assembling, gave the alarm. The enemy was here—the enemy was upon them!

Regina's majors had confidently expected to take Thrip's colony by surprise. When at last they were close enough to perceive her foragers and majors ranged along the rock and the mound, the ants in the front lines tried to stop but were carried forward by those behind. They had no strategy, no plan, beyond that single notion of surprise. Their own surprise and turmoil was now greater than their foes'. The heroic major, the one who had been praised by Regina for her intrepidity, was almost the only one among them to respond rationally. She at once ran around her army's flank to find a secure position for herself at the rear.

From cunning in a few, from indecision in many, from one ant behaving like another and none daring to take the lead, Thrip's daughters held their advantageous high ground on the stone and hill, squirming in anxious excitement, until the enemy was directly below them. Then the scent and sight of the intruders renewed their frenzy, and they surged forward into battle.

Behind them the youngest ants, those who had never before ventured out of the nest, were wedged tight together in the entrance, immobilized by the sense-rending shock of daylight, while the pressure of other ants behind them prevented their retreat. It was not planned—nothing had been planned—yet it was a perfect defense. No enemy could breach that living barricade to attack their brood and Queen.

Thrip's daughters had never been united. They were not united now, and it worked to their advantage. While they fidgeted and hesitated, they had instinctively clustered together according to their usual factions, like with like, full sister with full sister. When at last they went into battle they formed themselves into teams in biting, yanking, and sundering their adversaries. The majors stayed to the rear, moving forward with their slow, deliberate cunning whenever their smaller sisters had succeeding in immobilizing an enemy ant. Then their huge mandibles made quick unerring work, cleaving their victims in two.

On encountering, foragers fenced with their mandibles, which were both shield and weapon, parrying each jab until one managed to close her jaws on a vulnerable part—the face, a feeler, a chink in her opponent's armor. She then had the advantage, but not always the victory. Her desperate opponent would twist and writhe until she too had fixed her mandibles on a limb or a segment; the two would lock in a tumbling, rending struggle, unless one or the other had a sister who could come to her aid. Writhing clumps of ants tore at each other in a fury so savage and unthinking that sisters bit one another by mistake. A toxic stench of rage and fear hung over the battlefield, mingled with the tang of spilled hemolymph oozing from crushed and torn bodies. Mangled, mutilated ants staggered and convulsed with the shock of injury, yet still fought on. Those that had fallen, bodies torn beyond recognition, writhed in impotent, tormented hate.

Thrip's ants fought valiantly but could not hold out against the superior numbers of their foes. The battle began to turn inexorably in the invader's favor. A determined force broke through to the hilltop and began to batter at Thrip's callows, who were still wedged in the nest entry. Since they could not retreat, the poor callows were compelled to defend themselves, snapping frantically at their attackers with their sharp young teeth. Packed tight together as they were, their attackers could scarcely dislodge them without hacking them to pieces. They certainly intended to do so, but they had left their own gasters undefended. Thrip's big sentries began to slash and tear at the hindmost until Regina's ants were forced to abandon their assault on the callows in order to defend themselves. The bloated major who had bragged of her store of honeydew lost her life in defense of the nest, done in by her greed. The distention of her crop made gaps in her gaster armor that even the dullest mandibles could pierce. Her entrails trailing beneath her, she went on fighting with astonishing ferocity until at last she crumpled and fell, drained of hemolymph.

The assault upon the nest entry disarrayed the enemy's formation so that Keen, Spout, Rank and the young major found themselves facing pale, trembling conscripts—very young ants, almost callows, impressed by Regina's bellicose majors to swell the numbers of her vast army. The poor innocents were so dazed and disoriented, so terrified to find themselves suddenly confronting the enemy, that they could not fight, did not even know which way to run. They clustered like aphids on a stem, chirping and squeaking with terror. Thrip's foragers gleefully cut them down almost without resistance. As they died, did they wonder, bewildered, why it must be? They were young—death was for the old. Why must they fight, why must they die, here in this strange-smelling place so far from home, why, when surely there is land, and honeydew, enough for all? They were only the most ordinary workers, interchangeable, replaceable, with no distinguishing features other than their youth. Yet they sought powerfully to live with every particle of their being. No epic hero could struggle with greater ardor, and it was only to escape, only to go on living for a little while longer, that they twisted and writhed with such desperate, yearning intensity.

Methodically, pitilessly, Thrip's foragers chased down and executed Regina's callows. But in doing so they were drawn deeper into the enemy's lines, where they now encountered Regina's majors. The wiser foragers retreated at once, before the hulking majors could move to the attack. The others were trapped, hacked to pieces by the majors as easily as they themselves had cut down the callows.

The battle had raged for nearly five hours and now the heat of a hot summer day began to take its toll. A few very young combatants with only minor injuries dropped to the ground in a death as sudden and serene as sleep. The more intelligent of Thrip's daughters became aware of their painful thirst and desiccation and began calling out to their sisters to retreat. Many were too crazed by the battle and distracted by their wounds to perceive this new enemy; but as the sun passed its zenith they began, a few at a time, to withdraw to the nest. Then, with the frantic spontaneity common among ants, they all broke and ran at once, tumbling over each other in the rush to escape the heat. New sentries had come forward to take the place of those who died, but these inexperienced ants could not control the panicked horde. Many of the injured were wounded afresh, needlessly, in the scuffle.

Once inside, most collapsed into a stupor. Others, agitated by grief and fear that overcame their exhaustion, began slowly to circulate, questing with feelers and mouthparts to discover which of their favorite sisters had returned and which had not. After some wandering, Spout found Rank; both had recognized the young major among the defenders guarding the nest's main entrance; but the whereabouts of Keen was unknown. Spout again went wandering but returned a little later. Keen was missing, presumed dead.

Throughout Thrip's nest, the survivors licked each other's wounds, quivering with sorrow and fatigue. Had they won—had they lost? What would tomorrow bring? They huddled and caressed each other for encouragement but their crouched posture and drooping feelers signaled their dismay. Alone among Thrip's attendants, the Royal Alpha exerted her ingenuity to argue that they had won a great victory. First, she said, they had repelled the surprise assault on the nest, then held their enemies at bay, not yielding an inch of ground, until the raging heat of the day forced an end to the battle. She was certain, moreover, that the enemy's losses were as great or greater than their own. Perhaps Alpha only meant to comfort the silent, listless Queen for the loss of so many daughters, whose replacement would be so laborious. No one responded; no one took her seriously, not at a time when the air was heavy with suffering and lamentation.

The Royal Beta was tempted to ask the Alpha whether she proposed to follow up on their victory with a raid on Regina's brood chambers. But, twitching her feelers over the sad Queen, she satisfied her rancor by reminding the Alpha of pressing concerns. No food had been gathered all day; even the root aphids had gone untended, their honeydew dried up and wasted; the colony's collective crop stores had been drained by the exhausted army; they must eat.

This was undeniable. Hungry-thirsty, hungry-thirsty, hungry-thirsty … the call for nourishment rose up from the nurseries, from the depths of the nest, gaining urgency as it passed throughout the colony. Sisters wandered compulsively, soliciting each other for food but none was offered.

They murmured bitterly that their enemies nested at the roots of a nectar-rich shrub, suddenly, the antlions having been forgotten, a very desirable residence. *They* have food—*we* go without. Hungry-thirsty, hungry-thirsty, hungry-thirsty … The ants of the upper nest were no less hungry and thirsty than their privileged sisters below; but they were also exhausted and dejected. None would willingly go out to forage. And so they quarreled, each excusing herself and blaming her sisters, until they reached the usual accommodation. The elders must take care of their younger sisters. When the sun was setting, when at last the tortured earth began to cool, Rank was among the old foragers who were harassed and chased out of the nest to forage.

They scattered at once in twos and threes, most making a quick jittery run to the nearest aphid colonies, where they might fill themselves and return to safety with the greatest possible dispatch. Rank took only a few steps beyond the nest before she came to a halt, too worn-out to move. She knew that she would not be permitted to reenter the nest unless she brought back provisions. None of the foragers who had come out with her were true sisters, none would share their food with her. Her limbs crumpled and she crouched in numb, solitary despair. She had come to her end, surviving a great battle only to perish of hunger and exposure. A series of taps on her gaster brought her from her stupor. Spout was standing over her, spluttering as usual.

"I-uh-I-uh c-c-came uh," Spout tried, the words damming up in her ducts and then streaming out all at once, "help-you-old-help-can't-yourself-get-it-done," she finished in an awkward burst.

"Why must you be so absurd," Rank mumbled, embarrassed. Spout had hoarded a little honeydew and now offered a tiny droplet to her sister. It was enough. Revived by the sweetness coursing through her body, Rank picked herself up and began to move, rejecting Spout's offer to carry her.

The two sisters decided to go in the direction of the battlefield where, with luck, they might satisfy both curiosity and hunger. Many of the corpses would still hold potable juice—if they got to them before the beetles did—and they wished to survey the dead, to see if it were really possible that the Royal Alpha was right, that the enemy's losses were equal to their own. And, though they did not say so, they hoped to find Keen and observe the last rite of returning her substance to the colony.

The afternoon had been so hot and the numbers of the slain so great that most of the dead still lay untouched where they had fallen. Only now were the pavement ants and spider beetles coming forth in number to feast on the slain. The dead twitched and twisted in surreal resurrection as tiny scavengers gnawed them. To the two ants, surveying the battlefield from the rock, it seemed as though their homeland had been transformed into a vast midden. They folded their feelers in disgust and sadness.

The ants retraced the course of the battle as they passed through the field. The mutilated bodies of the foragers and majors who had died defending the nest were scattered about the entrance and the mound, some still locked in a fatal embrace with their enemy. Spout and Rank stepped carefully through the dead, applying their mouthparts to their sisters when they found them intact, drinking their juices through their gaping wounds. Most of the dead lay in mangled heaps—the severed head of one ant still clamped to the ruptured gaster of her enemy—limbs and segments strewn at random so that one could not tell ant from ant or friend from foe. In death they were indistinguishable. Further beyond the nest, they found evidence of a counterattack of appalling efficiency—here were ants hacked to pieces by Regina's majors, here Keen had met her end.

The ants rested for a moment on the underside of a leaf. It was more, much more, than they could comprehend. Spout at last ventured to put her thoughts into words; this time she hardly spluttered at all, but the ideas themselves, so alien and odd, could not easily be expressed.

"Such confusion, such madness. Ants shrieking in rage and torment, spraying poison in every direction, piling on top of each other in murderous knots. I know I bit some of my own sisters by mistake."

"Never mind about that," Rank answered. "Most of them deserve to be bitten."

"Muh-makes me think, how alike we all are. These enemy ants smell and look almost like sisters. They are workers just like us. Like us they work and fight to breed sisters, not daughters. Why can't we come together as one colony, producing greater numbers of eggs by combining our efforts?"

Rank's feelers shot up in surprise. "You think like a soft, freshly hatched nursery ant, Sister. War is about power, about controlling the most territory and the best resources. It has nothing to do with eggs."

"But what good does it do to have more food or more territory except to produce more eggs?"

"Eggs are the ultimate expression of power, that's all."

Spout still pursued her own train of thought. "Why this useless shedding of hemolymph? Our differences are not so great that we cannot come to terms!"

"It's lucky for you that you stutter, Sister. An ant could get herself dismembered for talk like that. You might as soon argue a toad out of eating you as convince an ant to do anything, or think anything, different from her sisters. They all hate and fear Regina too much for there to be any possibility of peace. Come on, let's finish and go home."

They drank the juices from a few more fallen sisters. Once they had filled their crops, the stench of ant-death, conveyed very forcibly by a freshening westerly breeze, was repugnant to them. Having fed, they naturally turned homeward. Had they ventured a little further, had they paused to question why the evening breeze carried such a powerful reek of death from beyond the battlefield, they might have made a great discovery. West of the battlefield, across the wide expanse of lawn, all the way, almost, to the midden of Regina's colony, lay a trail of dead ants.

When Thrip's forces had suddenly withdrawn to escape the heat, Regina's army, mistaking their retreat for a rout, had given chase—the majors urging their exhausted sisters forward. They swarmed onto the rock, abandoned by its defenders, but they were unable to penetrate the nest, its entrance now closed and guarded. Too excited by the heat to be rational, they milled in circles upon the burning rock until at last they also turned to seek shade and damp. They had waited too long. Their early morning march to attack had taken the most direct route, across the open, sun-parched lawn, and this route they attempted to take home. But it offered no shelter and no water, even though desperate ants overturned pebbles and squeezed the damp earth in their mouths for relief. The scouts who had led the outward march were scattered or dead; many of their less experienced sisters took the wrong way home. Desiccated, exhausted ants staggered from the path, not to return. For every ant who had fallen in battle, another perished on the terrible retreat. Those who succumbed to the heat were the youngest, ants whose cuticle was still soft and unprotected. Maddened by thirst, they stumbled after mirages until overcome by heat stupor. A few, a very few, were found and carried home by their older sisters. That day an entire generation of workers was lost. Had Thrip's army sought to counterattack at once, they might have scored a decisive victory.

But none of this was known to Thrip and her daughters, dismayed and overawed at being attacked in their homeland, their nest itself nearly breached. Only when the next few days passed without a renewed attack did they began to hope Regina's colony had also suffered great casualties. They themselves had lost many of their most daring and experienced foragers, whose ferocity had carried them too far into the enemy ranks, where they were cut down by Regina's majors. The surviving foragers were mostly novices, easily frightened and apt to get lost if they ventured much beyond the closest and most familiar aphid pastures. They must all be trained as quickly as possible. Spout and Rank now foraged singly, running back to the nest to recruit a junior ant whenever they found meat—patiently teaching the naive foragers the trails and hunting grounds, drawing them further from the nest on each foray. It was tiring and inefficient—they must be satisfied with small game and stale remains—but they could not chance losing an entire party of expert foragers and majors to a greedy toad or sharp-eyed bird. For the first few days after the terrible battle, Thrip's majors patrolled restlessly, expecting a renewed attack. A nearly disastrous encounter with a flicker persuaded them that it was wiser, after all, to keep to their guardrooms. A major should never risk her life needlessly.

In both colonies the focus now was on the nursery, on producing a new generation of workers to replace those lost. Thrip went on laying eggs, little lopsided eggs with hardly any yolk to them at all. There would be no royal brood to overwinter; she would be too spent to produce them. But if there were not more worker daughters, reared as quickly as possible, there might not be a colony at all. Anxious nurses hovered over their charges, feeding the hungry ones, devotedly cleaning them and carrying them from chamber to chamber in search of the right balance of warmth and humidity that would hasten their growth. They scrupulously separated the big ones who were inclined to bite, and continually checked the pupae for the restless movements of a full-grown ant ready to eclose, to step forth from her safe cocoon into the service of the sisterhood, now, in the most troubled and tempestuous period of their long history.

The commotion was hardly less among Regina's ants, although the Queen herself was obstinately or superiorly unaware of it. Aside from the heavy casualties of the disastrous retreat, the migration had itself produced social upheaval that had not yet been resolved. Several prominent nurses had been lost along the way, including the one who had formerly dominated the egg pile. The competition to take her place generated turmoil and negligence in the brood chambers. A few socially adept foragers took advantage of the confusion to wriggle their way back into the deep nest, while less assertive ants found themselves propelled upward to undesirable posts well before their time. Now the loss of so many young ants in the disastrous battle and retreat had depleted the number of workers within the nest: housekeepers, builders and even some nurses were among the slain. In a reversal of the usual social order, still more foragers and scouts left their posts for positions within the nest. Somehow—no one quite understood how it could have happened—the heroic major who had been credited with saving Regina's life took up residence in the brood chambers, along with two other majors who followed her lead, where they were not at all welcome but impossible to dislodge.

To preserve their mother from excessive exertion, Regina's Alpha had persuaded the head nurses to dedicate the current brood cycle to the production of new majors. It was a risky strategy: the brood would require more food and more time to mature. But since they had lost very few of their experienced foragers, there should be no shortages. The Alpha did not think Thrip's daughters—the daughters of a runt queen, after all—would dare to attack first. She easily persuaded her sisters to accept her plan, which might well have succeeded, if not for the three majors' presence among the brood.

Majors make very poor nurses. They are always either dropping the little ones or pinching them too tight in their unwieldy mandibles. They are inept at feeding time, clumsily spewing food at the larvae, often missing their little mouths entirely, then failing to clean the poor things properly. The other nurses tried to make up for such neglect and incompetence; but for whatever reason, the larvae had little appetite as long as the majors were around. They grew, but they did not grow big no matter how much nourishment their regular nurses urged upon them. They pupated late, just like a major, but anyone could tell from the size of the cocoons that they were only going to be ordinary workers after all.

Within Thrip's nest, daily life continued as before but accelerated by an unexpressed urgency, as if the signal to attack, or to flee, might be released at any moment. There was a unity and harmony to their actions that overcame their usual factious quarreling. No ant needed to be urged to her task. The Queen laid her eggs. The nurses tirelessly fed, cleaned and cradled the young. The builders repaired and widened the emergency exits, then just as carefully concealed them. Even the ambitious Alpha and the quarrelsome Beta submerged their differences and devoted themselves to the care of the Queen. No more discussion, no more debate. Once the brood has hatched and the swelling population of the inner nest impels more ants out to forage and fight—then our enemies will learn what we can do. If there was any shirking it was only among the novice foragers, who dared do little more than bring in the daily supply of honeydew. Since there was now no surplus to store, the majors were all sleek and battle-ready. Even they were unusually alert, if not actually busy, keeping to their stations in the upper nest and sometimes patrolling the nest perimeter. The brood at last began to eclose: the new ants were small—there had been too little meat to go around—but they were active and strong for their size. They soon began to push their nurses from the brood chambers, who in turn displaced the builders and cleaners. The upper nest was crowded with edgy workers getting their first prolonged experience of the sunlit world.

The new foragers were still unreliable, barely capable of subduing a half-grown worm. After so much egg-laying, the Queen was famished for meat. Rank went scouting under the linden on the chance of finding immature inchworms fallen from the leaves—the tree itself had been taken over by carpenters, who were as resentful of intruders as any other ant—when she came upon an extraordinary find. A freshly dead shrew lay stretched out upon a root, almost untouched. The flies, shiny green ones with red-garnet eyes, were on it already. Flies are always the first to anything worth having, planting eggs by the thousands on orifices and folds of flesh. But for the ants they would only add a course of tender maggots to the feast. Otherwise, there were just a few small, shy ground beetles worrying it as they searched for the soft bits. Rank raced back to the nest to recruit a party of majors and foragers to cut and bring home as much meat as they could wrest or steal from the beetles, who would soon claim it in large numbers.

Such an immense treasure of rich food could not go undiscovered long, and not only by beetles. Regina's scouts had chanced upon the shrew as well. Their foragers, who had run ahead, looped back to lead and encourage their majors, now lumbering near.

The two groups approached slowly, then stopped, grimacing fiercely. One of Regina's foragers charged to lock mandibles with Spout, then quickly stepped back. Rank retaliated by grabbing a feeler and giving the ant a good hard shake before releasing her. Ants began to express their poison glands with an angry murmuring along both sides. Having come forth for big prey, they were out of battle array—the majors in front, with foragers interspersed—and hesitated now between attacking and awaiting reinforcement.

The young major could hold still no longer. She charged one of Regina's big ants and instantly locked mandibles with a reverberating shock that stirred all their sisters to battle. The two wrestled ferociously, never breaking their hold on each other's jaws. Around them the other majors squared off and battled, if it could be called that. They tussled like stag beetles, too heavily armored to do each other much damage. Each neutralized her opponent but could do no more. It was up to the foragers: they boldly piled on top of the wrestling majors, nipping at any exposed flesh, gnawing away at limbs and feelers. Inevitably they bit their own sisters by mistake, but since their mandibles were too weak and their teeth too worn to break through a major's armor with one blow, it hardly mattered. And now it was terribly obvious that Regina possessed more majors, and that many of Thrip's foragers were timid and inexperienced. These ants did nothing but run back and forth to the nest. Even when there were no more ants to recruit, when every capable forager and major had been called forth to fight, they circled between the combat and their nest—too old to hide themselves in the nursery, too young to hold their ground and fight. At best they would snap their jaws at an enemy or, by mistake, a sister, then instantly flee for another looping return.

And why, after all, were they fighting? There was enough meat on the shrew to sate the appetites of a hundred colonies. Instead, while the two armies went to war over it, wriggling knots of rove beetles eagerly dug in. How delightful to feed on a creature that normally feeds on you! Little black pavement and yellow thief ants crept around them, furtively snatching their own tiny shares wherever the fur had been shredded away. The big slow carpenter ants came down from their tree to get themselves a few choice bits. Then three stout orange-barred sexton beetles, enormous brutes, alighted on the carcass and began shoving and brawling. One was lucky enough to have its mate arrive to join the struggle; the two of them soon got the better of their rivals. Repelled by the writhing hordes of battling ants, which they only now noticed, they preferred to raise their grubs in more peaceful surroundings. Putting their backs to it, they hauled off the shrew, still mostly intact.

It was now a battle without a cause, without a prize for the victor, but fought all the more viciously. Thrip's ants were being driven back towards their own nest perimeter, and there the young foragers found their courage and began to attack. Their teeth were quite sharp. They were able to cut into the segments of the big ants, then shoot poison at the wounds they inflicted. They began to fight better but not yet good enough.

Rank died on that battlefield, of her wounds, her exhaustion, her age. The wisest, wiliest of all Thrip's daughters: so much knowledge died with her. No sister noticed her fall. But the penetrating must of her great age stamped her as individual even in death. The young major, stumbling sideways in retreat, recognized her corpse. She felt a sharp little sting of unnameable feeling, a regret that was very near bereavement.

"Every ant is expendable," the young major reminded herself, "except the Queen." Then she had an idea. It must rate as the only time an idea, a really good idea, that is, has ever occurred to a major. The battle still raged around her. Before the decimated sides retired to escape the heat of the day, she must act. She called Spout to her side, and together they recruited a raiding party to attack Regina's nest before her army could return.

Regina's nest was defended by a cluster of majors too fat and out of condition to march. In their haste, in their arrogance, no one had thought to remove the bridges that provided safe passage through the antlion pits. When the majors left at guard duty saw a large company of foragers moving rapidly and confidently towards them upon the bridges, they only wondered why their sisters were returning without booty—surely not for reinforcements— not for them! When they at last realized a raiding party was on the attack they were too astonished to know what to do. They should have retreated to block the entrance with their massive heads. Instead—perhaps thinking a party of foragers with only one major among them could be easily with- stood—they did the next best thing, putting themselves in a ring around the nest entrance, prepared to slash any ant who tried to break through.

Carried forward by their fury, Thrip's ants ran straight at Regina's guard. Those of the front line were horribly hacked and maimed, but the second wave was able to climb over the combatants and attack the majors from the rear. Their swollen gasters, soft flesh gaping between the armored plates, presented an easy target. The smaller but quicker foragers bit savagely at the exposed flesh until Regina's sentries stumbled and fell.

One of their number, more intelligent or more self-interested than the rest, had thought to run to the deep nest and give the alarm. Timid nurses and callow attendants scattered desperately this way and that, some down, some up, picking up brood, then stumbling into other panicked sisters and turning back again. Few of the frenzied ants remembered the emergency exits or knew how to find them.

Thrip's forces had won their entry, slaughtering those who dared to op- pose them. But they could not find their way in the alien nest, in which a disturbing queen scent, akin to their mother's yet harshly different, drenched the air and fuddled their senses. It was a meaty, sharply sweet scent that compelled, threatened, pacified, all at once—a flesh-eating flower with a stinger concealed in its honeyed lure. Under the sway of Regina's des- potic essence, the ants felt oppressed, dominated, despite their rage. They clustered, twitching their feelers questioningly, before they again put them- selves in motion, struggling against a strange reluctance.

Recovering their urgency, Thrip's ants sought out the main gallery and surged downward. At first the nest seemed peculiarly like their home, constructed on like principles. But nothing was where it ought to be. The tangled roots of the overhanging shrub shaped the corridor into twisting detours that puzzled and delayed them. At last the delectable aroma of egg and the scraping, scrambling sounds of frightened ants taught them the way to the nurseries. Thrip's foragers greedily snatched up clutches of eggs and soft, plump larvae, as many as their mandibles could hold, then at once ran homeward with their plunder.

The young major was not interested in brood. She continued to probe the winding corridors, seeking the source of that penetrating, fatty sweetness that rose up from the depths of the enemy nest. She was alone, Spout and the other foragers all having been drawn by the egg scent to the brood. The distant stridulations of the panicked nurses were so like those her own sisters would make that several times she half-turned to run to the rescue before recalling that these ants were enemies. Not sisters, enemies. She hurried to escape the noise. Now, strangely, she had had no fear and very little rage remaining to her. She only knew what she must do.

Regina's Alpha stood before the royal chamber, held in her place by a prideful sense of duty that was more powerful than her terror. All the same, she could not still her trembling and she crouched before the intruder. She had nothing left to her but her eloquence. She pleaded, threatened, reasoned, so adroitly that the young major was momentarily confused, until she remembered once again her purpose. With a quick, savage bite she silenced the Alpha. The rest of Regina's attendants had already fled—some helping nurses save brood, others cowering in corners. The young major entered the royal chamber alone. Before her stood the old Queen, helpless, yet imposing—far larger than the major, greater than any ant she had ever encountered.

The old Queen—old she was, although still fertile and majestic—had refused to comprehend what the alarm and the frantic scattering of her daughters signified. Despite the obsessions that regularly took possession of her reason, those lurking nightmare intimations of insurrection and treachery, she had never permitted herself to doubt that she would triumph over Thrip. So certain was she of her power that she believed the uproar celebrated her victory and the novel odors emanated from the booty her troops were carrying home. Abruptly, as the major entered, the acrid scent of the intruder flamed across her sense. She knew, and she was afraid. She cried out. Where was her Alpha? Where were her soldiers? Again she stridulated convulsively in rage and terror—abandoned, betrayed! She snapped her toothless jaws in threat, intimidating with her size and scent. The major advanced slowly, as if stalking dangerous prey, then struck a single, sure blow to the neck. Regina died as she had always known she must, in the absolute fulfillment of her foreboding dreams.

Epilogue

Regina's army returned to find their nest plundered and ruined. All through that terrible afternoon and into the next day, the nurses who had escaped began to return, bringing with them the rescued brood: some struggled with big cocoons almost ready to eclose; others brought back sticky clumps of eggs and tiny larvae. It was not much but it saved the ants from despair. They, the survivors, would nurse the brood and forage for its sustenance.

The captive brood that were carried back to Thrip's colony met with a different fate. Most were promptly eaten. Others were overlooked or misplaced or spared day by day for one obscure reason or another.

Spout had something to do with these furtive, fitful acts of mercy. Following Rank's death she became very quiet. She still spluttered; but now she kept her opinions to herself, only she acted upon them to the extent of her powers. Rank had been right about her. She still thought like a nursery ant, and now she had a chance to behave like one. She hid alien brood throughout the upper nest, nursing them on her own, slipping them into the brood chambers whenever she had the opportunity. Out of ignorance, out of compassion, other young ants who happened upon the forlorn larvae also carried them down to the nurseries. Once they had lost the stink of the enemy nest, they were no longer food but sweet innocent little ant-grubs. Some nurses still bit and abused them, it's true, but others fed and bathed them, making no distinction between actual sisters and these adopted ones.

Back in Regina's ruined nest, after the last of their rescued brood had been nursed to adulthood, the ants began to disperse. Some sickened and became listless, only managing to stagger out of the nest, out into the indifferent daylight, when it was time for them to die. Some stolidly continued to forage even when there were few healthy sisters left to feed, until at last some antlion, jumping spider or tiger beetle relieved them of their meaningless existence. Because an ant must live with other ants and with brood, a few wandered all the way to Thrip's nest. There they were instantly harassed and chased away. But those who persisted, who kept coming back, succeeded in begging a little food from returning foragers. As their native nest smell faded and blurred, they managed to make their way into Thrip's nest and to find a home there. Within a short while, no one recollected how they had once been enemies.

VI.
Point-of-view
Ant

Individual ant workers do not fit the popular image of invariant replicas that perform like parts in a machine. Some individual peculiarities occur that are based simply on the learning of specific portions of the environment, an obvious means of improving efficiency. But other, often striking deviations exist that are something of a mystery. They are either accidents of development and learning—the irreducible noise in the replication process—or else represent an adaptive form of diversification by which the colony divides labor still more finely beyond that attained through the physical and temporal castes ...

   Division of labor has been elaborated in many species by elitism, defined as the existence of exceptionally active or entrepreneurial individuals within age-size cohorts.

–George F. Oster & Edward O. Wilson, **Caste and Ecology in the Social Insects** (1978)

Somewhere the author must break into the privacy of his characters and open their minds to us. And again it is doubtless his purpose to shift the point of view no more often than he need; and if the subject can be completely rendered by showing it as it appears to a single one of the figures in the book, then there is no reason to range further.

–Percy Lubbock, **The Craft of Fiction** (1921)

The problem of point of view was largely neglected in literary criticism before the advent of Henry James.

–Robert Scholes, James Phelan & Robert Kellogg, **The Nature of Narrative** (2006)

The truth was doubtless that really, when it came to any free handling and naming of things, they were living together, the five of them, in an air in which an ugly effect of "blurting out" might easily be produced.

–Henry James, **The Wings of the Dove** (1902)

She was almost capable of the violence of forcing this home, for even in the midst of her surge of passion—of which in fact it was a part—there rose in her a fear, a pain, a vision ominous, precocious, of what it might mean for her mother's fate to have forfeited such a loyalty as that.

–Henry James, **What Maisie Knew** (1897)

Dᴵᴅ ᴛʜᴇ ᴀɴᴛ make the choice, or had the choice made her? Her earliest sensations, still keen in recollection, had been of two rival attractive forces—the egg and the queen essences. Those newly eclosed ants who were more powerfully drawn to the egg began, almost as soon as they could walk, to pick up eggs, to lick them clean, to heap them together; then to rearrange them into fresh assemblages and to clean them once again. The evanescent delight of egg essence, melting upon their palps, wafted about them by their busy motions in the still air of the deep nest, was the aim and reward of all their endeavors. Immersed in the eggs, away from the Queen. Surely she might have gone to one rather than the other. But for her, at that determinative moment of her young life, the queen essence had exerted the greater urgency. Taking her departure from the nursery, she had presented herself to Thrip; she had been accepted. She possessed, in noble abundance, those attributes of grace, strength, fluency and beauty that are sought in a royal chamber attendant.

Her triumph meant another ant must forfeit her place. Compelled to acknowledge the passing of her time, the one who had held the position of Royal Delta departed in meek resignation. The fate of this superannuated ant went unnoted. She may well have perished in an unlucky encounter with an antlion or a sparrow, or with one of the more aggressive ground beetles; or in a minor, unrecorded skirmish with Regina's workers, one of the many such that took place during the anxious interval between the two great battles. Of her no stories were to be told, and she departs from ours, humbly, unprotestingly, not to return.

Our ant had been accepted by the Queen. She did not, at first, comprehend that she must also be accepted by her sisters, by the other preeminent ants who served the Queen. It was just the complications of this acceptance—delayed, qualified, adjusted, measured out in allotments, given then withdrawn in order to be given again—that prompted her wondering, obscurely regretful thoughts of the nursery and of the role she might therein have taken. The perception that one might choose, or at least might have chosen, one path or another was for her the origin of awareness. Her consciousness took shape from her belated knowledge of those divergent ways, out of a nostalgia, mistaken perhaps, for the one not chosen, if choice there was. It taught her to think of herself, in secret, as an entity distinct from all the presences surrounding her, pursuing their relatively oblivious ways throughout the vast swarm of society.

Hesitating still, though powerfully drawn forward, she had entered the royal chambers to approach the Queen, who had scanned her appreciatively, assaying her size, her youth, her merits. Found worthy, she began to groom the Queen. But not many moments had elapsed before she was brusquely thrust aside. She had held herself perfectly still in the effort to comprehend. The Queen had not rejected her service, but another ant, of intimidating aspect, had done so. Was it that she must not groom the Queen, or must not exceed some period of allowance?

Thrip then happened to turn slightly and to direct her feelers searchingly, lifting a fine imperial foreleg as she did so. Her new attendant understood the intent of these gestures: the Queen wanted nourishment. Having herself just come from the nursery plump with honeydew, she hastened to offer her mother a droplet, but was discouraged with a gentle backward tug at her feeler, administered by a quite different ant, followed by an explanation equally gentle in its tones. Her offering was unnecessary: to feed the Queen was the role of the resident Alpha. "You, my dear, are a delta," she said. "You need not undertake any primary responsibility. You will do very well, and very respectably, to assist your sisters when they call for your aid."

Our poor bewildered newcomer could not but respond gratefully to an address so civil, so seemingly helpful. Of course the tall, gentle ant who fed their mother was the Royal Alpha. Only an alpha would have that duty, she understood that now. That other ant, the one who had threatened her, must be the Beta here. Even in the nursery she had encountered sisters like that: envious, quarrelsome, vulgarly striving. Better to preserve a distance with such ants. The stately bearing of her interlocutor, forming such a contrast to the rough handling she had just received, struck our impressionable young ant so favorably as to suppress any immediate use of her critical faculty. Only much later would she reflect and judge; and then the verdict was against herself, to whom she showed no mercy, rather than any other ant.

The Alpha had designated her as a delta speculatively, casting out a covert challenge. When she did not object, the astuteness of this assessment was evident. An alpha, a beta or a gamma, however youthful and inexperienced, would not placidly accede to such a judgment or accept discouragement so unprotestingly. She had been placed.

This the Royal Gamma perceived at once. The latter ant was not tall, did not in fact greatly exceed the middle height; but her angular features were pleasing; and if her gestures were not as graceful nor as gracious as the Alpha's, they had a flair that marked her nonetheless as an ant worthy of emulation.

"Such a difference between 'mustn't' and 'needn't,'" Gamma blandly remarked, "or don't you find it so? You mustn't groom the Queen, and you needn't feed her."

If our Delta detected an ironic tinge to this remark, she chose to conceal her consciousness with a stout affirmation. "Yes, a very great difference," she replied.

"How good-natured of you to take your sisters at their word, just as you find them," then, addressing herself to the Alpha, "She is certain to be an ornament of our little circle, don't you agree, Sister?"

The Royal Alpha agreed, but with a dull, distracted gravity that might suggest, to a close observer, something more of disavowal than approbation. Any such observer would have been perplexed, nonetheless, to determine whether the ant objected to the trifling compliment expressed, or was rather reacting to some malign obscuration that, she perceived, would cast its long unwholesome shadow over almost any reply she might attempt. "Certainly, certainly," the Alpha brought out slowly.

Then, no doubt realizing her concurrence might have been several degrees too cool for a persuasive welcome, she addressed herself to their new companion, letting her know just how exclusive their little circle was. Only they four took permanent residence in the Queen's quarters. They admitted visitors at certain regular hours, when their antechamber thronged with the best society—latecomers could barely find "leg room" to suspend themselves overhead. Foragers were never admitted, despite the Queen's appreciation of their great service. They might bear disease and in any case they bore repellant odors, their own and those of the outside. Yet it was necessary to "know" the foragers, to draw upon their experiences as well as their all-important stores of food. The stories of each individual ant, or not stories so much as a jumbled multitude of incongruous impressions, reach the royal chambers after many safe removes, passing from sister to sister in accordance with their rank, from lesser to greater, older to younger. Each such impression, sensed and tasted by a succession of ants, was refined in its downward passage, purged of circumstantial dross. Whatever might transpire within or without the nest thus made its way here, to be evaluated and understood. Nothing is ever discarded from which a little sweetness or knowledge can yet be distilled. The extraction of such knowledge was the chief role of the royal chamber occupants, as their charming new sister would soon find for herself. Warming to her receptive audience, who was ready to accept any such attentions as tokens of the kindest sisterhood, the Alpha made herself comfortable, resting upon her hind parts to give her forelegs freer play of expression, in order to elaborate, *par exemple,* upon certain great discoveries she herself had made.

"Give us your news from the nursery, my dear," Thrip interposed at last, after a series of irritable twitches that suggested a less favorable opinion of the Alpha's self-regarding eloquence. "How many of my sweet little eggs have hatched?"

This question was far more particular than our young ant's state of information. She knew that there were a great many eggs—an unprecedented number for so late in the season, forming, in effect, a second summer brood. Still nestled among them, not yet big enough for their own nursery, were tiny larvae just beginning to wriggle and pout for food. But she had not expected to be called upon for an enumeration. She had only her remembered impression, spotted with a hundred incoherences and confusions, of devoted nurses hovering near, feeding her, bathing her, and helping her at last from her cocoon. This partial view she sought to fashion into an acceptable answer, portraying the nursery as harmonious, efficient, utterly devoted— unconsciously imitating the tropes and tones of the Royal Alpha, whom she already admired, as she elaborated her idealizing depiction.

"Never mind, dear," interrupted Thrip, with mild maternal scorn, "I did not mean to test you."

"It's just possible," she added in afterthought, but in a tone suggestive of unshaken skepticism. "It's certainly the report the nurses give of themselves! And one likes to think that one's daughters do come together to help each other, and their mother, in a crisis. I should like to think none of my eggs are being abused or neglected. It's been painful enough to produce them so suddenly and out of season. Ah, well, you are young and you may live to be a better observer yet. You have those around you who will task your abilities to the utmost." And on that, with a slight dismissive gesture familiar to her attendants, the Queen retired to her private alcove, accompanied, even half-carried, by the Royal Beta.

Her answer to Thrip's question *had* been shallow, unsatisfactory—our ant felt that, with her inveterate honesty, even as she cringed in mortification. But her mother did her some little, lasting injustice—Thrip made no time, now, for attending to the wounded feelings of her callow daughters—in slighting her powers of observation. It was her nature as a delta to be rapid and intelligent in her apprehension of others. Her subordinate status might even be understood as a consequence of her percipience, in that any rebuff or reproach was so intensely felt that she shrank from incurring its repetition. In this regard, she could not be more unlike the Beta, who never quailed at a challenge, who invited snubs and slights in return for those she freely gave.

Even at this instant of felt disgrace our Delta did not fail to take in rich impressions. Her attention had shifted outward to observe her mother, to gauge how she stood with her. That her failure had already been forgotten, dismissed, was evident: relief gave way to renewed humiliation as she reflected how little she must matter to her mother. The Queen had begun to turn away at a slow, strangely unsteady pace, punctuated by a faltering pause. The Beta stepped forward, mandibles parted in eager service, to aid her mother. The moment passed, but left, for our Delta, a wave of engulfing impressions in its wake.

The extent of their mother's exhaustion had been revealed to her, communicated in the Queen's slow deliberate motions, which, to a more casual observation, might have seemed properly expressive of a high, fine majesty. That air of remote grandeur, which had formed no part of Thrip's youthful character, was the mask she held in place to conceal her growing fatigue. The little she now said and did might be as nobly conceived as ever, but it was very little. It was as if she engaged in a conscious struggle to conserve and apportion her divided, dwindling powers of mind and gaster, as if even the little social energies she expended to maintain her pose, to express a few short phrases to her attendants, had their great price, that she drew them from a shallow spring that would one day run dry. Our Delta perceived all this and more, in an instant. As the Queen withdrew to her alcove, her absence could be felt: her penumbral aroma did not remain richly behind to fill out the void. Our ant understood from this where the exhaustion would end. The Queen's essence would begin to fade; the warm amber redolence that had drawn her from the nursery, that drew all the ants into fascinated orbit around her fixed maternity, would suffer some daily diminution, gradual, imperceptible, irreversible. It was already fading, although no one as yet knew it, no one but Thrip herself.

Delta realized with a start that the Alpha was again addressing her, in exquisitely modulated undertones.

"... health always delicate of course, so much we must always be doing, and now this crisis for her, for all of us, of *the troubles outside*. You are familiar—?"

Delta was familiar. What ant was not? She had been very young indeed, lost in the dreamy lethargy common to newly emerged ants, when the nest had first been attacked by Regina's army. She recalled the sharp shock of it: nursery ants rushing frantically back and forth, snatching up pupae and larvae, running for the emergency exits, then turning about to come back to the nursery—frenzied, frightened, bewildered. She herself had been at the awkward age of being yet too young to rescue brood herself, and yet too old to be snatched up and carried to safety. She had held herself tensely still, although trembling, jostled and trampled by her elders, until the crisis passed. The nursery sisters still talked of it—talked of little else. Delta's views were inevitably derived from theirs, although she had the good judgment not to claim them as her own.

"The nurses say they do not understand why we have not counterattacked. I realize of course that this second summer brood who are now in the nursery are meant to supplement and rebuild our forces. We must be bravely patient. But the nurses say we have limited our foraging activities so much from fear of attack that they wonder whether they will be able to feed the brood adequately."

Delta's circumspection was unnecessary. Alpha so relished an opportunity to expound her views that no observation could seem impertinent if it might be indulgently taken as a request for enlightenment. The colony, she explained, had experienced a disproportionate loss of expert foragers in the battle, who had been too unthinkingly brave in charging the enemy. That loss, not fear, was the reason why a somewhat less bountiful selection of food had been coming into the colony of late. The surviving foragers were training new ones; there would be food enough for the brood; and their maturation would allow us to field sufficient forces to attack the enemy on their own ground.

"Yes," said the Delta, doubtfully, "but if so many among these augmented forces are young ants, coming to the outside prematurely, will they have the skill to fight as well as seasoned foragers and majors?"

The question was for Alpha only a cue to continue. The enemy, she said, was surely investing their resources in the production of new majors. Majors were certainly the best ants at defense, at offense too. Roughly speaking, the tactical value of a major was equivalent to four ordinary workers. A force of only a hundred and ten majors might put an army of four hundred ordinary workers to flight. However, it took four times as much food, as well as precious additional time between molts, to breed majors.

"We have nearly five hundred eggs in our nursery, some number of them—some as yet unknown number of them—already hatched into vigorous little larvae. Let us say that Regina is bent upon breeding an additional one hundred and fifty majors to augment her already strong force. Her majors would overpower our new sisters, supposing the rest of our forces to be evenly matched. But, our new sisters will be ready for action while her majors are still pupating."

Delta was fascinated but not satisfied with this ingenious theory, which did not after all allay her original doubt. "But are four callow workers tactically equivalent to four experienced foragers?"

"When you are older yourself, you will no longer feel the urge to ask such a callow question." Beta had returned to follow this conversation in angry but not mute disapproval. Of a devoutly conventional cast, her attitudes proclaimed a distrust of subtlety, of glossy surfaces, of theorizing, of witty doubts and doubting wits—a distrust, in short, of the Royal Alpha and Gamma, and of the new Delta who was fast proving herself just such another dealer in civilized sophistries.

"Let us hope she will then be able to explain it to the rest of us," Gamma threw in with an easy mockery.

"Perhaps she can tell us now what we should do *instead*," Beta demanded, overflowing in offended propriety. "A great many inexperienced fighters are better than few or none. We might push this inexperienced ant out to the mound with the rest of them, and she'd at least help to block the entrance in her panicked retreat." The Beta held herself tall in menace as she spoke, uncomfortably reminding them how very little she lacked of an alpha, except that little was *this* Alpha's *all*—discretion, tact, finesse.

"Oh, yes," Gamma replied, "all problems are to be solved by sending out a great host of ants to wrestle with them, or die in the doing. But defeating a strong, cunning enemy is not like carving up a dead cricket." Then, pivoting her feelers to take in the Delta.

"Ah, we find already, my dear, how stimulating your freshness is to our jaded stock of conversation!"

A sister who mocks might be more formidable than one who shoves and blusters, but our Delta did not make this observation to herself. Gamma so beautifully fused irony and cordiality in her elegant articulations that the mockery, especially when it was not readily apprehended, was painless to its subject. She possessed to an eminent degree the art of mingling attractants and repellants, so that the recipient scarcely knew whether to be flattered or offended. If Delta nonetheless continued to feel a certain wary uneasiness in the company of this brilliant sister, she reminded herself that other ants also, the Beta, the Alpha, their frequent visitors, provided Gamma with themes for her light, gliding ironies, in which no harm, apparently, was meant. She herself might vacillate indecisively between admiration and mistrust, but she did not dislike the Gamma.

Thus the new Royal Delta began to find out her place among her sisters. The impressions of that first day were deepened and strengthened over time. Alpha was kind and affable; Gamma exercised a keen wit but its cruelty was mollified by the imperturbable smoothness of her manner; Beta was crude, caustic, domineering. Mother, of course, was goodness and justice incarnate, immune to criticism; her sternness was majestic, that was all.

Our ant clung so firmly to these impressions, sought with such persistence for their continued proof, that she risked leaving herself little room to make new ones—or rather failed to understand those that she inevitably did make. The very acuity of her sense had the odd, untoward consequence of inducing her to fix upon those crude initial conceptions—to take them as her trail markers in plotting her way through an ever-burgeoning thicket of incongruous perceptions. A stubborn loyalty held tight, for all life, to the primacy of those first impressions, arranging later ones, sometimes with excessive ingenuity, to conform to their model. Her understanding, as it expanded, folded in on itself, concealing any disquieting observations beneath others that were more comfortably or complacently digested, as though her awareness were bound within a larval skin too inelastic to develop such divergent ideas. There was just the faintest touch of arrogance and complacency, of willfulness too, in her maintenance of those first impressions, which were not to be effaced by vulgar experience. The reader may hazard a guess as to whether this great loyalty of hers, on which she rather prided herself, was not merely or even primarily to others, but to herself.

Once it was evident that the new Delta had no ambition to better herself, the Royal Beta had relaxed into a coarse-grained familiarity that was more repellant to its subject than her initial belligerence had been. "Little sister," she found occasion to remark, upon observing the ant's constant deference to the Alpha and Gamma, "I may as well call you that since that is what you've apparently chosen to be. Have you ever considered that too little ambition may prove to be as great and as dangerous a fault as too much?" Delta answered stiffly that an ant ought to sacrifice her personal ambitions for the greater good of society.

"*Ought,*" Beta responded, "oh, yes, unquestionably, she *ought*. And, since there are always other ants who risk *their* lives to gather *our* honeydew, we must conclude that a number of ants do as they ought, at least once they are pushed right to the brink of it. But I would advise you, for your own safety, not to enlarge the unselfishness of sisters to a universal law."

"It is certainly gallant of you to warn me" was Delta's rejoinder, to which Beta only laughed. Delta could find but one likeable trait in this sister's character: though she continually gave offense, she never took it.

Her discomfort with the quarrelsome Beta, the perplexing Gamma, the austere Queen Mother herself, threw Delta much upon the society of the generous Alpha. This agreeable personage was always ready to offer advice and conversation. From Alpha she acquired her understanding of society, of the intrinsically regulated place of every ant, of their own privileges at the apex of that order. From Alpha she learned what may and may not be said. Some subjects were too tremendous or too disquieting—the troubles outside, their mother's declining health—were only to be broached with consummate indirection. Their very awareness that the troubles outside had nearly come inside, that the nest had almost been breached by their enemies in the first assault—this awareness must be unspoken and could remain more easily unspoken as being so completely shared. The truth was doubtless that really, when it came to any free handling and naming of things, they were living together, the five of them, in an air in which an ugly effect of "blurting out" might easily be produced. They guarded their fragile, ailing mother with their words as other, lesser ants guarded her with their bodies.

Under such polite constraints, indirection flourishes, skirting solidities to wind through stony detours like the blanched yellow stalk of a seed planted at too great a depth. If our Delta was, by her nature, exquisitely sensible to social interactions, she was unprepared for the subtlety and brilliance of the exclusive circle in which she now moved. Her comprehension crept after the event, catching up with it only after much shy subsequent reflection. If the triumphant civilities, the gloating kindnesses, with which she had been met on her arrival had escaped her observation until the opportunity to oppose them had expired—she had remembered and pondered it all— how much else did she miss? Her companions might, to all appearances, be engaged in ordinary discourse, yet other meanings hovered and gathered, forming lucid pendants of congealed implication that then evanesced like dewdrops before she could begin to take it all in. An innocuous address to one ant might conceal a sting for another. Words of apparent praise were undercut by an oddly placed emphasis or by a slight, almost impalpable, acerbic tincture. The language of feelers, forelegs and glands were by these ants brought up to a complexity laden with more meaning than, perhaps, it could comfortably bear. Our ant's articulate awareness expanded upon these observations yet recoiled upon them too, in surfeit and confusion. Nothing was ordinary; nothing was to be taken for granted.

It was widely and rather lazily assumed that the royal attendants achieved their high station by youth and size alone, an assumption that went unchallenged even when such modestly proportioned ants as the current Gamma managed to win a place for themselves. Rather, these ants were remarkable for their immense powers of perception, for the quality and refinement of their sense. An ant of only ordinary perspicuity is satisfied to prolong her stay in the nursery, to take her turn at licking and fondling brood until stale maturity renders her objectionable and she must find a new position for herself elsewhere in the nest. Among the newly eclosed ants of each brood, only the most acutely observant are able to detect and discriminate the distant allure of the queenly essence, to comprehend its significance and to trace it from the nursery. There they fall naturally to the task of deciphering all the intermingled experiences entering the nest. No such experience, however trivial, was discarded; and if it came to them amplified or diluted, and always frankly muddled with other, possibly contradictory perceptions, the four ants then enjoyed the challenge of decoding it.

Alpha was brilliant at that, Delta thought. The others had nothing to contribute, nothing worthwhile. From rumors and surmise borne throughout the nest, from hazy perceptions and sensations haphazardly gathered up with the honeydew and prey, Alpha plucked a finer meaning, achieving clarity and order. No task—other than the Queen's egg-laying—could be more essential. Each individual ant, each minute vessel of thought and feeling, brought her experiences back into the nest to pour them into her sisters, at first detached and individual, then merged, blended, with every other such experience, into every other such ant.

Beta was persistently, unfailingly disagreeable in these discussions, as if it were prescribed to her by her role and not in her power to change. She made objections, found faults, caviled over minutiae. The edges of her conduct were always cutting sharp, honed for perpetual battle.

"You are overly fond of asserting that we have the advantage over our enemy by our longer residence—that we control the land, we know its features," Beta complained. "Haven't you ever put a feeler out into the gallery, into that jostling, striving confusion of ants? Do you think *those* ants are in control of anything, even of themselves?"

Alpha kept her dignity—how Delta admired her for that—and with great patience went over all her arguments again. Beta was reduced, at length, to smirking silence, as if she could answer back if she chose, only she chose not to.

"Maybe after all," Gamma murmured, with recondite wit, "we know only ourselves, at best—some of us not even that!" A saccadic twist of her feeler pointed this remark with barbed intention but it passed without response, since Gamma had more. "However we probe and sample and taste, we only come back to ourselves, recreating externals in the image that best suits us, orderly and controlled, or chaotic and pushing."

"*Thank you*," said the Beta with her heavy irony, "for supporting my position, however inadvertently, and at the cost of a slight."

No fresh impressions had presented themselves to qualify Delta's nostalgic recollections of the relative candor of the nursery. The attendants themselves only rarely left the royal chambers. There was no need. The passage of nursery ants back and forth assured them of a steady supply of food and news. The royal apartment, all of it, tasted richly, in the past almost oppressively, of the Queen. The taste passed outward, thinned and attenuated as it divided itself into a thousand minute shares, out to the meanest forager. But it was first passed from the attendants to the favored nurses. Among the latter ants, it was a privilege to be allowed to enter the royal apartment, to stay some little while, to bring a food offering that would come, as a point of etiquette scrupulously observed, first to the Alpha and then to the Queen and the other attendants. The ensuing conversation concerned the health of the Queen and the welfare of the brood—subjects of tremendous urgency now that replacement workers were so badly needed to protect the colony from their great enemy.

To their visitors' conventional query, Alpha always replied with the equally conventional pretense that Mother was quite well but not, at the moment, receiving visitors. They, the visitors, must be content with their own humble company. The visitors from the nursery made the expected gracious reply, and the conversation proceeded to the usual subjects: the sweet charm of eggs, the lively naughtiness of larvae (so hungry, so demanding!), the prospects for a few of the more precocious ones to begin pupating, and the latest intelligence from the foragers, which had been relayed through many removes from mouth to mouth until it reached the nursery and from there progressed at last to the Queen's own chambers.

One of their visitors, an ant of no great size but with a pushing disposition, found occasion to remark that the Queen seemed never to receive visitors, at this moment or any other; she hoped Mother was indeed in good health and spirits.

"Entirely so," Gamma replied soothingly. "Just today she mentioned her intention of paying a visit to the nursery, to find out for herself how her little ones are coming along."

The cool insouciance of this fib startled Delta almost as much as it did their visitors, although she concealed her surprise more effectively than the nursery ant, whose response was delivered too eagerly to be natural.

"That will be a delight—an honor! Why, our mother hasn't visited the nursery since I myself was a little new-laid egg!"

There was a lull now in the conversation, a certain complicated embarrassment reigning on both sides, until another visitor expressed, in tones of polite resignation, her regret at being unable to approach the Queen.

Alpha replied once again that Mother was feeling quite well but resting, "As you, I am sure, must know very well, it can be severely exhausting to produce eggs."

"It is really quite beyond *my* imagining," replied the largest of their guests, with a presence of mind superior to her nursery sisters, who had stirred uncomfortably at the Alpha's words. "You must tell us about it. It must be fascinating to witness, and such a privilege to be the first to scent and taste a newly laid egg." She paused only briefly, as if not expecting a response, then continued a little differently.

"Once the eggs arrive in the brood chamber, we nurses have so much to do we can scarcely spare a moment to enjoy the delightful aspects of our work—except, it does seem there are fewer eggs reaching the nursery these days. Every single one of them is needed, of course. The troubles outside—"

"Every worker egg, I'm sure you mean," interposed Gamma, smiling significantly.

The nursery ant continued as if not noticing, although a trifle incoherently, "we depend so much upon the foragers and soldiers, without whom—"

"They might display their courage and devotion, in the meantime," Beta put in tartly, "by bringing in better food. The Queen lacks meat and we all, I am sure, could do with some choice nectar in place of so much common root honeydew."

It was quite true but not the right tone; with Beta it never was. Delta felt how it jarred. Workers so often go about their lives with a discontented longing for what has been sacrificed in exchange for a high civilization: some mourn their lack of wings and independence; most wish for greater stature and fertility. Beta seemed rather to regret the want of a stinger.

It seemed to the Delta, as she followed these conversations, with their dizzyingly rapid turns and twists, that her Alpha and the Gamma were spinning a wondrous silken web of words. She almost felt the web, as she thought of it, suspended there between them. Each fresh utterance added a new thread, another vibrating strand of sense, wove it a little further into a still finer object. The sequence of their quick-flashing ideas entwined and interlaced with an inscrutable grace. She might not be able to fasten upon the pattern of cunningly knotted meaning represented therein—she was often in these conversations left well behind in helpless bewilderment—but she was certain it was there, almost to be grasped. She did not ask if this beautiful web she half-perceived, half-imagined, might serve, as a web, to trap unwary victims, to knit them up in its unapparent, tangled sense.

In all such conversations, Beta's mood was suspicious rather than interested, as if her assertively frank character resented such airy loveliness or even reared back in fear of it. These shimmering displays of wit invariably terminated with some envenomed interjection by Beta, although it would still be Alpha who instilled a final graceful phrase.

"We are all called upon to make sacrifices of our comforts," this ant now intoned, almost in mediation. And as if those words were a signal, although Delta could not guess of what, the nursery ants all rose to leave.

Our ant had settled early on that it was quite impossible to like Beta: no one could do so; no one, she perceived, did. It was very easy to like Alpha. Delta accordingly liked Alpha and disliked Beta; and where she liked she trusted, where she disliked, she distrusted, never considering that these qualities might not be truly coupled. She might have learned to question these indolent assumptions had she studied Gamma more carefully: Gamma was brilliant, Gamma was charming. Gamma's keen perceptions of others allowed her to be considerate with great deliberate cunning. But if Gamma was likeable, was she also trustworthy? Delta did not dwell on these questions, not fully recognizing their significance, believing that if she remained faithful to her Queen and to the Queen's Alpha, then that faith would ensure her security.

Her faith took the form of a readiness to second and affirm, with a super-fluity that was often painfully evident. Having been effectively discouraged from feeding and grooming the Queen, she was without a fixed or certain duty. It was the Beta who at last discovered a task for Delta, shortly after the conversation about eggs. This ant now proposed that Delta should have the responsibility for conveying the Queen's eggs to the nursery ants.

"I think you may be entrusted with them," she remarked dryly. "You ought in fact to have a fine natural feel for their care, since you are scarcely full hatched yourself."

That her relative youthfulness should become a subject for the Beta's sarcastic commentary puzzled Delta not a little. Of all the attributes and appendages from which an ant may claim merit, youth and stature—that she had both in full measure, she well knew—were the most commendable. Then it occurred to her that these invidious pleasantries—for there had been others on this theme—might rather be aimed at their two companions. Beta and our ant were both offspring of the summer worker brood, differing in age by some few days, a distinction that allowed Beta to demand precedence of her junior sister without obliging her to yield it back again at some future date. The Alpha and Gamma were of the previous generation. They had emerged in the smaller hatch of workers who had passed the winter as larvae in the same nurseries as the royal brood. It made a difference not merely of age but, suggestively, of temperament as well. Delta had been but half aware of this difference, only now giving it her attention.

These two were ants who had lacked some single but critical element, some minute endowment of a finer yolk that would have made them royals. They had emerged from their cocoons without wings, without ovaries worth the name; but might they, through their lengthy maturation, have gained something yet of the quality of a queen—her refined cunning, her exquisite social sense? This, dimly felt, is what made the two ants distinguished from the viewpoint of the Delta, what made them dangerous from that of the Beta. They were already to be admired; a more ingenious perception now had it that they might also be pitied. Informed by her quickened historical sense, our Delta began to glimpse the signs of a relation between the two ants, who had formerly seemed to her so nearly opposite in character—the one forthright and sisterly, the other enigmatic, a shape-changer shielded in brilliant irony. They were together a great deal; speaking very little perhaps, but exchanging light, allusive touches that seemed expressive of a quiet commerce of taste and perception.

Throughout the troubles outside, their mother had undertaken a continuing production of eggs far beyond the season of the summer worker brood. As the attendant in charge of receiving newly laid eggs, Delta became adept at judging each egg's capabilities, attuned to noting infinitesimally fine variations in form and feel. She would gather up the eggs with a gentle, nostalgic admiration. In their pure mindless perfection, eggs are free of selfish wants and hateful inequalities—or at least unable, as of yet, to manifest them. She said as much to her sisters one day.

"But which is it?" said the Gamma. "Are they in fact devoid of selfishness or only, being eggs, unable to act upon it?"

Delta had not expected to have her words taken up so sharply. She did not suppose, and said so now, that the tiny germ of an ant in becoming, so to speak, already dictated its character, which must rather be the product of experience.

"Yet that tiny germ contains every other form of potential," Alpha responded, with her inveterate fondness for debate. "The adult's six legs, her gaster and trunk, her feelers, her mouthparts, her integument and her internal organs—all these must be already present, à peine ébauchée, in the egg. If her physical character is already determined, why not her mental as well?"

Delta had no answer to that: Alpha's views were always supremely well reasoned.

"Then presumably you give no place to experience at all," said Beta, who had obviously waited for Alpha to take a position so that she might then adopt the opposing view. "But what is an ant's mental character other than the product of her experiences? An egg has no experiences, but a larva does. What she is fed and how well she is fed will affect her mental development—and her physical development too. If a royal brood egg, big and heavy with yolk, is mistreated or neglected by the nurses, depend upon it, that ant won't be a queen but an ordinary, if large, worker. Certain large ants of my acquaintance seem to entertain a private view of themselves as queens manqué—but no doubt you would argue they are only pathetically deluded."

"If you came to the nursery," said one of their visitors, who suspected a criticism in Beta's remarks about nurses, "you would find among even the tiniest newly hatched larvae that some are already bolder and more assertive than their sisters. We have to check them continually to protect the shy, quiet ones from being bitten."

"Precisely," said Alpha, "and these little larvae, manifesting their leadership abilities so young, are the ones who will develop into alphas and betas."

"Is that in fact so?" Delta asked the nurse with interest.

"I cannot tell you that," their visitor replied. "I did not say that. No nurse ever cares for an egg throughout its development. We always move the young to a new brood chamber each time they molt, and then again when they pupate."

"One should follow the development of the most and least active larvae, to see if they in fact mature to be alphas and deltas, respectively. It would be a most interesting experiment," Alpha remarked.

"Possibly," said the nurse, "but it would be unconventional and rather impractical. There are such a number of larvae present, with so many nurses to care for them, that they are continually shuffled about. We don't approve of singling out the young ones for special attentions. They must all be treated alike. Partiality is not our way."

"But we know they aren't all treated alike," Beta objected. "Not all nurses are as dedicated and skillful as our esteemed guest here."

To Delta's amused observation, it was clear that their esteemed guest was little gratified by this gracious exemption from criticism, although it indeed represented the Beta's very nearest approach to graciousness.

"Some nurses *do* bite or neglect their charges," that ant continued, obstinately. "We would never see so much variation in size among workers—I do not mean the variation between ordinary workers and majors, but between members of each caste—if nurses did not favor some of them with the best food while scanting others. I submit that an ant's character is determined in just this fashion, by the fondling and feeding she receives from her nurses, or the relative lack thereof."

"It is not invariably the case that the biggest, best-fed ants become alphas and betas," said Gamma. "Of course, I mean no reflection on anyone present. I only observe that size does not completely account for character."

"If all larvae were treated exactly the same," asked Delta wonderingly, "all worker larvae, I mean—would we then eclose as equals, no alphas or betas among us?"

"Perhaps you meant to say 'no gammas and deltas among us,'" Beta corrected, with an unpleasant smirk to speed her little joke to its target.

"I meant only to say that then we would, presumably, all be equals, all alike in size, matched in character, without dominance or rank, all truly behaving as sisters, not merely pretending to do so," Delta responded, with deserved asperity.

"Ants will never be without rank, without class, even if we were all the same size," Alpha pronounced, with the serene assurance of an alpha. "We would still have with us the inescapable class distinctions of age. Surely no one here would propose that an ancient, foul-smelling forager would be accepted into our circle. If we were all the same size, I believe the social striving would be yet greater as more difficult to resolve. I do not think we ever observe two ants of equivalent stature accepting each other as equals; rather, they posture and compete until one gives way to the other. I conclude that competition is natural, part of our character, imprinted in the egg and only waiting to be hatched in order to be expressed."

Nonetheless, Delta continued to believe in the pure innocence of eggs.

As eggs have their undeniable charm, there are always ants eager to caress and admire them. Delta had no sooner retrieved a newly laid egg, had revolved it in her mouthparts with practiced expertise, than there was a waiting nursery ant to whom it must be surrendered. There was no edict to bar Delta from carrying or escorting eggs to the nursery; only the flat superfluity of it, with so many nursery ants continually in attendance, stood in her way. She moved slowly, lingering with the eggs, turning them over and over again, delicately cleansing them as if the nurses could not be trusted to do so, and at last parting with them when her delays could be protracted no further without embarrassment.

Thrip had continued to lay eggs long after the usual season to produce the emergency second summer brood, sacrificing the eggs that should have been developed for the next season's royal brood in order to do so. Increasingly these eggs entered the world as scant, irregular creations, marred by the haste of their inception. When the latest batch were so deformed that not even Delta could feel affection for them, this ant did not know what to do. They had so little likelihood of survival that they did not belong to the nursery. Beta, perceiving her hesitation, discovered the cause and at once took action. She seized the poor misshapen things and placed them in the Queen's mouthparts with an exalted tenderness that Delta could never have expected of her.

"Dearest Mother," Beta said, so faintly Delta could barely catch her words, "you must spare yourself now. Take back these eggs to yourself, since all comes from you. The brood have all pupated, will soon begin to eclose. You will have daughters enough to serve you, and to die for you if need be."

"You are a good, loyal daughter," Thrip responded with a slow dignified motion of feelers and forelegs, touching the Beta caressingly on the brow. "I regret that I cannot protect you, either from these new daughters who will soon push their way forward, or from those already here. I lack the strength to exert control even over my own chambers. You must look after yourself."

"We know that, Mother," Beta murmured, "we know."

Delta could make little either of Thrip's cryptic warning or of the odd inclusiveness of Beta's response. She was lost in wonder at the mere fact of this exchange and the intimacy it conveyed. She had known this sister to be zealous in the service of the Queen—had found it out so unforgettably at their first encounter—but her devotion had seemed an act of crude possession, a public display of her power as the Royal Beta. The ant's real tenderness, along with their mother's answering trust, now gave Beta's motives a different character. Might her belligerence be expressive, not of vulgar, vindictive striving, but rather of a frustrated sincerity that distasted the sophisticate style of their sisters? Delta still could not like the ant, but she began to respect her.

The eggs of the second summer brood, upon reaching the nursery, had been carefully tended. None of them suffered from the conscious neglect and partiality that Beta had claimed to be usual. With the urgency that had possessed the entire society they were washed, cradled, and provided with every advantage of rich warm humidity until they hatched. The larvae were tended just as devotedly, although a shortage of food, so many foragers having perished, kept some unhandsomely small. They pupated normally, however. The assiduous attentions of the nurses and the warmth of the season brought them to eclosure not long after the Queen had produced those last misshapen eggs.

At first these new ants held themselves dumbly, meekly still; then the most forward began to wake up to life—to move about, to pick up eggs, to wash them and to put them down again in another place. They were pushed aside by the experienced nurses until, inevitably, they began to push back. The lower nest was suddenly crowded with jealous, jostling sisters, the new brood taking up pointed residence in the nursery, letting their elders know that their period of eminence had elapsed. The lucky ones kept their places, the unlucky ones moved upward, elsewhere, competing with all the wit and force of their characters to cling to their stations, or at least not be forced all the way upward into the company of the foragers. Civility became tense, fraught, pressured. Ants intrigued and combined to hold their own against the callows who aimed, with the brave crudity of youth, to supplant them.

Over the whole history of the society, it seemed as though each fresh generation was more striving, more on the lookout, more indifferent to traditional decencies than those they displaced. These new ants, from a generation unplanned, novel in its timing, seemed determined to make a break with the past and all its time-honored constraints. They had been brought into being to put an end to the war; they behaved as though they would put an end to everything. The older ants, alarmed at their boldness, felt as surely invaded as if Regina's raiders, not their own junior sisters, were before them—demanding, asserting, proclaiming themselves *for* themselves. They would take you up—quite up—lifting you in their sharp young jaws and putting you out of the room if you happened to be too much in their way.

When the royal attendants learned from the nurses that this second brood had, all but a tardy few, emerged from their cocoons, Alpha proposed that the attendants decide upon a plan of action for carrying the war to Regina's colony.

"If you truly suppose," said Beta, who missed no opportunity for argument, "that hundreds upon hundreds of sisters will faithfully execute your no doubt ingenious military strategies, I think you sadly deluded. Nothing amongst ants ever happens according to plan, not even the passage of brood to a new nursery or the construction of an emergency exit. Always some ant more persistent than her sisters pursues her *idée fixe*, tunneling or transporting brood in just the opposite direction, stumbling over her less imaginative sisters as she does so, eventually converting them to her views, convincing them that they themselves are in error, until all move just contrary to the original scheme."

"That is a revision of plan, not an absence of planning," countered Delta, who would indeed follow wherever the Royal Alpha led, and expected all her sisters to do the same. "Such movements are not random. An ability to prevision, to plan, is the mark of a high civilization. So, one might add, are good manners."

"Our enemies succeeded in marching an army to the attack," Alpha observed. "Do you suppose that we are somehow incapable of such discipline ourselves? For what reason has our mother laid so many eggs if not to launch an army against our adversary?"

"I objected only to the presumption that we can confidently plot a step-by-step campaign. Of course we must attack. If we do not, our enemies will think us weak and act accordingly," Beta responded, in surprising affirmation. Gamma and Delta suspended comment in wonderment, fixing their feelers instead upon their mother, awaiting her judgment on this extraordinary accord.

"Let them," said Thrip, breaking her long silence. "Let them think us so weak that they will dare to chase us to our hill. We will do nothing in the meantime but wait for them to carry out *their* grandiose plans—along with their inevitable, fumbling mistakes." Then, to that ant's astonishment, she turned to address the Delta.

"This daughter, the junior among you, perceived something that the rest of you have left quite out of your reckoning. As *you,* my dear Delta, correctly pointed out, we cannot expect naive inexperienced ants, who perhaps have never before ventured beyond the hilltop or the midden, to launch an offensive in alien territory. An ant always fights best when she has no retreat—when she knows exactly what she is fighting for, when the battle is for herself, for her home, for everything she knows."

There could be no argument. They would wait until the war came home to them once again. Gamma only tossed her feelers in well-contained amusement at Alpha's discomfiture. She kept always to a fine independence of outlook. So long as the troubles outside remained outside they were not greatly of interest to her, although she was glad to find they were so distracting and engrossing for her sisters. When an ant has no eggs and no loyalties, she can focus with admirable constancy on her self-advancement. The Gamma saw a little revolution coming for which she intended to be fully prepared. Delta's joy at being marked for praise was so acute as to be almost painful. Beta was instantly, pugnaciously certain that their mother was right, was wise, was always right and likewise always wise. To her credit, Delta noted, the Beta had never resented a contradiction or reprimand from their mother. Alpha grieved the loss of her beautiful scheme in private, certain that their delays would grant Regina the time to mature her majors and her plans of conquest. She also felt, confiding to the easy sympathy of Gamma, that the failure of her plan was the fault of the Delta and her ill-conceived questioning. Who had even known that their mother, at rest in her alcove at the time, had given the conversation her attention?

Thrip *had* followed her daughters' conversations, which had, by the oddest chance, paralleled the looping, circling track of her own restless self-questioning. Knowing her mother as she did, she understood Regina was likely tempted to invest in a production of majors. Her own inclination, conveniently supported by the pompous Alpha's theory, was to produce as many daughters as possible, trusting to their courage more than their bulk. Yet, like the Beta, she recognized the fatuity of planning and forecasting; and she had found the Delta's questions to be—no doubt fortuitously—quite to the point. The Gamma as always—a dangerous daughter, that one!—had cut through to the core of her dilemma in the senseless waste of it all. Problems could only be dealt with by producing immense numbers of expendable eggs and daughters. Immense, yes, but not infinite. She had never felt so utterly spent in her life, not even when she was anxiously awaiting the eclosure of her first brood of tiny daughters. *Then* she had merely been starving: now she was used up.

It still dwelt in her consciousness, as fresh as the moment, how her mother and her royal sisters had doubted her capabilities. She had proven herself great on the only ground that mattered: alone among her brood sisters she had founded a colony, from which her own winged daughters had gone forth to establish colonies of their own. Now she must prove herself again, on the meaner score of producing how ever many hundreds of worker daughters, producing them only to be stupidly slaughtered.

Now that it was done—now that they were hatched and ready—Thrip could not bring herself to stake all those daughters on a single rash attack. The struggle between the two colonies could only be resolved by the destruction of one of them—of at least one, she grimly reflected. But the outcome might just as easily be decided by one enterprising bird or mole as by an army of a thousand. She would wait; she would postpone; she would trust to the luck that had never yet deserted her entirely. To the disappointment of the young ants and their theories, she would do nothing. She hoped that Regina was likewise surrounded by ambitious ants with naively grandiose plans, and that she would commit the folly (hadn't she already?) of permitting her daughters to act upon them.

To escape the strained conditions of the crowded brood chambers, the nursery ants came many times a day now, pretending to an expectation of eggs. They were only too glad to stay and visit, although Beta took it upon herself to discourage those who lingered excessively. These nursery ants, whether lacking in refinement or preoccupied by their private anxieties, were frequently slow to read the meaning of pauses, conspicuous twitches and conscious neglect. It often took some prodding and yanking to remove them. Of late some of their visitors had included newly eclosed ants who were peculiarly unapt to receive the hints their elder sisters threw out concerning the lateness of the hour or the inordinate length of their charming visit. These visits at last came to be so pointedly prolonged that there might be doubts as to who was the visitor and who the resident.

"I wonder if you happen to recall a fascinating discussion, not so very long ago, on the subject of character development," said Gamma to Alpha. The latter bent her feelers inquiringly but said nothing.

"These fresh, pushing young ants rather prove your theory, I think," Gamma continued, after a pause.

"They are exceedingly impertinent for their size," Alpha responded, "and they begin to be inconvenient."

"While we perceive it is true that size does not necessarily correspond with rank, I think it is also not strictly necessary that the mature ant must give way to the juvenile, not if there are others who can be sacrificed in her stead."

"I certainly feel we owe it to Mother, in these troubled times, to try to preserve some continuity, some standards, in regard to her attendants," Alpha answered, with a lofty vagueness that was apparently to Gamma's satisfaction, as this ant only nodded and said no more. A seemingly somnolent and detached Beta had lifted her head and darted her feelers, attempting, belatedly, to follow the exchange that had just taken place. If more was to pass between them, it was not attempted now, not with the Beta quivering with aroused suspicion. No ants were more adept at communicating with obscure hints and signals than the Alpha and Gamma. A few slight gestures—towards their companions, towards their silent, mournful mother—communicated their shared awareness. The Queen was either too feeble or too preoccupied to control them—else she would have promoted their younger rivals, Beta and Delta, whom she obviously preferred, long before. Beta's vigilance could not reveal the key of their communications, and their junior sister was too dully trusting to suspect them. They could easily complete their arrangements, which needed only opportunity for execution.

The Queen had ceased laying for many days and then, quite unexpectedly, produced one more egg. It was a fine, well-formed egg, heavy with yolk, quite distinct from the flimsy, stunted ones that had lately filled the brood chambers. Delta turned it over delicately in her mandibles, marveling at its loveliness, so perfect and rounded and lustrous. She hesitated—possessively no doubt, yet also, as she insisted to herself, justifiably—over its relinquishment to these new, inexperienced nursery workers. Prolonging her moment of guardianship, she displayed it to her fellow attendants. To her surprised delight, Gamma suggested, with Alpha's quick concurrence, that Delta herself should convey the egg directly to the brood chambers, so it might be placed in the charge of the best nurses. To this sensible suggestion, however, Beta made objections.

"It is a fine, promising egg, an important egg, but it is yet more important that you remain in your place."

"Surely you do not expect she'll encounter impertinence and disrespect from sisters *outside* our loving circle?" Gamma parried with acid sweetness.

It was the vibration of some new tension, an unheralded exchange of roles that Delta could not comprehend, equally puzzled as she was by the one ant's advocacy and the other's opposition. Gamma mocked almost crudely, almost in the style of the Beta. Undeterred, unchastened, Beta insisted, proclaiming the impropriety of it in tones so strenuous that it was possible to detect the note of some urgent need, sharper and more emphatic for being unexpressed, for pleading, almost, to be understood as inexpressible. But at that moment Delta had consideration only for her own keen desire to revisit the nursery. She was unwilling to forego such a pleasure to appease her sister's readily aroused disapproval. As Delta departed, the Beta cried out after her in a final, dismayed appeal to stay. Obscured by the bustling confusion of the gallery, she could choose not to notice this appeal even as she wondered at it.

The nursery was so densely packed with ants that Delta could barely push her way in along the upper portion of a wall. All ants seek the society of other ants, assembling with warm rapid pleasure to cluster, to groom, to gossip; but our ant's keen perception caught the play of other, less sociable instincts in this tight, nervous throng. From the slight vantage of her post, she directed her feelers with questing attention, searching for some familiar nursery figure to whom she might entrust her egg—she could not help thinking of it, however absurdly, as hers. Groping her way forward on staggered footholds, she encountered just such an ant—a simple matronly personage who had oftentimes visited the royal chambers. But the nurse would not accept the egg, turning away in refusal. "Times are changing," was all she offered in explanation. "Surely you feel that for yourself!" Then that ant thrust herself—no, *was thrust* by the striving pressures of the edgy crowd—outward into the passageway.

Delta was almost expelled as well in the forcible discharge of superfluous ants from the overflowing nursery. She took a firmer foothold on a stony projection and again sent her feelers forward in anxious survey. Many in the throng were soft, teneral, shy creatures, dazed and trembling with the shock of emergence into a society of such fierce, overwrought tensions. Seething masses of ants, some cunning and determined, others with ill-concealed desperation, were milling about them, each striving to preserve a place in the deep nest and to defeat the humming motion and pressure of a hundred sisters who all wanted the self-same identical thing: not be forced up and outward into a terrible exposure.

In a scene of such turmoil, all Delta thought possible was to seek out the egg pile in the hope that responsible nurses still held it in their charge. She succeeded in tracing the delicious scent of eggs, letting herself drop at the spot. A large young ant loomed before her, crouched possessively over a sizable clutch of eggs. Brought abruptly face to face, the two ants made rapid acquaintance, their feelers engaged in a mutual survey of quickened curiosity. The touches Delta gave her interlocutor were those of sociable inquiry; the other's fairly bristled with intense interrogation that subsided once she had inspected the fine egg Delta bore.

The nursery ant's features were not lovely, were not even regular, but were rendered distinctive by massive feeler brows, which, our Delta confusedly felt, were tokens of something, of abilities beyond the ordinary range. Her figure was remarkably plump, her person drenched in the sweetness of eggs—an advantage she no doubt owed to her position upon the egg pile. The scent was so strikingly, deliciously rich that it could not but affect our ant favorably. Delta was attracted, to the point of envy, wondering if she herself might have been so imbued, might have achieved just such an advantage of presence, had she stayed in the nursery.

Her new acquaintance impressed her as possessing a great deal of assurance coupled, rather strangely, with a great deal of reserve. She had slowly raised herself up to sit upon the egg pile with her forelegs fully extended, her head held stiffly erect, her mandibles parted in an expression that was not especially cordial. Although the eggs were not so abundant as to grant her even a transient advantage in height, it was a place so apart, an accumulation so precious, that it gave a borrowed grandeur to the ant, of which she was manifestly conscious. After a few polite phrases of introduction and compliment, Delta expressed her surprise that an ant endowed with such distinction should never have visited the royal chambers. To this friendly overture the nurse replied, with chilly indifference, that she had no time for visits, no interest in mere talk; caring for her eggs consumed all her time.

Delta replied with determined civility that the Queen Mother greatly appreciated the dedication of the nursery ants. But surely the work—shared among so many sisters, devoted alike to the brood—might still leave her the opportunity to enjoy a few minutes in the Queen's presence?

"That *is* kind of you—but I doubt if the Queen would express any great appreciation of *my* dedication to the nursery."

Delta felt the mockery—her own manners were being mimicked back to her in coarse parody—but was more mystified than offended. Arrived at her destination, Delta had not thought to put the egg down; or rather, she had, and had then thought better of it. Her instincts were oddly at war with her reason: she felt the propriety of putting the egg in its proper place; yet she felt even more an urge *not* to do so. The nursery ant seemed so oblivious to the egg's great merit, having dismissed it from notice after an initial inspection, that Delta could not but question her competence and, despite her protestations, her devotion.

Although Delta's attention had been arrested by the large, striking ant who had seemed solely in charge of the egg pile, it now was urged upon her awareness that other young ants were situated nearby on similar if smaller egg piles. Some, like herself, held an egg or two in their mandibles, as if they too were uncertain where it should go, to whom it might be entrusted. The impression corresponded but poorly with the claim that the nurses were not partial, did not favor one egg or larva over another. Her observation was half critical, yet she had hardly indulged in it before she caught herself up to ask whether she, at that moment, was behaving any differently. She still clung to her egg—that is, to the one she had carried from the royal chambers. She might almost seem to have forgotten her business, she was so strangely reluctant to conclude it. But she justified herself that it was an egg of exceptional merit, deserving the best nurses. She would not have it bitten or neglected. She considered that her business was not done until she had understood the changes in the nursery, until she had decided upon the nurse to whom it was to be entrusted.

Before she had half plumbed the depths of these reflections, she was seized by a sudden wonder that there should be any eggs at all, the Queen having ceased laying for so many days. She stooped forward to brush her antennae along those nearest her, then drew back under the shock of two great surprises—the first that the nursery ant had moved aggressively as if to guard the eggs; the second, and greater, that the eggs were not the Queen's, were not even female. She did not need to inspect the smaller clusters of eggs guarded by the other nursery ants to know that they, too, were drone eggs—incapable, interdict, inadmissible drone eggs.

Our poor bewildered ant retreated to the corridor, scarcely knowing what she was doing, still less what she intended to do. "*My eggs*" the nursery ant had said—and she, Delta, had taken it all innocently, oblivious to the signs before her. Other sensations and recollections presented themselves as confirmation—the talk with the nursery ants about eggs, a conversation from which others, she now perceived, had drawn other meanings. It was a code to which she was only now in possession of the key. The ants who came daily from the nursery, seemingly so solicitous for eggs, for news of their mother's health—had they only come to gauge the Queen's weakness and their own resultant opportunities? Moving rapidly, but at random, under the spell of these perceptions, she collided with an ant who apologized very civilly, then flashed her feelers forward to establish an acquaintance with Delta's features. Those feelers took her in, comprehensively, her character, her burden, her dilemma.

"Let–let *me* have the egg," the stranger said, her earnestness made emphatic by a stammer—the pronoun strangely self-effacing and opposite in sense to that of the domineering nurse. It was not a demand but a plea, more than that, a promise. Delta surrendered the egg to the ant, who instantly turned to depart, as if to forestall questioning. Delta only then recognized that the ant was a shade too mature, too musty, to hold a station in the nursery. There had been something in her manner, nonetheless, that inspired trust; more, certainly, than the brutally triumphant ant who stood upon her egg pile, in rank assertion of a stolen privilege.

This encounter took place in the main gallery at a point nearly midway between the nurseries and the royal chambers. As Delta lingered there reflectively, she recollected the spot as one significant to her own history. It was here that she had paused, as she paused now again, when she had hesitatingly traced her way from the nursery to Thrip's chambers. It was here that she had first experienced the full allure of the royal essence, here that she had made her decision, had turned away from the nursery to seek out the attraction of the Queen. *She* was the same ant she had always been—sensitive, self-questioning, loyal—but the place itself was altered almost beyond recognition. A prodigious shift, an erosive transformation, hideous and sordid and sad beyond any power of speech to convey, had been steadily taking place, was now almost complete. The two poles of attraction were no longer in harmonious balance: the Queen's essence, ever more poignant, more beautiful, in its decline, had been overpowered by the meretricious allure of drone eggs. It was borne to her quickened senses that a young, well-endowed ant could now have no hesitation in choosing her path—would not even perceive the possibility of a worthwhile alternative. Delta turned to take her own way, chosen, not to be relinquished, back to the Queen she served.

Her doubts and misgivings multiplied, became clamorous and contradictory: it had been a mistake to give away the egg, a mistake to leave the royal chambers. She recalled the Beta's strenuous objections. What had she not understood? She hurried back to the royal chambers under the force of her dim intimations of trouble and change, only to find her way barred. Two fierce young ants—she recognized them as the most formidable and persistent of their recent visitors—blocked her way. She might not enter despite her anxious, her all but physical entreaty. She was not welcome. The Alpha would not admit her; the Gamma sent her fond regrets.

She was almost capable of the violence of forcing her way, for even in the midst of her surge of passion—of which in fact it was a part—there rose in her a fear, a pain, a vision ominous, precocious, of what it might mean for her mother's fate to have forfeited such a loyalty as hers. Turned away into exile, she stumbled in desperate confusion back into the main gallery. Something had happened, something final, terrible. All the ants were streaming upward, convulsed with great emotion, with intermitting rage and fear, and Delta was carried along with them. The successive shocks which she had undergone delivered her over to a state of excitation no less than that of the frantic workers into whose midst she had plunged. The scent of the Queen on her cuticle still marked her, however. By that scent the Royal Beta recognized her and drew her out from the surging mob.

Beta, too, had been forced out. Alpha and Gamma had profited by Delta's brief absence to combine with the two younger ants to overpower and eject the Beta. The upstart ants had declared themselves the new Beta and Delta, while Thrip their mother had been too weak, too ill, to object or even perhaps to take notice. It needed no emphasis—and for once Beta had the charity not to supply it—for Delta to comprehend that her own misplaced trust—no, her colossal ignorance—had brought down both ants. The ground of their quarrels dissolved itself: they had both been wronged;

their grievance had at last made sisters of them. Forgiveness was expressed by the Beta's firm embrace but Delta could not yet forgive herself.

Distraught, disoriented, she could scarcely follow what her sister was now telling her. That there were hidden reaches of the nest, obscure corners and cul-de-sacs where they might evade the mobilization now taking place. "It's the war, don't you understand? A half-hour ago it was just a squabble over food, over a dead shrew. Now it's a full-scale battle," the Beta said, shaking her sister with an urgent tenderness. "We aren't formed, you and I, to die in wars, not yet. We can hide ourselves—there are places, there are ways—"

Beta was proposing that they conceal themselves to escape the present danger—pulling the unresisting ant towards her retreat as she explained. They might, she said, maintain a respectably high station as long as the Queen's essence still clung to their persons, as long as they held themselves apart from the throng. They might make new alliances, win their way back into the royal chambers; their mother needed them, needed their loyalty. At worst they would take up some light domestic duty of cleaning and tidying, of moving bits of not-too-dirty dirt from this place to that—Beta knew how it was to be done—leaving the worst of the work for others. To Delta's view, this scheme conveyed a sordid prospect of lying, shifting, shirking. She made her choice: the immensity of it swept away grief and fear. Having gently disengaged herself from Beta, she hesitated for one long tremulous pause before breaking free altogether and joining the streaming mass of ants surging out of the nest, their individual natures cancelled out, merged into mere inexhaustible sisterhood.

"Stay—we *must* stay for Mother," Beta cried out, startled, astonished. The ant was already lost to the Beta, lost even to herself, jostled and thrust upward—some ants as always were doing the pushing and others being pushed. In her fierce glow of sacrifice, Delta advanced unresistingly, letting the surge bear her upwards all the way to the upper nest and then out onto the hill, where the florid shock of daylight, the hideous vacancy of space, stunned her sense, undoing her great resolve in an instant. But she could not retreat, could not even stay where she was. Savagely exposed, she could stop nowhere, tracing a restless circle between battlefield and home, between duty and safety, in the company of a hundred sisters all alike, rendered indistinguishable in their fear.

VII.
Stream-of-consciousness
Ant

Insects have thus been shown to learn in complex ways, to categorise, to generalise, and to integrate information from the different senses … Some authors argue that classical conditioning alone may prove that insects also possess some kind of consciousness or inner perspective, because conditioning seems to be impossible without consciousness in humans; however, this is controversial.
–Anna Dornhaus & Nigel Franks, "Individual and Collective Cognition in Ants and Other Insects" (**Myrmecological News**, 2008)

Let us record the atoms as they fall upon the mind in the order in which they fall, let us trace the pattern, however disconnected and incoherent in appearance, which each sight or incident scores upon the consciousness. Let us not take it for granted that life exists more fully in what is commonly thought big than in what is commonly thought small.
–Virginia Woolf, "Modern Fiction" (1925)

A lived event is finite, concluded at least on the level of experience. But a remembered event is infinite, a possible key to everything that preceded it and to everything that will follow it.
–Walter Benjamin, "On the Image of Proust" (1929)

The deathbed **topos** has been complicated or aggravated in **Artemio Cruz** by the presence of the modernist (and subsequently, postmodernist) theme of the multiplicity of the self, dramatized here through the fragmentation of the monologue into three discontinuous monologues, each using a different grammatical person.
–Brian McHale, **Postmodernist Fiction** (1987)

I survived. Regina, I hurt. I hurt, Regina, I discover that I hurt. Regina, soldier.
–Carlos Fuentes, **The Death of Artemio Cruz** (1964)

All the being and the doing, expansive, glittering, vocal, evaporated; and one shrunk, with a sense of solemnity, to being oneself, a wedge-shaped core of darkness, something invisible to others … This core of darkness could go anywhere, for no one saw it. They could not stop it, she thought, exulting.
–Virginia Woolf, **To the Lighthouse** (1927)

I am another now and yet the same.
–James Joyce, **Ulysses** (1922)

A COLLECTIVE SHUDDER passed through the twisting corridors of the nest, a spreading, enfeebling palsy. The ants, not so many in number now, who still made themselves busy were excessively so, urgently in pursuit of senseless tasks, excavating chambers that were not wanted, caching debris into those that were. The very busiest would come to a blank amnesic halt. Hesitating, loitering there for a while, then wandering off, their work unfinished. What now were they there for? What was to be done that mattered? They forgot what they had been doing, they gave it up, lapsing into a long apathy between hungers. Pointless. Someone else do it if they want it done. A decadent, disjointed rhythm prevailed, like the stuttering gait of an ant dragging herself forward on crippled limbs.

She knew it; she knew without leaving her cell, without being able ever again, under her own power at least, to leave her cell. The nest was mapped within her brain and nerve, tangle for tangle. She had visited almost none of it. But still nerve for nerve, pathway for pathway, she held it rehearsed and known within her. The rhythms of the nest traveled through her body, amplified, perhaps, by its hollows. At least she had never been so aware of them before, before they, she, faltered.

Hollow where my wings were, hollow where my eggs were. The gaster more powerful than the head she said. Not anymore dear mother not anymore. My head's all I've got left—more than you've got.

Mother who made me—who I unmade. Because what my daughters do I do. They are my legs, feelers, mandibles sent out into the world. Or they were. They're no one's now. Can feel the change. It's in them too. They went out to gather food, to feed their sisters and to grow new ones, unthinking, instinctive. Now they hesitate. Oh I can feel the change, nothing as it should be nothing as it was.

Nothing as it should be. It could be ignored, one could go about one's business—but still that sense, something askew, not right, missing. Ants paused to wipe their feelers, seeking clarity and direction. Direction, yes— no, that's not it, or not exactly. Up, down, here, there, oh that was always certain, those were qualities that never went away. Something else gone slack or missing, the dissolution of some essential bond. It had been oppressive, yes, they felt that now, but secure and comforting too, gathering them all together, giving them their tasks. Go ahead: wipe your feelers all you want you can't bring it back the way it was.

Direction—in fact there were ants who didn't seem to know up from down, below from above, ants who went down when they were supposed to go up. Ants who were here instead of there, ants doing things that didn't need to be done, senseless stupid things, avoiding those that did.

Ants paused outside her chambers, mostly those who had no business there. The nurses had ceased to come. The chamber itself felt desolate but that was not now, that was still to come. In times to come it would be abandoned to rot and wilderness, to nematodes, mites, maggots, beetles, to all the primitive unnamed things that cannot build for themselves but creep in to claim what ants have left behind. Now it was still occupied by ants, as it always had been, by a mother and her daughters. But something was lacking. Some fading or slackening, that was what made it seem empty, bereft, interrupted in being, despite the always presence of the ants.

Thrip crouched in the rear of her chambers, turned away from her daughters, from the rest of the nest. Her feelers pulsed in faint, almost imperceptible motion; she tapped sporadically at the dense smooth earth as if in concentrated question. Her attendants, clustered near the entrance, waving their own feelers in fitful discourse, could be ignored, screened out from awareness. Sometimes her attendants would leave, would wander off, down to the nursery or elsewhere, then return. The wait must be tedious for them. Sometimes the ants felt angry, irritable; other times unsure, a little frightened, sensing the emptiness that wasn't yet but would be. They crept toward their mother, close enough to run their feelers lightly over her gaster. She did not respond, did not register their presence. Then the Alpha offered to groom her.

No, go away, go away. No I don't want you to—go away.

These daughters. Always licking—licking, yes, and judging me. I don't doubt that. Not going to fool myself about that for a moment. That was a lesson she didn't teach me, one I learned for myself—never be the fool. I know what it's about—I know—the eggs. No never think about the eggs, only makes it harder. Think something else, and then they will just happen, one after another, like always, like it used to be, trickling out like slow thick drops of nectar trembling on a daughter's mandibles. There! Think pleasant thoughts!

Get away! Be off! They are still afraid, just a little. Enough to get a few minutes peace. I'm bigger than they are, bigger than any of them, that never changes.

Inside is what shrinks and shrivels and wastes. Oh my so charming so affection-ate daughters I know you. You will trade on my essence, my fading essence, and then what will you do. No never think about that does no good to think.

The reek of memory embedded in the hard-packed earth of her cell, thick, thick, all around her. No forgetting, but no recollecting either—a dim undif-ferentiated past that concreted itself into ring-like layers, summer followed by winter, bounty by famine, the fast warm season of egg-laying then the slow winter brood. Deposits of impressions resolved into one—the whole sum of yesteryears one year, of yesterdays one day, the repetitions indistin-guishable, without character or savor. Season upon season: eat and sleep; egg, larva, ant, death. Then again: eat and sleep; egg, larva, ant, death. A worker perishes, a new egg quickens. Those were her seasons—the other ones, the ones out there, she knew only from the food brought in by daugh-ters. Once only had she gone up, revisited the upper world, scented the greenness and sweetness in the flowing air.

Trapped in your cell, in the cycle, trapped by your own egg-swollen body, inert, helpless, having to be fed, having to be carried from place to place. Egg, larva, ant, death. Now the cycle breaks into a stuttering repeat of death, death. Daughters perish, no more come forth to take their place. Why they cluster around, probing, testing.

What if no more eggs can't feed myself can't do anything myself.

Cool season, slow brood; warm season, fast brood. Your ovaries were the clock that set the seasons, set them for you and for your daughters too. A richness of food—worm or grub or scavenged bits, spider eggs sometimes, big creatures' droppings and leavings, other mysterious findings—these things, coming in all of a sudden, marked a change in season that you oth-erwise did not feel or sense. Your body, though, detected it, moved and changed with the season, effortlessly, inescapably, through no will of your own. Eggs would be laid again, another cycle beginning, the slow one this time. Fine big eggs, full of yolk, dropping down one at a time, to be gath-ered up and given to the nurses; fed, when they hatched, with the special rich food. Put to sleep for the winter, coming forth in the spring as a new brood of royals and big robust workers.

Then, when the days grew warmer and longer, as that brood of winged ants left the nursery and the first good meat of the season came into the nest, passing always first to *you*—heart, mind and maker of this nest that is yours, that all came from your body. Then the eggs would drop again, a faster, flimsier brood, the summer replacement workers. Always needed. Because with its bounty of meat and nectar and honeydew, the season brought predators hunting down your daughters. Every day workers went out and did not come back. Ants creeping laboriously over the land, making their slow progress over stick and stem and leaf, so easy for the big-eyed hunters to find. Not that it was much better for those with wings—the nuptial flights—who ever knew what became of them? Exhausting each time, but each time you did it, season after season, brood upon brood.

Spending all those eggs for a second summer brood—a mistake when it turned out the war was ended by a single ant. A major took her head right off, cut right through, just a single blow did it they told me. That was luck, should have trusted to luck. A mistake to lay those eggs, that second summer brood.

Was it though. Oh it was unnecessary as things turned out. But a mistake is something you choose that then turns out wrong. Eggs lay themselves she said. The loss of so many daughters—taken by predators we thought at first, till we found out the truth. Then the battle itself, so many dead. My body felt it, the emptiness and the need. The eggs came on their own—their decision, not mine. I didn't reason it, will it, choose it. Eggs lay themselves she said. Not anymore they don't.

They will. They must.

Then the terrible winter, long, unrelenting. The older foragers, the ones we all relied on, unable to go out, or going out and dying, perishing of cold. Many daughters that died. Remember waking up, hungry, hollow inside. Terrible winters, or just the opposite, long hot droughts—there was always food for the Queen. Brood could be sacrificed, would be sacrificed, rather than the Queen go hungry.

There is no brood they said. Calling me their dear mother saying there wasn't any brood. Do you think I'm a fool do you do you. Always hard to control the egg-layers with their drone eggs even when I was healthy when I had good loyal daughters around me. Must be plenty of them now, take advantage my weakness fatten themselves—big larvae and little ones, hidden away somewhere, ripening on stolen food. Maybe not even hidden, right in my own nursery. Who'd stop them now. Once they'd be seized and brought to me. Wouldn't need to give an order, just be done. Zealous daughters, patrolling the nursery, seizing drone eggs that lacked my stamp, bringing them to me as my food, stolen from me. Lying to me, think I'm a fool do you. Not a fool, worse than that, weak, helpless, hollow, spent. Not spent yet. The eggs could come back, they could.

Lost control to my daughters when the eggs stopped. These attendants none of my choosing, disloyal, dangerous. Too old to be laying their own eggs or that's what they'd be doing. Just figuring what I'm still good for, what they can gain by me.

Let them have their drone eggs let them what do I care what difference does it make. Something at least will leave my nest on the nuptial flight. Sent forth my drones and queens for however many seasons now. However many—five or six or even seven maybe. All blurred together now all the same.

However many seasons. Cool season, slow brood; warm season, fast brood. You no longer know, you can't remember. Time now only measured by hunger, sometimes not even that. Too tired, too weak to feel your hunger, to summon food. Your attendants still holding their places in the royal chambers but no longer coming about you, not licking not testing you anymore. They know, but they keep their places, turning away the curious, guarding the secret. Trading on your faded essence. No, not even that, now. Trading on the memory of the tradition of your faded essence. Guarding their places in the royal chambers but not coming about you much at all anymore.

Thought ebbed and flowed. For some period of unmeasured time, moments or maybe days, nothing, emptiness. Then thought and memory would trickle back until an overflow of fear and anger sent you back into your vacant torpor. *I've come to this—empty, needy, powerless.* Some subtle rhythm your body yet obeyed—the ebb and flow of thought—where did it come from? Did the rhythm of day and night reach you somehow even deep within the earth? It was a lesser rhythm, unimportant, unnoticed within the great cycle of seasons and broods. But still a rhythm, a marking of time. You are alive in the now, the today. You might very probably be so in the next, the tomorrow. Time turned trivial, counted out in drops and slivers.

From the blur of season after season brood after brood—what? Almost nothing. Except once, so vague so dim now, once you went back to the surface, to the hilltop. Your feelers and palps tasting all the harshly sweet things, coming upon your sense with a burning or biting even when they were sweet. And the vast strangeness—utter alien strangeness. Your sense suddenly awakened, tingling and alert after so many seasons in the restful dark. Now, searching, you try naming the things out there, gathering together words like nursery eggs, words for half-forgotten things: sun, shadow, breeze, bud, stem, leaf, flower. What was it that brought you there—some bother about daughters and their drone eggs. But there you were in the warm sun moving slowly but by your own power circling the hilltop. Eyes long blind but who needs eyes. Your feelers and palps filled up with fresh quivering sense.

A big brood that year what difference could one selfish worker with a drone egg make then. That was a good year—a big brood, favorable weather, some daughter or two might have survived to tear off her wings and dig her hole and raise her brood and never—

Long prosperous career of egg-laying. May you send forth your own flights of winged daughters, she said. Well I did didn't I. She lied oh she must have lied when she said hers dropped effortlessly. Not trusting not liking her daughters that was the truth.

You also found it difficult to trust. Some daughters you had who were honest and devoted but they were gone so soon. Hardly had you noticed their devotion before they were chased out in defeat by younger bolder ones. It had not seemed worth the trouble to intervene. The new unpleasant ones would lose their places in due course. Always more daughters, more dying, more eggs.

You are not comforted in the least to think that you have descendants whose colonies flourish. You naturally enough resent those who survive you. And to tell the truth—if we do not tell the truth now, at last, then when?—you have always resented your daughters. Eggs torn from your reluctant substance one by one with a shudder, a spasm, each one with its tiny attendant pain, pain at that loss of substance.

When is it? When are you? Where never changed, never had changed, not since you, exhausted, terrified, dug your hole to lay your eggs. How long ago was that? How long since the war, since the disastrous winter? Without your body's working to mark the time there were no seasons you could tell. You come to slowly, aware of your emptiness and hunger. Far off a confused jumbled rhythm, it might be ants fighting ants. It barely registered. It was not important. You were alone, you were hungry.

Daughters! Food! Daughters, Daughters!

I wanted them to leave me alone and now they do now they do. Can't do anything can't feed myself.

My sisters wouldn't feed me, stole food, faster smarter than any of them. This is different this is now.

Hardly come around me hardly bother me at all now. Maybe I sleep more, don't notice don't remember. Hungry, can't go, can't do. Daughters! Daughters!

Abandoned. No not abandoned—forgotten. Like I'm no longer here. Barely am here barely am. Can't feed myself. Can't do anything myself. Don't want to think anymore don't want to feel anymore. Sleep now only sleep.

Your lethargy deepened and lengthened but was not entirely dreamless. You drifted into a featureless realm—no longer life, not yet death, fitfully populated by memory and desire, nostalgia and resentment. A daughter comes to you in your delirium. Not one of these daughters, one from the past, a good loyal daughter long dead by now must be. How long has it been. *Good daughter, loyal daughter,* you mumble in your haze as she offers you food. That daughter long gone, daughters die so soon. *Good daughter, loyal daughter,* you mumble to the phantasm. But her honeydew revives you, just a little.

It becomes a pattern of sorts, irregular but recurrent. When you are alone, asleep or awake or something in between, abandoned or forgotten by the daughters who were once your attendants, the phantasm approaches. You begin to suspect she is real. Why not? Why couldn't she be? When you are desperate, can't your desire for some necessary longed-for thing bring it into being? The things you need invoked by the conjugative force of that need. Not the eggs anymore, you can't bring back the eggs. Other needs, other longings, another sort of fertility at work. Many incredible things are real; many quite conceivable and preferable ones are not. Real, not real, a trifling, niggling distinction. You don't care. *Good daughter, loyal daughter* you say, and she feeds you.

It is not enough, that sip of honeydew, to make a difference. To be frank, nothing can now make a difference. But your sad, sad ending moves off a little, baffled, like a mantis that has missed its prey, preens its scissor legs reflectively, resumes its wait. Death stays for you at a little distance as everything is now at a little distance, slipped into hazy indistinction. The nest and all your numerous, once numerous, daughters—they move away from you or you from them. Better that way.

You are elsewhere, going over things, probing your past, as much of it as you can reach. The years of your maturity so indistinguishable—good loyal daughters or cunning selfish ones, the anxiety of raising a royal brood and then getting rid of it. The loss of so many worker daughters, going out to forage and not returning—the eggs, always the eggs, always more eggs. Body bloated beyond recognition. You had never known, never suspected this, back when you were young Thrip, a winged virgin, liked by no one but free and quick and cunning. On your own, always on your own as you are now once again—except now you are trapped and enfeebled, almost to paralysis. Your cunning, if you yet have it, cannot help you now, can it?

How long ago did you tear off your wings? How long ago did you dig your hole with such frantic, terrified haste, shattering your teeth and claws on the stones? Dug your little chamber on this very spot, only not so deep. Must still be there, that first cell, probably a guardroom or a larder now. Those first little daughters, timid, harmless, loving. Now these.

Eggs have a power, she said. Led this way and that by influences we do not recognize and forces we cannot control, she said. Then going ahead and giving all that advice on ruling my daughters. But the same forces controlled me controlled them.

Thought she was in control or said she did. But she was afraid, I remember that. Well, events proved her right didn't they?

Wouldn't their own mother. It's my helplessness, started with those first eggs, swollen, weakened, scared of everything, anything. Wasn't afraid of my daughters then. Little things, the first ones, timid, sweet, died so soon, so easily. Daughters die so soon, have to replace them, more eggs.

What a cheat everything was. A baited trap, a sticky web of causes and consequences. You ought never to have flown, or, having flown, never to have removed your wings. Everything that happened afterwards, it all started then.

Just the wing stubs left to mark me as a queen, that and my size, still bigger than any worker. Wings. I tore them off—why? can't remember now. Everything useless must be eliminated she said. I was frightened, wanted to creep underground safe. Better without wings.

No—wasn't that. Didn't think just did it. Felt compelled, had to tear them. Didn't choose. There was no choice. Some compulsion of the eggs to trap me, cripple me, compel me to take care of them. That's what it was. It was the eggs doing it for themselves not me for myself. Just the stubs of my wings to show me what I am what I was. Not in control never was in control. Led by my gaster this way and that. Only thing she said was true.

Nothing but the stubs of wings. Shouldn't have torn them, shouldn't have let the eggs—

Lapsing again into a stupor but not that of death not yet. Senses still alert despite exhaustion and indifference—cautious, catching hints, perceiving, deducing. Something happening. Again a distant scuffle and alarm as if a battle—a predator broken into the nest maybe it was, the now half-empty nest. Or was it war, like before? No. The alarm confusion dying down now.

Daughters at war with each other that's what it is. Nothing to control them each wanting to be an alpha, a drone-queen even, laying their drone eggs in my nursery, fighting amongst themselves. Nothing to be done about it without my own eggs nothing no help.

Lapsing again into a stupor but not that of death not yet. Now the phantoms visit you again, fitful, vague, circling incessantly, eluding you each time as you try to grapple them with a question. Your mother among them but amorphous, unrealized, evading you as you try to ask your question. Lapsing again into a dreamy stupor— then senses suddenly alert. Something here. Someone. Not a dream, a presence, a stranger, big, bearing a sharp, harsh tang of something recollected only as danger, fear—

Who's there—what do you want—why have you come? A big ant, a big major, they don't come here. They wouldn't. Not me not my own daughters not like that. Go away—let me be!

No it's all right she's harmless. Food yes, yes, I'll take a drop. Oh—the taste, a sharp tingling taste added to the sweetness—what is it?

It's the outside she brings it with her it's in the food. Fierce jumbled savor of the outside. A forager come all the way into the deep nest into my chamber never used to happen never allowed. Never that taste not for so long something gone and past coming back.

This time, instead of the good loyal daughter who was dead, a big harsh-scented major entered your chamber. Came right up to you. Never such an ant before, a major, a forager, permitted in your chamber. You thought of your mother, of the war—had it come back again, had it never really ended? You were frightened. Everything without purpose must be eliminated. But the big major was a harmless good daughter after all. She fed you. Only the meaty sweetness of that drop was charged with an exotic tincture—riotous, rich, adulterate on your surprised and trembling palps. For all the long years of your maturity you had not experienced its like. All your food brought to you by many removes, passing carefully from daughter to daughter from mouth to mouth until it reached you at last, distilled to bland purity. This drop impure, intense and vivifying—like the food your first shy tiny daughters brought you famished, near death then too, that moment collapsed into this one, then submerged again as other recollections are called up. Longer ago. This—like the food you, a winged virgin, wheedled from the returning foragers of your mother's nest, harassing them with your hunger and your questions.

Too tired now for questions too tired too late. No must remember what that taste when

The vapors of lost time gather, coalescing into the long-forgotten forms of things. The past returns to you. Transfixed, enthralled, you remember.

Still tingling on your palps, the savor of that food, a meatiness and sweetness impure and violent, laced with the pungency of the big daughter who bore it. No longer young, that one—must have been from the winter brood before the war. No more daughters to come forth—but never mind that—the scents she brought with her, the tastes still clinging and tingling—redolent of—what? So many once potent impressions, faded to incoherency but still, still perhaps recoverable.

Outside, out there. The air that is never quite still. How it would pass over every hair on my tegument, setting them in motion, transmitting a tingling of alarm. Foragers get used to it, the old ones lose most their hair anyway, don't feel it anymore. Remember it so vivid, the tingling, sensation of being touched all over, running all through me. Though it was only being touched by the strange light dry air that's out there. Didn't understand, ran straight back into the nest that first time. Came back out, had to find out what it was. The old foragers not minding not feeling it anymore.

Came right back up again, more curious than scared. Or enjoying almost the prickle suspense of the fear, brought up so alive and vigilant by it. Then the seeing things. Matching the shifting eye shapes of the foragers and scouts to the feeler sense of them. Everything else, immense, impossible, jumbled up just like that taste. My big slow sisters still below, barely out of the nursery, none of them daring what I dared.

The foragers coming back to the nest bulging with food. Thrip they said it's that Thrip again. But they'd give me the food and it tasted like that. Just like that.

Thrip, it's that Thrip again. When they wouldn't share I stole my food and got away with it. Quicker and smarter than they were and not afraid not at all back then.

I was fast wasn't I. When no one fed me I stole. Sometimes I wasn't fast enough and then I got bitten and slapped. No, no. They could never catch me. No they never caught me.

The nuptial flight, never meant to join it. A major caught me up and forced me out. Suppose it'd been different. Suppose I flew off on my own. Suppose I'd hidden then slipped back into the nest. Thrip, it's that Thrip again, coming back, just waiting her chance then off again so quick.

It was all such a jumble. Who knew what really happened? Why not remember it a better way?

With an effort, she could remember setting off on her wings all alone. The outer world was so dimmed to nothingness that for some time she could not get beyond that one thought of setting off on her wings all alone. She could not remember what would happen next; but all the same she rehearsed that one theme over and over, capturing the delighted sensation of being borne upwards on an easy breeze into the thick humid light of late afternoon. Stumblingly and haltingly at first, she began to make her way through a labyrinth of branching possibilities, finding out her right path, the one she should have taken, the one she would yet.

Out of mumbling rambling memory, the elements of her story came to her, offering themselves up like the phantom daughter with her honeydew. Things she had been told, long ago, almost forgotten, remade by reversal. A party of returning foragers, heavy laden, picking their slow laborious way over a tangled mat of stubble, suddenly beset by smaller, quicker thieves. She would be that thief. A renegade infiltrating the queen's brood chambers, gobbling up eggs and replacing them with her own. She would be that vagabond queen. The unsettled fringes, the indeterminate borderlands of shifting uncertainties, of disorder and misrule—she laid her claim to them; they would be her realm. Abandoned passageways left open to thieves and rogues and imposters, forgotten chambers populated with marauders and shirkers and fat lazy majors overstuffed with nectar. Her own galleries now—but never mind that. Not really her—it had never really been her. She, Thrip, was young, quick, cunning, living off the efforts of others, getting the better of any ant who opposed her, the shirkers and hoarders as well as the dull, dutiful ones. She gathered up the pieces of her story and put them in their order.

A young ant queen named Thrip, cunning and quick, left home on her wings long ago. Her wings carried her up and down, wherever she wanted to go, faster and more agile than any other ant. She gulled workers out of their honeydew and—when she hungered for meat—stole the eggs of her rivals and enemies. No one could catch or contain her—she was clever, that Thrip!

She left things out. She put things in. The things indifferent, too small or too big to matter, were banished from her recreated, triumphant memory. The green things were all one green, all one thing. A riot of exuberant tendrils coiled themselves into a lush, mildly improbable thicket that set the limits of her world, that neatly excluded the big unmanageable things, the birds and toads, the unnameable things too, they also could not penetrate her thicket of entwining green. Anthills there were aplenty, where the wingless daughters of other queens became her easy marks. She only lurked and waited—then she stole, flying off again before anyone could stop her! A world made for her and from her, replacing the failed exhausted nest that housed the failed exhausted Queen Mother. The nest that faded and fell away around her as her daughters died off—perishing in the intractable plodding reality in which they, lacking wings, were helplessly hopelessly trapped. Not her daughters—the other Thrip's daughters. The false Thrip, the one who had let herself be tricked and defeated.

There were two Thrips now. There was the Thrip who was weak, hollow, helpless and failing. And there was the strong, the undefeated Thrip—the one with cunning and agility, the always capable Thrip. This Thrip did not believe in the other one. There was a struggle. Thrip of a thousand wiles won out over Thrip of a thousand daughters, the one who was shrinking and fading. They, the daughters, those that yet lived, forgot her as she dwindled to insubstantiality—being now only the word mother, the memory mother. Her daughters had forgotten her—so let them. If she was no longer real to her daughters, why then her daughters were no longer real to her. She deleted them as irrelevant, supernumerary, not germane to her story of the other, truer Thrip—Thrip the undefeated—no one could hold her, the earth could not contain her.

She detested the weak, she despised the decrepit, failing Thrip. She shunned her, just as her daughters did. Leaving that weak, failed Thrip abandoned and exposed. She turned to the other Thrip, the one who had never been trapped or tricked or defeated, not by other ants and not—most emphatically and especially not—by her own body.

In her story she was all capable, independent, resourceful, solitary. She was everything she needed in and for herself. On her wings she flew from stem to stem, harvesting wild honeydew or stealing it from tame, stupid ants who snapped their mandibles in vain, she was there and gone again so fast. With wings and wit she escaped and hid, evading all her enemies, foiling and disgracing her earthbound rivals.

In some tellings of her tale she did not lay eggs, not a one, not at all. In others she did, at will, carelessly, letting them drop to the earth to take care of themselves. No, better yet, she slipped into other queens' nests, leaving her cuckoo eggs behind to be raised by their workers—never losing her wings, never crippled by her egg-swollen gaster, laying eggs at will, carelessly, or not at all, not caring about eggs at all anymore.

It was a wonderful story—the story she told herself of an ant named Thrip. The story went on and on. How Thrip escaped every trap, how she triumphed over tame fools, over the ants without wings.

The chamber was no longer there. It dropped away, out of awareness. She rose up on her wings, out of it, away from it away from her daughters away from the nest. It's far away below her now, tiny, tiny, insignificant, really. She can no longer perceive it, she has already forgotten it. It never really existed, it was there only for that other one, the false Thrip, the one who tore her wings and dug her hole and laid her eggs in it.

Her wings lift her and she is gone, gone again as on her nuptial flight and this time she will never come back to earth. Nothing, nobody, can catch her—she will never meet her end.

Long ago and yet to come, always and endlessly, a clever young ant queen named Thrip kept her wings and lived by her wits without any daughters at all.

VIII.
Postwar
Dystopian
Ant

I have at different times during several years observed in my artificial nests a most curious phenomenon among ants that had long lived amicably together. Several or many workers were seen standing around one ant as if holding a court of inquiry concerning this associate. Sometimes the associate is proscribed, sometimes rent limb from limb.
–Adele M. Fielde, "The Progressive Odor of Ants" (1905)

With the repudiation of omniscient narration, and in the face of inherent limitations in dramatized reliable narrators, it is hardly surprising that modern authors have experimented with unreliable narrators whose characteristics change in the course of the works they narrate ... Authors in the twentieth century have proceeded almost as if determined to work out all of the possible plot forms based on such shifts.
–Wayne C. Booth, **The Rhetoric of Fiction** (1961)

In the twentieth century, the dark side of Utopia—dystopian accounts of places worse than the ones we live in—took its place in the narrative catalog of the West and developed in several forms throughout the rest of the century ... Works such as Yevgeny Zamyatin's **We,** Aldous Huxley's **Brave New World,** and George Orwell's **Nineteen Eighty-Four** came to represent the **classical**, or canonical, form of dystopia. In a more diffused manner, works that shared the cultural ambience of the dystopian imagination (though often with irony or ambiguity) appeared on the margins of mainstream literature ... In the direction of popular culture, a more overt dystopian tendency developed within science fiction, and this resulted in "new maps of hell" as Kingsley Amis put it, that appeared after World War II and continues in the dystopian science fiction of recent years.
–Raffaella Baccolini & Tom Moylan, **Dark Horizons: Science Fiction and the Dystopian Imagination** (2003)

In their original form human societies bore no resemblance to the hive or the ant heap; they were merely packs. Civilization is, among other things, the process by which primitive packs are transformed into an analogue, crude and mechanical, of the social insects' organic communities ...
   Brave New World presents a fanciful and somewhat ribald picture of a society, in which the attempt to recreate human beings in the likeness of termites has been pushed almost to the limits of the possible.
–Aldous Huxley, **Brave New World Revisited** (1958)

Pleasure is an egg ... If I have an egg, what more can I want?
   In reduced circumstances, the desire to live attaches itself to strange objects.
–Margaret Atwood, **The Handmaid's Tale** (1985)

Introductions

They call me "Old Major" in that ugly new way they have, tagging an ant with a name like a bad smell. But I'm not old, only a bit over a year, which isn't old at all, not for a major. Still in my prime. But there are few of us majors left, maybe a score at most, which makes me stand out as individual whether I want to or not. A dozen or so of us still keep our posts in the guardrooms, just like in the old days. The rest are skulking in their hide-aways in the deep nest, hoarding juice and wheedling favors in exchange. A few died heroically in the war. *The fly* got the rest of them—got them in the final battle, when they couldn't flee or resist. That's a horrible death, makes me shudder to think about it, and I've seen all kinds of dying. I've been in an antlion's pit and lived to talk about it!

Just a chance of war, I guess, that I was spared, or maybe it was meant for something. Most things are chance, some things are meant.

Our meeting—that means something. I knew you at once—knew you for a true sister, the last of our kind. You didn't want to come away with me. I had to carry you off protesting. But you have found it out for yourself now, haven't you? When I touch you, when you touch me—don't your feelers and palps tell you we're alike? Different from all the others?

What's that? Oh, *the fly*, you don't understand about *the fly*. No of course you wouldn't. It must have happened to them at the final battle. That would be about the right time for it. A real bonanza for the flies. They smelled the battle from far off, probably. They could have met and mated right overhead, then come down and laid their eggs without a struggle—just one quick hard thrust to drill a hole and plant an egg in it.

Oh, their victims probably felt it, or maybe not. Maybe they just thought it was a blow or a bite from another ant. Even supposing they noticed the flies coming down at them, what could they have done? If they stopped to fight off the flies, then one of Regina's majors would have cut them down. That would have been the kinder death, of course. But no ant ever thinks of it like that. We all just want to live another day.

And that's why, if they knew, they kept quiet about it after the battle. After that first sharp jab, they probably didn't feel anything for a long time. But there was a maggot growing inside them all the while, feeding on their hemolymph at first, getting bigger and bigger while the poor ant got weaker and weaker, still hiding the truth of it from her sisters, from herself, maybe, too. At last the filthy thing tunneled into her head, to feed upon her brain. Then they must have known for sure what was happening, because most of them managed to stagger out of the nest before the end came.

That's common decency among ants, or used to be. If you know you're sick, really sick, you get out of the nest to die. So there were my fellow majors, staggering out of the nest, onto the mound and the stone, crazed by the maggot chewing away inside their heads. Still struggling to live, to stand upright. Then, when the filthy thing inside knows its time has come to pupate, it spits out some special poison it's got. The head falls right off, and there's the filthy maggot cocooned inside the head so tight and neat that you can't get at it.

I was on sentry duty at the time. I knew what was about to happen when my sisters started staggering around with their heads lolling and their feelers gibbering senselessly. I'd seen it before. But it's still an awful thing to witness. One head landed right at my feet. I couldn't help but recoil in disgust. Then I went after it, biting and spraying and doing all I could to get at that maggot. But you can't crack open the headpiece of a major. Some fly figured that out long ago and now we can't escape them.

So all those maggoty headpieces and headless corpses got dumped on the midden—with the flies safe and comfy inside their head-cocoons. Eventually they emerged, of course, and now they're out there, or rather their daughters and granddaughters are by now, searching for fresh victims to feed the next generation.

But *the fly* isn't going to get *me*. I'm done with patrolling and foraging. Why would I go out there, risking my life, for what—to feed a nursery full of drones? If it were for the Queen—of course I'd die for the Queen. But most of the good food is going to the drones, or worse yet, to the rove beetles. I'm not dying to feed drones and beetles.

What's that? Wasn't I in the battle—how did I escape? I was on a special mission. I led the raid on Regina's nest. I'll tell you all about it another time. I remember everything about the war. It was glorious.

Being young, being just a nursery ant, *you* might think it was the war that changed everything for the worse. I've heard some say that—in private, of course—nobody dares to say much of anything in public anymore. But the war itself, the death of however many hundreds of sisters, couldn't matter that much. Sisters die every day, you know. More come forth to take their place. The war was noble, the war was glorious—the war made us pure sisters, all of us, filled with devout fury, ready to die for the sisterhood. Nowadays every ant behaves as though *she* were the queen. If that's what peace is like, give me war!

No, it was what the war did to our Queen that changed everything. She couldn't keep the pace, she began to fade. Now it's almost as though she's no longer here. You have to go all the way to the royal chambers, almost, to find her essence, and even there it's just a thin, floating vapor—still lovely, you know. I like to linger in the gallery near her chambers and feel it. But not powerful now, not a force.

Maybe they call me Old Major because I remember the past, insist upon it. No one else wants to do that. I'm not that smart, never claimed I was, not like my poor lost sisters—*our* poor lost sisters, though you never knew them. But I remember. I must give you my memories, share them like honeydew, so they can be yours too. I remember our orderly, sisterly society, our many acts of beautiful sharing. That's what I remember most about the war—how we all came together, how—

You can go ahead and call me Old Major, if you like. If that's what it means—that I remember the old ways—then it's not an insult, not at all. I'd like to call you by a name, if you don't mind. A nice name, a good name. I'd like to call you "Young Keen."

Back when the Queen was healthy and strong, we didn't know about true sisters and half-sisters. Her essence marked us all—*made* us be sisters to one another. Oh, there were little hints and signs that nobody ever quite understood at the time. There were sisters you trusted, sisters you wanted to cuddle and groom with, and all the others you tried to avoid.

There were never many like *us*. We've always been an elite, all hunters and scouts and warriors. No cowering nurses or sneaky egg-layers among *us*. There were four of us sisters in the war together. Our leader—she died in the first great battle. She was so keen and quick—that's what did her in, I suppose. A restless kind of ant who never held still, never shirked her duty—and that's what it got her. I say she was our leader because she was our scout, but we had another sister who was as wise as they come. A wily old survivor. But she didn't survive the war, either. She saved my life once but I couldn't save hers.

I survived, along with a fourth sister, no older than a nursery ant, very young to be out there foraging and fighting. She was brave for her age, I had to respect her for that, but she was always a bit embarrassing. Said the strangest things, and stuttered too. They called her Spout, if you want to know the truth. She survived the war, then just disappeared.

No, not in one of the Desegmentations, though she's just the sort of ant who'd get picked for it. Poor silly thing never knew when to hold her peace. Not that I'm saying anything against the Desegmentations, mind you. That's about the only one of the new ways that makes sense to me. The royal attendants started them soon after the winter fast, when we were all still slow and dull with the cold. That first one woke us all up, I can tell you. Anyone who says I'm against the Desegmentations, that's just wrong. They're a check on the ones who hoard outrageous amounts of food and the ones—you know—who are just too different, who can't get along. I just wish they'd go after the egg-layers too. Those ants have it coming to them.

The Desegmentations are really the only thing that still brings us all together as sisters. It's the suspense—who will it be this time?—and maybe a little secret thrill of fear, followed by the pleasure and excitement when it's someone else, someone expendable and generally disliked, who gets it.

No, I think Spout must have perished during the winter fast—a horrible cruel winter, coming after the war, making everything so much worse. A lot of sisters froze, starved, got tossed out on the midden come spring. You probably wouldn't know about the winter—you were just a larva then, I guess—anymore than you'd know about the war.

I thought there was nothing left in the nursery but drones—and here you are. It gives me hope.

What—you're asleep? You're young yet, can't help it. Silly to be talking to myself. It's the sort of crazy thing that Spout would do. Poor silly Spout—now there's an ant who could never stop talking. Never cared for her like I did for the others, for Keen and Rank, but she was still one of us, a true sister. I went searching for her before the winter fast, thinking we'd cuddle up together, but I couldn't find her.

Guess I'll sleep a little too.

Scrobe's Nursery

"Sister, Sister! Young Keen!"

I woke up and you weren't there. I couldn't believe it. Why, *why* would you wander off—didn't you understand, even yet? We're true sisters, you and me, the last of our kind. We have to stick together, take care of each other.

So I went searching for you. I'm still searching.

I asked myself, where would an innocent young ant go off to by herself? The answer came easily enough: back to the nursery, of course. The young ones are all like that. It's not that way for majors, of course, nursing's not for us. We leave the nursery as soon as our cuticle firms up and we never go back. These days, you'd think they—the callows—would recognize the difference between caring for the Queen's own brood and looking after filthy drone eggs, but they don't. They'll still linger in the brood chambers as long as they can, trying to lick eggs and nurse larvae, even when the egg-layers keep chasing them away.

Oh, it occurred to me you might have your own little nursery secret that you were going back to protect. But I didn't really think so. You'd didn't have that drone-egg stink about you—and like I said, we've never been that kind.

I never have occasion to go to that part of the nest so I was shocked to find out how thick the rove beetles are down there, like flies on carrion, lying in wait, curling their ugly abdomens and wheedling for honeydew.

Some of them pretend to be ants, holding themselves the right way and touching your mouthparts the right way. So if you're not alert, you'll be feeding them honeydew before you realize—faugh!—it's another dirty, tricky beetle! Then the beast veers off before you can catch it. The others— the ones that are nothing like ants—just try to get you to lick their glands. Get you a little soft in the head that way, with their strange liquors, and then while you're feeling no pain they'll get you to give up your juice. The big ones, if they come upon a tender young ant in a lonely place, they'll get her stupefied and take *all* her juice—if you get what I mean. In the old days, we majors and the alpha workers always chased down the beetles and threw them out of the nest. Now it seems like there's more of them than of us.

"Pretty-pretty, feed me!"

"Sweet-sweet! Give sweet—take sweet!"

"Get away, you filthy beetles," I said to them. "I don't want your filthy liquors or your dirty kisses, and you're not getting any juice from *me*."

They just kept on jabbering in their beetle-speak. I've been told they understand a lot more than they let on. Or at least they can repeat anything said in their presence, which makes them useful spies. Another reason to keep chasing them off.

They have some beetle way of figuring out who's got food. I make sure I keep my crop full of good honeydew these days, when you never know what might happen, when you can't depend on your sisters to share anymore. But I'm careful not to store so much juice that it shows. So long as your gaster isn't stretched, nobody's going to notice if you've got an extra share or two stashed away. Except the beetles could sense it somehow and they kept on coming after me, making me—me and my plump crop—a bit more conspicuous than I cared to be. I kept stopping to snap at them till they backed off, finally, still coaxing and wheedling.

I had to push my way into the nursery. A couple of the bigger nurses tried to discourage me. I wouldn't be surprised if a rove beetle or two got in while I was arguing with them. Majors aren't for the nursery—but good luck trying to keep one out who really wants to get in. I got in all right, and then I went to work searching for you.

I remember the nursery the way it used to be—all the brood arranged neatly by age, in their proper chambers, all cared for equally by devoted nurses. Of course it's nothing like that now.

Now the brood are clumped in little piles—eggs and larvae all jumbled together, the big larvae biting the little ones and mostly getting away with it. Each pile under the care of a single nurse—its mother—who was generally doing a bad job of it. The ones who had the bigger piles of eggs and larvae were struggling, with a quiet sort of violence, to push away other sisters who kept trying to creep up to their brood pile, whether to steal something to eat or to sneak their own cuckoo egg into the pile, I couldn't tell you.

For a moment, though, they forgot their little rivalries, they were so upset by my presence. Some hissed and snapped at me as I wandered around, still searching, always searching, for you, my sister. But I think I was actually relieved not to find you there, in that big filthy stink of selfishness.

"Big Sister is watching you!" one of them called out after me, and I turned to find out what she meant.

I'd been making rounds starting at the edges of the chamber, where the less successful ants were guarding their tiny broods, figuring that's where you'd most likely be. I'd been gradually moving in closer towards the center, so I wasn't all that surprised to turn and find myself confronting a big, proud ant straddling a wriggling mass of well-fed drone larvae.

"Big Sister means *me*," she said in an ugly way, doing her best to intimidate me, as though I were a callow nurse and not a seasoned major. "What brings you into *my* nursery?"

"It's the Queen's nursery," I answered, "for the Queen's eggs." I knew who she was. The scared little drone-mothers call her Big Sister to flatter her, but everybody else just calls her Scrobe, on account of these peculiar feeler grooves she's got.

"Oh, well, if the Queen were ever to lay an egg again—that's very doubtful, of course—I'm sure we could accommodate her little brood. Egg-laying is open to all. Every ant may lay an egg in my nursery."

A nearby ant sniggered appreciatively, and I turned my indignant feelers on her. She had the same oversized carinae forming the same deep feeler scrobes—a sister, Scrobe had a true sister! "She can lay it but she can't keep it!" another ant added. She was a true sister too—that was obvious. Now I understood how Scrobe managed to dominate the nursery. She had two sisters to help guard the brood and get food for it—easy enough to do by grabbing eggs from the timid ones ranged around the edges of the chamber. None of them, probably, ever came to one another's aid. Each just hoped it would be someone else's egg that got taken, until inevitably it was her own.

"But everybody knows smelly old majors don't lay eggs," Scrobe continued, now advancing towards me, while her two sisters took her place in guarding the brood. "So what *are* you doing in my nursery?"

Well, I wasn't going to tell her that. None of her business if I'm searching for *my* true sister. "It's the Queen's nursery," I said again. But I found myself retreating.

That nursery stink—there's something about it that—. Now to you it's probably attractive. You're just an ordinary worker, and a young one at that.

To a major, it's repellant. I couldn't help backing away as that ant kept coming towards me. I certainly wasn't afraid of her. She might be intimidating to an ordinary nursery ant but she's still puny compared to a major.

When she'd gotten me off towards the entrance, she seemed satisfied with her work, just giving me one last smirk and then going back to her brood heap, guarded by her sisters all this while.

While I was edging my way out, I stumbled over a little ant who was clutching a single egg in her mandibles. She shuddered with fear, probably thinking I was going to snatch it from her. She didn't budge, though, just held tighter to her egg, as if to defend it with her life.

"Look here, you silly fool," I said, letting my irritation get the better of me. I wasn't feeling at all comfortable with how things were turning out. "You're wasting your time with that drone egg. He's not going to be ready to fly until midsummer—long after the nuptial flight takes place. So what are you going to do with him then? Let him fly off by himself to feed the birds?"

Drooping her head a bit, she touched her feelers to her egg, whether with shame or doting maternal love, I couldn't tell you.

"*Pleasure is an egg,*" she murmured, more to herself than to me, as if she were repeating something she had heard somewhere. "*If I have an egg, what more can I want?*"

I called her a fool once more, just for my own satisfaction, and got out of there. As soon as I stepped back into the gallery, the beetles were after me again.

"Me double-plus-good! Pet me, love me!"

Double-plus-ugly is what you are, I thought, but I was mostly wanting to get away. The beetles were homing in on my full crop again. The gallery was crowded now, and a few ants had paused out of curiosity, directing their feelers to figure out what the rove beetles were after so intently. I didn't like that. There are spies everywhere, and they say you could get denounced for Desegmentation for just a little extra juice—even though of course majors are *supposed* to store juice. It's one of our most important duties—*the* most important in peacetime.

Luckily enough for me, I spotted a worker who actually was feeding a beetle, while the ugly beast stroked her head and crooned and soothed her. She was cooing right back at it in the most disgusting way. "*Hug me till you drug me, honey, kiss me till I'm in a coma.*" And that's exactly what some of these beetles—the most dangerous kind—will do to you, if you're not careful.

"Here, you!" I said, with a loud squirt of indignation. "What do you mean by feeding that beast—don't you know we're short on food these days!"

She didn't let go of the beetle, just went on cuddling in the most brazen way.

"*In reduced circumstances, the desire to live attaches itself to strange objects,*" she quoted mysteriously.

"And just what does *that* mean?" I asked, still loudly, though I wasn't feeling quite so anxious now. The ants who had paused to check out the commotion were now showing more interest in her than in me, which was a good thing.

"Only that I wanted a pet," she said. "If I couldn't have an egg. Just something that was—mine."

"I'm *so* glad I'm a major," I answered with disdain, to show I knew a good line or two of my own. It was something I'd learned in the nursery ever so long ago.

So here I am alone, more alone than I can ever remember feeling. Thinking about how even that Scrobe has true sisters to help her and I have nobody. And talking to myself like a fool, like some crazy ant with a maggot in her head. But I'm not quitting. I found you once and I'm going to find you again.

When I do, this time I'll keep you.

Coming Together as Sisters

The message went round the nest, one ant running up to another, passing it on and on. A Desegmentation, in the great hall, everybody in attendance, hurry up now, don't be late.

I went, of course, and I made sure to get there as quick as I could, hoping I would find you. I never dreamed you wouldn't come. I just worried whether or not I'd be able to pick you out in such a mob. You'd have to come. Wouldn't be safe or wholesome not to. They say somebody counts or checks or something, though I don't understand how they could. The two younger royal attendants, the Delta and the Beta, are always at the entrance, making believe, maybe, that they are counting or checking or something like that. Or maybe just making sure nobody can get out until after the selection's been made.

So I made sure to get there early, meaning to stay out in the gallery as long as I could, scanning each wave of new arrivals in search of you. But the Royal Delta spotted me and said, "Hurry up, you—you're wanted inside." And the Royal Beta added, snapping her jaws at me, "Move it—you're blocking the way."

I'm a big ant, maybe the biggest of all, saving the Queen. I'm not used to being talked to like that, so disrespectful. I didn't answer back, though. After all, it's because I *am* big that I was blocking the way—and I *was* wanted inside, to take my place with the other majors. We're important. We're needed, more often than not, to deal with the bigger pieces, and even some of the little bits can be stubborn to crack. So we generally line up in the front, flanking the two older royal attendants, the big one, the Alpha, and the little one, the Gamma. The Queen is never there. I suppose she isn't up to it these days. But I do think she'd enjoy it, the festivity of having all of us, all her many, many daughters, come together in one place, not just for the winter fast.

I was disappointed that I didn't get a chance to search for you. But I figured I could try again when the Desegmentation was over.

I found myself side by side with an old comrade, one I'd done sentry duty with during the war. I'd never liked her much, to tell the truth. A cynical kind of ant. It was rumored she had mites, so naturally I'd avoided her. I hardly gave a thought to the mites now—I was so glad for a familiar presence. She must have felt the same. We crouched close together, touching each other with friendly feelers, getting reacquainted and catching up on things while the hall was still filling up.

"I always enjoy our coming together like this, all us sisters in one place. And the Queen's Alpha makes such wonderful speeches. How do you suppose that little bitty mite of ant ever got her place as Royal Gamma?" I said, just for a little friendly gossip, not meaning much by it.

"Hush," said my companion, "it's the Gamma who controls the whole show, everything. The Alpha does the talking but Gamma does the thinking.

And those two ants at the entrance answer to Gamma, the Beta as well as the Delta."

We were close to the Gamma, who might have had a feeler out on us. So I figured the cynical major wanted to flatter her.

"Oh, yes," I said, loudly, "the Queen's Gamma is a fine ant, a wonderful ant. I couldn't agree with you more."

"Hush!" she said again, more urgently. Well, there's no pleasing some. I didn't want to be unfriendly, though, so I told her what I'd found going on in the nursery. This interested her, I could tell. All ants love a bit of scandal.

"They ought to do something about those egg-layers," I complained. "Dozens of them, laying their drone eggs, trying to outdo each other, and all of them squabbling and gobbling up each other's eggs whenever they can. Then there's that big one—Scrobe, calls herself Big Sister. She's got the biggest brood of nasty drone grubs and she's grabbing up every bit of food she can get to keep them fed. Now there's an ant who needs to get desegmented!"

"Oh, they'll never do that," she said mysteriously. "You're only a traitor when you're weak. Scrobe's not weak."

"Scrobe's the biggest traitor there is!" I said indignantly, but then I thought about it a bit. The ants who got selected for Desegmentation did tend to be a puny lot—old, small, unpopular.

"It'll never be us, at least," my companion said, as if to make peace, or maybe just to get the last word.

"We're too important," I agreed.

"Too hard to yank and hack us to bits," she came back. "The Gamma wouldn't take a chance on a bad show. No matter how much juice we hoard." She slapped her gaster lightly into mine to let me know she'd detected my bulge—as I'd noticed hers, though of course I'd never be so rude about it.

So there you go. Just as mean and cynical as ever, if not worse. Well, nobody ever claimed an ant gets sweeter with age. I was sorry now I'd been so friendly and I started worrying about the mites. But then it started, and in the excitement I forgot all about this sister and her cynicism.

The Royal Alpha stood up tall to make her speech. A fine speech as always, about sisters coming together in solidarity, standing by each other, sharing and sacrificing. Caring only for each other, for our home, and most of all for—our Queen, our Mother. And it was beautiful how she put it. No one could touch the Alpha when it came to making a good speech. Her modulations, every time she came to the bit about our Queen, our Mother, and she repeated that a lot, were so eloquent, so moving, that all around ants were wiping their feelers with emotion. Only, she continued, modulating so exquisitely from tenderness to sternness—the transition was thrilling—only there were some ants who wouldn't share, who were in it for themselves—not for their sisters—not for their Queen, their Mother.

There are the ones who shirk their duty, Alpha continued, the sternness and majesty of her tones ever deeper, richer, more thrilling. There are those who will not forage, although it is their time in life to do so. There are some who hoard food—I half expected the cynic to give me another slap on the gaster but even she was too awed for that—there are some who squander food on rove beetles and other parasites, Alpha continued, and I wanted to cheer for that one, only the silence was so great all around us. An awed, terrified, paralyzed silence. Who was it going to be this time?

But the worst traitors of all, Alpha continued, the worst traitors of all are—the egg-layers!

"So there!" I hissed softly, nudging my companion.

These ants—I will not call them sisters—steal food not just from their fellow workers, but from the Queen's lawful brood. They betray their sisters, their Mother, their Queen—for what—for drones, *their drones*.

The older ants—the shirkers and hoarders—began to feel safe now, so they murmured and tapped their forelegs in approval. The Queen's Beta and Delta had slipped quietly into the crowd, stalking their victim. With perfect timing, they seized her in their powerful young jaws. She gave one shriek of fear but didn't try to fight. The crowd parted as they dragged her forward, then closed up again, everybody now pushing and jostling to get closer, to get their piece. Fear gives way to a panicked jubilation—not me, it's not me this time, it's *her*—Let's get her! Traitor! Egg-layer!

Her legs and feelers were seized by the lucky ones in front, who tugged and bit until she began to desegment. One ant near me got off with most of one feeler, all but the scape, but she wasn't allowed to keep it. One segment per ant is our rule. So as she moved away from the traitor with her prize, other ants pushed up to her to take a piece.

Until the Desegmentations began, I'd never realized how many parts there are to an ant. How many parts to her legs, for example? Oh, you say, that's easy, let me see … and doing some rapid arithmetic, you'd probably say there's five to each of her six legs, making thirty in all. But that's wrong, because each tarsus has its own six segments, including the pretarsus, and then there's the claws and spurs to count too—so you end up with seventy-eight parts to be shared out of just the legs. The mouth and palps are really intricate too. Shiver all the mouthparts into bits, and you'll end up with another fifty-two pieces, if you do it right.

By now all the appendages have been yanked free and subdivided. And that's when we majors step forward—to deliver the death blow, of course, but more importantly to desegment the head, trunk, waist and gaster, as fairly, neatly and completely as possible, to yield the maximum number of pieces. Not every sister will be able to walk away with a souvenir, but I've never heard that any complain or try to snatch a piece that doesn't belong to them. It's a beautiful act of sharing, about the last we have left, certainly the only one you can rely on. The tender juicy bits—the crop, fat body and ovaries (if present)—are not given out. That's because the juices of her delinquent daughters naturally belong to the Queen. The royal attendants drink them up and bear them away to her.

"So there!" said my cynical companion triumphantly, while we were at our work. She flicked her feelers at the ovaries. They were small and withered. But I already knew this ant was no egg-layer because I'd recognized her. It was the ant who'd been feeding the rove beetle.

Well, I felt a little sorry for her, and I wondered if I'd gotten her into trouble. Still, she shouldn't have been feeding beetles. And she would have been an egg-layer if she could—she said as much herself. Mistakes do happen. I remember in the war, how easy it was to bite a sister when you meant to aim your jaws at the enemy.

I guess the Desegmentations *are* a sort of war, waged inside instead of outside. They bring us together, just as the real war did. Maybe the royal attendants figured that out. It's a new kind of us against them, with a different enemy each time.

I miss you, Young Keen, but I still believe I will find you. I believe the Queen will recover her health and begin to lay eggs again. I believe these things because I must. I don't want to live for myself alone, but for others.

Nothing Doing

I went up to take my turn at sentry duty. I still do that, you know. Still do my duty in the guardrooms.

I could tell, as I moved upwards, that it was a fine glorious spring day out there. A little quickening of tempo—sisters standing a little taller, moving more briskly—told me that. The sun beaming down on the stone was warming the whole upper nest. A fine day at last for the foragers to harvest some good food, whether sweet or meat. A fine day too for taking a little snooze in a guardroom. I hurried up a little, lifting my legs with pleasurable anticipation. When things are bad, an ant can still take pleasure in a fine warm day, providing she doesn't actually have to go *out there*. That was for my partners.

My partners—well, all the majors have partners now among the foragers. A sort of private sharing plan. My partners deposit their surplus juice with me and I hold it for them in case of a shortage. That sort of thing would never happen in the old days, of course. But these days ... even the most decrepit, beaten-down forager takes offense at the idea of knocking herself out to feed Scrobe's drones. And once you give your food away, you can't be sure you'll get any back when *you* need it. There's just no trust these days, I'm sorry to say. So it's only prudent to bank a little juice with a discreet, reliable major. I don't see anything wrong with it. It's the majors who are lurking in the deep nest, so bloated they can't budge under their own power, not ever doing their turn as sentries—those are the shameless, selfish ones.

"What's doing?" I asked the major I was relieving, just for something to say.

"Pretty dry," she answered, as she made off.

"Huh?" I didn't get that—but she was already gone. It wasn't dry at all. I didn't need to probe to realize that the ground outside was delightfully moist. It must have rained recently, maybe last night, and now the sun was sparkling on the damp gray stone overhead. Perfect weather—can't ask for better. I turned toward my fellow sentry, wondering whether she had overheard. But her feelers were folded back on her head in a peaceful doze. I settled down and got comfortable too. My partners would nudge me awake when they came back with their crops full of juice.

It was late when I came to—the day had gone dim and chilly. A pair of smelly old foragers were cleaning themselves up nearby. They took off when I came towards them—not my partners. I prodded my fellow sentry.

"Huh?" she said, coming to.

"What's going on?" I asked. "Where are all the foragers?"

"They've quit, most of them. No one wants to go out there anymore, not to feed a nursery full of drones."

"But—that's not possible. The nest needs fresh food every day. The Queen—"

"Oh, the Queen! But no one much believes in the Queen anymore."

I gaped at that—couldn't find words. But she just went on as if not noticing.

"So your partners quit, eh?" she asked in a confidential whisper. "Tough luck. Only two of mine are still going out, and they'll probably quit soon too. Nobody wants to do the work anymore, not when you can get by with harvesting grass root honeydew instead."

That news took me back a bit. I repeated, a bit stupidly, "Root honeydew?"

"You'll probably find your partners there, in the tunnels where they herd the root aphids. But maybe it's better not to find them. They may be wanting to make a withdrawal instead of a deposit!"

She picked herself up to go.

"You can't leave!" I said. "We haven't been relieved. Who'll guard the nest against enemies?"

"What enemies?" she answered, "We are our enemy. Nothing's going to try to come in here except maybe more of those oozy rove beetles." She wiped her feelers and stretched herself, shaking loose her leg joints. "Or maybe something that *eats* rove beetles—that'd be a pleasant change. Anyway, I've had my little nap. I'm off."

I didn't leave. I stayed at my post until another sister came to relieve me, a major who wasn't yet in the know. I didn't tell her anything. Let her find out for herself.

"Pretty dry," I said, when she asked.

A Dead End

I wandered around a bit, searching for you as always, still hoping I'd find you—or that you'd find me. I can't believe you meant to desert me. You wandered off and something happened. Maybe you're in trouble, you need me. So I keep searching.

I had turned out towards the tunnels where the root aphids are put to pasture. I was feeling a bit empty by now and thinking I might find some of my partners there—hoping they wanted to make a deposit and not a withdrawal, of course.

It was never a place I'd had much occasion to visit in the past. The tunnels were more extensive than I remembered, but still very narrow, meant only for the smallest ants, the ones who aren't worth much even as foragers. I bumped into a lot of the foragers passing through, some with bulging crops, but none that I knew. I realized I didn't really care if I found any of my partners. There's nothing very appetizing about root honeydew, not unless you're really hungry.

I wandered along, then realized I wasn't bumping into foragers anymore. It was an old tunnel, I suppose, the roots gone dry and useless. I started to turn back, when I detected a presence ahead—another ant, a sister. She was perfectly still except for the slow motion of her feelers, as if she was aware of my presence too, but didn't want to make herself known. As soon as I stepped forward, I knew who it was.

"Sister, Sister!" I cried out, "Young Keen!"

But you weren't there. Nobody was there. The tunnel came to a dead end just a few paces further along.

Found and Lost

Things seemed bad enough around here until they got worse. The foragers have mostly quit, except for harvesting root aphid honeydew—poor food, unless you're hungry and can't get better. Nowadays lots of ants *are* hungry: the young ones, who don't know how to forage; the egg-layers, desperate to feed themselves and their drone grubs, but not desperate enough to leave the nursery. Any egg-layer who leaves the nursery will come back to find her sisters have devoured her young, whether egg or larva or pupa. No one ever used to eat pupae, but now they will, for spite if not for nourishment. I've known plenty of sisters who were mean or lazy, but none of them ever matched the egg-layers for spite. They seem to get more pleasure from destroying a sister's brood than nursing their own. Maybe even they realize it's too late in the season to be laying drone eggs. What we need is more workers, but—

Some are saying that the Queen will never lay again. I don't believe that, I won't. She just needs time to recover her health, after the strain of the war, the extra brood, the terrible hard winter.

The Desegmentations are daily now but they don't seem to make a difference. No one behaves as she should. We're only together as sisters, sharing as sisters, when we're tearing another sister apart. Today it was an ant accused of food hoarding, but when we majors sliced her up, her crop was almost dry. She had a bit of fat on her because she was young, that's all.

I didn't say anything. It wouldn't be wise. But the cynical major couldn't help herself. She poked me and whispered, "So maybe she wasn't hoarding, but now she'll *be* hoarded, eh?"

I don't know what she meant by that, and I didn't ask. It's better not to ask questions. Rove beetles and other spies everywhere. Suppose the answer to your question is treasonous—then your question is too, isn't it? Anyway, it just draws attention to be asking questions, and nobody wants that.

After the Desegmentation was over, I went wandering again, into out-of-the-way corridors and corners. Mostly I wanted to avoid my partners until I could figure out how to refill my crop. I could always bully some aphid herder into giving up her juice, but my partners had deposited good stuff. They didn't expect to be paid back in root honeydew.

I suppose I'd used up a lot of juice wandering in search of *you*, my sister.

But I wasn't thinking of you just then. Still talking to you, as though you were there, but not actually thinking of you.

Preoccupied with the state of my crop, not really noticing my surroundings, I'd gotten myself into some derelict half-abandoned corner of the nest—an unhealthy smelling place. I was just about to turn and retrace my steps, when I caught a hint of a figure crouching, hiding, just out of feeler reach.

"You—Sister! Young Keen!"

I gave chase. I wasn't going to let you get away again. Majors aren't all that quick on their legs but I ran fast with love, with longing, with anger and rage and hurt. Longing and fury blended together like some sweet poison. I cornered you. I caught you up in my great mandibles.

"What have you to say for yourself now, Sister?"

You said nothing, only recoiled, and I realized how tight I must be holding you. I put you down.

You touched me on my mouthparts and asked for food in a polite, formal fashion, as if I were a stranger.

I fed you.

I fed you when you asked, my sister. Because I promised to take care of you, and I always will.

Did you notice, when you were done feeding, that my crop was now emptier than yours? Did you care?

No. Because all you said was: "Can you get me some meat?"

Then you caressed my head as though—as though—you felt sorry for me. Not as though you cared—only because you knew I was puzzled and hurt and angry. You would not answer my questions—would not even let me ask them. That one touch was all the answer, all the reward, you were willing to give me. It would have to do.

It will have to do.

As if I had said yes—and I hadn't, only I hadn't said no—you said you would meet me there again tomorrow.

So: I know your secret now, Sister. You've got your own drone egg, or eggs. Actually, you must have at least one larva or you wouldn't be wanting meat. I suppose my questions *have* been answered, without being asked. It was smart of you to find a hiding place for your brood. In the Queen's nursery the egg-layers are all devouring each other's babies, out of hunger or spite or both. You wouldn't have had much of a chance there. Somehow you figured that out in advance. We've always been a smart bunch. Rank was the smartest ant of all time, and Keen was really smart too. Spout was plenty odd but nobody ever called her stupid.

So: I'm to risk my life to feed drones after all. Because there's no other way to get meat these days, except to forage on one's own, as solitary as a fly.

At least it's for my own nephew. Or nephews.

I wonder how many there are.

Evened the Score

The major up in the guardroom thought I was there to relieve her. "Hey!" she said, as I walked on past her, "Hey, where are you going!"

"Hey yourself," I said. "Stretching my legs." And I sauntered on out, as though there were no such creatures in the world as starlings and toads and antlions and decapitating flies. As though I was just taking a stroll. Even though I might quite possibly die out there, my sister.

But it wasn't my time. I hadn't gone all that far before I found my prize— a young linden looper, fallen out of the tree and wriggling like mad, as if to let me know it was there for the taking. I put an end to its wriggling, picked it up and started running straight home.

I shouldn't have done that, of course. I was excited, that's all. In the old days that's how we always did it. If you found something good you could manage somehow, anyhow, to carry back on your own, then that's what you did. It meant less time outside, where it's dangerous, and it meant your sisters could help you carve it up in safety, inside the nest, congratulating you on your fine catch and listening to you tell your story.

I suppose I wanted to tell *you* about it, Sister, knowing how you would want to listen and how you'd admire the big fat prey I got for you. I didn't think about how I was going to lug it past the sentries and all the nurses and rove beetles and spies and everyone else who'd want their cut of such fresh, juicy meat.

I started out fast but soon I was staggering from the bulk of the thing. I think I must have ended up going in circles. It was too hard to tell which way I was going, and of course it's been a long time since I'd been outside. Most of the old trails have been obliterated and I didn't know the new ones. I was getting tired, but I kept up the struggle, turning this way and that to force my way through the grass and the gravel with my burden clenched in my jaws.

Then—I got stuck. What was it now—what had gone wrong? I moved over a bit, and tugged again—still stuck. Tried again—almost got it free—then stuck fast. Maybe I was just tired. I put it down for a moment.

Oh, now I knew what the problem was. A cobweb! Not a fresh one, and luckily no longer occupied, but still sticky enough to catch hold of my looper.

Well, that *was* discouraging. If I couldn't pull it loose, I'd have to do without my trophy and just drink up as much of the juice as I could hold.

A little movement nearby scared me half out of my wits. Was there a spider still at the web after all? No—it was another forager—one of Scrobe's true sisters. That couldn't be chance. I wasn't close enough to the nest for that. She must have followed me out, spying on me.

"Oh, Sister," I said, all innocently, "you're just in time! Help me with this looper that's too big for me. If you'll just catch hold of the other end, we can carry it between us without too much fuss."

Well, she did what I asked and blundered right into the web. Squeaking with fear she writhed back and forth, getting herself tangled up even worse. What does a nursery ant know about spider silk!

Or about spiders. Because it turned out there was one still working that spot after all. It was fresh silk that held her fast. While the spider (probably disappointed to find its latest tidbit was only an ant) wrapped her up in silk, I went ahead and drank the juice of my looper.

"Nice day outside," I said to the major on duty, who was too astonished to notice my bulge.

I knew you would want to hear all about it, Sister. How I got such a big juicy bit of prey for you. How I evened the score with Scrobe, so now it's one sister each.

Only you didn't.

You said: "Thank you."

You said: "Can you bring some more?"

You said: "Please don't follow me."

Once Again

"Can you bring some more?" I know now that you don't much care how I do it or at what risk. Just do it, just bring it, that's all. So I came back with more, not saying anything, not volunteering any information, since you don't want to know, aren't interested.

It could be I went scouting, this time, through those abandoned root aphid pastures. A callow nursery ant might think that's perfectly safe. After all, you're still underground, still in the nest. Well, it's not. Once ants move out, all sorts of other creatures move in—some dangerous, some tasty. Could be I found a white grub, which is both, and I managed, with my special skill and cunning, to bite off a big piece of it without getting bit myself.

More likely I went out of the nest again. The sentries probably thinking I had a maggot in my head and was just taking longer to die than usual. Can't expect to find a nice fresh looper every day. This time probably I had competition.

You're young, you've never been outside. You might think that if so few foragers are going out of the nest these days, there'd be food just lying around, waiting to be harvested. Well, that's wrong. Instead, there's much less, because our competitors—our own kind, the pavement ants, the turf-grass ants, the acrobat ants with their spiny backs and pointy gasters, the little cowardly thief ants—have all begun to poach our territory. I might have to grab a bit and run for my life—or fight them off—in order to bring you some more meat for your brood, Sister.

A big patch of something fatty, right on our nest stone! These things just show up sometimes, maybe dropped there by a bird—who knows? Of course it belongs to us—it's right on our stone. But an anthill loses territory the moment its workers stop patrolling and scouting. Right there on our own stone were the pavement ants, swarming all over that fatty stuff.

I'm lots bigger than they are. Even you are bigger than they are. But there were already twenty or thirty of them swarming over the food, and they'd swarm over me too, if I tried to get some for you.

So instead I found a spot on the underside of a nice shady leaf that gave me a good view of the action, and I just waited. Didn't have to wait long, actually.

More pavement ants showed up, from another colony this time. Both sides sent for reinforcements, and pretty soon there was a full-scale battle taking place. Now I could make my way safely to the grease and lap up as much as I wanted.

Could be that's how it happened, but you'll never ask, you'll never know.

In fact, my crop—so much bigger than yours—still had a good load of looper juice. I didn't go anywhere. I just idled and waited for you to come back for more.

This time, I didn't say anything to you. I made you no promises when you said "Please don't follow me." So I did follow you, lurking well behind, as you pursued a winding way through disused corridors and musty chambers, pausing and hiding when other ants approached, like a guilty one, like a criminal.

I followed you through secretive back passages all the way to the upper nest, to the abandoned root aphid corridor where once before I thought I had found you. I followed you all that way—then you were gone. I went further along the passage you had taken until I came upon a dead end, nothing.

There's something going on here that I just don't understand.

So I crouched down in thought, if it could be called that. Sheer blank bewilderment is what it was. But then I caught the hint of a presence—you were still here after all! There must be some little niche nearby where you had hidden yourself, just in case I followed, and I went right on past you like a fool. That was clever of you. But I can be clever too.

So I held still, as if I knew nothing, as if I were dropping off into a doze and then—I leapt out at you! I missed, but I got enough of a feeler trace that I stopped in surprise, not giving chase.

It wasn't you. It was an older, bigger ant—a worker, but much bigger than you, as big as the Royal Alpha herself, although of course it couldn't have been the Alpha.

There's spies everywhere—everybody says so. Only I thought they were just snooping on hoarders and shirkers, listening in on conversations and the like. Why follow me all that way? Was I the one being spied on, or was it you, Sister, you and my young nephews?

Good thing you slipped away from me like you did. Wouldn't want to lead a spy right to you. I'll be more careful next time.

Almost Back to Normal

Now my crop really was empty. I'd been mostly successful at avoiding my partners, but I did have to pay up to two of them. They were surprised to get bug juice instead of good blossom and bud honeydew like they had put on deposit with me. But I said to them, what are you complaining about? Count yourself lucky—*other* majors are paying back *their* partners with grass root honeydew. They didn't say anything to that—they knew it was true.

I wasn't eager to go back out of the nest. And I kept worrying and wondering about that spy—was she still on my trail? I tried hiding in corners and doubling back, and a couple of times I thought there *was* someone there who halted or veered off. But of course when you're a big ant like me, the stalker has the advantage. The spy—if she was there—wasn't fooled by my trying to conceal myself in cracks and niches that were too small to hold me.

I was loitering in the upper nest, still making up my mind about going out again. It's quiet up there these days. There's just the sentries dozing in the guardrooms—those who still take their turn—and a few foragers too old and set in their ways to quit foraging. All the others are squeezing into the root honeydew tunnels, pretending to be busy. And it's quiet because–because sisters have died and because no new sisters have come forth to take their place. That scares me—it scares everybody. We've got all the drones and rove beetles we could want, but we have no new sisters coming from the nursery. And now you can feel it, the vacancy, the empty places not being filled. So maybe I can sort of understand about the ones crowding together in the root aphid tunnels, pretending they're needed there—

Maybe I dozed off a bit because I came to all of a sudden with a startle. Ants were streaming out of the nest, running right over me in their haste. "War—a battle!" I thought with a quick surge of joy—but, no, that was wrong. They were being chased out by younger, stronger sisters, who were themselves being chased upwards by still younger ants—each slapping and snapping at the gaster of the one in front of her. A few—panicked into courage at the prospect of being forced out to forage—turned on their assailants. Pretty soon the guardroom was a writhing mob of dueling ants. One spreads her feelers to block her opponent from heading back into the deep nest, then starts pounding her head until she crumples into a submissive crouch—only to get pounded and bitten worse until she finally gives up and gets out. Others compel their rivals out with a series of ferocious jerks and snaps—little by little the losers keep giving ground until there was no where to go but—*out there*. The math was easy enough for anyone to work through: if *she* goes out, then *I* stay in.

I moved out of the scrimmage as soon as I could and joined my fellow sentry on the sidelines. We figured it out between us.

The spite and the famine in the nursery had boiled over into an uprising. Scrobe and her true sister had combined with a few of the biggest nurses to chase the others off their brood piles and out of the nursery altogether. Now it truly was Scrobe's nursery. There were no other young workers capable of laying more eggs.

These bereft drone-mothers were the same ones I'd found trembling over their precious egg piles, each hoping that somehow her little ones would be spared. They'd all been too stupid or selfish to cooperate and fight back. Once they lost their place in the nursery, though, they got over their meekness. They were going to stay in the deep nest no matter what. So each found an older or smaller ant to push and shove and bully into moving upwards. And that's how it went.

The bullies did their job so well that now we had a surplus of foragers, which wasn't such a good idea, because a third of them, probably, will be dead within a week. Send out just a few new ones at a time and they've got a better chance to learn some skills from their elders, the cagey old survivors. Still, we need the food. We need more workers too, but food comes first. When they're dead—but let's not think about that. The Queen will lay more eggs. There's still time to start a summer worker brood.

So things are almost back to normal. All I had to do was settle down and wait for the foragers to come back, then pick out the ones carrying prey juices. I could have done with some sweet for myself, Sister, but I know you need meat for my nephews.

There are no partners anymore. Most of the ants who went out today were terrified novices, all on their own. There are no rules anymore, except the primal rule that the bigger ant wins. I'm so glad I'm a major, Sister, glad for your sake as well as mine.

Juice always flows from smaller to bigger and from older to younger. That's the natural order of things. But in the old days we used to be polite about it. "It's your turn, your time of life," we'd say, nudging the old ones out to forage. And then it was "please" and "thank you" to get the juice they brought back in. But that's all gone and forgotten now. So when a returning forager acted like she was reluctant to disgorge her juice, like she was saving it for someone else, I backed her up against the wall and rapped her with my feelers until she gave it up.

That's what we've come to. It's the selfishness of the egg-layers, spreading until it infects us all. But I got you your bug juice, Sister, and that's all that matters.

I've been thinking. It was wrong of me to follow you. Now that I know there's a spy trailing me, I won't try that again. My first plan was the right one, and I don't know why I didn't stick to it.

Next time you won't leave me. Next time I'm going to keep you.

Not at All What I Thought

Now I know, now I really know. I imagined you. You aren't my sister at all.

You had the scent of a true sister on your cuticle—that's what fooled me. That, and my loneliness. I do have a sister but it's not you. It's Spout.

This time, after I gave you the juice, I grabbed you and held you, not letting go until you gave in and told me everything.

You were very stubborn. You kept still for a long time. But I just held onto you, hardly even shaking you. You'd have to give in, eventually, and you did. You told me everything.

I wish you hadn't told me everything. I like my version better.

You aren't my sister. There are no nephews. You and Spout are hoarding all that juice to feed some big fat larva that Spout just found somewhere. Some other ant, some stranger, gave Spout this oh-so-special egg, and now you are risking your lives—and mine!—to nurse it in secret.

You do realize, of course, you could get desegmented for this. I'd be awfully sorry if that happened, even though you're not my sister, but you really shouldn't be doing this.

Oh, yes, I know, you told me. Spout says it's the Queen's own egg, that it's a royal one. Then why are you hiding it?

She's crazy—you don't realize that. She's been your nurse, your only nurse, so naturally, or unnaturally, you believe everything she tells you.

Spout was always crazy about eggs. She got chased out of the nursery too young and she never got over it. That's why she saved you from being eaten, of course. And it's why she's saving this larva and making up preposterous stories about it. She'd nurse a beetle grub or a caterpillar if there was nothing else to be cared for. And she'll convince herself—and you—that this foundling, this cuckoo, is the Queen's own egg, even though everybody knows the Queen stopped laying long ago.

Oh, it's clear to me now. Spout got that egg from Regina's nursery, the same place she got you, and she'll say anything to keep it.

It occurs to me that you might know exactly where this mysterious egg came from—that you might be protecting your own true sister and playing Spout and me for fools. But I wouldn't like to think that of you. I'm so used to caring about you, and talking to you as though you were here, that I hardly know how to stop.

You told me everything, more than I wanted to know. Then you asked: "Will you still help us?"

I said: "I don't know."

The Alpha Will Know What to Do

I thought and thought and finally I decided: It's too much for me. I'll go to the Royal Alpha. The Alpha will know what to do. If it's the Queen's own royal larva, a princess of our line, then the Queen will acknowledge her, and the royal attendants will ensure the very best nursing care—better than you and Spout can provide, hiding in dirty neglected corners, full of mold and disease.

Oh, I know what Spout told you. But that's absurd. Scrobe, maybe, but I don't think even Scrobe would harm a royal larva—why would she? And the Queen's Alpha can prevent that from happening.

Maybe—oh, I hate to think it, but I keep coming back to it—maybe it's a cuckoo, a survivor, like you, from Regina's brood chambers. And you know it—so you take advantage of poor crazy Spout's obsession with eggs to raise your cuckoo sister. Well, I'd hate to think that, but of course it would explain a lot that—you ... I ...

No, it's too much for me. I'll go to the Alpha. She'll know what to do.

But she wasn't there. No one was there. In the old days the royal chambers were crammed to bursting with ants, all the young ambitious ones hustling to get a place, all the nurses coming for a taste of the Queen's essence. Now it was empty, void.

Not quite. I ventured in, swiveling my feelers from side to side, until I found her. In the rear of the smaller, inward chamber—an ant, a very large ant, all by herself. Her essence grown so weak, so faint, that I had to taste her with my palps before I knew her for sure.

"My Queen, my Mother," I said. Not at all the way the Alpha says it. In my own way, feeling surprise and shock first, then sorrow, "My Queen, my Mother."

She stirred, touched my mouthparts with her feelers, then recoiled. Recoiled because she didn't know me, because she was afraid. But I'm her daughter! Surely her touch told her that.

I touched her again, caressingly, soothingly. "I'm your daughter," I said, "Mother, Mother. I'm one of your daughters, one of your many loving, admiring daughters." She was very hungry, very weak. She took a drop from me, a single drop, and then she was gone again, sunk back into a deep trance, where no word or touch of mine could reach her.

And then I understood many things I did not understand before. That Mother is very ill, that she will not recover. I sat there for a while beside her, touching her still form, working it all out.

Sister who is not my sister, I said when we met that I would tell you about my special mission, about what I did during the last battle.

I led the surprise assault on the enemy nest. They had left few defenders at home, never expecting we would dare take the offensive. We cut our way through a ring of fat, infirm majors at the entry. Regina's nurses scattered in terror, some rescuing brood, others rescuing only themselves. My sisters, Spout among them, followed the egg scent to the nursery and seized all the brood they could find as spoils. Did she tell you that? Perhaps she carried you herself, carried you back from Regina's nest and hid you so you wouldn't be eaten. She never left off being a nursery ant, bringing up a secret brood of cuckoos and aliens and interlopers.

I went on, by myself, to the royal chambers. The scent of the enemy queen was overwhelming, filling the nest with her foreign egg reek. It was a scent that maddened, that compelled, that overcame every other sense. But I remembered what I had come to do. I followed the scent down, down, through strange twisting corridors, all the way down to the royal chambers. Only one attendant had remained to guard the entrance, and she didn't put up much fight. The enemy queen had been abandoned by her daughters, just like Mother now.

Regina scented me, she knew what was coming. She cried out, calling for help to her attendants, to the Alpha that was dead and the Beta, Delta and Gamma who had deserted her. But I was quick about it. I struck just once, right at the neck, and that was the end of her. Never spoke of it much, never boasted. Killing Regina killed her colony, the survivors eventually coming over to us, begging and wheedling like rove beetles, getting accepted, most of them, and becoming fellows with us. Hard to tell them apart now. Certainly I didn't know *you* for Regina's daughter.

You're not my sister and you're not here. I'm talking to myself, or I wouldn't be telling the story at all. Because there's something new that's been added, that wasn't part of the story before.

I had never approached a queen before that day. That's not for majors. So the size of the enemy queen—well, it was hard not to crouch down before her in fear and amazement. But I did it all the same, I killed her, I struck off her head with one quick blow.

And now—after touching my own mother, after giving her food, I know something about her that none of her other daughters could ever know. I am the only ant who knows this thing.

I will keep my mother's secret forever.

Too Obvious

Something has happened—something very disturbing—as if I didn't have troubles enough!

As I was leaving the Queen's chambers, I cannoned right into another ant—the spy! We were both startled but she was the first to recover her wits—I suppose because she's so used to sneaking. She ran her feelers over me.

"You've fed her—good," the spy said. "I didn't find you here and you didn't find me here. Remember that."

I started to protest at that, remembering my innocence and my motive for coming. She interrupted me.

"I know who you are. I know your sister and what she's doing."

I was speechless with confusion. That ought to prove to you—if anything could—that you and Spout are nursing a cuckoo. And now you've gotten *me* into trouble with a spy!

I was terribly flustered but I went up to the guardrooms to do my turn as sentry all the same. It's comforting to have a routine, and on a nice warm day the upper nest always feels like my right place to be. Things are mostly back to normal there, or what passes for normal, now that foragers are going out again.

"Where have *you* been?" said the major I was relieving. "You weren't at the Desegmentation."

"Must have slept through it—in a corner somewhere." I made that one up pretty quick. Now at least I understood why the royal chambers had been deserted. "Anyone I know?"

"I would say so!" she said darkly, drawing it out, knowing she had my full attention. "It was one of us."

"No!" I said. "No! You mean they caught one of the ones who've been hiding out in the deep nest, hoarding juice?"

"Oh, they said she'd been hoarding juice, but that's not where they caught her. It was your special friend, the one you're always chummy with at the Desegmentations."

"They *called it* hoarding juice," she went on, thoroughly enjoying herself, knowing she was giving me a scare that was even bigger than her own must have been. None of us ever thought a major would be—could be—deseg-mented. "But it could be she got it for talking too much— Hey, where are you going? It's my turn to be relieved!"

"Yeah? Well, it could be you talk too much," I said, as I went off.

I started to detect a pattern, a spider web spun all around me, closing in. The pathetic little worker outside the nursery who I'd talked to—deseg-mented. The cynical major who was my partner during the ceremonies—desegmented. Then that spy following me, threatening to expose me and you and Spout, when I confronted her. I'm next—if they catch me.

So I guess I'm on your side now, Sister who is not my sister, your side and Spout's.

Only I still don't know how to get there.

Right now I need to hide out in some little corner somewhere. Wait till a few other Desegmentations take place, wait till they've forgotten about me and gone after someone else. Plenty of other ants who can be desegmented. So I started slipping through those back passageways and disused chambers that I'd come upon when I was following you.

I was all alone, except I wasn't. Little fresh traces of life, sometimes a rustling or tapping ahead of me, behind me, to this side or that. If I went for the spot where something had moved, there'd be nobody there. It was a bit unnerving. At first I thought it was beetles and maggots and nematodes and other nasty things that sneak around in dirty neglected corners. But sometimes I'd catch the scent trace of ants, other fugitive sisters, who heard me coming and got out of the way.

Well, what can I do? I'm a major, I'm big. I wouldn't make a good spy. Not like that spy who's always following me.

For the first time in my life, I began to wish I was littler, like you, or even smaller.

While I was searching for my hiding place, I came upon one of those majors who've been lurking in the lower nest with their stores of stolen juice. She was so bloated she couldn't slip away and hide from me. In fact, I don't believe she could have left that musty little hole of a chamber if she'd wanted to, not unless the entrance was specially widened to accommodate her.

I recognized her. She'd been a good soldier during the war—did her duty as a sentry and didn't shirk in battle either. She'd killed her fair share of Regina's daughters. And now she was so swollen with juice she couldn't stir.

I let her know what I thought of her. I didn't hold anything back. "Hoarders like you give the rest of us majors a bad reputation," I told her. "They think we're all hoarders and shirkers."

"An innocent major, a very special friend of mine," I continued, "recently got desegmented because they had her pegged as a juice hoarder, and she was only tanking a little tad extra for a few friends."

"So? I just have more friends than she did—better and more important friends. No one wants to be giving away juice to the ants who are tearing us apart, the ones who got us into this mess."

"Never mind about Scrobe and her drones. They can't excuse everything that's gone wrong around here," I said. "There's hard-working sisters that could use the juice," I said, "and even Mother, the Queen herself—" Remembering all of a sudden how I'd found her alone, so weak and hollow and hungry.

"And how do you know I'm *not* storing juice for the Queen?" she answered me back. "Anyway, what are you making such a fuss about it? Seems to me we're on the same side, or close enough."

"And how do you make that out?" I asked, all sarcastic.

"What's with the pretense? Do you really think I don't know who your sister is and what she's doing?"

Again! But how did *she* find out? I couldn't imagine—except that you and Spout have been careless. I understood her gambit all right, though. She'd denounce me for Desegmentation to save herself. Denounce me because of you and Spout—when all I'd done was bring you a little bug juice, not even knowing what it was for. I didn't answer a word—I turned right around to get out of there. This was the wrong part of the nest to hide in.

I got out of there fast, but not so fast that I didn't detect a presence lurking nearby—aware of me as I was aware of her.

The spy!

Using My Head

I need to find you, Sister. I need your help. You know hiding places that I don't.

Wait—I forgot. You're not my sister. And you never said anything about helping me—only about my helping you.

I calmed down a bit as I put a little distance—more moldy passageways and crumbling side chambers—between me and that bloated, double-talking traitor and the spy.

I was pretty sure the spy had slipped into that chamber after me. Now, of course, I knew where the bloated major had gotten her information. The spy was one of the "better and more important friends" that she boasted of having. That gave me an idea—I could denounce the spy before she turned me in. Then it occurred to me that we'd probably both get desegmented.

It was a mistake to confront that bloated major. My indignation got the better of me, that's all. I'll be more careful from now on. Creep a few steps forward—freeze—a few more steps—freeze again. I'll be very, very careful and quiet until I find a spot that'll hold me.

I headed upwards, still keeping to the unused galleries, slipping into little corners whenever I thought someone might be following, or whenever I just felt tired. To tell the truth, there were lots of places where I might have hidden myself. I was surprised how many empty passageways and chambers there were. It seemed like half the nest had been abandoned to ruin. And I realized, well, it had been.

The housekeepers had been shirking their tasks, just like the foragers. All these chambers should have been rubbed and cleaned and repaired. But I couldn't recall a single instance of a negligent housekeeper ant being desegmented, which seemed a bit unfair. But of course there was nobody here, nobody using these chambers and corridors, which is why their negligence hadn't been found out and denounced. Then I realized how many sisters must have died without anyone particularly noticing—with no new sisters coming forth, ever again, to take their place. An emptiness that's growing and spreading. Better to close off these unused chambers, block the passageways connecting them, so we don't have to know, don't have to witness how we are dwindling, wasting away like Mother herself.

I was too agitated to hide myself, only pausing for a minute or two to rest or groom, then moving on—still worrying and puzzling over it all—the spy always following me, you and Spout hiding that larva of yours, the poor frail Queen left by herself, so weak and hungry. I puzzled and talked to myself, or to you, just keeping it very quiet. Nobody was near, nobody could listen in.

I had made it to the upper nest, and it occurred to me that I was pretty near to the spot where I thought I'd traced you—twice!—only you weren't there. It was the place where I'd first been sure of the spy.

I rested there and thought some more. All of a sudden, I had a really good idea—one of my all-time best. Majors don't have big heads for nothing. I could put mine to use. It was safe to try. The spy wasn't after me this time. I had checked and checked and nobody was trailing me.

I put my head down and ran, hard, right at the wall. It gave way at once.

Who Are You Calling Names?

"Clumsy idiot!" said the ant I landed on, showering her with debris. I turned my feelers on her.

"The spy—it's the spy!" I burst out, swelling with surprise and indignation.

"You clumsy fool! Who are you calling spy? I'm no spy. I'm the Royal Beta," she answered me back, with her own little puff of pique, drawing herself up to her maximum height as she did so.

"You're not the Royal Beta. I know the Beta and she's a much younger ant. You're nothing like her."

"I'm the Royal Beta until the Queen dismisses me from her service," she returned, just as haughty and proud as an ant could be.

We were facing off, our feelers whipping and tingling. I pulled my feelers away for a moment to map out where I was. I made you out. You were busy repairing the breach where I'd broken through the wall. Someone else helping you. I knew her at once. Three ants—the spy, you, and Spout. A frowsy old abandoned chamber, stinking of mold and unclean things. Three ants—and a big larva, an incredibly big larva. But the spy who called herself the Royal Beta was still snapping her jaws at me. That was twice now she'd called me a name and I didn't like it. It was incredible—she was right there among you and you didn't know your danger!

"You're a sneaking spy and a traitor—" but just then you came up and stroked my head that way you have of doing, that comforts me and calms me down. It did calm me down, even though you're not my sister.

"Call her Beta, won't you?," you said in your soft way to me. "It pleases her to be called Beta, and she's been a good friend to us."

"I don't like what she called me," I complained. Just then your other friend, your special friend, came over and put her feelers and palps on me. I might have called *her* a name—she hadn't treated me at all well. But I was dignified.

"Sister," I said stiffly, acknowledging her greeting.

"Dear, dear sister," she gushed, "my dear, my very dearest sister, that last of our line." That was vintage Spout. Quite as if she wasn't embarrassed at all, as if she didn't owe me some explanations and apologies—especially the latter. I pointed this out to her.

"When she came back to me," Spout said, indicating *you* with her feeler, "and told me about the big ant who had carried her off and claimed her for a sister, of course neither of us knew what to make of it. Then she told me the name you had given her—Young Keen—and I knew it must be you."

"Well?" I said, coldly. I didn't like to be reminded of that. I didn't like remembering the true sister I had lost long ago, and the new sister I thought I had found, the sister *you* were going to be for me.

"She told me other things as well. How you had praised the Desegmentations. It made me wonder, well, if I could trust you. Even though I longed for you. I didn't want to take a chance of endangering this royal one here." Waking up at her touch, the larva demanded to be fed, waggling its fat body and clicking its baby teeth. Spout turned away to nurse it, crooning and spitting food into its mouth until it had finally had enough and gone back to sleep. Paying no attention to me in the meanwhile.

Not trust me! I was terribly offended. It's true I might have said something or other about approving of the Desegmentations, but everybody said that. It was expected. Later on, of course, I had my secret doubts, and then when they went after a major who hadn't done a thing wrong— But not to trust me! Over such a trifle!

"*I* would never have deserted *you*," I said bitterly. "Not for *that*. It's big but so what? Where did it come from and whose is it?"

"I know whose it is," I went on, before Spout could answer. "It's Regina's— you brought it back from Regina's nest and now you're trying to pass it off as Mother's."

Oh, I was angry!

"It *is* the Queen's," said Spout.

"It *is* the Queen's," you said. But what would you know? You just repeat what you've been told.

"It *is* the Queen's," said the spy who calls herself the Royal Beta. "I knew it as an egg—I recognized it. The Queen produced it just before the final battle of the war. The Queen's Delta lost her life to save that egg. And I lost my place."

You were all together on this and I didn't want to be left out.

"All right, it's the Queen's," I agreed. "Now what?"

"It needs more meat," said Spout.

I might have said something mean, because I was still angry at Spout. But you spoke up, touching me again in that way of yours.

You said: "Can I go with you?"

Young Keen, I Named You

"You stay close to me," I said. "Keep your feelers on my gaster. None of your wandering off."

It's a shock to any young ant, that first trip to the outside—the bursting glare of vision, ghost-images flickering and dancing before you—that would be enough to make anyone dizzy and disoriented. But every single sensation is new, except for the warm must scent of the earth itself. So you did just what I told you, like a sensible ant, keeping close behind, your feelers tapping gently on my gaster.

I don't think any ant needs to be told what to do if something big and birdlike puts you in its breezy shadow—dart quick into a crevice or to the underside of a leaf, then freeze. That's just instinct. But there's lots else that has to be learned. I started to tell you a few things—how a good scout can use sunbeams to find the shortest path home, which of the animals that creep along—slugs, millipedes, worms, and such like—have bristles or a stinky spray or a sticky ooze they can use against you, why springtails aren't worth chasing—when I realized you weren't tapping me on the gaster anymore.

I veered round in a hurry, scanning for you, making a few quick little runs this way and that, trying not to lose my way in my panic—then I found you. You were poking around the tarry, evil-smelling wood that borders the flower beds. Just as I was running up to tell you that was wrong—to complain about your wandering off like that—you lunged and pulled it out, wriggling like mad—a termite!

A termite's just about the best and juiciest meat there is. We don't find many of them hereabouts, not enough of the good rotting wood they like. I killed it for you and got ready to drink up the juice, when you stopped me.

You wanted to take it back as whole meat. You said it would be good for the royal larva to have something to chew.

Oh, I understood. Your first game—a real prize. Of course you wanted to carry it back and display it to Spout and that ant who calls herself the Royal Beta. You said I could distract the sentries while you ran past them with your game clenched in your mandibles. I didn't think it was likely to work, but it was your prize so I said yes.

It turned out to be easy. I didn't need to distract the sentries because they were already distracted. Everybody was. The message was going round the nest, one ant running up to another, passing it on and on. A Desegmentation, at the nursery, everybody in attendance, hurry up now, don't be late.

At the nursery. Nobody ever expected that. They were actually going after the egg-layers this time, after Scrobe herself. I wasn't going to miss that—nobody was, except of course you and Spout and a few other hideaway ants.

The Royal Delta and Beta were at the entrance as usual, not so much counting or checking or anything like that this time. Just making sure the ants trapped inside weren't able to get away. As soon as I found a place for myself inside, I made out where the Queen's Alpha was, there in the fore-front, as always, along with those of the majors who were still alive and still showing up. The majors had already pinned down the nursery ants—three of them—two big ones who must have been involved in the coup when all the littler egg-layers were expelled, and Scrobe's sister. Scrobe wasn't there.

The Alpha probably expected to be making her usual speech about sisterhood and sharing, only she never got the chance. The displaced nursery ants came charging in, full of fury and hate. The majors were so surprised they dropped their captives and got out of the way.

I always said no one compares to an egg-layer for spite, but these ants, who'd all had their little ones stolen and eaten, took it to a new level. One of them let off the contents of her poison gland, and then another and then another. In that little space, it drove everybody berserk. Sisters were all over each other, biting and pounding away.

I didn't expect any of this, but I was ready for it when it happened. I'd been scenting the wrong trail for a long time, but once I got straightened out, I'd done some fresh thinking. Figuring things out for myself without asking any questions, without saying a word. The cynical major claimed it was that little bitty Gamma who controlled the whole show. But it's hard to take an ant that small seriously. No, it was the Royal Alpha I went stalking through that riot of biting, spraying, quarreling ants—remembering her grand speeches and that special way she had of saying "our Queen, our Mother." I caught up with her from behind—snip!—off went one hind leg. She fell over, coiled up in shock, neatly presenting me with my next target—snip!—off went the middle leg on the same side.

She writhed and twisted in spasms, making it harder for me to pick out the rest of my targets. But, unluckily for the Alpha, I'd gotten a lot of good practice at those Desegmentations of hers. I hit square at the joint each time—snip, snip, snip, snip. When I was done with her, she was stumbling on two middle femurs and one front trochanter—all the other legs taken off clean at the coxa. I trimmed her feelers for her too. Whether any sisters wanted her segments as prizes, I couldn't say, but I cut them up neatly just in case. We wouldn't be getting any more "our Queen, our Mother" speeches out of her.

Grudges were being settled and paybacks administered all around. Most ants were too excited or too stupid to know who they were biting and why, but some had singled out their quarry just as I had mine. The Royal Beta and Delta who'd bullied so many of their sisters were under attack and doing badly, though not so badly as the Alpha. The Gamma must have gotten off somewhere. I would've given her a trimming too if I'd found her. Scrobe's sister had been torn to bits by the pack of vicious displaced nurses. I'm not sure how many realized they'd had to settle for the sister instead of Scrobe herself. Maybe it just made them meaner. Those three big nurse-bullies all got pulled apart and ground to pulp first, then they tore up the drone larvae that had been left in the nursery. Then they still weren't satisfied and went back to biting and lashing out at random sisters. I'd done my little job so I got out of there. When it was finally over, when all that hate and poison had exhausted itself, I'm told there were torn limbs strewn all about the chamber, still twitching, some of them. The Queen's nursery it once had been, turned into a battlefield.

I suppose you and Spout are holed up with your precious larva. Spout must have been pleased with the termite. Pleased and impressed, if you told her how you caught it yourself.

I tested you on the return, letting you lead, wondering if you would find your way. I knew it of course, but you, a young little nursery ant on her very first hunt? You ran straight home, taking the shortest way, and you reminded me so much—

Young Keen! But of course you're not my sister. Not her sister either. Yet so much like her all the same. And I thought—maybe we keep coming back, repeating at long intervals like the seasons. As though there were only so many ants, with only so many stories, arranged in some pattern, maybe, or more likely it's just chance, whatever happens now, or long ago, or in times to come. Ants die, others come forth to take their place, and eventually it's the same ants again, or others so much like them that—

Young Keen—I'm just sorry you don't get to live out your life in a healthy colony, like this one was in the old days, where you'd be the elite scout and everybody would know it. But that's for other ants in other places. Some things are meant, most things are chance.

All Things Come to an End

I'd gone back up to the guardrooms to take my turn at sentry duty. Things are back to normal now, or what passes for it. Normal being: The older, smaller ants get chased out of the nest every morning—the ones who are just a bit younger or bigger snapping and whipping at their gasters all the way, forcing them out to forage. They bring back food, if they're lucky—or else they don't get past us sentries. They try to slip back to the deep nest with their booty, but they get stopped along the way and bullied if they don't give up their juice willingly to any ant who's bigger or younger. They always hope they can keep enough juice and work their way deep enough so they don't get chased out again the next day. That's what passes for normal.

I'm so glad I'm a major. When I need food, I just block one of these little ants and back her into a wall, boxing her head with my feelers if she doesn't give up quickly. That way I can always feed myself and you and Spout and that ant who calls herself the Royal Beta.

She came up for a visit and sat down beside me. She's not a bad ant at all, quite pleasant really, if you remember to call her Beta every now and then. We rested side by side for a long while, talking and not talking, getting acquainted.

She told me that it was the Royal Gamma who had tipped off Scrobe—that the two of them had gathered up her brood of drones, or as many of the pupae and bigger larvae as they could manage, and got out of there before the Desegmentation began. So Scrobe abandoned her own true sister, while Gamma played a double game—setting up the Desegmentation and then helping its chief victim escape. Now they were in hiding together, standing guard over the surviving drone brood. In a dying nest, any eggs, any larvae or pupae, even drones, have value.

"My sister better be careful," I said, "with dangerous ants like Scrobe and Gamma roaming around."

"It is a danger," my companion agreed, "but it might also be an opportunity. They have drones. She has a queen. It's a game she can win if she plays it carefully."

"Happen to come across the Queen's Alpha on your way up here?" I asked coyly. "I understand she's not getting around as well as she used to."

Calls-Herself-Beta perked up at that. "So that was your work, was it? Nice job! She's not getting around *at all*, anymore. Couldn't hobble fast enough to get away from the rove beetles."

"No!" I said, delighted. "The rove beetles got her, eh?"

"They haven't been getting much honeydew lately, so they had to settle for ant—crippled, can't-get-away ant. An ant's not all that tasty, of course, not like honeydew or stolen eggs or larvae. So they chewed away at her slowly—took a bite or two, wandered off to search for something better. Came back and chewed on another bit, and so on. I checked on their progress once or twice. Finicky beetles took all night to finish her off."

"Now there's a story with a happy ending," I said.

"Yes," she said. "One of the few."

She told me how she'd first met Spout, how they'd both gone into hiding around the same time. How she kept creeping back into the royal chambers to visit Mother, bringing her food whenever she could, getting it from that bloated major I'd encountered. So we sat together and chatted for a long time, getting acquainted at last.

You came for a visit too—I appreciated that—and you told me your news.

The royal larva has spun its cocoon, so we can all take a well-deserved rest. But Spout took fright when she learned that the Royal Gamma and Scrobe were renegades wandering around in the emptier parts of the nest. She grabbed up the pupa and hid it somewhere, in one of her secret places. Even you don't know where it is.

And you told me about Spout's crazy scheme—how she thinks she can bring back the old ways, make us all like sisters again, by mating her royal one with Scrobe's drones. I'm sorry but it's a dream, a fantasy, a nursery tale. It's not going to happen. Those ants, when they emerge, will smell our age, our sickness, our decay. They'll fly away and leave us. Because we've come to our end. It took her a long time to get it out, but Beta finally told me her real news, what she had come to say.

Mother died today. Or maybe it was yesterday. Beta wasn't sure. It might have been yesterday. That would make sense—that would explain why Gamma set up the attack on the nursery and then forced an alliance with Scrobe. Yesterday, today. It doesn't really matter. Her death is ours. We won't survive her for long. The ending is set down for us all, to perish in here or out there. Which will you choose, Young Keen?

IX.

Postmodern

Postcolonial

Ant

The modes of communication found in the social insects are awesomely diverse. There exist the expected tappings, stridulations, strokings, graspings, antennations, tastings, and puffings and streakings of chemicals which evoke various responses from simple recognition to recruitment and alarm. We must add to this list other, often subtle and sometimes even bizarre effects ... various forms of dominance and submission relationships, programmed execution and cannibalism, necrophoresis, and still others.
–Edward O. Wilson, **The Insect Societies** (1971)

The literary text is always metaphoric in the sense that when we interpret it we apply it to the world as a total metaphor. This process of interpretation assumes a gap between the text and the world, between art and life, which postmodernist writing characteristically tries to short-circuit in order to administer a shock to the reader and thus resist assimilation into conventional categories of the literary. Ways of doing this include: combining in one work violently contrasting modes—the obviously fictive and the apparently factual; introducing the author and the question of authorship into the text; and exposing conventions in the act of using them.
–David Lodge, **The Modes of Modern Writing** (1977)

The Aleph was probably two or three centimeters in diameter, but universal space was contained inside it, with no diminution of size. Each thing (the glass surface of a mirror, let us say) was infinite things, because I could clearly see it from every point in the cosmos. I saw the populous sea, saw dawn and dusk, saw the multitudes of the Americas, saw a silvery spider web at the center of a black pyramid, saw a broken labyrinth (it was London), saw endless eyes, all very close ... saw tigers, pistons, bisons, tides, and armies, saw all the ants on the earth.
–Jorge Luis Borges, "The Aleph" (1949)

They collected black ants only, and the ant-farm was already enormous, the ants appeared to be furious and worked until nightfall, excavating and moving earth with a thousand methods and maneuvers, the careful rubbing of feelers and feet, abrupt fits of fury or vehemence, concentrations and dispersals for no apparent reason.
–Julio Cortázar, "Bestiary" (1951)

They always had a new labyrinth traced out with different substances which they prepared from day to day, and for this game ants were a necessary element.
–Italo Calvino, "The Argentine Ant" (1952)

WATCH OUT!

Down there at your fictive feet. Reader, you nearly stepped on them. Please be more careful!

There they are, spread out upon the pavement, streaming in and out of their inconceivably separate unreachable world. First an ant then an ant an ant next an ant another ant oh it's another ant yet another ant one more one more ant keep going not done yet an ant an ant keep on an ant an ant an ant can't stop yet because they aren't stopping. An ant an ant another and another and still another ant oh will there ever be an end to them and what are they doing anyway?

No don't do that—that's not nice!

Just look at them being so busy about something. First an ant then an ant next an ant another and another and another. And what are they doing anyway?

No, they're not lost. See that little semi-circle of dirt pellets next to the edge of the walk, with the little black hole in the middle? That's where they live. Some going in, some going out, but most circling around like that on the walk, or clustering together in that funny way that could be fighting or loving or something altogether different.

Each one an each one, charged with some intention only we don't know what. Look over there at that group clumped together, putting their heads close and flicking their antennae at each other so intently. Who knows what that's about? They're too small to see clearly. Not that seeing would tell you that much.

Go ahead and try if you want. Lie down on the grass, put your head where your feet are. (Like your shoes, by the way.) Oh, oh, too close. They noticed you noticing them—they're scattering—heading back down that black hole into that unreachable unknowable separate world of theirs. Too bad. Might as well get up again. Not that seeing would have told you that much.

So much of what is going on, above ground or below, cannot be seen. The ants speak to one another in a squirty oozy streaky gassy language, emanating from a dozen or so distinct little glands. They speak to one another, waving their expressive feelers to listen or to comment, with alkanes, alkenes and alkadienes; with alcohols and ketones and esters; with offensive acetates, startling aldehydes, alluring alkylpyrazines.

If we can't know what they're doing clustering and circling around like that right at your feet, in plain view, then of course it's impossible to know what's going on below within that chambered darkness.

True, you could stick a tiny camera in there; it's been done in some of the better nature documentaries; but the ants will be no more natural in its presence than you are when a doctor sticks a scope into your dark, winding, cavernous spaces. Even had they not commented on your presence by scattering, you could never be sure whether you were in fact observing ants being ants or observing ants being observed.

Perhaps you, Reader, stiffened and looked away with self-consciousness or surprised displeasure at being thus addressed by your author. (Still avoiding eye contact, you glance down at the recto running head and murmur to yourself, "'Postmodern Ant,' well, I suppose it's expected, almost a requirement.")

But I imagine that it startled and slightly annoyed you to be so addressed. Especially if you do not like your feet. Some people don't. Alternatively, you may have been pleased: you may be wearing some brand of shoe to be noticed, to be respected, admired, envied; endowing you with a sense of well-being that suffuses slowly upward from your toes through your genitalia and viscera, where it lingers warmly, upward to your heart, lung, liver, brain, suffusing warmly slowly sweetly upward to wherever the soul may or may not reside. You know of course that I cannot have witnessed your shoes; yet I recalled them to your consciousness and so gave you pleasure. Reader, you're welcome.

Or you may be a different sort of reader, one who is bored by coy postmodernist games and you tap that foot impatiently—in which case, Reader, I hope to please *you* with the announcement that this section is only nineteen pages long, roughly eight thousand words. We will return you to a regularly structured story shortly. Here I only ask you to consider how, surprised at being addressed when you had thought yourself unobserved, you might have moved your foot—whether shuffling backwards like a startled crab, or flexing your ankle to display your shoe to its best advantage, or tapping impatiently—communicating so unmistakably before any conscious intention shaped itself in your awareness. No subsequent words, however well formulated, can entirely efface the message conveyed in that movement.

Movement. They're back, streaming in and out again. Each one an each one. The ants give out messages, to each other if not to us. Antennae flickering like the fluttering of eyelids, who's to say the fluttering of an eyelid isn't a code, a signification, yours for instance, just now.

Messages. We can see their antennae flickering back and forth, if we bend down close enough and squint—gathering or exchanging information. The perpetual waving and tapping and slapping of their feelers at or upon one another—that *must* serve some aim, must *mean* something. Since feelers are also smellers and tasters, we can't know if the flickers are giving information or gathering it or both at once, hieratically nuanced, establishing identity, class, place. In some instances the flickering clearly takes on the character of a gesture, like you tapping your foot or clenching your fist (which may of course mean a great deal).

A shuffling of feet, a rustling of pages, a bit of restlessness. I sense your resistance, Reader. Real ants, you say, are automatons. They release pheromones in response to specific stimuli, a response that is hardwired, instinctive, unthinking. To fictional ants you grant broad artistic license. You wouldn't object—you might see it as a gain in credibility—if Thrip, Regina and Carina wore skirts and batted their eyelashes while they flirted with confident, swaggering, masterful drones. But real ants! Tiny, insignificant, squashable. (*Please!* I asked you not to do that!)

Those real ants circling so inscrutably down there at your imagined feet: you say they must be automatons, executing simple robotic tasks with a minimum of neural circuitry. Consider the paltry size of their brains, less than a quarter of a small pinhead, as Darwin remarked in *The Descent of Man, and Selection in Relation to Sex*. (You'll find it on page 145 of the 1871 edition or *vide supra* page vi, quoted as one of my four epigraphs; you might want to take another look at them right around now.) But millions of molecules can dance on the head of a pin, shuffling and recombining, coding and transmitting. Anyway, Reader, as one who takes an extra small in hats, I am personally unmoved by the Argument From Size.

In the same passage Darwin noted that the cerebral ganglia of ants are enormous by insectile standards, many times larger than those of the less intelligent beetles—a generous acknowledgement, given how fond Darwin was of beetles. And, let us not forget, worker ants are able to apply their quarter-pinheads to their problems with great efficiency, since they are entirely freed from worrying about *Selection in Relation to Sex,* which is probably all a beetle *ever* thinks about.

Think, Reader, what you and I, with our enormous cerebrums, might have accomplished if we had not devoted so much of our attention to sex—how to get more or better, and whether last night ...

A gap expressed as dot-dot-dot: our familiar code for something omitted or incomplete ...

In the late Victorian era, at a time when scientists could be less inhibited in their speculations, Erich Wasmann proposed that the antennal flickers were a sort of Morse code: dot-dot-dash, tappety-tap-tap, tap-tappety-tap. Not that Wasmann thought ants were intelligent: he didn't. In his book on the comparative psychology of ants and higher animals he alluded disdainfully to *The Descent of Man,* dismissing Darwin's anecdotal accounts of intelligent behavior in higher animals and capping them with anecdotes about ants. Anything apes can do, ants can do better, he argued. The intelligence apparently displayed by the ants is fully as great as that apparently displayed by primates, which goes to prove that apes are only brute beasts, unrelated to divinely endowed man. Wasmann was both an eminent scientist and a Jesuit. To be true to his faith as well as his science, he acknowledged evolution only insofar as it explained variations among lower species. His own research focused on the mimetic adaptations of rove beetles to their host ants. In this instance, Reader, characterizing ants as instinct-driven automatons (a view ultimately derived from Descartes), was the defensive reflex of a man made uncomfortable by a threat to his God-given sovereignty over creation.

You insist that ants are unintelligent, mere reflex machines. But ants, it turns out, do very well at learning their way through a laboratory maze, almost as good as rats, who are, as you know, old hands at the business, bred to the trade. Perhaps that's not so surprising when you consider ants live in a maze. Although—and this is worth noting—the labyrinths of the laboratory are nothing like home. In the lab they are wiped down or replaced between trials, so that the ant, when she must retrace her journey, cannot rely upon chemical signposts to mark her way. She is deprived of the use of her best sense. It's as if, Reader, you had to find your way through a dark wood with only the inexpressibly remote light of the constellations, which you had never quite troubled yourself to learn, to guide you.

Each one an each one. That can be verified. The members of a small research colony can be color-coded for individual study. A palette of four colors, used to mark head, trunk and gaster with three little dabs, creates a code that provides sixty-four unique identifiers. Dot-dot-dot: this one is red-white-yellow, call her RWY. Another three dots of paint, blue-white-red this time, she'll be our little BWR. Red-white-white, that's RWW; white-blue-blue, WBB. Four ants will do nicely: we certainly don't need all sixty-four.

BWR was tidying up the middle regions of the nest. Nothing too strenuous. Pick up a bit of something; carry it a little ways; but not all the way to the midden, never that. Not her place. Leave it for another ant to carry out. By chance or design, she came a little closer to the brood chamber than usual. The tender sweet-scented brood! A little further, another turning, she was almost there. Only her way forward is blocked: she has been found out. Outraged by the ant's presumption, RWY snaps her mandibles and whips her feelers harshly at the offender's head.

BWR cowers respectfully but RWY is not so easily appeased. Nothing will serve but she must turn to run back to the middle nest where she, BWR, belongs. There she encounters an inferior, RWW, who is quite properly engaged in carrying debris to the midden. BWR chooses to take offense, even though RWW is only completing the work BWR left unfinished.

RWW cannot be so easily intimidated, however. She once ranked as high as RWY among the nursery ants. Her age has condemned her to midden work but her temper is as formidable as ever. The two ants exchange feeler slaps in a back-and-forth duel, first one then the other. Their rage subsides: it is ritual now. When they feel their status has been confirmed, their rights defended, they turn and go their separate ways.

Meanwhile, RWY has had a nasty surprise. On returning to the nursery, her position has been challenged by another. WBB senses weakness in RWY. She might be wrong about that: it might be only a whiff of the older weaker BWR clinging to RWY's cuticle. But it's nonetheless true that only a certain elect number can enjoy residence in the brood chamber. RWY retaliates, answers back. But WBB is not the sort of ant who backs down. She keeps at RWY; other nurses also take sides against RWY; and within a day or two she is compelled to leave the brood. She has to do something so she begins to tidy up the middle nest. Nothing too strenuous. Pick up a bit of something; carry it a little ways; drop it for another ant to carry out.

Plainly visible to the human eye, social striving of this sort typically takes place in small queenless colonies in which the sisters are all equally capable of egg-laying and equally reluctant to be forced out to forage. But it seems unlikely that selfish rivalries have been extirpated in larger, more stratified societies. At dusk the office towers spill their contents onto the street. Drab multitudes move at a measured mechanical pace: but there is not enough room in the elevators for all; there are not enough seats on the trains and subways and buses. There is no shouting, no overt intimidation, no obvious pushing. But by means of oblique maneuvering and posturing, by skilled placements of knees, elbows, briefcases, some among them—the alphas and betas, no doubt—are assured of a good place.

Drab multitudes spill out upon the pavement. First an ant then an ant an ant next an ant another ant oh it's another ant then yet another ant. On and on, apparently endlessly. But of course we know there can't be that many of them. Thrip is dead. She left no eggs. The colony is dying. It must be the same ants repeating themselves. One after another, coming out from the dark nest, circling, retreating, coming out again to circle and retreat. One after another, looping forward then backward with an easy twist of their slender waists, coming again and again to the beginning, evading the ending.

Hold on, wait a minute, you say, frowning a bit, wrinkling your brow with surprised annoyance. What are we talking about here? Real ants or imaginary? Both, Reader. Real ants as studied in artificial nests in research labs and fictional ants as found outside, under the walk, not too far from where I sit at my desk, although I cannot see the anthill from the window, which, anyway, is behind my back. They reside under the walk of my residence, at least some of the time. They are portable. I carry them with me. They move blurrily through remembered and imagined space.

In the back story, I place them in the yard of a dilapidated farmhouse recollected from a childhood spent in the warm south. There was no walkway to the house, just a dusty beaten path up the hill from the road to the wide rickety steps of the porch; but I supply one for the ants with a few slate tiles spaced generously across the swell of ground leading up to those same rickety steps, foreshortening that long path from the road, which was excessive and inartistic. Time passes, space shifts. Now, in the outer suburbs of a northern city, the farm having been bulldozed, the farmhouse given over to decay but still intact and marginally habitable, the ants relocate to the edge of a development filled with hostile symmetries, big square houses on small square lots. Then comes the river, slow, thick, melancholy. But the river must wait; we have not yet come to the river.

Blurring superfluous details, telling only what I am capable of perceiving, perceiving only what is essential to the telling, I find fictional ants easy to apprehend. It's the real ones—although you, Reader, are not yet convinced of this—that are quite, quite inconceivable.

Try putting yourself in the ant *umwelt*, try imagining what it's like to be an ant being an ant among other ants. I struggled with this, Reader. I was ambitious to get it right. I tried to put myself within that dark labyrinth, finding my way, recognizing my friends, avoiding my enemies, entirely by the use of my feelers. Not the tap, tap, tap of a blind human's cane—it's not like that at all. Within the nest, ants can recognize their friends and enemies from a sizeable ant-scale distance of one or two centimeters. My feelers are a mobile pair of exquisitely sensitive nostrils, able to track odors to their source. They are tasters too, able to sample the chemistry of felt objects. With my feelers I can trace my way confidently through the twisting corridors of my home. I don't need, can't use, my eyes, knowing easily where the Queen is, where the brood, recognizing my friends, avoiding, or trying to avoid, my enemies.

Only I don't have feelers. I imagine my hands fastened to my forehead, probing the space before me, gropingly, then remind myself that my hands must also be noses and must be able to taste whatever they touch. But I keep cheating and using my eyes, if only to witness my botched attempts at being an ant. I have no awareness of the familial forms that must be looming all about me—sisters, mother, brood. I am aware only of myself, with a grotesque pair of hand-nose-and-tongue antlers projecting from my forehead.

What is the subjective experience of an ant being an ant among other ants? Such a question could not be considered good science today: ants assuredly have experiences, but one may not ask what they are. One may ask questions about their sensory information processing. It is now possible to trace the nerve signaling pathway stimulated by a pheromone, thereby identifying a discrete cluster of brain cells that encode its unique "odor image" in the insect brain. Not my own clumsy expression, Reader, but one I find in the scientific literature, set between scare quotes to signal the researcher's embarrassment at the want of a better term. Ah, the impossibility, again, of understanding the inner being of a creature for whom odors are images!

But at the turn of the last century scientists were less inhibited in their speculations. I ask Google Scholar and Google Books for help, shuffling and recombining search terms, trying for the open sesame. Again and again they send me to smart commercial sites that ask for my member password or my credit card number. At last, grudgingly, the surly librarians pull out their rusty keys to the vaults, offering up PDFs of old volumes so degraded by careless scanning that they resemble Gothic blackletter. They provide me not only with the Jesuit myrmecologist Erich Wasmann, but also with the myrmecologist-psychiatrist Auguste Forel of Zurich and the myrmecologist–Presbyterian minister Henry Christopher McCook of Philadelphia.

In his defense of the dignity and supremacy of man, Wasmann took aim primarily at Darwin but did not spare fellow entomologists his scorn when he found them guilty of anthropomorphizing their subject—not even the harmless Reverend McCook, who believed God placed ants upon the earth to teach civic virtues to mankind. (Seeking the truths that God intended us to find in them, McCook found himself espousing socialism, eugenics and suffragism.) Forel, a free-thinking socialist reformer, was a more formidable opponent. Forel's monumental work on the ants of Switzerland was cited respectfully, but Wasmann attacked his opinions freely: "He, who seriously points to the complete socialism and communism of mixed ant colonies as models for human socialism and political economy, is sadly in need of a nerve specialist."

Forel no doubt caught the barbed allusion to his views, but it was the objectionably strong whiff of incense clinging to Wasmann's arguments about evolution and intelligence that drew an answer from him. He countered with his own monograph on formic psychology. Unlike Wasmann, Forel was fully prepared to accept evidence of intelligence in the ant. "All the properties of the human mind may be derived from the properties of the animal mind," he declared. "And all the mental attributes of higher animals may be derived from those of lower animals." Forel supposed the complex behavior of ants to be ninety-seven percent instinctive, but three percentage points of intelligent activity were sufficient for his argument. Tiny and insignificant though they may appear, ants make an effective rebuttal to Cartesian dualism.

Google Books classifies both works—Forel's and Wasmann's—as juvenile nonfiction. Could there be a crueler dismissal than that? True, Google Books is only an unthinking automaton—but still, how mortifying! All alike in death, flung out upon the vast midden of intellectual history, giving a fitful twitch or two of afterlife as a few scholars scavenge their remains for research topics.

In a time when scientists could be less inhibited in their speculations, Forel wanted to understand how the ant senses her world. The ant's chemical perceptions, he said, are so refined, so exact, that they provide her with the spatial awareness that we achieve with vision. To know what it is like to be such an ant, Forel suggested we imagine ourselves with olfactory hands that are in continual vibration, examining everything in our path. Moving thus through her world, he said, an ant perceives not merely sweetness or muskiness or pungency but round odors, rectangular odors, elongate odors, soft or firm or hirsute odors.

Did Forel succeed in understanding, really understanding, how an ant senses her world? Or was he groping in darkness, gathering words together, moving them about, finding two or three that fit well together—then, with growing excitement, piling on others that fit the blank on the page, the gap in the thought. And only when he had put the words together did he know what he had meant to say by them. This work of clustering and compiling, putting like with like, is called stigmergy when it is social insects, mindless automatons, who do it.

This swarm of neurons and corpuscles that, for convenience, I call I. (There's also that other swarm of neurons and corpuscles that, despite the obvious potential for confusion, you call I.) They speak to one another in a squirty oozy language, emanating from a tangle of synapses: aspartate and glutamate, glycine and gamma-aminobutyric acid, acetylcholine, norepinephrine, dopamine, serotonin, histamine. Continually busy, doing and undoing, promoting and censoring, suggesting and deleting.

The I of this particular swarm of neurons am not too sure of my way right now. Creeping along mostly, sometimes rushing ahead to find myself at a dead end: nothing to do but backspace and delete. Finding my way more cautiously now, phrase by phrase, sentence by sentence; lines wrap, paragraphs spill over to a new page. Some of it's rubbish, will have to be tossed out. But not yet. Move it around a little. Maybe it's just in the wrong place, or there's something else still missing that belongs with it. Leave it alone for now. Better to keep moving, come back to it later.

The aptitude of ants for learning their way through mazes was established in studies performed some ninety years ago by Theodore C. Schneirla. At first the ant is understandably upset and uncooperative. She will repeatedly attempt to climb up the walls, which will not help her; in her panic, she will try the same blind alleys over again. On repeated exposure, her movements through the maze are slower and more patterned. When forced to turn she employs a strategy of alternating her direction—left, right, left, right—and she will be badly stumped if any of those turns are dead ends. Schneirla explained this behavior mechanistically as "centrifugal swing," suggesting that the ant is robotically carried along by her own momentum. But, Reader, I tell you that if I were in some humanly comparable dilemma—let's say I was lost in a dark wood with only the constellations, which, frankly, I have never troubled myself to learn, to guide me—I would do the same thing as the ant (and the rat), I would attempt to pursue a straight course. Once the ant learns her counterintuitive way, she will remember the combination for unlocking that maze for days to weeks: turn right, then right again, then take the next left—home at last!

With that laboratory maze, one can ask an ant several important questions about herself: How fast do you learn? How long do you remember? How, actually, do you find your way? The answers are not always consistent or easy to interpret, but one can ask objective questions and get publishable, career-advancing answers. The Russian myrmecologist Zhanna Reznikhova asks yet another question. She asks if that ant can teach the way to other, unaccompanied ants. In partnership with her husband Boris Ryabko, a coding theorist, she has found that ants can impart simple directions: "Turn left, then left again, then take the next right: you'll find the food there." By analyzing the time required for directions of differing complexity to be transmitted, the researchers conclude that the ants use a unary code. Not dots and dashes. Just dots. Or just dashes. But they do communicate.

Picture the scene, Reader. The nest has gone without food for two days. On the third day, upon leaving home on her lonely quest, a scout finds herself in one of those strange, blank, dreamlike mazes. She wanders, not quite hopelessly. She has had this dream many times before. Down one of those diverging pathways, turning, as it happens, left at the first two branchings then choosing to turn right, she discovers—it is no dream!—a thick delicious drop of sugar syrup! (Not honeydew: having spent all their lives in a laboratory nest, she and her sisters have never tasted honeydew, only sugar syrup and the occasional cutup mealworm.) Quickly she drinks up a bit of it and turns to run home, pausing only to press her hind parts to the surface every few steps, thoughtfully leaving a trail for her sisters to follow.

On her return to the nest, she rushes up to one of her favorite sisters and offers a sample: "Just taste it, Sister, so pure and sweet!" Their antennae flash intently over the news. Then the scout grabs her sister's mandibles in her own and gives them a meaningful tug: she will lead her to the find. They will go together, then recruit other sisters to help carry all the delicious food home.

But before she can do so, the forceps of the gods descend and she is gone, just like that!

To get more food, her sister, on her own, must follow the trail left by the scout. But there is no trail. The inscrutable unknowable gods have removed the maze and replaced it with another maze, identical to the first except for the only two features that could matter to this solitary ant. It has no scent trail; nor is there any sugar syrup she might possibly discover for herself by detecting and tracing its luscious sweet fragrance.

What does she do? She proceeds bravely into the strange, blank, dreamlike maze. She turns left, and then again left, then proceeds right at the next forking of the way. There the gods reward her piety: a pipette descends from the heavens, delivering a miraculous drop of sugar syrup. It all ends happily: the famished ants will get their food; and the scout, spirited away so mysteriously, will be restored to her sisters.

A simple story, but one that leaves unanswered essential questions of character, discourse and motivation. The researchers speculate only by proxy, with a reference to the antennal code theory of Erich Wasmann.

If I cannot achieve anthood by conscious effort, can I dream myself an ant? I prime the subconscious for the effort, reading about ants late at night, poring over photos of ants while drinking red wine (excellent, in my experience, for vivid dreams). A dream comes, but a false, cheating dream straight from the gates of ivory: I am trapped in a small space with many other people—strangers, we are all strangers to each other. The air is heavy with repressed disgust and hostility. We are pressed so close together we are touching; we cannot escape contact with each other's bodies—unpleasant, hateful! At last I wake up.

I look at real ants, those out there under the walk; and when they make their occasional forays into my house (they do so mostly in springtime, when they are fattening the royal brood for the nuptial flight), I capture them and subject them to my observation. I study how they move, their interactions and their body language. At last, unsought, another dream comes. In a cavernous space—it seems I can see in the dark after all—I see three ants behaving quite naturally, beckoning with their feelers, siren-like. They rest upon a ridge at a little distance from me. Maybe that is why they still seem small, still almost ant-sized although distinct and plainly visible. I try to come closer, to see them as they would see each other. They melt into the darkness and I wake up. I had asked too much.

I wanted to imagine for myself what it is like to be an ant among ants. I was ambitious to get it right. But readers are kind, readers are credulous, readers are willing to meet the author halfway. It is only necessary not to get it obviously wrong. You, Reader, peering right through the pages, will follow my ants through their labyrinth in any old makeshift fashion that your mind spins out from moment to moment, confidently relying upon your eyes despite the utter darkness of your surroundings.

It's true that I cannot, even yet, after so much time and so many pages, follow the ants through their underground maze, finding my way, recognizing my sisters, solely by the use of that hand-nose-and-tongue feeler apparatus fastened to my forehead. All the same, my fictional ants are for me less imaginary than you are, Reader, although I can readily picture your feet out there beside the anthill, in a kaleidoscopically shifting variety of shoes and self-conscious attitudes (the colors are yellowish-white ranging to a burnished brown-black).

I say that I can visualize your shoes. But, whether there are holes in your socks, whether your socks are clean or you are without socks altogether, whether your toe nails are neatly trimmed, whether you are afflicted with bunions, hammertoes, corns, warts or common ephemeral blisters, whether you have the regulation five toes on each foot or some other number—into these questions I will not go, Reader! I will content myself, humbly enough, with your shoes, which, as I say, I can visualize rather clearly.

Yet my eye, the mind's eye, that is, keeps trying to crawl up your leg (bare or trousered? and if the latter, jeans or khakis, casual or dressy—surely casual, to suit the informality of the occasion). I have you, right now, in olive khakis with a dark red plaid shirt. You've decided to be male. I'm not sure why. Must try again.

Why do I picture you as a man, Reader? Statistically, in terms of the gender composition of the fiction-reading public, you are more likely to be female. This is not a new trend. From its beginnings, the novel has been a female art form: relating, with the intimacy of two friends sitting together on the sofa, stories of handsome, good-hearted foundlings who win heiresses and of young ladies lacking dowries who, not without struggle, find love and happiness. Here we have a novel in which the mammalian rules are reversed: the females are in charge; the males are decorative. Won't female readers be fascinated with these six-legged amazons, as I am? Then again, there's no romance among ants and hardly what you would call marriage— a quick one-time scramble mating. Maybe women won't be interested and you, Reader, are in fact a guy.

Olive khakis and a dark red plaid shirt. Outdoorsy. Not overly concerned with appearances. More an ant than a novel person, I would guess. But you never know.

I cannot resolve this issue. It is better to focus on your shoes. I can picture them quite clearly—or rather a series of possible, plausible shoes, shuffling through them like a deck of playing cards, pausing over the images that appeal to me. They are unpretentious, well-worn, comfortable shoes—a bit boxy for most women's tastes, I'm afraid, although they seem too small to fit most men's feet. But about the shoes, at least, I feel quite certain. Brownish, sensible shoes, somewhat scuffed. It occurs to me only now, as I pause the images to make my selection, that I haven't imagined sandals. Why not? Because, as I tap the keys right now, visualizing the ant colony under the sidewalk outside, just beyond my window, it is a chilly October morning. I did not, in those shifting images, allow for the possibility that you, Reader, are located elsewhere in space and time.

Need I add that those brownish, sensible shoes, somewhat scuffed, are my own, tucked, at this moment, under my desk?

Why, if they are my shoes, situated both inside under my desk and outside next to the anthill—why is one pair of them being worn by a man? Because (I'm only guessing) the self is always the same weary inescapable self, but the imagined Reader, secret object of countless authorial hours of longing and struggle, is the Other. You are not just any reader who might happen to page through a copy of my book. You are the Ideal Reader, opposite in gender, identical to me in every other aspect of your being.

But I didn't want you to be me with a gender change. I wanted you to be you, someone else entirely. I create you in my image, yes, can't help that: but I want you to be free to choose.

Skip the clothes, Reader. Wear whatever you please. I will pass over your body along with all those vexing questions about the feet inside your shoes that seemed, initially, so easy to visualize. I want to see your face. I want to know what you are thinking. Are you here because you like novels? Or ants? Or both? I confess, Reader, despite all postmodernist posturings, I am anxious to please you.

What is it like to be you, in your own separate unreachable inner world, thinking your own inconceivable (to me) thoughts?

The mind's eye glances nervously from your shoes to your face, Reader, or tries to. Images flicker in uncertainty, the possibilities are shuffled through once again until my eye settles upon its choice, grainy and soft-focused but handsome. A handsome face, sternly beautiful one might call it. A strong female face, it might be, or a sensitive male one. I can't quite tell from here. But a fine, intelligent, noble countenance. I am drawn to it. Reader, I like you very much!

Yet you do not meet my eye. You look down, at the ants, I suppose, or maybe at the page. There is a soft roundness to the eyelids but otherwise your face is smooth and stony, your mouth straight, the lips compressed. At least you don't look like me, but that's hardly a triumph of the imagination. You look suspiciously like everyone, anyone, genderless, ageless, raceless, a tritely photoshopped image of the model reader.

But the expression—the averted eyes, the almost frowning mouth—how should I read it? Oh, I'm so nervous, meeting you like this for the first time, I can hardly stand it!

If I cannot know you as you are, Reader, I can easily invent you. I can choose your gender and your age and your personal attractions. I can dress you up anyway I please, give you your gestures and tics, collecting your wardrobe and your mannerisms from friends, family, passersby, doing so with sufficient finesse as to evade any potential libel claims. But, Reader, Character, whatever you wish to call yourself, when I try to visit the twisting corridors of your thoughts, the pulses and pangs that creep in darkness— then I am lost, I founder, unless I play the jaded tricks of the two hundred and sixty year old trade.

Shuffle the words around a bit. Take out the commas or the verbs or the commas and the verbs. Keep sentences short. Make the sentences extravagant, ingenious, lengthy, plump with surprises like raisins, made up of rolling clauses rumbling tumbling one after another in rhythmic waves. Stylistic sleights of hand to distract the audience's attention. You won't realize that you, Reader, Character, whatever you want to call yourself, are wearing my shoes, thinking my thoughts. Readers are kind, readers are forgiving. The reader will play along. The reader *wants* to believe in the trunk with the false bottom, the magical escape from the inescapable locks and chains, the wooden dummy with the square hinged mouth.

If there's no love or romance in this book and if that's a flaw (which I do not admit), what about something happening, you know, between you and me, Reader? A work of fiction as a cry for understanding, for companionship, a 120,000 word personal: Aspiring, slightly solipsistic author seeks gentle, understanding, cultured reader.

Oh, I'm not after your money. What difference is $18.50 going to make to my life? (Particularly when you consider my cut is only $3.26, barely enough for bus fare.) I seek only your understanding, Reader, your sympathy, your affection, and only for the few brief hours we may be together. That would be enough for me. I ask nothing more.

This is my first time. No, really. A few short stories, nothing serious, nothing lasting. Be gentle with me, Gentle Reader.

Almost no love or romance, except there *is* going to be the almost obligatory surreal sex scene coming up in Magical Realism Ant. Still in the planning stage. Going to be hellishly hard to write. I don't have to make anything up—that's not the hard part—making up is easy. Drones, male insects in general, have an elaborate copulatory apparatus called the aedeagus. Their pride and joy, as you may well imagine. Retractable, comes with a set of claspers and (at least in the deluxe model) a reamer. More like a Swiss Army knife than anything you're used to. Fills up … never mind, you'll get to it.

The drones exist only for this one-time sex scene, lasting perhaps a minute, if they are lucky enough to get cast for the role. Succeed or fail, they all die soon after their nuptial flight. They struggle mightily to find a female, clasp her, penetrate her. Other drones are trying to mount her too. It's such a scramble that it's impossible for us, as alien observers, to tell whether victory goes to the strong or to the lucky or to the one the female chooses. It seems random. Yet the lives of ants are so relentlessly structured in all other aspects—can it be that for their one minute of a sex life they, males and females alike, are out of control? Surely, if she can, the female would want to take great care in choosing the father or fathers of her twenty thousand daughters.

After about thirty seconds, the female struggles to break free from the male, turning, twisting, biting him. He needs his claspers now just to hold on. Is it painful for her? Is she testing him, making sure he's the strong healthy one she needs for lasting happiness and prosperity? Or is she urging him to hurry up, get his business over with, so she can go off and dig her hole?

I'll let you know, Reader, in due course, when we get to the big sex scene. I am no scientist and have no scruples to inhibit me from inventing answers to unanswerable questions.

What, Thomas Nagel famously asked, is it like to be a bat? Or, one might add, an ant? He put the question in order to declare it unanswerable. It is not possible to extrapolate the inner life of a bat from one's own case, he said. Or, one might add, of an ant. Far from being an impasse, to me it's a way out. I do not gaze down upon my page to find only another wretched mirror reflecting my wretched inescapable self. Or, sticking more strictly with the usual postmodernisms, a wretched labyrinthine hallway of fun-house mirrors filled up with me, me, me, still recognizable throughout all the infinitely reflected distortions. I set myself the task of imagining something fundamentally incomprehensible, something utterly not me. To be sure that the imagined ant will not metamorphose (after uneasy dreams) into me, me, me, masquerading in an ant suit, I deflect the question. I ask what is it like for Moll Flanders or Struthers or Emily St. Aubert or various members of the Bennet family to be an ant.

These specific ants at your fictive feet—no laboratory research can tell us about them. If we can't know what they're doing wandering around like that, in plain view, then of course it's absolutely impossible to know what's going on inside, in the obscurity of that chambered darkness.

Fortunately, I have it on the best possible authority that in this particular instance the ants are circling above, and also below, in their labyrinth, in a state of great anxiety and indecision. They are circling very much as you yourself might circle if you are waiting for someone who is late, someone you counted so much on seeing, who is perhaps not coming at all. They are circling very much as you yourself might circle when you feel trapped or anxious or indecisive. They feel all those things themselves. There is a reason for their agitation, their alternating bouts of hope and desolation.

It's the nuptial flight. It took place yesterday. You, Reader, missed it because it happened in the white space between chapters, off-stage as it were. Not that there was much to see. Some two dozen drones—which was more than any ant had guessed to exist—came crawling up from the main gallery, or from emergency exits in abandoned galleries, most eagerly enough, others pushed and prodded by their mothers. They didn't take off at once. Instead, they wandered around on the stone for some hours, excited but needing encouragement. No one wanted to be first. Or it wasn't time yet. Their long, sensitive feelers and big eyes searching and questioning the void, wanting a signal to depart. The workers catching some of the excitement themselves and coming out, then going back, coming out and going back. A nuptial flight that was only a few drones, hopeless, hopeless! This was what they had come to! But it was still a nuptial flight, something to leave the nest, maybe continuing their story in another place and time.

The weather at least was perfect. A warm day, overcast and misty in the morning, clouding up in the afternoon. Rain—let's hope not! Just a few drops, the big heavy drops that nearly do you in but not many of them, luckily, and then the sky cleared again. The drones felt it was time, they must have sensed something—instinct, intuition, no one knows how drones decide these things. They opened their wings and a light lofting breeze bore them up. Just two dozen frail fluttering shapes, getting smaller and smaller. Soon out of sight.

The last nuptial flight, just a scattering of drones, semaphores of improbable desire and yearning. Within the drones were elements of all the majors, drones, virgin queens, callows and foragers who had belonged to the colony. Each drone was packed with codes that, reassembled, might spell out once again the story of Thrip—spell it out only partially and subject to much editing. But if one of the drones should live for the next few hours, if a single drone were to mate and his queen survived, then the story would live on to be continued, however changed and translated. A tiny flight of drones, messages flung out at random into the bright unfathomed void. A nuptial flight that was only two dozen drones, more than anyone had known to exist, but still—no, it was hopeless, hopeless!

Undetected, unobserved, with only a single worker to assist her, a virgin queen emerged from a hidden gallery and took off after the drones.

We see what is left: a recursive procession of ants, feelers touching gaster, one behind another, one before another, leaderless, directionless, circling in upon themselves, tracing wandering ellipses across the blank slate that covers their nest. Directionless, circling in upon themselves, as if to find something lost that could not be regained, not that way—as if they could find the colony that had been lost.

Now that there was neither queen nor brood the nest had become a true labyrinth. The ants lost themselves in it. Even a straight line can be a labyrinth if you find yourself without a motive either for leaving or for staying. It is better to pretend that you have misplaced the exit or misjudged the time; it is better to pace, pace, pace your little chamber within than to bear up against the alien world without. Some did so. But now it was almost as dangerous within as without. Darkness had overtaken the nest, not the warm full-scented natal darkness of safety but that of sickness, anomy and oblivion. Beetles and nematodes and other vicious, secret, nameless things taking it over now, hunting them down for food. Within forgotten chambers, the dead grow gardens of sinister flowers, shedding a dim dust of spores into the empty corridors. Perish within or perish without, that's what it had come down to.

Each one an each one, except it's mostly the same ants over again, repeating themselves, stepping back into the nest, looping back to the outside, passing in, passing out. With an easy twist of their slender waists, coming again and again to the beginning, avoiding the end. In this way they find a mechanism, regrettably tedious, of postponement, evasion, indirection.

Each one an each. Each one a story. Everything is a story, even a blade of grass, even a stone, even a letter of an alphabet. One ant had her eggs stolen and eaten; another saved hers and raised two fine sons who flew away yesterday to found great kingdoms, she believes, though they would do nothing of the kind. That one came from one of Regina's big heavy eggs and might have been a queen herself if only she'd been tenderly nursed and nurtured. Feeling, each one of them, the anguish of unimportance, of being untold, of coming to the end.

They are seen spilling out onto the blank slate, following one another in dazed, distraught, wavering lines, inscribing upon the stone their alien illegible unintelligible (to us) significations. From above they look not like ants but alphabets—cryptic notations composed of loops and lines, dots and dashes, ascenders and descenders, an active, moving, living script, graphemes bristling with unknowable sense. But one can guess at their meaning. They write upon the stone their anguish, their bewilderment, their overmastering sense of loss and futility, tracing their meaning up and down, not knowing how to pass beyond it, feeling they have reached their end.

But something always happens next, if not for them then for some other ant.

Four ants, one following another, detach themselves, stepping from the stone to a tuft of grass and descending it to the ground below.

The tendency of modern writers to multiply narrators or to circumvent the restrictions of empirical eye-witness narration are signs of the decline of "realism" as an esthetic force in narrative.
–Robert Scholes, James Phelan & Robert Kellogg, **The Nature of Narrative** (2006)

"Only one ant!" Yes, it is not much in the vast fecundity of nature, and is easily replaced. But it is an atom in the world's order that no human power can restore.
–Henry Christopher McCook, **Ant Communities and How They Are Governed: A Study in Natural Civics** (1909)

A miracle of creation—I pursue the thought but it eludes me like a wisp of smoke. It occurs to me that we crush insects beneath our feet, miracles of creation too, beetles, worms, cockroaches, ants, in their various ways.
–J. M. Coetzee, **Waiting for the Barbarians** (1980)

Four ants, one following another, detach themselves, stepping from the stone to a tuft of grass and descending it to the ground below.

Young Keen:

I stayed to the rear. I do as I am asked and no one thought, for quite a while, to ask. Major started off briskly, or as briskly as she could. But she could not pull herself away from the old paths. We walked and walked but still were no farther from the nest, from the stone where the others of the dying colony still circled in despair. Then Nurse tried to lead but she also grew confused and hesitant. She could not free herself from the old paths.

I could, of course, and finally Major thought to have me lead as scout. I was the only one who could lead them from the place that was not after all my own, my mother's nest.

Afterwards they asked me: How did I do it? How did I know which way to go?

They asked at first with amazement, later with resentment, as we began to understand what our lot would be.

Which of the possible answers is the one to be given: That if you walk in any direction you are sure to find ants, including eventually your own kind? That my senses are keener than yours? That, not being one of you, not having a home, my senses are open to perceiving all the other places where I will also never be at home?

They asked at first with amazement, later with resentment, as we began to understand what our lot would be. As if it could have been better elsewhere.

I walked straight to the foraging trunk trail of our kin, as if I knew the way. My senses are keener than theirs. I know why that is. Someone once told me that I was meant to be a queen. And would have been a queen, if only I'd been tenderly nursed and nurtured.

Beta:

I ask myself why I did not stay on the stone, or inside, dying with the nest. That would have been the proper thing to do. A good loyal daughter, one who was the Queen's attendant, the Royal Beta, ought not survive her mother.

I had never been outside. There was no need. Even after the Queen's essence had faded from my cuticle, I retained my authority. It's a matter of bearing, of assurance, and of size, of course. Other ants gave up their juice to me. I would never have needed to go to the outside.

It was horrible, stepping out into such an incomprehensible torrent and stench of sensation. The sickening flicker of vision, the flood of bizarre, stupefying aromas. A treacherous, deceitful, dangerous world, into which I never needed to go.

I wanted to turn back. I would have turned back, but always there was another ant at my gaster prodding me. They would not let me leave. Forced to continue with them, I summoned up my strength. I remembered who I was. The way became less horrid. I began to perceive patterns, regularities. Now I went ahead bravely. It's a matter of bearing, of assurance, and of size, of course.

Old Major:

I led but my grief led me. I could not find the way. I kept doubling back to the nest despite myself. Then Spout came forward. Spout. She's forgot how to do anything except nurse stolen eggs. No more eggs for her now, unless she'd like to adopt some spider eggs. It was Young Keen who did it, who led us away.

She headed due east. I don't know why, or if she knew why. We walked and walked, and the way was hard. The grass came up so thick that we had to take long winding detours around and over and between the stalks. But there were hardly any other obstacles to our passing—no sticks, no pebbles, no holes, hardly, of any kind. Fewer crevices, even, than you usually find in hot weather like we've been having.

It worried me a bit. It would worry any ant with a little experience of the world, who knew what she was about. You depend on there being plenty of those crevices and holes. Where were we going to hide if a jumping spider or a ground beetle went after us?

Then it came to me how few animals there were in that thick uniform grass. No burrows, no smells or other signs of the bigger things, like toads and mice and shrews. Hardly any beetles either—who would miss beetles, you say—but still it was strange that they were absent. Of course there were gnats and mites and springtails—they're everywhere—but fewer of them even. No predators that we noticed—that was to the good—but hardly any prey or anything worth scavenging either. A vast, monotonous, lushly green wasteland—how to make sense of that?

Then Young Keen led us right up to the strangest thing of all. It wasn't a trail and it wasn't a gallery. It was something in between—a broad long path just under the surface, covered over with dirt and debris so you'd hardly know it was there.

"Ants built this," Spout said, wondering at it, as who wouldn't wonder. "A foraging path with a roof over it. Protection from wind, sun and rain and even from most predators. Think how many ants it must have taken to build it, and then to keep it in repair!"

"But what kind of ants?" I said. "No kind of ant that's kin to us or would welcome us."

But Young Keen said no, they were our kind, our kind and our kin. But whether they would welcome us or not …

Whether, or not. We hesitated there for a while, not quite daring to enter, not knowing what else to do. Then it was Calls-Herself-Beta who went ahead. The rest of us followed her.

She's forgotten that now. That she was first and the rest of us just followed her. Now when everybody's complaining or sulking, and she's complaining or sulking the most, she's forgotten how she went first. The rest of us just followed behind her.

Spout:

We knew they must be different from us, just from discovering this path they had built for themselves. I thought how many sisters must have worked together, truly cooperated and shared, to accomplish such a great work. It occurred to me that this might be a better, fairer society than the place we had come from. It might be a place where sisters were equals, were kind to one another.

I thought these things but I didn't say them aloud. I have learned to be silent. And that's lucky, for if I had shared my hopes, my fantasy, then they would have blamed *me* later on, at those times when everyone's grumbling or sulking, which now seem like most of the time.

I thought it might be a place where sisters were equals, were kind to one another. That didn't mean they would be kind to us, who were not their sisters. I thought back to the time after the war, when the survivors from Regina's ruined colony came to us and begged. They were bitten and chased away at first. But a few ants, more generous or less alert than their sisters, less sensitive to differences, fed them. Eventually they managed to join us, to merge, until no one remembered, or hardly remembered, that we had once been enemies.

I thought it would be like that. Now I ask myself why it has turned out so badly. Was it really because they would never accept us? Or were we finally unwilling to merge with them, to give up our identities and our past? To be accepted by these ants, to lose our own ways, would be a kind of death. Maybe some of Regina's daughters felt like that too. Staying at the periphery of our nest, clinging to each other, wanting shelter but never wanting to be one with us, clinging to Regina's remembered ways until age and hardship made an end of them.

Beta:

Of course I was nervous. We all were nervous. This is when one shows oneself a leader—the Royal Beta, or the Alpha as I should have been. I reminded myself that we were among ants, not beasts. That it would be safer to venture onto their sheltered trail than to stay exposed to the outside. I held myself tall and I led the way.

It was mid-afternoon, a time when most foragers would have retreated to the nest to groom and share and rest. But a concealed trail like this can be used at all hours, and it gave access to a network of connecting trails and tunnels where root aphids are pastured. So we soon began to encounter ants. They showed no interest in us, barely turning a feeler toward us before passing on. "Ants," they said to us with their indifference, "just more ants." And there were such a great many of *them*.

We had walked a long way. We were hollow for want of food. So I did a bold thing, something none of the others would have thought or dared to do. I went up to one of the strangers and tapped her mouthparts. Not as though I were begging—as though I deserved. She gave me a drop of food then hurried on her way. I shared it with the others.

An ant had fed us. The rest took no notice of us. We were elated. It seemed, incredibly, we had already been accepted or at least tolerated.

The trail debouched near the nest mound, or what would have been the mound. The entrance was concealed, placed deeper in the shade than most ants would find comfortable or convenient. We didn't trouble to reflect on what this meant: they must have enemies; there is something that they fear.

I was confident. I held myself tall and went straight for the nest entrance. I did not realize my companions were staying prudently behind, waiting to find out what would happen to me.

I had put myself among a group of returning foragers. The first sentry passed me, not noticing or not caring. But the second stopped me. She opened her mandibles in threat, or so I thought, and I began to edge away. Then she lunged for me, trying for a grip on my neck. Missing, she slashed at my trunk, then placed another blow on my gaster as I turned and fled.

I was hurt. My sisters, at this moment we were truly sisters, all of us, licked and cleaned my hurt for me.

Spout:

After Beta was attacked, we retreated to the nest midden. We spent the rest of that first day there and much of the next, scavenging a little, not too successfully, for food among their waste. We were terribly dejected. It would have been easy to stay there, numbed by grief, exhaustion and exposure, until we were midden stuff ourselves.

It would have been easy to give up. It was our feeling for ourselves as sisters that saved us from it. My sister Major licked the wounds of my sister Beta with all the tenderness of a nurse for a new-laid egg. My Other-Sister and I crept back toward the nest entrance, hoping to find another way into the nest.

"All we have to do is avoid one ant," I told Other-Sister, I told myself. "Just one ant. The others don't mind us." And it seemed true, or seemed as if it might be true, at the time.

We noticed other ants crouched around the nest environs, some solitary, some clustered. Some waving their feelers slowly toward the entrance, others seeming as if they had dozed off. Most had found themselves a better spot for waiting than we had, more sheltered and secluded. Still, it was strange. Ants don't do that—ants don't rest outdoors, where it's always dangerous.

"What are they doing," I said aloud, making it a question but not expecting an answer.

"They are waiting for the changing of the guard. Some sentries must be easier to pass than others."

"But other ants are passing in and out freely," I objected.

"Those are the ones who are the same. These others waiting outside are the ones who are different. Maybe other refugees like us, or maybe the ones who are old or crippled or stunted or otherwise objectionable. They have to wait for their chance to get in. They know what it is, and if we watch we'll know too."

And it was just as Other-Sister said. We detected a little commotion at the entrance that might have been a changing of the guard. And shortly afterwards the ants who had been waiting got up and joined the stream of foragers entering the nest.

"How do you know these things?" I said, this time intending it as a question. But this time she chose not to answer, or else did not know the answer.

Young Keen:

Beta took the lead. Should I have tried to stop her, tried to warn her of the danger? She is too proud, or she was then too proud, to listen.

I could have said: We must be patient, hiding in their midden, begging food, running away when challenged. We must wait until our alien nest smell fades and blends with theirs.

I could have said: I know these things. I was the alien in your nest, where only some ants, the kindly or the less perceptive ones, called me sister. Beta had never been one of the ants who called me sister. She has had to change. We have all changed.

Once Beta was well enough to move, we waited for the proper time, then slipped in one by one. I was very frightened—why was that? If we made a mistake, if we were detected, we could veer off before the sentries attacked us. They were majors—too slow and clumsy to catch *me*, at least. No, it was frightening to succeed, to get inside the strange nest. It was frightening to be surrounded by strangers, so many strangers. Their nest is enormous, teeming, confounding. I was afraid of not finding the ants that I call my sisters.

I did find them. We clustered together in a side chamber, an old unused storeroom, staying close to each other, staying close to our old familiar ways, keeping our difference intact. And that soon became our pattern. When we are not at work, we cluster tight together, guarding our familiar scent, our familiar ways, keeping ourselves separate.

I was very frightened those first few minutes after slipping into the strange nest. I was afraid of not wanting to find the ants that I call my sisters. Because I knew these strangers were also granddaughters of Regina, just as much related to me. I might have merged with them, blended, been as much a sister and as much at home as I could be anywhere. Would that have been better?

I did not have to make that choice. My called-sisters found me, claimed me. Pressed so close together, always together, there is nothing we do not share except our thoughts.

Beta:

Except for that one, the major who attacked me, most of them leave us alone. Working alongside us, sometimes sharing food with us, but otherwise making us feel the difference. None of them ever grooming with us. We were made to know our place almost immediately. It's the upper nest for us, and none of the better quarters in it. If we want a clean corner to rest and groom in, we must clean it ourselves.

Major and I work with the honeydew gatherers in the surface tunnels dug beneath the grassroots, carrying the harvest back to the nest. For the major this is easy work. I am not used to it; the stretching of my gaster pains me; but otherwise we might not be able to feed ourselves. Our sisters, who are smaller, must work each day at maintaining and repairing the trunk trail. I do not think they admire it so much now.

We go in and out of the nest with the other unwanteds, the crippled, the stunted, the old, who do not even want each other. It seems to me that even the unwanted ones take care to avoid our contact, no matter how crowded the passageway might be, as if they did not want our savor on their bodies. Sometimes we are unlucky with the sentries. Then we must wait outside the nest a long hour or more, my gaster swollen and uncomfortable, before we can safely return. And the one who attacked me still remembers my taste. I must always be alert, even inside the nest, even when I am tired, even when I am so tired I hardly care.

Once we are inside again, once our work is done, we go to our chosen place. It's small and musty; but if we cleaned it up other ants might evict us, take it for their own. In our chosen place we share the food that Major and I kept back for ourselves. Then we cuddle and we groom and we talk about things that do not matter, avoiding those that do.

Odd how those two always put Regina's daughter between them. They're true sisters, although that doesn't seem to make for much love between them. Or maybe it does: much love *and* much hate.

The major was always saying the royal ones wouldn't stay and repopulate our nest. Her sister might have resented that, particularly when it turned out to be true. They flew away on their nuptial flight and never came back. Being smarter than your sisters doesn't go toward making you popular with them, though of course the major's not an ant who has to worry much about that.

They keep Regina's daughter between them as a buffer, as an insult, as a contest to be her favorite—which is it? Do they even know?

I never needed to be loved by my sisters, never expected it. I served the Queen my Mother, but she didn't, couldn't, protect me from the hate of sisters. And in the end I couldn't protect her. If she had made me the Alpha, it might have been different. I would never have deserted her. She would have lived, she would have laid more eggs.

My wounds still trouble me, but that is not my greatest cause for grief.

Spout:

Bickering, always bickering, those two, Beta and Major, finding fault, seeking someone to blame. Beta at least has some reason for it. Her wounds still bother her, and I think she is afraid, though she would never say so. I do not mind her bickering as much. But my sister—nothing has happened to her but she is always finding fault, especially with me.

She doesn't understand, even now. We must stay together. We must be as true sisters to one another. While we yet live, the life of our homeland, its story, the only story we have ever known, continues.

We are not as proud, Other-Sister and I, as Beta and Major. We save a little food and share it with other unwanted, outcast ants who work on maintaining the trunk trail. They begin to like us a little and to tell us a few things. There is mockery in it, because we are the newcomers. They tell us things that may be true or false or right or wrong—always holding something back, breaking into smirks at our ignorance. They are friendly and they are also malicious.

They tell us the sentry who attacked Beta is called the Enforcer. They say she mostly attacks newcomers but any ant, if she's despised enough, different enough, will be a target. It's been safer for us since you came, they laugh—so thank you, that makes you our friend! They laugh at us for the words we don't know, for our customs that are different. But some of them are refugees and immigrants too and are trying to mingle, to blend. I know which ones they are because Other-Sister told me. It is another one of those things that she knows, can sense, somehow.

You will never be enough like them that they'll treat you as sisters, I say to them. No, they answer, but the Enforcer will leave us alone. Watch out, watch out, they say, sometimes the Enforcer remembers an ant, and that can be very bad! But they are being mean. They want to frighten us. And I'm sorry for sharing food and for trusting them the little bit that I trusted them. It is better to be separate, to keep to ourselves.

When we are working together, Other-Sister sometimes edges away from me, comes nearer to the other ants. It occurs to me then that she might think: Here are a hundred ants who will treat me as an almost-sister, an other-sister—a hundred instead of just three ants, three aging, unpopular, vulnerable ants. But it's not true! We treat her as a true sister—why else do we always place her between us, so that she is more like one of us, as much as she can be.

I think but I do not say: I nursed you, I saved you from the destruction of Regina's nest, you belong to me! And then, thinking these things, I am jealous, as jealous as Major. So I pull her away with me. She does not resist. She comes, almost, willingly. I am afraid of losing her. And then we would be only three ants, three aging, unpopular, vulnerable ants.

Young Keen:

When we are together, the four of us, grooming and resting in our corner, in the squalid space permitted to us, the air is thick with unspoken regrets and resentments.

Major is an ant for whom the present is always hateful, always inferior to the misremembered past. She thinks: why did we leave our home; and she thinks there is some ant, perhaps me, perhaps Nurse, who is to blame. As if we could have stayed in a ruined, sick, despairing nest without despairing and sickening ourselves. She wants to remember it different from what it was, heightening the contrast, feeding her discontent and bitterness.

When Nurse is quiet, we all know what it is that preoccupies her: she thinks of her princess, her royal nursling who flew away on the nuptial flight and never returned. As if that were not what royal ones do, what they have always done. I wonder which thought is more bitter for Nurse, that her beloved princess fell to predators or that she abandoned us.

Beta's silence is sorrow and indignation blended. How she might have saved her mother Thrip. How her mother might have saved them both by making her the Alpha. How all of this might not have happened. As if it were ever that simple. As if there were a single turning, a moment of choice, when things could have been otherwise. As if we were not held fast within a web woven of thousands of implicated causes, both tiny and vast.

And as for me, what is there for me to regret and resent: if my mother Regina had not waged war on her daughter Thrip or if my mother had not lost the war; if Nurse, who saved me, had not also starved and stunted me; if these things had not happened I would have been a royal one myself. And

I know what I would have done. I would have flown away on the nuptial flight and never come back to a ruined, sick, despairing nest.

None of these things can be said but the silence is contaminated by them. The silence must be filled and rendered wholesome, or at least endurable. We must talk of something, and that something will be flavored with our resentments. Usually our topic is all the things that we dislike, all the things that are different from home, that we will never accept, that will never accept us.

First comes the food. There is no end to complaining about the food—bland and savorless, cloying yet unsatisfying. There is always much that can be said about the food. This is Beta's favorite topic and she handles it well. But even this topic is unsafe. Inevitably, Beta and Major are drawn into their reminiscences about nectars and honeydews that were so much sweeter and finer in the old days, flavored as they now are with nostalgia. This makes us all sad, and it takes an effort to pull ourselves back from the past, to return to trivial complaints about the food.

We grumble, we bicker, we console each other, exchanging roles from day to day. One day Major might say: This sort of life is not worth living. If Beta is feeling irritable, as she usually is, she will be the one who replies: No, no, you're wrong—any life is worth living. Another day it is Beta who declares this life is not worth living, and Major who argues with her. The argument passes back and forth between the two of them like the dull savorless root honeydew on which we now subsist. In this way they expend their resentment and unhappiness in abstractions.

Complaining, bickering, grumbling: that is how we conceal our thoughts. That is also how we multiple ourselves, our persons, filling up the intolerable silence with our words, so we are not just four but many more, we are our lost sisters too.

It is easier to think "our lost sisters" than "their lost sisters." When I am weary, discouraged, why shouldn't I think as they think, if it is easier to do so? I must share their fate. Even if they did not always put me in the middle, including me, excluding all others—even then I must share their fate.

Old Major:

We were going on about the food again, smirking at something clever that Beta had said, when Spout came out with it: "I know what it is about the food," she said. "The flavor of a food doesn't come from the aphid or the plant but from the sisters who share it with one another. It's savorless to us because we can't taste our homeland in it." We drew away with shock and embarrassment. Only Spout could blurt out something like that, something that should never be said. It's better for all of us when she keeps still, silently mourning her lost fantasy of keeping her princess, her royal nursling, home to repopulate our nest. Her princess who repaid her devotion by flying off to feed the birds.

For the rest of us, silence is not good. We are noisy, complaining and bickering, to escape our thoughts. When silence falls between us four, it means we are thinking: What happened, or is happening, to all our sisters, the ones we left behind? Did they disperse, like we did, finding their own meager places in some distant kin's nest? Did they just sicken and die of despair and exhaustion? At the time, it seemed unthinkable that the colony could continue without Mother, without even a brood of drone eggs. But maybe it did. Maybe they're still there, and if so we made a terrible mistake.

There wasn't an ant left behind that I cared about. But whenever the silence falls down on us I have such a feeling of sickness, of loss, like I can never be whole again. And the stupid thing that Spout had to say made the feeling so much worse!

But I'm pretty quick for a major. I thought of something to say, something to take away the silence that meant so much more than any of us could bear.

"Why are they always so spiteful," I said to my sisters, who knew what I meant—they being always them and we being always us. "We earn our keep. We work for our share. It's not like we were trying to sneak into their nursery to lay our eggs."

But I made the mistake of phrasing it like a question, when I meant nothing of the kind. Spout had to give an answer, which I didn't want, which I wasn't asking for.

"It's because they are all true sisters, with just one drone for a father to the whole nest. Not that it makes them any sweeter to one another. They still fight and compete, each one trying to keep a place in the nursery or the royal chambers, trying to force the dirty dangerous work on others. They're so much alike we can hardly tell them apart. But they can tell *us* apart. And they can all join together like sisters in chasing us out. Then letting us back in when we bring them their food. Then chasing us out again for the sport, for the meanness of it."

What can you do with an ant like Spout, who just can't keep it to herself? We all got quiet again, until we dozed off, cuddled up close together like we always are, like we always make ourselves to be.

Spout:

Rain. A long soaking rain first, then building to a storm. It lasts all night and into the next day. No ants can leave the nest. The sentries close the entrance but do a bad job of it. The rain is coming in there and at other places too.

Fortunately, our little corner in the upper nest isn't wet at all. It stays pleasantly damp without puddles or drips. We don't know why that is. Perhaps there's a stick or a stone right overhead that blocks the rain from coursing in. The main gallery is too wide and straight—we have often re-marked on that—it means the ants in the deep nest are getting wet—hah! We laugh at that—for once we have the good spot!

We are cozy. We are almost cheerful. We pass around a few drops of food and we groom one another.

Other-Sister says how much work this is going to make! The trunk trail will be in ruins after such a rain.

Major says it shows how silly these ants are. The things they do never make sense. So much work for nothing. Why a covered trunk trail in a land so barren of spiders and toads and such like?

But there are enemies, Other-Sister says. Enemies that destroy whole nests. That's why there are so many other refugees here. They don't come from dying nests, like us, but nests that were destroyed.

That shows how much time she spends with other ants, listening to them, learning their ways, much more than I realized. None of us knew this thing.

It makes us quiet and a little dejected, until I think of something to say.

Yes, I say, there will be *so much* work to do that even the ants from the deep nest will have to come up and help!

Hauling away twigs and debris! says Major.

Beetle frass! says Beta. Getting themselves dirty picking up beetle frass!

We laugh and now we are cheerful again. Today we are the fortunate ones, we say to one another. We have the dry spot. We have the good spot.

How could we have been so stupid.

Did we think no one would notice? Did we think they would leave us alone?

Old Major:

We weren't paying attention. Feeling warm, cozy, well-fed, cheerful. Maybe imagining or pretending we were back home.

Then came a sharp mean jab at my gaster. I jumped with the shock and knocked into Beta without meaning it, without knowing what was going on. It was the Enforcer, looking for something to do, somebody to terrorize, and now she'd found Beta. She seized her by the mandibles and shook her, hard, then set off with her.

We didn't do anything—what was there we could do?—except follow at a safe distance. The Enforcer went straight to the entrance, probably intending to eject Beta from the nest. Give her an nasty bite or two to remember, then toss her out of the nest. That was probably what the Enforcer had going on inside her dull ugly mind.

But of course the entrance had been blockaded to keep out the rain. The Enforcer stood there stupidly for a full minute, still holding onto Beta. You could almost sense the thoughts—she never had many of them—going through her head. She had grabbed Beta to throw her out of the nest but she couldn't get out. Now what to do?

A problem she couldn't work out. So she just started running around the upper nest, into this corner, into that, as though she were looking for another exit. The longer she held on to Beta the more crazed and berserk she got, tearing and gnawing at her, running back and forth from one end to the other.

Ants who were feeling bored or irritable got interested, following along, taking a nip or a pull themselves whenever the Enforcer passed by with her prey. A new sport for a rainy day! Another major wrested Beta free and started running up and down with her. Then she got bored. Beta might have had a chance then. But the Enforcer snatched her back, more furious than ever.

The Enforcer was getting tired. She put Beta down and stood over her, keeping her feelers poised over her victim. If only Beta had held still, played dead! But she must have been a bit crazed with shock because she kept trying to creep away, and then the Enforcer would start it all over again, rushing from one end of the nest to the other, gnawing and shaking Beta as she went.

Eventually, when she put Beta down and stood over her, whipping her feelers over her prey, Beta didn't move. The Enforcer carried the inert body around for a while longer, at a much slower pace, maybe just showing off now. Finally she dropped her at the entrance. Someone must have carried her out to the midden after the rain stopped. I don't know. We didn't check.

The rain stopped. Beta was gone.

And what was I to do now? To work all by myself among strangers, kegging their honeydew and bearing it back to the nest?

Let's do the same work, I say to my two sisters.

No, Spout says. You can't do our work. You're too big.

Let Young Keen work with me some of the time, with you some of the time, I said, getting angry.

But Young Keen spoke up and said she was used to the work she was doing. She wouldn't know anything about how to gather honeydew.

She stroked me on my head that special gentle way she has. But it meant nothing.

Spout:

We never spoke of Beta again. As if she had never existed. We missed her that terribly.

Everything was worse now. We quarreled openly. Mostly it was Major who bickered and complained, she was so unhappy about being alone in the field while Other-Sister and I got to work together.

There was less food. Other-Sister and I didn't say anything at first. But we both must have been thinking: Is that it? Will she starve us into doing what she wants?

We had barely enough for ourselves and no food at all to share with the other ants we worked with on the trunk trail. Now it was all malice and no friendship. They said we were hoarding food and they taunted us. "We hear the Enforcer's looking for a new victim. Who wants to be next?" How I hate them—and begin to fear them too, just a bit.

It could not go on. Finally I spoke to Major, I asked about the food.

No, she said. She was bringing back the same amount as ever. Did we think there weren't ants inside the nest keeping tabs? Checking to make sure the harvesters didn't hoard extra shares in their crops?

No, she said. She was bringing back the same amount as ever. That wasn't the problem. That wasn't what had changed.

"I'm just one ant," she said. And that was the closest we ever came to mentioning Beta.

We had to give in to her, let her have what she wanted. Other-Sister began working as a harvester on alternate days. I must work alone with ants who are hateful to me, who seek out ways to spite me.

It was a mistake to share food with them, a mistake to be friendly. If only we had kept to our own ways, never speaking, never sharing with those others who now resent me, who smirk at my loneliness, who wish me harm.

Young Keen:

Again, once again, I know it would be no use to warn of danger.

I could say to Major: Your sister says nothing but she is afraid to be alone with the other workers, who grow more and more threatening. You are big. There would be no danger for you in working alone.

I could say that to Major but I would not be believed. It would only make for more bitterness. They cannot escape their fate, and I also cannot escape. I am the prize that the two of them must battle for.

Now I go with Major on alternate days, leaving Nurse alone. Field work is hard, but I find I do not mind it. I stand over the aphids as they feed, ready to catch the honeydew as they let it drop. When I am filled up, I carry it to Major and then go back again. We must work very fast to gather up the honeydew before it falls, because whatever is wasted attracts pests and grows mold. There is no time for friendship or malice among the harvesters. That is why I do not mind the work.

Usually Major and I manage to leave and return to the nest in the same group. Usually I can go to her when I am filled up, but sometimes she is busy or far away and I go to another one of the big ants who carry home the honeydew harvest. This means Major is still alone among strangers for most of the day, which is the thing that made her so unhappy—and so am I, and so is Nurse.

When I bring her my honeydew, perhaps we hold our mouthparts together longer, touch each other more, than other ants do when they bring their honeydew to the majors who carry it back to the nest. Is it this that makes Major more cheerful? Or is it scoring a victory over her true sister?

I sometimes try to calculate how much of love, how much of hate, combine to make up such feelings as they have for one another. I cannot work it out.

This latest change becomes familiar, like all the other changes we have had to undergo. It is now the rhythm of our days. With a little effort we can forget that things were ever any different. As always they keep me between them when we three are together. I must share their fate. That is how it must be. It seems impossible to leave them.

Old Major:

When we went to our spot at the end of the day, she wasn't there. I just couldn't understand it. How could she not be there?

I went searching for her. I went back to the old spot, the one we had vacated after Beta's death. I went up and down through every part of the upper nest—all the parts where we were allowed to pass.

It was getting late. The sentries had blocked the entrance. No more ants would be returning to the nest. She would not be returning.

Now there was just us two. I went back to where she was waiting for me, my sister who is not my sister.

Young Keen:

Every day ants leave the nest and do not return. No one asks what happened to them. And we do not ask either. Nurse was old, she was working alone among ants who did not like her, who would more willingly hurt than help her.

Now Major seems much older too. She moves slowly, as though she were very cold. Yet she holds herself apart, keeping a little distance from me now when we are together. The last daughter of Regina and the last daughter of Thrip.

If I groom her in the way I know she likes, she will seize me in a grip so tight it's painful. So it's better to let her be. She is getting calmer and calmer and colder and colder. I understand that things will not continue like this for much longer. I am sorrowful. I am patient.

We go out each day to the honeydew harvest. I must prod her sometimes to get her to go out, then again to get her to come back to the nest.

At last comes the day when prodding does not work, when she does not move. I go alone to the harvest. When I return, I do not go back to that spot, so I do not know whether she has been taken to the midden or not. Instead, I seek out another part of the nest where I will live out my days.

X.
Magical Realism
Ant

It is no coincidence that the famously altruistic insect societies provide the most compelling examples of spite. In the course of social evolution, insect workers have become actually or effectively sterile, thus overcoming the major obstacle in the evolution of spite—cost to personal reproduction.
–Kevin R. Foster, Francis L.W. Ratnieks & Tom Wenseleers, "Spite in Social Insects" **(Trends in Ecology and Evolution, 2000)**

The constitutive feature of magical realism is a powerfully appealing hybridism of the realistic and the fabulous … García Márquez's novel neither settles comfortably into the secure realism of George Eliot or Gustave Flaubert, nor faithfully inhabits the region of pure fantasy we associate with the works of J. R. R. Tolkien or Lewis Carroll. **One Hundred Years of Solitude** refuses to resolve the cognitive and social-historical dissonance between realism and fantasy. Unlike the gothic novels of Anne Radcliffe or the Sherlock Holmes detective fiction of Arthur Conan Doyle, in which supernatural occurrences are invariably explained away by reference to a scientific-materialist understanding of the physical universe, the magical events of **One Hundred Years of Solitude** cannot be assimilated to a rationalistic worldview.
–Michael Valdez Moses, "Magical Realism at World's End" **(Margin, 2002)**

"The ants!" she exclaimed. And then she forgot about the manuscripts, went to the door with a dance step.
–Gabriel García Márquez, **One Hundred Years of Solitude** (1967)

The old man climbed on a horse and ambled slowly, mumbling advice and recommendations, prayers of wisdom and enchanted formulas, to the ants.
–Isabel Allende, **The House of the Spirits** (1982)

You sense for a moment just how mysterious and incomprehensible life is, and how tiny a part of what life could be we actually call by that name.
–Victor Pelevin, **The Life of Insects** (1998)

SHE WAS A PRINCESS, a very great, a very large princess, the last of an illustrious lineage.

She lived with her old nurse in a chamber of ramshackle magnificence. The Princess and her nurse agreed to notice only its magnificence and to pay no attention to its mildewed and crumbling condition. That, and the greatness of the princess, were the sole points upon which they were able to agree. They got along perfectly well all the same by virtue of discreet silences and dignified forbearances and polite disregard of anything tending to the argumentative. The discreet silences were contributed by the Princess, whose manners were exceptionally agreeable. She had never been known to utter a negative, nothing stronger than a maybe, elegantly varied from time to time with a perhaps.

The old nurse was quite, quite mad—that the Princess had settled for herself long ago, almost from the moment of her eclosure. Nurse said the oddest things, and stuttered too. She was old and she smelled bad. But she was devoted to the Princess, who therefore forgave her her age and her smell. It was obvious that the old nurse had gone mad for love, love for the Princess of course, a love that must go unrequited, although the Princess magnanimously forgave her all these faults, her age, her smell, her stutter and her madness, in recognition of her devotion.

They lived alone in their magnificent, mildewed chamber. They rarely went out, and when they did, the old nurse proved herself to be the most jealous of duennas, blocking and boxing the head of any ant who dared to approach the Princess.

The old nurse said the oddest things. She spoke, feelingly, stutteringly, of generosity among sisters, of the duty of those endowed with eggs to be considerate towards those without. She spoke of danger, terrible danger, if the Princess were ever to go anywhere or do anything without the nurse's advice and protection. It was all madness, and the Princess felt the kindest thing was not to listen. When a silence warned her that Nurse expected a response to her peroration, the Princess gave a gracious maybe or an agreeable perhaps. Maybe she did agree that a responsible young virgin ought not to abandon her dead mother's nest. Perhaps it's true that ants are meant to creep through hollowed earth and that wings are much too dangerous to be used. Maybe it's true that all ants, regardless of caste and class, can work together and cooperate. Perhaps it is also the case that common worker ants are very dirty and the Princess must never let them near her.

They have few visitors. A musty old major brings them bug juice, nectar and honeydew. She is introduced to the Princess as the ant who beheaded Grandmother. The nectar she brings is excellent, but Nurse insists that the Princess, for the sake of her delicate and all-important health, drink the bug juice. The major is usually accompanied by the Princess's aunt, the last of Grandmother's many thousands of daughters. The Princess likes her aunt because she never gives advice and she does not smell. The family is quite small: just this one aunt and some two hundred worker sisters, none of whom are ever admitted for a visit or allowed to approach the Princess during her rare excursions, always accompanied by the nurse, in the relatively inhabited portions of the moldy, crumbling, depleted nest.

"Why are there not more visitors?" the Princess took occasion to ask in one of her infrequent utterances.

"Keep out—dirty—for your sake—disease," Nurse said, spluttering and spraying the words in her eagerness to impress the Princess with the many dangers threatening her from which she, her nurse, would save her.

"Disease," the old nurse reiterated with dark foreboding didactic intent. "Juice-sucking mites, vermiculated brain frenzy, glabrous palsy, the white patch pox, the feeler shivers, the sporulating chills, the paralytic gapes ..."

But the Princess was no longer listening. There were already so many voices in her head, competing to be heard, that Nurse could not hold her attention for long unless what she had to say was of the most diverting oddity.

The voices had begun soon after she pupated. That had not surprised her. Nothing ever surprised the Princess. Then they had been vague, muzzy, dreamlike. It was only when they continued after her eclosure that they began to annoy and puzzle her. Why were all these ants gabbling in her head? One would begin by giving her advice, much like Nurse. Then another would break in and argue. Then another and another until they were all talking at once.

She should fly away said one. No, no, said another, she'll be eaten for sure. She should mate with the drones within the nest. What! cried another. When have we ever allowed our noble line to inbreed! And on and on. She hadn't the faintest notion what they were quarreling about and the noise left her feeling tired and confused.

Occasionally the babble would recede to a distant mumble, allowing two distinct voices to be heard. She figured out who they must be. Mother and Grandmother, of course.

Mother and Grandmother got along much better than she would have supposed, knowing their history. But they spoke so quickly, trying to get it all said at once before the other voices interrupted them, that she couldn't make out what they wanted of her. And of course they contradicted each other too. It was a lucky hallucination when she could finally get something straightened away. To appease their restless spirits, and in hopes of exorcising them, she readily agreed with everything they proposed.

"Yes, yes, Mother! I promise! I'll do just that!" she would cry out, quite unnecessarily. She had failed to grasp the self-evident fact that the voices inside one's head can overhear one's thoughts. "There's no need to shout," said her grandmother severely. "Sorry, Grandmother," said the Princess, still rather loudly. "Sorry, sorry, sorry."

Which confirmed those around her in believing that the Princess, though large, though fat, though reekingly fertile, though unquestionably everything a princess should be, was an utter imbecile. Which was so much, they agreed, to the good. She would be easier to manage, the agreeably vacuous Princess.

When Grandmother and Mother talked in her head they often were drawn into long dull logistical analyses of the battles they had fought against one another. It was Grandmother's position that she had won the war—that properly her daughter would be dead and she would still be alive. It was all the fault of the Princess's nurse and the major, who had violated the conventions of honorable combat by decapitating a queen and carrying off her brood.

"My daughters simply have more imagination than yours," Mother answered. "Like this one here, who thinks she hears us talking in her head." And they both laughed at that, a little unpleasantly.

The Princess was of age and her nurse was anxious to arrange her nuptials, concerning which she held confused but impassioned notions. It was part of Nurse's madness that she had kept the Princess in such carefully guarded seclusion, admitting only Nurse's true sister, Old Major, and the Princess's aunt, Young Keen. But others who were just as obsessively interested in the Princess's fate could no longer be excluded.

The three visitors kept a respectful, sanitary distance from the Princess as they were presented, murmuring their compliments on her size and fertility. Beta said the Princess had been a big beautiful larva who had grown up to be an even bigger more beautiful ant. Gamma vowed to serve her with the same devotion and loyalty she had shown to her late Mother, their beloved Queen. "The Mother of us all, except that one," she added, indicating Young Keen. Then Scrobe came forward and attempted to introduce herself to the Princess as her future mother-in-law. Fortunately, the Princess, distracted once again by her voices, had not been paying attention.

Scrobe's inept attempt to overleap the preliminaries had a chilling effect. It was by no means agreed that the Princess should be matched with Scrobe's sons. Inbreeding was felt to be undesirable, particularly if the result was to perpetuate a line of Scrobes. Yet, if the Princess were to take her nuptial flight in search of more suitable mates ... Nurse shuddered at the danger.

At first they carried out their negotiations in the Princess's presence, until Old Major suggested that maybe she wasn't quite as stupid as she appeared—a shrewd observation which, considering who had made it, was its own confirmation. They left the Princess in the charge of her aunt, who was too young to be included in their deliberations, and adjourned to a smaller but even more dilapidated antechamber.

"Why are there voices coming from the wall?" her aunt asked the Princess once they were alone.

"You're mistaken," the Princess answered. "They are coming from my head."

Young Keen hesitated, finding the Princess's explanation unconvincing but being too polite to dispute it. Overcome by curiosity, she edged over to the wall and examined it, probing and tapping, until finally, her suspicions confirmed and her interest aroused, she began to dig. The wall was hollow, giving entrance to what proved to be a vast passageway. Oddly enough, the occupants seemed initially less interested in the Princess than in her aunt.

"Ah," said Regina, "so you've come too. You know you've been a great disappointment to me, Daughter."

"But what have I done?" Young Keen asked, stupefied.

"It's what you haven't done. You've haven't got wings and gonads."

"But that's hardly her fault," said Thrip. "There wasn't enough meat to raise two queens. My daughter naturally chose to favor her own sister over your daughter."

"It was stupid," Regina insisted. "If she'd asked the major for help sooner, she might have raised both of them properly. Then my daughter could stay here to mate with the drones. No issue of inbreeding with grandnephews, or not as much. And your daughter could fly off and take her chances."

"Don't be too upset, dear," Thrip said, quite kindly, to the bewildered ant. "After all, you might just as easily have been eaten."

"That's true too," Regina acknowledged. Forgetting Young Keen, they went back to arguing military history.

Conversations that were not about the Princess could not hold her interest. She wandered further along the passageway, which teemed with dead queens, rows upon rows of them, all directing their feelers toward the Princess, all, as usual, talking at once.

"So you're not in my head after all!" The Princess was not haughty and could laugh at her own mistakes.

"Certainly not! Not enough room in *your* headpiece!" they chortled. It was not as rude a remark as it seemed, given their numbers, which the Princess tried to count but got confused after she reached thrice-six-six.

"How many of you are there?" she asked.

"Exactly one hundred million," they replied. "We are your forebears, from your unfortunate mother to the great Ur-Ant herself."

"I would like to meet her."

"Impossible! You could never walk that far, not at your pace."

She was walking slowly along their ranks. As she approached, the ancestors were stirred to a mock life by contact with her living, fertile flesh. They began to posture, mothers trying to outdo daughters, daughters striving to excel their mothers. They drew themselves up, each wanting to appear taller, forgetting the unpleasant realities of death. Their decayed joints snapped under the strain; and some of them, on collapsing, disintegrated entirely, showering their neighbors with powdered mummy.

"Am I to understand," the Princess asked, "that this passageway tunnels through time instead of space?"

"Nonsense! How absurd! How can you imagine such idiocy!" they sneered in unison.

"Then how do you come to be here?"

"We have come to you because you are the one hundred millionth and one queen since our race began!" the ancestors announced with momentous solemnity.

"And is that really worth making such a great fuss about?" the Princess asked incredulously.

Ghosts cannot endure even the mildest skepticism. Dismayed, the specters dissolved with a shudder, even the ones who were only disintegrated mummy, reassembling from their dust first and then fading backwards through the walls. The annoying babble of ancestral voices had been silenced. She had defeated them.

She returned to her chamber and her aunt sealed off the passageway, neither of them making comment on the experience. Only her mother and grandmother continued to mumble from time to time from behind the wall, giving advice and admonitions, not much different from her old nurse. And now she knew she could escape listening simply by moving to the other side of the chamber.

The nuptial negotiations, conducted primarily by Beta and Gamma, had advanced to the point that they agreed to introduce the Princess to the drones, who had likewise been hidden away all this time. The occasion was managed with cautious formality. Beta, Spout, Old Major and Young Keen had taken their places alongside the Princess. Scrobe proudly ushered in her sons while Gamma prodded them into their places, reminding them, in a carrying undertone, to hold still and keep silent. "Your mother will set you the example," she added meaningfully.

"Seven!" said Old Major, after a pause. "Such an unlucky number! Why ever did you go to seven?"

"Yes," Beta said, backing her up, "especially since one is just like another. No one can tell them apart. Had you made one provender for the others, they might have turned out bigger."

Scrobe was provoked into an indignant defense of her sons so rambling, so absurd, that even the Princess smiled: The drones were each of them individual, each with tremendous talents and virtues. They were all of them big, handsome, robust, and stuffed with sperm. And they all simply adored their mother.

"But of course they do!" said Spout, who hastened to reassure Scrobe, apologizing for such thoughtless comments, and complimenting her on the outstanding health and bigness of her sons.

Scrobe's feelers twitched with the rapid vacillations of her feelings—with suspicion and surprise, with assuaged hurt, with gratitude and sisterly affection. She opened up. She told all her troubles. Spout listened sympathetically and said yes, yes, she knew just what it was like.

They talked, the two of them, of the terrible anxieties they had undergone in nursing their charges, their terror of beetles, of disease, of shortages. From there they proceeded, gushingly, to subjects of greater intimacy, reliving their tenderest memories of nursing, sharing the most tedious and embarrassing details of every molt their little ones had undergone.

From their separate hiding places, they had feared and plotted against each other so long, so utterly, that, when at last they confronted one another, hate and distrust had festered into fellowship and good manners. Spout was by no means persuaded, as yet, to mate her princess with the other's drones; but already she had begun to address Scrobe as The One Who Really Understands What I've Been Through, More Than My Own Sister Ever Will.

This salutation is far less cumbersome in the original Antic, in which it may be communicated simply by selecting among the hundreds of inflections and modifiers available for the word *sister:* big, old, mean, true, sneaky, smelly, and so forth. In a society in which everyone, even Young Keen, was called sister, only by shuffling and combining these modifiers was it possible to make oneself understood. Otherwise, even an utterance as simple as "Sister, did you notice sister pretending not to have any honeydew when sister asked?" would be impossible without pointing and pantomime. It was a language ideal for gossipy insinuation, since it was easy to pretend innocence if confronted: "No, Sister, I didn't mean you sister I meant sister!" In this instance, what Spout had said, more literally if still roughly translated, was Sister-like-me-like-true-sister-but-more-so, and there was no mistaking her meaning.

Old Major dropped back on her haunches in shock and disgust. She had never held a high opinion of Spout but she had never been disloyal, never called her a name to her face, never anything more barbed than a cool True-sister-who-could-be-truer-if-she-really-cared. And that was only once or twice, when she was really angry. Her sense of betrayal was absolute but might have been short-lived, were there not other ants who would stroke and feed it.

Beta and Gamma, who had anticipated an invigorating round of intrigue, treachery, double-dealing and paybacks, were likewise appalled by this new intimacy. There was nothing for them to do but forget their grudges, pledge lasting friendship, and proceed with their best efforts to thwart and punish Spout and Scrobe for disappointing them. They perceived that the major would be available for their use.

Once the ancestral voices had been silenced, the Princess could hear her own thoughts. She now discovered that she had some. She was no longer stupid, although she continued to have an absent air. She continued to answer questions, however inappropriately, with a maybe or a perhaps. But that was because she had a great deal of thinking to do.

She understood now what the ancestors had been babbling about. Her nurse, gone mad for love, poor thing, expected her to stay at home, a moldering, decaying, crumbling home, breed morganatically with Scrobe's sons and rear a brood of daughter-grandnieces. Some of the voices, she recalled, had approved of the plan. She'll be eaten for sure, they had cried, if she flew away to found a colony of her own. Even the Princess knew that couldn't be correct: there were, after all, other ants in the world, an immense number of them. She asked Mother and Grandmother and they in turn attempted to consult the ancestors; but the ancestors, offended by the Princess's disrespect, were no longer speaking to them. Relying, then, on their musty recollections of their own nuptials, Mother and Grandmother put the Princess's odds at one in a thousand. She would not be eaten for sure, only with a very high degree of probability.

Spout had made her such a lengthy, splutteringly earnest speech on duty and sisterhood that it had taken some time for the Princess to understand her. "You mean," she said at last, "you want me to mate with one of those drones. Now, without a nuptial flight."

The Princess tried a maidenly perhaps, a bashful maybe, but Spout would not be put off so easily. She could not be. She had already pledged that the Princess would be amenable.

Spout and Scrobe had come to a private agreement, which they now announced to their sisters. They would offer one of the drones, Scrobe's eldest, to the Princess as a mate. If he proved sufficient for the task, then the Princess would lose her wings and stay at home forever. If not, then they might still dare release the Princess for a very brief nuptial flight, provided that she promised to come straight home.

"But what does all that mean?" demanded Old Major, who did not neglect her opportunities for quarreling with her True-sister-who-could-be-truer-if-she-really-cared. "'Sufficient for the task' 'lose her wings'—I don't believe either of you know what you're talking about."

"The drone gives sperm to the queen," Scrobe snapped, "and then the queen can have daughters. Every ant knows that."

"How do they do it—what exactly do they do," said Old Major just as nastily. "You don't know that and neither does any ant here." And she was, in her blundering way, perfectly correct. But none of the others were willing to admit it.

"The drone has a thing and the queen has a hole it fits into," Spout suggested.

"No that's not it. The queen has a bag for holding the sperm and the drone give her his sperm to carry for him," Scrobe said.

"It comes to the same thing," said Spout.

"No it doesn't," said Scrobe.

"Neither of you know what you're talking about. And what does losing her wings have to do with it?"

"She can't lay eggs while she has her wings," said Spout, who was beginning to sputter. "At least, I don't think she can. Or maybe when she feels maternal she doesn't want them anymore. I mean, after all, she has no time for wings."

"You mean you don't know," Old Major said. "And if you want to make sure she stays home, you'd better clip her wings right now and mate her to as many drones as it takes because otherwise ..." A barrage of hisses and slaps silenced her.

The Princess might be listening. The Princess *was* listening although she was careful to give no sign of it.

"Why do *we* need to concern ourselves with the minutiae," Gamma said. "It can't be very complicated if it's something a drone knows how to do. Not all drones, after all, are as brilliant and versatile as our dear sister's seven magnificent sons."

"There's an order to things," Beta said slowly. "A queen fills herself with sperm first and then she loses her wings. That's how it's done. There must be a reason for it."

The Princess wondered whether those last words might have been said for her benefit, to reassure her. In either case, she must be very careful if she wished to keep her wings. The major who beheaded Grandmother might take it upon herself to clip them. And, if Beta was correct, she must not let herself get filled with sperm, not until she had had a chance to fly. When she was alone with her aunt, she sometimes fluttered about the ramshackle chamber. It was not satisfying. She ended up covered with dirt, whereupon her patient uncomplaining aunt, without commenting on her folly, would help the Princess clean herself.

Spout, in her role as jealous duenna, had never permitted any of the drones to approach the Princess. Left alone—a point upon which the Princess had insisted—the two winged ants feelered each other with curiosity. The Princess was reassured to find that the drone was barely a third her size, with a slender, fragile-seeming build and feeble, ineffectual mandibles. She felt certain of remaining in control of whatever it was that was about to happen. Something about the drone having a thing that fit into her hole.

The drone greeted her eagerly. Up until that moment, his ignorance had been as great as his mother's. That the drone gives a queen his sperm to carry for him was the extent of his knowledge.

Now, encountering the virgin queen, running his feelers over her plump, fertile form, the drone conceived the idea, as all his ancestors had in their own day also conceived the idea, the ineffable and prime idea that fills the expanding universe with life. It is the idea of stag beetles clashing in armored combat. The idea of the moth tuning his great feathered antennae to decode the amorous messages of the night. The idea of the pollen adrift on the breeze, finding their way to the ovule deep within the flower that blooms always and only for them. The idea of the seed awakening at long last to genial warmth. He shuddered with the splendor of the idea.

Under the power of the Princess's enchanting aroma, the drone knew the one great thing. His being churned and throbbed with an all-comprehending passion. He must have her or die! He must have her and die!

Still, some polite preliminaries were required. He contained himself with difficulty while he opened his mandibles, gaping amorously at his queen and releasing his own intoxicating scent.

"Very well. I consent," she said grandly, and the drone mounted her. He scrambled, then found a footing, aligning his hinder parts with hers. In the swift metamorphosis of love he sprouted two new appendages, stout hairy ones that clamped to her sides. Another pair of hidden body parts shot out and were planted, this time, on her terminal segment, while beneath them yet another pair latched into position, yanking her open. She twisted in surprise, not yet in pain, and as she did so their hooks dug into her flesh. Three pairs of royal ushers—blowing the trumpets, bullying the bystanders, laying the carpet and sprinkling it with rose petals. Make way for the king! The king slid in easily. The king asserted himself. The king lay claim to his surprised, indignant queen.

"Ow!" she cried out, giving a sudden twist to wrench herself free.

"Ow!" the drone echoed. She had bit him, hard, and he let go of her, just like that, landing on his back like a clumsy scarab. With a shocked and self-pitying air, he twisted to his side to lick the hemolymph trickling from his wound. He was very spoiled and good for nothing, not even for the one thing he was intended to be good for. He deserved his bite.

The Princess was curious to know just what it was that he had thrust into her with such violent efficacy. His apparatus now dangled nakedly at his rear. Two thick hairy clubs, shaped like stumpy mandibles, enclosed two pairs of hollow pegs, one pointed and the other hooked. Between the pegs was a bladder, partially deflated but still enormous. It tapered to a hard-edged tip that was furnished with spines on top and teeth along its outer edge. It had all been concealed within him somehow, though the bladder alone was bigger than his gaster. Only the tips of the outer weaponry had peeped, in apparent benignity, from his abdomen when she had feelered him a few moments before.

"Fascinating," she said slowly, "a bit disgusting, to be sure, but fascinating."

The drone, believing he had been complimented, waggled his parts for her. She examined them from every aspect as she worked out the mechanism. The hairy club-like members were claspers to get the correct alignment on her gaster. Then the pegs were shoved into place to pry her open, with the barbs of the bottom pair acting as pincers to grip her flesh. That had not been so bad. The real pain had come as the bladder inflated, driving its wedge of teeth and spines into her insides. Had she not acted promptly, the fully inflated bladder would have been locked in place until the drone had pumped out all his sperm. And what then would have become of her wings?

Fortunately, only a small sample of sperm had passed into her body before she had broken free. The Princess began to form a scheme of confused and baroque contingencies.

A little recovered, the drone was attempting to repackage his parts into his gaster. Jelly oozed from the tip of the bladder as it deflated.

"I don't think that was done quite right," said the drone, who was worried. His bladder would not yet retract, still emptying and trailing behind him as he tried to right himself.

"On the contrary, it was perfect," said the Princess. "Be sure and tell your mother what a good job you did. No need to go into the details."

"Well, it's done," the Princess said to her old nurse after the drone had dragged himself away. "And I hope you're satisfied. I didn't enjoy it one bit."

Trembling with excitement Spout asked her, tried to ask her— she spluttered horrifically and the Princess pretended at first not to understand. The old nurse, spluttering with excitement, wished to know whether—you know—whether it—you know—the, uh, her, uh, receptacle was, um, full.

After considering the possibilities of noncommittal answer, the Princess had an inspiration. "I really don't know," she said, in almost plausible imitation of her nurse's ignorance. This was a new answer. She had not thought of it before. Before she had had only her polite silence, her maybe and her perhaps. This novel response had many possibilities and at least two variants, possibly more. Or at least she thought "I really don't know" and "I don't really know" were different. She would have to try them both.

"I don't really know," she said in a tone of deep reflection, having decided she preferred the variation.

Nurse conferred with her sisters. Maybe it always took more than one. Hadn't their mother had multiple lovers? They would send another of Scrobe's drones to the Princess. They did so. Then another drone, and yet another. The Princess became more sure of herself. "I don't think so," she would reply after each encounter, wagging her head demurely. "Not yet," she said. The drones staggered away, enfeebled, exhausted, refusing the food their mother offered them. The eldest was by now plainly dead, though his obstinate mother persisted in tempting his corpse with honey-dew and nectar.

"Those drones of yours are no good," said Old Major to Scrobe, who trembled with indignation and fury. "We ought to find some others." Scrobe had not been the only egg-layer, only the most successful. There must be more drones somewhere in the colony; there were in fact more drones elsewhere in the colony; but their mothers, horrified by the rumors that reached them of the Princess's insatiability, had hidden them carefully away.

Gamma said little. She suspected a trick on the Princess's part but did not know how it was done. Now she regretted her indifference to mating technics, since it was clear the Princess understood far more than the rest of them. She guessed the Princess's motive after observing how she preened and fluttered her wings. The silly fool! It would serve her right if a wasp got her. But it would not serve Gamma right.

Gamma knew exactly what would serve Gamma right: continued comfort and the prestige of being once again a royal chamber attendant. She knew that a young queen's first daughters were small and timid. They would be easy to dominate. They would be chased out to forage while their elders kept their privileges. What happened to the nest when Gamma was no longer part of it did not concern her. She sought out the major to tell her that she, Gamma, appreciated all her wonderful ideas and suggestions, even if her true sister did not. Old Major lapped up the flattery like honeydew.

"Let's not be hasty," said Beta, after the sixth drone had staggered from the Princess's chamber. "Let's give our dear sister one last chance to prove her drones were worth the rearing. There's still one left, the one that should have been provender to fatten up the others."

Having witnessed his six elder brothers' fate, the drone approached the Princess warily.

"Well?" said the Princess, "Don't you know what to do?"

"Wouldn't you like to hear a story first?" asked the drone.

"What kind of story?" Nurse told her many stories, all dull and moralizing.

"A really good one!" Not risking a refusal, the drone began his tale.

"There once was a colony favored with great prosperity. No rival ants challenged them for territory. Honeydew and game abounded. Their queen was young and fertile. In the autumn of the third year of her reign she produced her first royal brood.

"In their pride and prosperity, they grew careless. One chilly night, when the nurses were stupefied with sleep, an intruder appeared in the brood chamber, a great hulking monster. It bent its feelers over the brood, clawing at their tender skin with its bristly forefeet.

"The brood awoke at the monster's touch. They trembled and clicked their baby teeth in terror but their careless nurses did not stir. The monster seized upon the biggest of the larva and carried it off.

"The next night, when once again the nurses were sunk in torpor, the beast returned, selected the fattest larva and went away with it. The brood that had been clawed by the brute as it selected its prey began to sicken and pine, which was fortunate for them. Because every night when the beast returned to take another victim, it rummaged with jaws and forefeet until it found the one that was most plump and succulent.

"The brood was so plentiful that many terrible nights thus passed before anyone noticed the losses. And then the nurses only quarreled among themselves. At last someone thought to set a guard over the brood, who roused the nurses to attack the intruder.

"Alas! The beast was invulnerable inside its heavy body armor. Its feelers were retracted into deep scrobes, and even its mouthparts were protected, concealed beneath a hideous overhanging lip. The attack of the nurses did not even distract it as it made its slow gluttonous selection. When the nurses sought to follow it to its retreat, the beast released a foul fluid from its hind parts. They were so overcome with disgust that they could do nothing.

"Desperate, they divided the brood up among many smaller chambers so that some of them might be saved. But still the beast tracked them down and took its nightly prey.

"At the end of the winter sleep, only two of the royal larvae, a queen and a drone, were left of the brood. Before they pupated, they each made an oath not to fly until they had avenged their slaughtered sisters and brothers.

"Their metamorphosis was accompanied by strange dreams.

"The drone dreamed that he wandered alone through a winding passage-way until he came to an eerie, ill-smelling brood chamber where the larvae, all unattended, were still deep in their winter sleep. When he touched one to stir it, it shattered into brittle fragments. He understood then that he had found the remains of his royal sisters and brothers. All had been drained dry of juice. Only something was stirring in the gloom beyond the heaps of dead. Something that moved with great stealth despite its bulk. Something that moved swiftly to block the exit and then sprang forward to grip the dreaming hero in its bristly forelegs.

"'Who are you—what are you?' asked the dreamer, trembling in the hor-ror of his dream.

"'My name is *Cremastocheilus*,' the creature replied, as it lifted its head to strike.

"Oh my," said the drone, breaking off his story, "think of the time! I've overstayed my minute. My mother will be waiting for me."

"Finish your story," the Princess commanded.

"I will. Later. I promise. And I'll tell you another."

His mother was overcome with amazement when the drone returned from the Princess's chamber in cheerful good health. "She wants me to come back later" was all he would say. "We're not done yet."

The drone finished the story of how the courageous drone and virgin defeated the brood-devouring scarab *Cremastocheilus*, then began another about a worker ant who escaped winter by clinging to the feathers of a robin. He told the Princess story after story, always taking care to break off the telling at a moment of suspense. His stories were filled with marvels— enchanted silverfish and wise old earthworms, malign beetle grubs of un-canny powers, workers who flew to paradisial lands on the backs of dead leaves, and yet more improbably returned from those lands laden with pre-cious nectars.

The greatest improbability of all was that a drone should know so many stories and should tell them so well. But the truth is that little intelligence was required. Through some odd mutation or genetic recombination, the drone had evolved a natural story generator. With it, he could plot his way through tangled thickets of incident, character and motivation—seeming to wander haphazardly, yet always finding the quickest and truest way home again, even when it seemed they must be irretrievably lost in the storied wilderness.

Sometimes the Princess would test him. "Tell me a story," she might say, "about a lazy worker, a crafty rove beetle, and a quest to steal spider eggs." And with scarcely a moment of hesitation or reflection, the drone would oblige. The story generator did it all. That is because there is only one story, endlessly edited, amplified, abridged, stylized and reformulated, but always still derived from the Ur-Story, made up of precisely thirty-one plot elements. By shuffling and reordering those thirty-one elements, the drone could produce, with little conscious effort, an endless stream of stories, seemingly fresh but actually very old.

The workers were at a loss to understand why the drone kept up his visits to the Princess.

"What exactly have the two of you been doing in there?" Beta demanded.

"Just talking," said the drone.

"Talking?"

"I've been telling her stories," the drone answered with naive authorial vanity, then leapt with a start as his mother slapped him.

"Fool!" she hissed, "Wasting everybody's time."

The Major, outraged, chased the drone from the chamber, not realizing, as none of them realized, that they had in the drone the perfect means to keep the Princess at home. Over the course of many, many stories, so fascinated that she missed out on the nuptial flight altogether, she would have accepted the drone as her mate and stayed in her natal nest. It might have happened that way. Indeed, it must have happened that way somewhere, among other of the ten thousand trillion ants upon the face of the earth, in the trees and woodpiles of the earth, in the underground labyrinths of the earth, within the walls and the woodwork and the cellars of the houses of the earth—but it did not happen here.

"Where's that drone?" the Princess asked, for the last story had been interrupted, as always, just at the most teasingly suspenseful point, after the evil earwig had imprisoned the heroine in a drainpipe, coercing her to lay drone eggs to sate its foul appetite.

"Where's *my* drone?" the Princess asked. Pining for the resolution of the story, she again grew absent-minded, forgetting to eat, losing a little of her magnificent amplitude. Her worried aunt went searching for the drone up and down the crumbling passageways of the nest but was unable to find him.

The drone had gone into hiding. He would emerge for the nuptial flight, when he would win a fine strong fertile queen to bear his daughters. That colony would thrive at first. But a storytelling bent had fatally weakened their line. Workers grew discontented with their lot. No longer satisfied to listen in their leisure moments to the marvelous tales of a few elite bards, they all wanted to be storytellers. The ants became self-conscious and developed annoying mannerisms. A shift in genre to a more realistic style brought them back from imminent disaster, for now their stories of proletarian struggle must be drawn from life. Again they went out to confront predators and gather food, though they did it now only for the sake of the stories they would tell. But these stories turned out dully drably alike. That's because a story generator driven by a reality engine has far fewer than thirty-one plot elements. The ants decided that they preferred stories that had nothing to do with daily life; what's more, the ants decided that they preferred stories to daily life. Their idleness and self-indulgence was as crippling to the colony as an invasion of rove beetles. Within a few seasons they and their storytelling came to an end.

No one but Young Keen noticed the change in the Princess, who was again abstracted, dreamy, indifferent. Not because of the ancestors—the voices stayed put behind the wall now. Rather, the Princess was lost in speculation about the fate of the ant imprisoned by the evil earwig who seized and ate her drone eggs. Did she save herself—and if so, how? Did she find a secret exit from the drainpipe? Did she lull the earwig into relaxing its guard? Or did a rescuer, not previously introduced, intervene? That would be sloppy plotting, the Princess decided, who had developed into a critic. Maybe the ant hid one of her drone eggs, nursing it in secret, and her son, when he emerged, helped her to defeat the earwig. Improbable, the Princess felt, even contrived, but just the sort of story her drone had liked to tell.

"Plots and counterplots," said Young Keen, immersed in her own sad reflections.

The Princess gaped, swiveling her feelers in surprise. Was her aunt now in her head too, just as the ancestors had been? Maybe her aunt knew how the story ended.

"What *is* the plot?" she asked. It was her aunt's turn to startle. She had not meant to speak out loud.

"Oh. It's nothing. I was just thinking about the others. How they've stopped caring about what's best for the colony. Now it's each ant trying to get the better of her sisters. They don't include me in their scheming but I can feel how things have changed. Now it's all blame and recriminations and double-dealing—plots and counterplots."

This was a new idea for the Princess. She dismissed the story of the ear-wig and the imprisoned ant as remote, irrelevant, ridiculous. How could she have been entertained by such nonsense—when there were real plots and counterplots going on right now, all around her! Right now, *about her,* as she readily understood, although her aunt was far too discreet to say so.

Plots and counterplots. The fragile accord reached among the five work-er ants had broken down in acrimony after the Princess had drained and discarded the six drones. Her nurse and the drones' mother were no longer so friendly—she had noticed that, without really caring. She had noticed a great deal without really caring. Now she began to put these observations together, shuffling and augmenting them, finding the patterns.

All of them, except her doting, love-crazed nurse, must realize now that she had somehow duped the drones. The major who beheaded Grandmother must be talking once again about clipping the Princess's wings. The drones' mother was rather stupid but her fury over the wastage of her sons rendered her dangerous. About the others she was uncertain. She must be careful. Plots and counterplots.

Nurse at least was safe. Her poor, mad nurse would believe whatever she, the Princess, told her.

"Oh, Nurse—dearest Nurse," the Princess said, drawing the surprised ant aside. The Princess was normally so evasive with her. "Such a pity all those drones went to waste like that."

"W–w–we're trying to find you some more drones," Spout answered. Old

Major, pleased by Gamma's praise, had been inspired to try to hunt down hidden drones, bullying suspected mothers and poking around disused corridors. She made herself too obvious and had no success whatsoever.

"Oh. But that would turn out just the same. Drones just aren't any good with their sisters or their aunts. They're not excited enough so they can't inflate their bladders properly and—oh, but I know you aren't interested in the technical minutiae." The Princess was very pleased with her experimental glibness.

"You—you knew this all along?"

"No, dear nurse. How could I know such things? I began to suspect it with the first one. He was on me just a few seconds before he fell off and flopped on his back like a dying cicada.

"But I didn't want to disappoint you," said the Princess demurely. "So I thought I'd give the rest of them a chance. You aren't angry, are you, Nurse? After all, it's hardly my fault if those drones didn't find me sufficiently attractive."

Flattered, exalted that her beloved princess had confided in her at last, had spoken to her—her alone!—nearly a dozen complete sentences, Nurse agreed completely. She could have no sympathy for drones who did not find the Princess sufficiently attractive to do the one thing they were good for. She went off to tell her sisters the news.

It made a sort of sense. Why would there be nuptial flights—why indeed would ants have wings—if ants could mate with their kin just as readily as with strangers? Even Gamma felt it was plausible, if only because she didn't believe the Princess to be intelligent enough to invent such a story on her own. Here she was doubly mistaken. The Princess was intelligent and the Princess had had help. The bickering of the ancestral voices about the disadvantages of inbreeding had given her a few essential hints. She had also, without knowing it, without ever being grateful, learned a great deal from the storytelling drone. One kind of plotting is much like another. From the drone she had learned how to invent, how to excite credulity and create suspense, how to manipulate expectations. She was doing so now. The workers were not at all sure what would happen next, but they were closer to accepting the inevitability of the nuptial flight—except for Old Major, to whom the intellectual effort involved in accepting new ideas was always distasteful.

"That doesn't change a thing," she said. "It just means we have to find where the rest of the drones have been hidden away by their selfish mothers. If we keep tossing drones to her, she's bound to get filled up eventually." Her obstinacy conveniently furthered the Princess's plot. The major who beheaded Grandmother would be too preoccupied with terrorizing former egg-layers, suspected maternal holdouts, to give much thought to clipping the Princess's wings.

"Our princess seems to have developed a sudden comprehension of matters that are beyond us ordinary workers," said Gamma. "Perhaps she can now tell us just how full her sperm bag is."

Ah! The Princess understood that there was a price to pay for glibness. She pondered the possible answers—none of which seemed sufficiently vague to protect her plot from their counterplots. Half empty, after all, was half full: they might decide to keep her at home rather than risk her loss in the nuptial flight.

"Not nearly full enough," she answered, then paused to build suspense as their feelers, aroused, waved in questioning wonder. "Not nearly full enough to restore the colony to its former glory."

Ah! The Princess hoped Mother and Grandmother were listening. They were the only ants who could appreciate her cleverness. As it happened, they weren't: they were debating military history again. Her grandmother was proving to her mother that they had each neatly anticipated and countered the other's moves at every phase of the hostilities. Since the major's move was unlawful, it must be considered null; therefore, the war was still taking place; the war, properly speaking, would go on forever. But the Princess's cleverness had been noticed nonetheless; she had too poorly disguised an undertone of triumphant glee. Gamma understood at last that they had badly underestimated the Princess's cunning.

The other ants—all but Old Major who was talking to herself again—had been greatly impressed by the words *restore the colony to its former glory*. They repeated them to each other until the fragrant words lingered in the still air of the chamber, growing in density until they begin to shape themselves into odor images. The image of a warm, clean, crowded, gossipy nest, with a great troop of scouts, foragers and majors going out each day and returning with rich food. The image of a hundred winged ants taking off from the nest to found new colonies in faraway lands. Yes, yes, that was it! That was what the words meant! Even workers, even those who must stay behind, forever earthbound, feel the thrill of the nuptial flight, the air is so saturated with perfumes that work a spell on every heart tube. *Restore the colony to its former glory.* They forgot that they were only a few workers, getting smelly with age, plus one complacent, if agreeable, princess. The chamber smoked with wraiths summoned up by that incantatory phrase. *Glory, glory, restore the colony to its former glory,* they whispered, as the phantasmal shapes of once and future ants floated around and above them. Their ancestors and descendants whispered back to them, in the vague echoic fashion of ghosts, *glory, glory, former glory, restore to us our former glory.*

And then the floating essences thinned and dissipated; the echoes died away. Or seemed to do so. In fact they were diffusing throughout the vast nest, passing along the vacant galleries, slipping through every chamber, until all the other ants, the two hundred or so surviving daughters of Thrip, those to whom the Princess was only a remote presence, hardly more than a rumor, felt it just as much as those who had experienced the Princess's words directly. They understood that they had a princess; they might again have a queen. Usually it is only feelings of rage or fear that can penetrate so potently and thrillingly throughout a nest.

"But she said she wasn't nearly full enough," Scrobe answered in bewilderment. Gamma had taken her aside to stir up her latent animosity but was finding it hard going. Even Scrobe had chanted *glory, glory,* to the gaseous spirits, forgetting her anger over her dead and dying sons, especially as she had not yet admitted them to be dead.

"Let's suppose she's half full," said Gamma, with labored patience. "If she stays in the nest, then all her daughters will be *your* granddaughters. But if she flies away and fills up her sperm bag, then only half her daughters will be descended from you."

"It's the same number of granddaughters either way. And why wouldn't I want some other ant's drone to sire all the foragers and cleaners? *My* granddaughters shouldn't have to do the dirty work."

Gamma had failed to reckon with the obtuse partiality of a mother. She tried a fresh track.

"I thought the Princess's nurse was so mean to you," she treacherously oozed, "after pretending to be your friend!"

Scrobe flickered her antennae uncertainly.

"How little she appreciates your sacrifice of your sons!"

Scrobe gaped then dropped to her haunches with a stricken air. The sacrifice! My sons, oh, my sons! She grasped at last the fact that her drones, drained and discarded by the Princess, were all dead or very near so.

Realizing that she was dealing with an ant capable of retaining only one idea at a time, Gamma wisely chose not to elaborate but to repeat: "So great a sacrifice—all your big well-fed sons—and so unappreciated, unacknowledged!"

Scrobe's character was all cruelty and sentimentality, joined in nearly equal proportions. Her big beautiful sons were dead, dead, all of them, all gone! If, at this moment, her youngest and still very lively son had come running up to embrace his mother, she would have struck him such a blow as to render him senseless, or even as dead as his elder brothers. She was not an ant to be contradicted.

She said nothing. She only brooded, nursing her sense of injury, which became more precious to her than any drone could be.

Ants do not keep secrets well. Their passions are leaky, seeping out of their pores. Scrobe's feelings escaped her as an insidious but penetrating fume. It made them all irritable. Old Major picked fights with her true sister whenever she wasn't patrolling the galleries, harassing suspected drone-mothers. Her comings and goings spread the ill will throughout the nest. Ants remembered old grudges and invented new ones. The Desegmentations would have made a spontaneous return if only the ants were able to settle on a victim. Two or three might unite momentarily to bully a smaller, older ant. But they had hardly begun to pummel her head and yank at her appendages before they realized how much they detested one another—had always detested one another.

Young Keen got the worst of it, everyone suddenly remembering that all their problems had begun with the war and that she was Regina's daughter. She disappeared, apparently gone into hiding like the drones. She was the most rational, well-behaved ant in the colony, and, after the Princess, the most agreeable. Yet no one missed her, no one asked what had become of her.

An epidemic of spite had infected the colony. Perhaps the wave of hope and unity that had swept through the nest with the Princess's inspiring words had left them vulnerable to an opposing force. With no brood to nurture and protect, with no queen to calm and control them by her essence, the ants reverted to waspishness. Now they would rather starve themselves than go out foraging to feed sisters who were so hateful and mean to them. Hunger made bad tempers worse.

Everyone felt it. The Princess thought the workers had gotten smellier than ever. It occurred to her that she need not return after her nuptial flight, that it would serve these ill-tempered foul old ants right if she founded a new colony of her own. She felt a sudden, powerful urge to fly, to get away, that she mistook for spite.

She told her nurse that she wanted to sun herself on the anthill. Spout felt a surge of fear and possessiveness that she mistook for spite. She snapped back that the Princess was going to stay put, right where she was.

"I think you stink!" said the Princess, overcome by hurt, "I hate you!"

Spout collapsed to her haunches in shock. The Princess had become disagreeable!

"I didn't mean it," said the Princess, relenting.

"I didn't mean it either. But you mustn't go to the anthill. Too exposed, too dangerous."

The epidemic, having climaxed, began to subside. Hungry ants went out to forage and grudgingly shared a bit of food with the ants who used to be their favorite sisters; then shared with the ants they really didn't mind so much; then with the ants who had been mean to them, because what's the use of stirring up trouble? The days were longer now; the sun was warm and honeydew was plentiful. Drones began to slip out from their hiding places, venturing into the upper nest and from there out to the anthill and the stone. The workers felt it was nice to have them there, like old times. The season made almost everyone agreeable again.

The Princess was doing her best to convince her nurse to let her out to the anthill. Winged ants crave sunlight as much as their wingless sisters crave darkness. Why couldn't she go out to sun herself?

"Birds," said her nurse, with dark foreboding didactic intent. "Starlings, house sparrows and wrens, robins and other thrushes. And flickers that practically *live* on ants."

"And that's just the birds," said Old Major. "What about digger wasps, what about ground beetles, what about antlions?" said Old Major, relapsing into spite. "Tiger beetles! Jumping spiders! Decapitating flies!"

"And those are just the ones that feed on the ground," said Nurse. "If you were actually to fly ..." She could not bring herself to finish the sentence but her sister could.

"Swallows and martins and waxwings! Robber flies! Dragonflies! Assassin bugs!"

"But my sperm bag isn't nearly full enough," said the Princess. "Without a nuptial flight how can I restore the colony to its former glory?"

The words made no impression. They had lost their potency for a colony weakened by an acute attack of spite, which had left the ants dispirited and prone to take a prudent and conservative outlook.

"It's better to be safe," said Nurse, with chilling practicality.

"You won't miss your wings at all," said Old Major, "once you settle down to motherhood. I'm glad I don't have wings. Maybe you don't even know what wasps do to ant queens. They're worse than decapitating flies, if you ask me. Much worse."

Spout made no attempt to suppress her sister. She wanted the Princess frightened into staying home. From ant queen–kidnapping wasps, Old Major went on to tell of her own experiences with antlions and decapitating flies. In her eagerness to impress the Princess, Old Major made the mistake of clumsily embellishing her account with narratorial tropes and tricks that the Princess recognized from the stories of her drone. Consequently, the major's experiences seemed less credible, as less skillfully related, than her drone's fabulous tales of enchanted silverfish and talking birds. She was not frightened, she was critical.

For days the drones had been creeping out from their hiding places to the upper nest and from there venturing all the way out onto the mound: Was it time yet? Surely the day must be near! Querying the air with their big eyes and long, sensitive feelers, they were too excited to attend to danger, ignoring their mothers' many warnings. They had to go out, they said. How else would they know when the day of the nuptial flight had arrived?

Old Major rushed into the Princess's antechamber with a crumpled drone gripped in her mandibles.

"There's more where this one came from," she announced triumphantly. "The upper nest stinks of drones. Send him in to the Princess and I'll fetch another."

"Mother, save me! Mother? Mother?" the storytelling drone pleaded but was ignored. Once he had disappeared into the Princess's chamber, however, Scrobe indulged herself with a fresh display of grief and rage. "This one too—the last of my sons, restored to me only to be lost forever!"

"Let me think," said the drone, nervously, after he had been prodded into the Princess's presence. "Where did we leave off? Oh, it must have been right after the earwig sealed off the drainpipe."

"I'm not interested in stories anymore."

"You're not? How about flying—aren't you interested in flying?"

"Of course I am!"

"Then we have to get going! It's the nuptial flight—it's happening today, right now, this very afternoon. If we don't hurry we'll be late!"

"They won't let me out. And now they won't let you out either, until you do your job.

"So get on with it," she added crossly. "It's your own fault. You were a fool to let the major catch you."

"Do I hear someone talking inside the wall?" the drone asked, trying rather hopelessly to distract her.

"It's only the ancestors mumbling again—just ignore them," the Princess answered, then paused as she realized there was a new voice, vaguely familiar.

"Who's in there?" she asked.

"It's me, your aunt," the voice answered. "I've been hiding here. Are they still feeling spiteful?"

"Not so much. But they're being very mean to me. They've started sending me drones again and they won't let me out of my chamber. Aunt, you know how much I want to fly, don't you? You'll help me, won't you, Aunt? Is there an exit from your hiding place—an exit to the upper world?"

"No," said her aunt. "No, there isn't an exit."

"You mean 'No, I won't help you.'"

"Princess, no one who really cares about you will help you escape to the nuptial flight. It's just too dangerous."

The Princess gaped. She'd been going about things backwards! It was the ants who *didn't* care about her who would let her out to fly. Surely there was enough spite still circulating in the colony to bring it off.

"Well, no one much cares about a drone, do they?" she said to her aunt. "In which case maybe you can help this one escape through the exit that isn't there."

"Oh, thank you, Princess," the drone cried out, as Young Keen obliged by opening a passageway for him, "Good luck, Princess!"

The lucky Princess passed out to the antechamber to find the two most spiteful ants of the colony waiting in attendance on her. Beta and Spout had left with Old Major to corner the remaining drones before they could take flight.

"Worthless, completely worthless," the Princess announced gaily. "His six brothers were all sorry stuff but this one was even worse. He no sooner put his thing in me than he shriveled up and vanished!"

Scrobe rushed past her and searched the chamber. Yes, he was gone, gone! Her last, her most beloved son, taken from her, like all the others, by the Princess!

"Such a bother, such waste of time," the Princess said. "Not that I'm blaming you, of course. I'm sure you tried your best. We'll just have to hope that Nurse, Major and Beta come back with some better-equipped drones. Because the nuptial flight would be too dangerous for me to try, what with swallows and starlings and robber flies and ..."

"Oh, no," said Scrobe, swelling with rage. "No, the dangers of the nuptial flight are greatly exaggerated. I really think you ought to go on it. In fact, I'll help you."

Gamma heard it all. Gamma did not intervene. Rational self-interest should have prompted her to prevent the Princess from undertaking such a foolish, quite possibly suicidal course of action. But Gamma had always relished the sufferings of others, a taste she'd indulged freely during the Desegmentations. Naturally enough, given her character, she had been badly infected by the spite she had stirred up in Scrobe. She could not resist a malevolent urge to let the scene play out, to find out what would happen.

"I couldn't stop them," she said when the others returned to the empty chamber. "After all, they're bigger than me."

Spout, distraught, rushed to the upper nest to save the Princess.

"Too bad. Such a loss to us all. You should have trimmed her wings while you could," said Gamma to Old Major.

"Somebody needs a trimming," said Beta. She had stayed relatively placid during the epidemic of spite, only because she was so lost in maleficent thought, pondering how she was going to get back at Gamma for past wrongs.

"Don't you remember, Major?" she continued. "You told me once how you wanted to give a certain ant a trimming, just like you did for the Royal Alpha. Only she had gone into hiding."

"You're right—I did say that."

"No time like the present," said Beta, as she moved to block Gamma's escape. "Now that we're alone and she has nowhere to hide."

Like all the other drone-mothers, Scrobe had memorized the locations of the emergency exits. She led the Princess to the nearest one, then encouraged her from behind as she made her way out into the daylight.

"Goodbye, Princess," Scrobe called after her. "What will it be? Flycatchers or starlings or robber flies or wasps? Wasps, I think. Yes, a wasp would be ideal."

As she turned to retreat a forceful push propelled her out of the nest. Scrobe was the bigger, younger ant, but she was panic-stricken to find herself outside, in the open, for the first time in her life. Spout went for her feelers first, then her legs.

"Keep on wriggling," Spout said to her. "That's the way to draw a wasp to you, or a jumping spider, if you're that lucky." She sealed the emergency exit as she reentered the nest. Along with Old Major, Beta and Young Keen, who came out from her hiding place, along with all the surviving ants of the colony, she took up the vigil on the nest stone.

The Princess has made her way to the swarm, following the last of the escaping drones. Fastidious in her lovemaking, she accepts a series of odorous, well-endowed drones, allowing each his twenty or thirty seconds before she bucks him off and replaces him with another. She mated her drones in the air, in the center of the swarm, the safest place for her to be. When she knows herself to be full of sperm, she casts her last lover aside.

The turmoil around her has become more than amorous: the birds and robber flies have found the swarm. The Princess must escape to safety, quickly, at once! The nuptial swarm has drifted on a light breeze until it is very near Thrip's decaying nest. The ants below, her sisters, running back and forth on the stone in their anxiety and excitement, cannot make out the swarm, cannot even perceive the rapacious devouring birds. But a gentle rain of dying drones is beginning to fall. If the Princess yet lives, she might easily return to them, she might restore the colony to its glory. But that is not what will happen.

Would she have come back? No one knows that, not Spout who loved her, not the giddy indecisive princess herself, not I, her narrator, because, as it happens, she cannot. A front is moving in: the light breeze gives way to a gusting surface wind and she is carried aloft. She passes above the sprawling housing tract, at the edge of which poor unhappy Thrip had founded her family in the front yard of the derelict farmhouse, now tenantless, soon to give way to two new luxury homes. She passes above the weedy half-lot with its narrow scrap of woods where her all-powerful grandmother had ruled in despotic grandeur.

That narrow scrap of woods was all that remained of the vast forest in which her ancestors had flourished for thousands upon thousands of generations. When the settlers arrived, when the trees were cut down, they moved to the stumps, laboriously gnawing small galleries, creeping unhappily between bark and wood, root and soil. Then, when the farmers came, when the stumps were pulled and the ground was plowed, what place was left for them to go? That was almost the end, they were pushed almost to oblivion. But a few colonies had founded themselves along a ditch, a few more in a scant hedgerow. They came back, they restored their numbers, although never to flourish as they had in the forest. Then, when the developers came, the hedgerows were razed, the ditches were filled, the entire land leveled; again they were pushed nearly to extinction, again they changed and adapted. Those lucky ones in the weedy half-lot and the farmhouse yard who had escaped the bulldozers now seeded their daughters into thick turfgrass lawns. There they went underground for good, relying on root honeydew for their sustenance, coming forth only for the nuptial flights.

For the Princess, the ground below was only a shifting, transforming blur of brown, blue, gray, green. Tiny, negligible, antlike. She floated over roads and houses, over parking lots and strip malls, over golf courses and over parks crisscrossed with asphalt trails, their tame brown streams contained within stone-and-mortar channels. The dimness of her unfamiliar eyes rendered the world below as a canvas of hot, drab symmetries, nothing but lines, rhomboids and rectangles placed with insistent regularity on a monotonous brown or green ground. The choppy wind had lessened; other, more practical-minded queens had taken their chances and sought out a relatively green landing site. The dreamy princess drifted onward over bigger swatches of brown and gray, where an immense concourse of roads centered upon a vast shopping mall. The wind was dying, she was slipping downwards in a confused flutter.

As she passed above the mall, the seething heat of capitalism—its aphalt expanses, its cars, its flat-roofed superstores—generated a violent updraft that flung the Princess high above the earth, not as high as the clouds, certainly, but well above the usual range of ant queen–preying birds and insects.

Tossing and churning around her were other eolian wanderers. Thrips, barklice and aphids were everywhere, she knew, but she would not have expected them up here and in such great numbers. They scarcely troubled to work their flimsy wings; buoyed on the rising thermal, they waited with imperturbable stupidity for the winds to deliver them to new feeding grounds. The air teemed with tiny rotifers, mites and tardigrades; bigger creatures— silverfish, firebrats, springtails and bristletails—were also tumbling up and down beside her; and it took the Princess several moments of confused reflection to realize why it seemed so strange to find them there—none of them had wings. Not that wings seemed to matter much. The air was full of spiderlings floating on gossamer sails. Bagworms were blowing about as well, some ballooning within their woven bags, others dangling nakedly with only a strand of coarse silk to catch the wind. All riding the bubbling vortex of hot air.

Although cars still streamed into the lots, although the rooftop generators throbbed with all their might, the thermal began to weaken as the sun dropped toward the horizon. The strong fliers, the beetles and the flies, having reached a useful altitude, began to work their wings, heading toward the declining sun. The bristletails, silverfish, and other wingless creatures began to drift downward. Some, falling onto shoulders or into shopping bags, would actually survive.

The Princess was a weak, inexperienced flier and she had fluttered about stupidly at first when she might have taken it easy by circling within the updraft of the vortex. As the thermal dissipated, she had the good sense to follow a crane fly that appeared to know where it was going, or at least where it was not going. It was not going down to the barren parking lots or rooftops directly below. Another, weaker thermal carried her along a roadway. She used much of her remaining strength to cross it, then rode an updraft created by a narrow stand of trees, then sank precipitously as she encountered an unexpectedly strong downdraft on the other side.

Now she was above the river, dangerously close to its surface, with a cool breeze pulling her downstream where, eventually, the river joined a greater river, which emptied into the bay, which opened into the sea. But she would not make it that far.

What happens next? Most likely she will fall exhausted into the river and be drowned. Alternatively, she may be snapped up by one of the swallows who sweep ceaselessly over its surface, or by one of the damselflies and dragonflies who patrol its banks for prey just as avidly. Or, trying to make for higher ground, she may mistakenly alight on the expressway that roared alongside and across the river, where its bridge deflects the wind.

After so much struggle, after making her triumphant way through such a tangle of circumstance, contrivance and coincidence, is it really possible that she will end as a splotch on a heavily ironic windshield? Very possible indeed, as anyone who has driven a car on a sultry June afternoon can attest.

The Princess's fate hangs in the balance. One side is labeled Realism, the other Romance. Now, *you* might think that Realism is weightier than Romance, despite the latter's bulkiness, and you would be right, if not for the fact that it is *my* balance. Like a dishonest butcher, I apply my thumb to the side I wish to favor. Romance it is—bestowing upon the Princess a prosperous and happy ever-after.

But why not have it both ways? Around her other ant-motes were fluttering downstream in the same river breeze. *They* were snapped up by the swallows skimming above the water's surface, by alert chubs and shiners in the riffles and shallows, or by the damselflies and dragonflies of the banks, if they made it that far. *They* dirtied the windshields of the cars on the expressway. At its height the nuptial flight had numbered a thousand queens, courted by ten thousand hopeful drones. Birds and robber flies were the first to batten on the rapidly decimated swarm. Returning to earth, inseminated queens and exhausted drones blundered into spider webs or were torn apart by rival ants or were snatched by jumping spiders or digger wasps or tiger beetles. Some survived to dig their holes and lay their little eggs, only to perish in a crude anticlimax before their first brood matured. Nine hundred and ninety-nine grimly realistic endings. Having posited their stories, let us return to the Princess, to whom none of these statistically ordinary endings would apply.

Instead, she made landfall on the island, the one that is on no map, undiscovered, unexplored, the island that was as yet without its ants. Where the expressway interrupted the river, the island had grown up. First it had been just a knot of debris, the trunk and branches of a sycamore that had come unmoored from its eroded bank upstream, that then captured more debris—an old tire, a tangled mass of construction fencing, some plastic shopping bags, the latter plucked right out of the air by the broken members of the sycamore.

The very first flood might have carried it all away, if not for the bridge that perturbed and mired the sullied waters washing past its supports. Instead, the rains that scoured the insulted, asphalted land upstream brought to the island its pebble and sand and silt and seed. Cottonwoods planted themselves in the moist bare soil, took root and flourished, gathering more rich silt about their roots. In the summers the island blooms with purple loosestrife, drawing bees and butterflies from the mainland, and the cottonwoods are visited by ventriloquating birds who leave their rich droppings behind.

Making landfall on that sweet, temperate island, a land of honeydew and termites (for it had already aphids on its trees, beautiful ones with black-veined wings, and it had termites, carried there in their bark of rotting wood), planting herself like a seed, an ant-seed, at the foot of the biggest of the cottonwoods, the Princess dug her hole and laid her eggs. She was fruitful: her little daughters, when they eclosed, at once set about grooming and feeding her. Her long painful fast ended at last, the Princess laid more eggs.

The colony was nearly lost in its second year when a terrible flood inundated the island for three days and three nights. But by some lucky chance her worker daughters had constructed the main nest chambers with high vaulted ceilings that retained a precious bubble of air while all else was under water. Thereafter her daughters extended the nest upwards through the bole of the tree, following the tracks left by cottonwood borers. Unknowingly, or perhaps obeying some faint ancestral voices of their own, the workers had returned to the ways of the ancestors who dwelt so long ago in the immense unbroken forest.

In her prosperity, the Princess did not forget everything her old nurse had tried to teach her. At each nuptial flight she kept one or two of her daughters at home, mating them and granting them a portion of her island. Her offspring multiply into a supercolony, her daughters and granddaughters marrying her sons and grandsons, the colony spreading itself, multiplying into the tens and hundreds of thousands. Each springtime flood brings another deposit of dirt from the tormented lands upstream. Each spring another brood of ants has more room to build. They fill the entire island but the island grows to accommodate them.

The daughters sent forth to found colonies of their own would, most of them, inevitably perish. Those few who survived the birds the robber flies the dragonflies the wasps the spiders and the assassin bugs—those few daughters naturally sought out a landing site like their natal nest. But they could not, with their weak eyes, distinguish water from asphalt. Any flat reflective expanse with an outcropping of green rising out of it attracted them. How could they know the difference between a river and a street, a lake and a parking lot? From the air the oily glimmer of asphalt was so like a river that they had torn their wings and dug their hole and raised their first shy little daughters before they discovered the terrible trick that had been played on them. What could have prepared them for something so surreal, so outlandish? So they founded their colonies in traffic islands, in median strips, in slender weedy archipelagos between parking lots—finding, when they could, a little parched islet in an asphalt sea. Here they could not thrive, not like in the homeland; but here they survived for a time, for some few seasons, even sending forth their own modest nuptial flights of drones and winged virgins before they perished from famine or fumes. Meanwhile, the ants of the river island prospered.

With every heavy rain a tasty flotsam of drowned bugs and worms washed ashore, not that there was ever a shortage of food. Each year the muddy river deposited more rich silt and the island grew. Each year as the island grew the colony grew with it, teeming, busy, blossoming. It might have gone on flourishing so forever, and surely it would have gone on flourishing so forever, if not for the war with the newts.

But that's another story.

And so proceed *ad infinitum.*

www.ingramcontent.com/pod-product-compliance
Lightning Source LLC
Chambersburg PA
CBHW071535260626
47170CB00002B/644